Sal,

Thankyou for always being your epic self.

With love,
victoria&james
x x

THE *Only* EXCEPTION

A ROAD TO WONDERLAND STORY

L.J. STOCK
VICTORIA L. JAMES

The Only Exception© 2019

L.J. Stock & Victoria L. James

All rights reserved. No part of this book may be reproduced in any form without written permission from the author, except that of small quotations used in critical reviews and promotion via blogs.

This is a work of fiction. The names, characters, places and incidents are products of the author's imagination only. Any resemblance to actual persons, living or deceased, events or any other incident is entirely coincidental.

Front Cover Design: Lou Stock of LJDesigns

Formatting: Lou Stock of LJDesigns

Editing: Claire Allmendinger of BNW Editing

Victoria L. James is in partnership with Francesca Marlow as co-creator of the Wonderland stories, with L.J. Stock and Charlie M. Matthews being creative partners. The characters of this series, unless used in the works of Izzy, Paris, Ethan, and Scott, may not be used in any other book without express permission from Victoria L. James or Francesca Marlow beforehand. Nor may storylines from the Wonderland Twitter pages be used in other works from previous participants who are not Victoria L. James, Francesca Marlow, L.J. Stock or Charlie M. Matthews.

- THE ONLY EXCEPTION - 5

ACKNOWLEDGEMENTS

This book isn't being released to garner thousands of new readers, hit bestseller lists, or make an impact on the book industry as a whole. We couldn't care less if only four people read it. Some stories simply need to be told. This book—Izzy and Ethan's powerful love story—is something we're doing for us. For Vic and Lou. For the years we spent on Twitter writing these two characters to a live audience, unscripted and unrehearsed. For the memory of what brought us together as friends first and foremost, as well as writing partners. Not a lot of people believe in destiny and fate, but we believe that we were meant to meet in some way or another. It was never going to happen with one of us being in America and the other being in England, so the Internet brought us together. When it did, Izzy Moffit and Ethan Walker came to life. We lived and breathed them while roleplaying on social media for two years straight, day in, day out.

It sounds like hard work. The truth is, it was some of the best times of our lives.

We grew confident as writers, and we learned how to tell the stories we wanted to tell.

Because of that time and people's encouragement, we're able to live this dream job of ours on a daily basis. Before we thank anyone else, we have to thank each other for the friendship. For the dedication. And for the drama-free way we work together without hiccup, intolerance, or negativity.

Our main thanks goes to every single person on Twitter who started following us in 2013, and who has stuck with us ever since. You know who you are. We write this story, not just for us, but for you, too. #WLSL and TBC will forever have such special meanings to us all. What an incredible thing we were a part of. We're so sorry it's taken us 7 years to get this HEA out to you, and while we can't promise you it will be the same story as it was back then, we CAN promise you it'll be just as thrilling, and most definitely worth it.

To our editor Claire Allmendinger, we love and appreciate everything you do for us, always.

To Wendy Shatwell, we thank you and Bare Naked Words for always being Team Wonderland.

To Francesca Marlow, Charlie M. Matthews, and Amy Trevathan, we thank you for the years of roleplaying creativity, friendship and support, and all the memories we created together. Though many have tried, we have a bond that can't be broken by anyone anymore. That's special. Let's forever keep Wonderland on lockdown from now on, huh?

To Sue Hollingmode—the first person to ever comment on us as unknown authors and say, "Hey, I love your writing. I'd like to know where this story is going. Please tell me you'll write more (or something very similar to that)—you, out of everyone, have been someone we feel utterly blessed to have stumbled upon. Selfless, funny, and 100% genuine, you're everything we need in a friend and more. Never leave us.

To Mary Green, we love you for your enthusiasm for everything we do. We really wish you'd have stayed around in Wonderland to play your character back in the day, but we'll take your friendship, support, and eagle eyes instead.

To Kristina Hanicar, we love you and your generous heart.

To so many others from the Wonderland days… this one's for you.

To all the new readers we've gathered over the years, thank you for giving us a shot.

To our families, always, you are our everything.

Our street teams, author and blogger friends, and to anyone who has been a positive aspect of our life, we thank you, also. To the people who have been negatives in our lives, we also thank you for the lessons and making us the people we are today—stronger, wiser, bolder, and a lot more relaxed than we ever used to be.

Now.

Most importantly.

More than we can ever begin to explain.

We want to thank Izzy and Ethan.

These two, more than any other character, are our first loves. They're as real as we are, and we are so happy to finally be able to give them this journey.

We hope you all enjoy reading it as much as we enjoyed writing it.

With love and Wonderland hugs.

Lou & Vic x

10 - THE ONLY EXCEPTION -

A NOTE TO THE READER

The Only Exception is the Fifth in a series of releases, all written by different authors who came together with one idea in mind: to be part of a team that could create a world away from reality, where struggles are dealt with today in order to find a better tomorrow.

The Only Exception is written by both L.J. Stock and Victoria L. James from the perspective of Izzy and Ethan.

This is the continuation of Izzy and Ethan's journey into Wonderland.

You can follow both LJ and Victoria on the following social media platforms:

L.J. Stock Facebook: /LJStockAuthor
www.ljstockbooks.com
LJ Stock Instagram

Victoria L. James Facebook: /VictoriaLJamesAuthor
www.victorialjames.com
www.instagram.com/victoria_ljames

12 - THE ONLY EXCEPTION -

BEFORE YOU DIVE IN...

Please note that, while technically this story could be read as a standalone, we strongly, strongly advise you to have read The Trouble with Izzy by Victoria L. James, and/or A Fight for Ethan by L.J. Stock beforehand.

Both the above stories provide you with the history needed to fully understand this book. It's the journey that leads to this moment, with Ethan standing on Izzy's doorstep. Some things could become confusing without these earlier facts in mind. Trust us, they're worth the read.

Also, to the original Wonderland fans who will be here thinking they know how this is going to go because of the storylines they followed back in 2013... erm. Sorry. We've changed it all. Haha. Izzy and Ethan are going in a brand new direction, but we can assure you that they're going to leave you breathless and as hungry for more as always.

In our eyes, this is better than the original, so strap yourselves in for their epic, epic ride.

Enjoy.

14 - THE ONLY EXCEPTION -

DEDICATION

Francesca Marlow, Charlie M. Matthews, Amy Trevathan, Sue Hollingmode, Mary Green, Claire Allmendinger, Wendy Shatwell, Kristina Hanicar.

And the Wonderland #WLSL fans from 2013-2015. This one's for you.

16 - THE ONLY EXCEPTION -

CHAPTER ONE

Ethan

Monogamy.

It was nothing more than a word, and it was one that had never found a place in my vocabulary before. At least not until Izzy Moffit finally stepped into my path and became more than just a fantasy. I'd lusted after her for more than a decade. Every woman I'd flirted with, kissed, touched, and fucked in between those years had been compared to her. Yet, not one of them had come anywhere close. They hadn't measured up. Not one of them had warranted a second date because no matter how hard I'd tried to make things work, they were all missing something...

They weren't her.

Now, there I was, at this woman's door after a disastrous first date, my heart hammering in my chest, my smile broad, and my mind completely focused on her. I hadn't driven there for any reason other than to spend more time in her company. I wanted to be close. I wanted to watch the blue in her crystalline eyes sparkle when she laughed—to try and understand what every brush of her hair over her shoulder and sly smile meant

Izzy Moffit was my *Great White Buffalo*.

One afternoon in her company— including a date that ended with Izzy running from me— beat every other date I'd ever had. Izzy had, for all intents and purposes, rejected me, and the first thing I'd done when she'd called to apologise was to jump in my car and make my way to her.

Now, beautiful Izzy with her long blonde hair, perfect figure, and sparkly blue eyes was looking up at me, holding the door to her home open like it was the door to her life.

I stepped into her house and gave it a cursory glance before turning my attention back to her. She didn't so much as glance at the door as she closed it behind us. She was as focused on me as I was on her.

"This isn't too presumptuous?" I asked, glancing down at her legs and double taking when I saw cute little ducks swimming across her pyjamas in a lake of mint material. My cheeks were already aching from smiling so fucking much, but my lips seemed incapable of doing anything else. "You're in your jammies. Cute."

"If you don't like ducks, we could already have a problem here." Her chest expanded as she pulled in a breath. "And you're nothing but a pleasant surprise," she said quietly, her face lighting up like the sun.

Taking a chance, I leaned in closer and brushed my lips over hers.

No matter how much I wanted to pull her against my body and drown in her, I wasn't there to get laid. I didn't want her to think I was, either. Her request for me to take things slow had stuck. I wanted to honour that.

For a while, anyway.

Though the ducks made her more fuckable than I'd ever thought she could be.

"I'm glad you called," I said quietly, reflecting on the surprise I'd felt at hearing her voice after she'd run away from me only hours before.

"I'm glad you came."

"I want to kiss you again."

Way to take things slow, Walker.

"I wouldn't stop you."

I swept my arm around her and pulled her against me. Everything in me was driving to take, claim, and conquer. I wanted to pick her up, press her against a wall, and explore her. I wanted her legs around my waist, that small mewl of sound falling from her lips as that undeniable chemistry flared to life between us.

I wanted and wanted and wanted.

I made myself wait, holding her body against mine as she bathed me in. I dragged out the moment just long enough to ensure that when I kissed her, she fucking felt it.

Our lips connected, our tongues stroked, and every corner of my brain was trying its very best to keep my touches respectful.

I'd wanted to leave an impression on her, but she'd imprinted herself on me.

Even her fucking freckles were sexy.

Her hand slid up my neck, the tips of her fingers brushing my hair as she lost herself to it—to us—before she let them slide back down my jaw, touching me as though I wasn't real. The kiss lasted a minute before her breath caught in her throat and she slowly pulled back. Her eyes remained closed, and she held me only an inch away.

"Was that part of rule five?" she asked shyly.

I rubbed my thumb over her bottom lip, the damnable smile right back where it had been before I'd kissed her. "No more rules, remember."

"I remember." She smiled, her eyes opening fully, aimed at me and mine. "Is that the kind of greeting I should get used to?"

"You can have that anytime you want it. I don't think I will ever get tired of kissing you."

"According to the great romance novelists of the last century, you really shouldn't lay all your cards on the table after the first kiss. A little mystery goes a long way."

"Then it's a good thing I'm trying to behave myself."

"What would happen if you *weren't* trying to behave yourself?"

"Mystery, Izzy. You'll have to wait and find out."

"Can I offer you a beer or something?"

"You realise you're doing nothing to dispel me of your perfect woman status, don't you?" I asked, pushing my hands in my pockets to stop myself from reaching for her again. I'd never felt a pull to another human being like I did with her. My hand twitched to drag her back in for more.

"Perfect is something I'll never be, Walker Texas Ranger."

"You have no idea."

"Do you want that drink or not?"

"I'd love a beer, cheers."

With a quiet chuckle to herself, she spun from me, her carefree mood filtering through the atmosphere as she sashayed away, her tight arse pressing against those mint green, duck-covered pyjamas, which would look utterly ridiculous on anyone else.

Reaching the partition at the end of the corridor, Izzy hooked her hand against the wall and glanced back at me with a smile before disappearing through it.

I took the moment I had to myself to palm my dick before it got too uncomfortable against my zip. The woman made my body act like it had when I was a geeky preteen. Nothing I did seemed to stop that inherent horniness around her. If anyone could have been in my head and heard my thoughts, they would have thought I had a sex addiction. It was one of the dependencies I didn't suffer, but I had a feeling that the first time I got a taste of Izzy, I would find my newest drug of choice.

Taking it slow could be a blessing in disguise.

I followed her into the kitchen, peering around the wall where the ducks bounced indecently from her arse, half-hidden behind the fridge door as she dug for beer.

"I like your house," I said.

"Thank you."

The compliment had made her smile brighter as she uncapped the beers and slid one across the island sitting in the middle of the kitchen.

She offered a tip of her head before she looked all around the room, like she, too, was seeing it for the first time. Her eyes roamed over the white and grey walls, before rising to the subtle silver lampshade above her head.

"The minute I walked into this place I knew it was for me. It was the first house to ever really feel like home."

"I felt the same way about my apartment. I'd never had somewhere that was… *mine.* I went from my parents' place and bunked with people, always had a roommate of some kind." If that was what you called your dealers and other addicts in rehab. "The moment I had the money and got my own home, I felt like something slid into place. It was the same with the club really."

On my second glance around to reiterate my point, I saw some of the smaller touches. The goofy pictures of Izzy and

Paris from a photo booth as teenagers held in place on the fridge with magnets. A small dying plant on the windowsill. The kitchen roll with some cartoon printed on it. I could see the parts of Izzy's personality that she'd injected into the place. I just didn't want to be the creepy guy to point that out when we'd only been on one date.

She leaned over the island, her elbows resting on top of it as a hand cradled her beer.

"I'm going to get straight to the point on this one and dare myself to ask about your club. What made you go down that route? Not that I'm judging."

I linked my hands at the back of my neck. "The club," I said, bringing my elbows together before letting them open again. "I met a girl at a party. She danced on a pole at a club. She and I started talking about it. I made the mistake of calling her a stripper and absolutely offended her, so she explained the business to me. She explained how much money she made, how much the club made, how she could still look her parents in the eyes when she talked about work. After that, I didn't think about it for a while. Then I graduated from night school and realised I wanted to be my own boss. The first thing I thought of was a club. The poles and dancers came after. They make money with their clothes on, and we make money letting them do so. It works."

She studied me, and I wasn't even sure she knew she was doing it. "I write stories for a living. Sometimes, in those stories... people do messed-up stuff that others would judge them for, and I make money from it. The money isn't much." Izzy stopped to release a laugh at a private joke she hadn't shared with me. "But I get it, Ethan. It's business."

"Sex sells. I run a clean club. I keep the drugs out, and I have people to protect the dancers. We don't just cater to horny men fantasising about beautiful women. We have as many women there, too. Some flirt with the girls, others ask them to teach them how to dance. One of the girls teaches a class in the club on Sundays while it's closed." I leaned forward, mirroring her position on the island. "Can I read some of your stuff?"

"My *stuff*?"

"Your stories."

"No," she mouthed through a smile. "Absolutely not."

"Why?"

"Because it's fantasy, and I'm tired of living there. You want to get to know me? Do it in reality first."

"Tell me something I don't know about you."

"Like what?"

"Anything."

"Anything?"

"Yep."

"Okay." Izzy tilted her head, her ponytail falling with her. "I love Paramore."

"The band?"

"Yeah," she laughed quietly. "The band."

"My brother had a thing for Hayley Williams," I lied. *I'd* had a thing for Hayley Williams. We'd managed to get tickets from a supplier. The little sprite bounced on stage with all of her teenage angst—though she'd been in her twenties. There was something about her that had reminded me of Izzy. "They make good music. I saw them live once."

"You saw *my* Hayley *live*? Are you kidding me, Walker?"

"I shit you not. 2008, the band were recording the *Live in the UK* album, right here in Manchester." I put weight on my arms and leaned in closer. "You didn't go?"

"I think you should get out of my house before I kick you out."

"Just think, if we'd been married, you'd have had my fourth ticket." I grabbed my beer and drank, trying my best not to smile, hoping to fuck my dimple didn't give me away. Scott, my best mate, called that dimple my wanker button.

"I'm serious." She raised her chin and gestured to the door. "You know how to run, right?"

I pointed the neck of the bottle at her. "And if I get tickets again? Should I call you then?"

"You should *only* call me then. With a letter of apology sent a week in advance."

"Not a chance, beautiful. You're stuck with me now."

Her eyes lingered on mine, and I could see she was fighting her smile. "Is that so?"

"Yep. Aren't you a lucky lady?"

"Hmm," she mused, drumming the fingers of her free hand on the kitchen island. Izzy started to move, carrying her beer with her as she rounded that island and came closer towards me in her little duck pjs. Stopping a foot away, she held out her hand, not saying a word as she waited for me to take it.

I took it, my hand wrapping around hers as I watched her and… waited.

She was a wonder.

"If I'm stuck with you, we may as well get comfortable," she said with more confidence than I expected.

With a gentle tug on my hand, Izzy led the way, her steps slow and assured as she hit the bottom stair before ascending the staircase, only glancing back at me once with a look of certainty.

She wanted this.

She wanted it as much as I did.

How was this my new reality?

CHAPTER TWO

Izzy

Trust was something that didn't come easily—especially not after one failed marriage and a young love gone wrong—but even I couldn't deny that every part of me was screaming one thing and one thing only:

Ethan Walker was one of the good guys.

That perfectly placed dimple that only ever showed up in his left cheek drove me crazy.

Those hazel eyes studied me like I was the only thing he'd ever looked at with any interest.

The words he spoke went straight to the softer parts of my heart.

His rough, firm hand felt right in mine as I guided him to my bedroom. I pushed the door open with my eyes on him as I led him through to my safe place.

White walls lined with pictures, posters, and fairy lights made it look like the home of a teenage girl. There I was in my thirties, taking him to the one place I allowed myself to be vulnerable, and showing him who I was as a woman. No makeup. No heels. No prepping this place to be something it wasn't to try and impress him. If Ethan wanted to see my soul, this was the best place for him to start.

He looked around; his smile soft as he took everything in. His hand tightened around mine when his eyes landed on the bed. "You're going to think I'm insane, but this room feels like you."

"Feels like me, how?"

Ethan glanced down at me. "To me, you've always been the lass in the Foo's shirt and Converse. Comfortable in her own skin and surrounding herself with things that matter. I only realised how right I'd been when we started talking."

"I never knew anyone was paying attention to someone like me."

"You underestimate your prowess." Giving my hand a tug, Ethan stepped towards the bed and lowered himself to the edge of it. "It's hard to ignore you."

"A little secret for you. You're the first man to ever come into this room. You're the first guy to ever sit on that bed. I hadn't even realised that until just now."

"You're trying to kill me, aren't you?"

"Definitely not." I smiled.

Pulling our linked hands to his chest, he rested my palm over his heart and offered me a cheeky smile as his heart pounded quickly against it. "Feel that? You're the only woman that's ever made it do that. That's one of my secrets for you."

"Are you trying to kill me as payback?"

"No." He wrapped his other arm around my waist and

pulled me against him so that I landed on his lap. "I'm just enjoying the new experiences."

I didn't think about my next move.

I kissed him carefully. The tips of my fingers rising to run through his short hair. Ethan let me set the pace, our lips moving together intimately as his warm hands ran up my back, holding me to him. He pressed his tongue against mine, seeking more. I responded, letting him have it. His tongue massaged mine, those lips of his soft enough to make a small moan rise in the back of my throat. Ethan obviously knew what he was doing, but it was the way he made me *feel* when he kissed me that really blew me away—the way I felt safe yet excited in his grip.

It took all of my will power to pull away. My eyes flickered open, and a dopey smile came to life.

"Sorry," I whispered. "Couldn't help myself."

"Never apologise for kissing me."

"You're a really good kisser."

"Ditto."

"What do you want to do now?"

"Don't really care, as long as I do it with you."

"We need music." I placed a small kiss goodbye on his cheek and reluctantly peeled myself away from him. If I were to stay there on his lap, I'd only need to see his dimple one more time, and I'd be throwing him backwards and climbing onboard. That was not part of the *taking it slow* plan.

Even though I'd promised him there wouldn't be any rules, I also knew that taking it slow was something I had to at least *try* to do. My heart broke easily, and I wanted to protect it in ways I hadn't done so many times before.

I made my way to an old CD player I'd had for years, too set in my ways to be a full-time member of the digital age. One of my favourite CDs held soft rock ballads from my favourite bands—Foo Fighters and Paramore included. I slipped it in, hit play, and then shrugged out of my duck pyjama shirt, leaving myself in a plain cream vest as I turned around to him and let the sound of *Everlong* float through the air.

Ethan was now on his back in the middle of my bed. He had his arm under his head, and his ankles crossed as he watched me.

He. Looked. Edible.

Holding out his free hand for me to take, he unleashed another of his smiles on me. One that shone with confidence. "You gonna come and join me?"

"Sure," I said, feeling a rush of heat rise to my cheeks.

Stop being a baby, rang in my head on repeat as I slowly walked towards the bed before I sank my knees into it and crawled nearer. When I got close enough, I knelt above him, dropping my arse back onto the heels of my feet.

"Do you just make yourself at home wherever you go?"

"Not really." He looked amused and reached out, his fingers twisting with mine between us. "I'm just preparing myself to be here a while. I have a million questions that have built up, and I'm pretty sure you do, too."

"What do you want to know?"

He glanced down at our joined fingers. "I'm really fucking happy you called me tonight. What made you change your mind?"

"I'm a real sucker for the arseholes out there." I smirked, watching his reaction. "And you were too much of a temptation to resist."

I saw his dimple before the curve of his lips. "A temptation?" he mused quietly. "I'm trying to be a gentleman here, and you're using words like temptation while sitting there in the sexiest damn duck pyjamas ever made. I think you were sent to test me."

"Are you going to pass?"

"I really fucking hope so." Sliding his hand to the back of my wrist, he bent forward and planted a kiss on my palm.

"Me, too."

"Do you have any siblings?"

I shook my head, my smirk turning into a smile as I eyed his face, his hand in mine, his shoulders—everything there was to see. "Not that I know of."

His lips traced their way up to my wrist. "What's your favourite movie? Cinematic tastes are a deal-breaker."

"*Rocky 1-4, Rocky Balboa.* We don't talk about *Rocky 5*, and that's the best answer I can give you. I'll throw in several honourable mentions, including *Top Gun, Cocktail, Minority Report, Gladiator*, and damn… this is hard."

"I'll give you those." Giving a tug on my wrist, he caught me off guard when I rocked forward. A quick roll of his body and I was lying on the other side of him, tucked against his chest, our faces only inches apart. "Can I take you out again? The cinema is playing *Road House* for a limited time. Let me show you I'm not a complete fucking imbecile."

"I wasn't lying when I told you that I wanted to go on adventures with you. It's why you're here… on my… bed." The last word came out as a breathy exhale.

"I think you might just have been made for me." His eyes met and held mine, while his fingers made idle strokes over my bare shoulder.

"Will you stay with me tonight?"

"I'd be honoured."

"You can take your shirt off, too, if you wanted to get a little comfier." I smiled. "Or you can just kiss me again and we'll worry about the shirt later."

Ethan didn't hesitate. With a roll of his body, he was

hovering over me, his lips crashing down against mine. This kiss was filled with passion, lust, and arousal, all edged with a hint of restraint from him. He nipped my bottom lip with his teeth, eased the sting with a gentle suck, then continued, exploring every inch of my mouth with his tongue as he went. He had one hand on my hip, his thumb brushing the exposed flesh above it as though at war with himself to go any further.

I was all out of thoughts, too high to care about the fall as I lost myself to him. The only other sound I registered was the soothing voice of Hayley Williams as she sang about having found her only exception.

Laid there beneath Ethan Walker, I wondered if I may have finally found mine, too.

CHAPTER THREE

Ethan

I stayed with Izzy all night, just as she'd asked me to. We mostly talked, both of us asking questions as inane as the first few I'd asked her. I wanted to know everything there was to know about her. We'd fallen asleep at some point and woken up as tangled together as we'd drifted off. It was the first date we should have had, and I could have stayed there all day. Probably would have if the damn alarm at the club hadn't gone off.

Driving away that morning after the worst cup of coffee I'd had in my life, I couldn't stop the aching smile on my lips. Izzy was more than I'd ever imagined. Nothing I'd experienced, no woman I'd spent time with, had ever held my attention with this much clarity.

It was fucking terrifying.

I had no idea what the fuck I was doing. I had no clue how

to go about setting us the date I'd planned for us as she'd dozed in my arms, but I knew a man who did. So, I dug my mobile from my pocket and dialled the number to one of the men I'd friended at the narcotics anonymous meetings.

"Mr Walker," he answered in his smooth, upper-crust accent. "It's been a while."

"Adrian, how you been, mate?"

Adrian Hobart was from a noble family. One of his ancestors had been an Earl or something of the like. Adrian had been arrested for cocaine possession, and he'd traded public condemnation and family humiliation for a year in the narcotics group of his choice. We were the arseholes lucky enough to be stuck with him. We'd had a couple of beers over that year and traded emails when he'd finally served his term.

"I'm clean, working for dear old Dad, and bored out of my skull. I think that about says it all."

"How long do you have left?" His family had included a clause in the terms of his rehabilitation that stated in order for him to get his inheritance, he had to work five years in his father's company or be cut off. He had no problem in admitting that was not an option, so he'd taken the job in London and settled in for the long haul.

"Three of the five years are done, but you didn't call to rehash my daily penance. How can I help you?"

"I have a date... with Blondie."

"*The* blonde?"

I smiled again. "The very same. I had an idea, but don't know how the fuck to execute it. I was hoping you could point me in the right direction."

"Tell me more."

I did. I explained my idea in detail. As I'd expected, Adrian knew a guy who could help me set it all up. He promised me an email with the details I would need before he hung up, thanking me for a project he could work on outside of the shit his father gave him to do.

I'd been floating on a natural high when I finally pulled into the car park of my apartment. I was ready to nap and shower before heading into the club to get some work done later that afternoon.

I never made it for my nap. I barely had my car in park when Scott was climbing in on the other side, looking hard-faced and drip white.

"What happened?"

"The club–"

"The alarm?"

"It wasn't a false one, mate. It's been broken into. Sapphire took the call and went in to check. Some fucker took a crowbar to the back door and trashed the place. Even managed to get into the stockroom and destroy half the inventory in there. Poles were beaten to shit, the speakers were gutted, and all the glasses were smashed. It's a fucking mess. She called the police in. We should get there at the same time."

"Son of a bitch!"

"Doesn't seem like a random, does it?"

It felt personal. If someone wanted to break in for money, they would have gone for the tills at the bar or headed to my office where there was a safe and computers. If it had been kids, I was pretty sure they'd have stolen money and booze and left it at that. To destroy the place meant they were trying to hurt us. There had to be a connection.

I'd soon find out. One of the companies that had their delivery doors facing ours had cameras. I was pretty sure they'd give me the files to find the arseholes who'd done this. Even though I had a pretty good idea, even after all this time. Tommy had warned me Jason Dagson was a dog that never let go of the bone. I'd have put money on my place being raided by his henchmen. While he couldn't follow the lead being in prison, he sure had plenty of arseholes to do it for him. Including Tommy.

Pulling up outside the club, I saw the flashing lights of the police cars lined up outside, and the gawking faces of passers-by trying to figure out what the hell had happened. The front doors were standing wide open, and Sapphire was leaning against the wall beside it, her hand waving in front of her face as she looked sick.

"Jesus."

"Yeah. Doesn't bode well, does it?" Scott said, pushing out of his side of the car with a huff of annoyance I felt to my bones.

The day had started off so fucking well.

I pocketed my dying phone and climbed out of the car as I headed towards Sapphire. Close up, she looked green, and I dreaded to think why that could be.

"Ethan, you really don't want to go in there, doll."

"How bad?" Scott asked.

"Bad enough that one of the fuckers shit on the girls' makeup. They shredded their wardrobes, smashed through your office door, and pissed over every file they dropped on your floor. Your leather sofa is shredded, and that five-pound note you had in a frame is smashed to fucking high heaven."

I actually felt sick. "Is there anything left?"

"Not much. I'm so sorry, boys."

There wasn't much I could say to that, and when I finally did find the words, the police had found me. They asked their questions, led me through the club asking what was missing at first glance, and who I thought might have done this. They finally made a trip to the place behind us to get the video file in hopes they would have clear images. It was never-ending, and by the time they left, I was drained, both physically *and* emotionally.

They had also given me the go-ahead to start putting shit back together.

I just had no idea where to start.

Finding a stool that hadn't been ripped apart, I set it upright and parked my arse on it.

The place was worse than I had imagined. Every piece of glass, including mirrors, had been shattered. Furniture had been sliced and gutted. Tables were upturned, and most of the poles were bent in fucked up angles. I didn't want to think about the changing rooms. I didn't want to think about any of it anymore.

There was only one person I wanted to talk to, and I wasn't even sure how to explain this shitstorm to her, let alone why it had happened. But I selfishly needed to hear her voice.

I dialled Izzy's number and waited for her to answer.

"Hello," she panted, barely able to catch a breath.

"Izzy?" I rose to my feet, suddenly panicked. "You okay?"

"Ethan? Oh, shit. Hi. Hi." The grin in her voice was obvious, but her breathing was laboured as fuck. "Sorry, I have my earphones in and couldn't see who was calling when I answered. I'm fine. Just… running. Woah. Hey, *arsehole*! Watch where you're driving!"

I covered my eyes with the palm of my hand, half-amused, and half distracted. "Please be careful."

"I am careful. It's idiots in cars they can't drive who are reckless." She paused, and I could hear the pounding of her feet on the road, her breaths heavy into the speaker of the phone. "You okay? You sound weird. Jesus Christ, I nearly tripped over a cat."

I choked out a laugh, unable to help myself at the sound of her exclamation. "Just needed to hear your voice. I had a hell of a morning."

She exhaled heavily, her pace obviously slowing. "What's wrong?"

"A couple of arseholes broke into the club and destroyed it. Had the police round most of the day. It finally went quiet. Needed more of that smile you put on my face."

There was a long pause on the other end of the line, the only sound to be heard being the cars flying by her and her calming breaths. "Is it ruined completely? Or can this be fixed?"

"It's a mess, but we can get a crew in here to clean and see where we go from there." I ran my hand over my hair. Just speaking to her made this seem less harrowing, but the implications of this scared me.

If they saw me with Izzy, would they use her against me?

"Do you know who did it? Have the police got them?"

"No, they're still out there. The business behind us has a camera. I'm hoping they're able to get something from that."

"Are you at the club now?" she asked, not sounding like the Izzy who had answered the call and almost broke her neck on a cat only moments before.

"Yeah," I sighed. "You wouldn't believe the state of it. They relieved themselves in here as well as smashing this place to shit."

"They *relieved* themselves?"

"They used half my property as a public toilet. Disrespectful little twats shit and pissed over the girls' things, too. It's a mess around here." I looked over to where Sapphire was talking to one of the girls by the locker room door.

"Are the girls okay?" she asked, her voice full of genuine concern for a bunch of women she'd never even met.

"The girls are fine. The ones who are here, anyway. We've called the rest and told them to stay at home. A couple have shown up, but they're more pissed than upset."

I could tell Izzy had started to run again. "You're a good boss, Ethan. You'll get this straightened out. I know you will. You'll do it for them probably more than you'll do it for yourself, right?"

I chuckled, drawing the attention of Scott, who was walking by. He stopped, even as I waved him by. "Look at that, we have something in common."

"What's that?" she panted.

"We're both nurturers."

The moment the words were out of my mouth, Scott started cackling like a ninety-year-old woman. I picked up an undamaged coaster and threw it at him, mouthing the word twat in his general direction.

"Is that going to be a problem? Us *both* wanting to protect the other all the time?"

"Nope," I said, throwing another coaster at Scott and nailing him in the forehead.

"Good." Izzy blew out a breath, the sound of her voice echoing all around at once. "Then maybe you can stop throwing shit around your already wrecked club and look up sometime soon."

I looked towards the door and felt my smile grow. Blonde hair pulled into a tight tail. Skin-tight running gear. Izzy looked fucking hot, even as a trail of sweat fell between her breasts, drawing my eyes to her cleavage.

I suddenly didn't give a shit who was watching.

I made my way through the broken glass and foam littering the floor, and I walked straight into her, my arms folding around her damp body as I swept her from her feet. I'd never been so happy to see someone in my life.

My lips met hers in a brief kiss as catcalls echoed around us.

I couldn't have cared less.

"You're here."

"Not to save you, just to hold you," she whispered, her shy smile and rosy red cheeks on display for only me to see. "But if holding you saves you, then it's win-win for me."

"You'll have to be careful. I may get used to this." I pressed my forehead to hers briefly. "Thank you."

"I'm sorry this happened to you."

"Shit happens."

"Literally," someone said as they passed, the crackle of glass giving their steps away.

It wasn't an image I wanted Izzy to have in her head.

"Are you going to introduce us, E, or are you going to stand there like a fanny all day?" Scott asked, stepping up beside us, looking like the cheesy bastard he was.

I guess there was no avoiding it now.

"Izzy, this is my best mate Scott. Scott, this is Izzy. Please don't be a dickhead."

CHAPTER FOUR

Izzy

Scott stepped towards me with a confident smirk in place. The second he did, running a hand through the long lengths of his curly dark hair, I recognised him. As a favour to my editor friend Lauren, I'd interviewed Scott in this very club years earlier. By the looks of things, this cheeky chap hadn't changed a bit. My hand was swept up into his in a heartbeat, and he bent at the knee as he kissed the back of it, looking up at me through hooded eyes.

"Izzy, believe me when I tell you that having you here is a goddamn pleasure."

Ethan's eye roll was strong, and I chuckled down at Scott as I curled my free arm around the exposed slither of skin around my waist. I hadn't exactly planned on seeing anyone when I dressed for my run, and even though this was a gentlemen's club of sorts, I was suddenly *very* aware of the fact that I was standing in front of Ethan's friends for the very first time in sweaty black running leggings, and an even sweatier black running bra.

"Hi, Scott. We've met before, right? I interviewed you when the club first opened."

"Shit, that's right. I remember. I made a good impression, didn't I?"

"You were…"

"Sexy? Endearing? The one that got away?"

"Let's go with *memorable*."

"Now you're stuck with this arsehole." Scott gestured to Ethan. "Tough luck, Blondie. I've been stuck with him for years, and it's no picnic. You should get out of here while you still have running shoes on those sweet little feet of yours."

"Probably best you shut up before I shut you up, dickhead," Ethan said, a pointed look in Scott's direction.

Scott raised his brows—a confident smirk locked in place.

I interjected, stepping closer to Ethan again. "As lovely as you clearly are, Scott, I like my men to listen more than they talk." I raised a brow.

Ethan gave my arm a brushing kiss. "Listen to the beautiful lady, Scotty."

My skin burst into goosebumps, a small shiver I couldn't hide passing over me as I watched Ethan. Scott rattled on in the background, and the two of them joked back and forth. Their easy banter reminded me so much of my relationship with Paris.

"Does he just keep talking like this no matter how much we ignore him?" I asked Ethan quietly.

"Scott doesn't have an off button," Ethan mused playfully. With his free hand, he reached for Scott but grasped at thin air as he dodged out of the way.

"That goes for all areas of my person," Scott replied smugly, glancing down at his crotch.

Ethan growled in response.

"Calm your tits, E. Jealousy is an ugly shade on you."

"And on that note…" Ethan said, making another grab for Scott, the arm around my waist ensuring he took me with him.

"Oh, we could have fun with this," Scott cried out, bouncing back on his toes, his amusement clear.

"We could, but when have I ever given you that much satisfaction?" Ethan gave Scott a smug wink and stepped away from me to shrug out of his coat. "You fancy a cup of tea, Iz?" he asked, wrapping the warm material around my shoulders.

I sank into it, careful not to moan when the smell of his aftershave surrounded me. Pulling it closed around my chest, I glanced around the club, taking in the excessive damage for the first time. This was Ethan's business. His heart and soul. It was his life.

"I'd prefer to help in some way if I can. Put me to work."

"You could help me in the office."

"Uh," Scott choked out, trying his best not to laugh.

I aimed my answer at Scott, a smile tingling my lips. "I would *love* to help you in your office, Ethan." I turned back to Ethan. "Just keep your hands busy, okay?"

His warm hand slid over the bare skin of my torso. "We'll get nice and sweaty."

"Lead the way," I said, a little rasp I couldn't control tainting my voice.

Ethan smiled smugly as he led me through the club, followed by the curious gazes of the other employees with brooms and bin bags in their hands. He didn't seem to notice them as we passed through an arch, started up a staircase, and led me to one of the three doors at the top. Ethan kicked the splintered black door aside before he turned to look at me. He didn't bother looking around—his eyes were on me.

"I'm really glad you came," he said, that voice of his making me suck in a breath.

"You doing okay? I know this can't be easy."

"I've had better days. It's just stuff. It can be replaced."

"Stuff you worked hard to have. Just because it's material, it doesn't mean it doesn't matter."

He folded his arms around my waist, his hands resting on the top of my arse. "We worked our fingers to the bone to get where we are, risked everything to make it work, and to see someone destroy it all… yeah, it pisses me off. But we're insured, and eventually, the anger will go away." He paused again, watching my face. "I'm okay."

"You wanna know what I do when I'm trying to hold it together?" Rising on my toes, I pressed a soft kiss to his lips and fell back down. "I clean. I mean, I *really* fucking clean. I get that brush out and I sweep like crazy. Hoover? I beast that thing around the place. Give me a duster, some polish, and I can take on the world. There's no better feeling. A clean space means a clean mind, and I don't mind getting dirty for the peace of it all. Honestly, you'd be doing me a favour if you let me get to work around here."

Ethan stared at me for the longest time, his hazel eyes studying my face.

"You don't have to help. You can watch. Just… let me do something," I added.

"You always manage to surprise me. There's something really sexy about that."

"Oh, well, you're going to find me irresistible then. I surprise myself every day. Now, let me clean."

Ethan's grin was bright as his eyes searched mine again. "Let me grab some supplies. Just watch your step; I have no idea what surprises lay under this mess."

He was making his way to the door when I called out to him. "If you wanted to bring a Corona up, too, I wouldn't be angry about it."

"You get more perfect every time you open your mouth, Izzy Moffit."

He'd gone when I spoke again, my grin too big given the state of my surroundings. "I am in so much trouble." I sighed heavily. "So. Much. Trouble."

CHAPTER FIVE

Ethan

Watching Izzy do her thing was proving to be a huge distraction for even my most basic skills.

She was a force of nature. After pulling off my coat, she'd demanded I put on some music and got to work, pointing me at the things she'd wanted me to do along the way. The golden hair held in a ponytail swung as she danced around the room, her perfectly pert arse bouncing from one side to the other, drawing my eye to it as she passed.

I'd been caught leaning on the handle of the broom just watching her four times already. Each time, I'd seen the humour sparkling in her eyes before she waved me back to work and continued on her way. If it had only been that easy. It wasn't just that sublime arse of hers that dragged my attention away from what I was doing. When she folded herself at the waist to pick something up or scrub a stain from the carpet, the view I got down that sports bra was more than I was capable of processing. The number of times I disappeared into some waking fantasy of bending her over my desk and burying my face between her legs was indecent.

At least Izzy was too busy to notice. Nothing seemed to distract her. Two hours of hard labour and my office finally started resembling what it had been before the break-in. The carpets were spotless, the bare surfaces of the bookshelf were polished, and my files were neatly stacked on the gleaming surface of my desk. Even the sofa cushions that had been slashed had been taken to the wheelie bins out the back.

Izzy wasn't shy about telling me what she needed me to do, throwing dusters at me, whipping me with the tail of a towel as she passed to throw it on another stain and scrub. Standing with the hoover in my hand, I was currently distracted by the sight of sweat making rivulets down between her tits, and imagining my tongue following them.

I realised too late that she was watching me.

"Erm. You're an absolute legend," I said, trying to cover my distraction, wishing Izzy's eyes were elsewhere so I could rearrange my zip for the hundredth time that hour.

Izzy held out her cloth in one hand, the bottle of polish in the other as she performed a small curtsy. "Some women are good on poles; others are good with polish. The important thing in life is to play to your strengths." She wiggled the can of Mr Sheen in her hand.

"Come over here," I said, setting the hoover upright and holding my hand out to her.

She did as she was told. Surprising us both as she dropped her cloth and polish atop my desk and coming to a blunt stop in front of me. One hand slapped her thigh, while the other slipped into mine. "Yes, boss?"

I cradled her jaw in my hands and tipped her head back, stealing a kiss before she could protest. I took my time with her lips before pressing my tongue against them, seeking permission to enter. The taste of her sank into me as she gave in and joined me, her lips parting wilfully.

The things I would do to this woman when I finally got her into bed.

The thought alone made it hard to focus.

I took from her, deepening the kiss and groaning as her tongue pressed against mine with her own hunger. I only slowed when I felt her breath rush across my lips at the impact of her back coming against my office wall. I had no idea I'd so much as moved, but if I continued, if I stayed pressed against her warm body swallowing her whimpers of approval, I was worried I'd do something we weren't ready for.

"I... I'm sorry," I whispered against her lips.

"Don't be."

"You just look extraordinarily sexy when you're in hyperdrive."

Her lashes fluttered, and her chest expanded. "I enjoyed every second of it."

I brushed some strands of hair back from her temple. "Forcing myself to stop was... difficult."

"I don't want you to have any regrets."

"I can assure you, anything we do together won't have the word *regret* attached to it. I just don't want to taste you for the first time in an office that's been destroyed by a set of wankers on a mission."

"Where would you want to taste me?"

I swallowed hard, feeling the ride of my Adam's apple against my skin. I leaned in—my mouth hovering inches from her ear. "Let me show you."

I was so erect it was becoming painful. This woman was intoxicating.

Dropping my hand between our bodies, I place it between her legs, and I ran my thumbnail along the seam of her leggings there. The heat from her told me she was as aroused as I was.

"Goddammit, Izzy."

"Sorry," she rasped, not sorry at all, her head falling back against the wall with a thud as she stared at me.

I tried my luck, my fingers moving, trailing up the seam between hip and thigh to the waistband of her skin-tight leggings. I ran my fingers along the border slowly, feeling the pebbling of her skin. My breaths were coming heavily as I tested again, slipping my hand under the material.

The corner of her mouth turned up, even when a nervous stutter fell from her, and her breathing grew quicker. "It's okay," she whispered. "I won't break. I trust you."

I pressed my forehead against hers again, feeling every hurried breath pushed from her. I should have been responsible. I should have pulled away and been better, but I was helpless to my own desires. Flattening my palm against her stomach, I slid my hand under the material and made my way to cup her in my hand, my fingers venturing over the seam of her damp pussy hungrily.

Just a taste.

That's all I wanted.

Slipping my fingers between her folds, I felt her thighs fall apart in welcome. I bent my legs and met her blue eyes, waiting for permission. She gave it with a small nod.

I pulled back, watching her face as I slid my middle finger inside her, grunting quietly when she clenched around the single digit. She was so hot and wet, the animal inside of me wanted to rip the tight material from her body so I could explore her—watch her body as it accepted me inside it.

I'd only asked for a taste, though, and no matter how much my mind flashed with filth, I would honour that request.

I pulled back slowly, slipping my finger out of her tightness and brushing her clit as I removed my hand from her clothes and stared at her, waiting for those eyes to meet mine.

If her reactions to this were anything to go by, sex with Izzy was going to be mind-blowingly arousing. Her eyes flickered, revealing the sparkling blue, and she watched me, waiting for me to taint any innocence she'd managed to hold onto.

I smiled at her, slipping my finger between my lips and tasting her for the first time while she watched.

Bad idea.

Her reaction only made me want her more.

Her own lips parted; her eyes focused on my finger in my mouth. "Do that again," she breathed.

I stepped into her body, my hips pressing against hers so she could feel how aroused I was. I kissed her, hoping she could taste herself on my lips as I took from her hungrily. I was playing a dangerous game, kissing her like this, but my sex-fogged brain still held some logic, and as I pulled back slowly, I met her eyes again, a small smile on my lips as I shook my head.

"Not here. Not today."

"Party pooper," Izzy mouthed.

"I promise you, this is harder for me than you can possibly imagine. But when you and I finally do this, it's going to be somewhere I can explore your body, spend time touching every inch of skin, giving you the best sex of your life."

"I believe it."

"Ask me to back away," I whispered against her lips. "My self-control is slipping, and I can still taste you."

She shook her head, rolling it slowly against the wall. "You're going to have to be the responsible one. I'm already too far gone."

I breathed in. The hint of Izzy's arousal still hung between us. I dropped my forehead to her neck, even as my hips rocked against her again. I wanted this woman more than I wanted to breathe. I wanted her more than I'd ever wanted that next fix.

"For the record," I said, pressing my hands against the wall on either side of her. "This is taking all of my willpower."

I pushed away with a groan that I felt in every part of my body and stumbled back.

Her shoulders sank against the wall, and Izzy took a moment to close her eyes, while a smile rose on her lips. I watched her, taking in the fluttering of her eyes from behind her eyelids, the brush of her lashes on freckled cheeks, and the run of her tongue over her bottom lip as though she could still taste herself. It was erotic. I didn't think I would ever want a woman the way I wanted her. My self-denial was proof of that as ironic as that sounded. I didn't even want to think about the other women I'd had in this office. This erased every last one of them, and all I'd done was touch her.

Intimately.

Longingly.

Hungrily.

I watched, waiting for her to say anything, yet content just to study every sweep of her tongue over her lips. Eventually, her hands came up to cover her face, and I heard the small huff of laughter falling against her palms before she peered up at me over the tips of her fingers and shook her head again.

"I should go," she said through her fingertips, her eyes sparkling with excitement.

"I'm not ready to let you go."

Her palms shifted to her flaming cheeks. "You're not ready for me to stay, either. I don't think either of us are."

"Can I take you on a proper date tomorrow night?"

"I'd love nothing more," she answered almost dreamily, her happiness crinkling the corners of her eyes.

"Can I give you a ride home?"

"I think I'm going to run. I have a lot of tension to drop off along the way."

I huffed out a laugh and nodded, reaching for her hand. "Let me walk you to the door, then."

"What? No fireman's lift now you've already had a taste of me?"

I growled. "If I put you over my shoulder, my hand is going to slip, and I won't be sorry."

She wrinkled her nose. "Probably best we just kiss and say goodbye here then."

Sweeping her against me, I kissed her. It was softer than the last one, more respectful as the words battered against my skull. I could be a gentleman.

She responded with her whole body, her arms folding around my neck, her soft lips working with mine, and stirring that hunger inside of me. The insatiable hunger that I would be stuck with until I managed to get home and fall into my fantasies.

When I finally eased back, I was breathing heavily.

"Thank you for making this really shitty day better."

"You're welcome, Walker Texas Ranger," she whispered, placing her hand over my heart and feeling the heavy thud of it as she stared at in wonder.

I realised that she did this a lot—took quiet moments to take in what was happening, not really caring about the silence they created, or the quiet intensity they could sometimes carry with them. When she looked up, she smiled. "Whenever you need me, I'm ready."

"Be careful running home and text me when you get there. No more cats."

She grinned against my mouth before she pressed a gentle goodbye kiss to me. Then she turned and left with a small glance over her shoulder.

I watched her go, but the moment she was out of sight, I fell forward and pressed my head against the wall. This woman was either going to break me or make me, and I foolishly couldn't wait to see where this went. Grabbing my phone from my pocket, I hoped for a miracle as I dialled Adrian's number.

CHAPTER SIX

Izzy

*S*he braced herself against the wall, her body tight with want and her breaths tearing at her throat. She'd felt fire before in her life—been touched by the flames only to jump away and stare at the sting—but this time had been different. This time with him was like the very first time. Edward wasn't just fire. He was the scorching heat of the sun. He was the fire saved for Hell. Edward was the kind of flame you were scarred by, never the same once the touch of his…

"Izzy, have you seen my red shoe?"

I blinked hard and stared at the document on the screen of my laptop, the words I'd written beaming back at me, foreign and unfamiliar.

"Izzy?"

Scrunching my eyes shut, I sighed heavily and called out, "No, Goose. I have not seen your red shoe!"

"Well, I haven't, either. One of us must know where it is!" she cried, her voice getting louder and somewhat closer.

"Considering it's your shoe, maybe that should be you."

Within a breath, her head peered around the edge of my bedroom door, her unimpressed face staring at me as I flushed red and quickly closed my laptop. "Don't you knock anymore?"

"I've never knocked." She scowled.

"Well… you should."

"Why?"

"Because I could be doing anything in here. I could have anyone in here."

"Oh, please." She smirked. "I know when to make myself scarce and when I'm safe. Ethan isn't here, Izzy, and since you walked back through that door yesterday, it's pretty obvious he's the only guy you're going to be having around in the future."

I frowned, wishing my emotions couldn't be read as easily as they could by this woman. I loved her, but damn, she sure could be a pain in my arse, too.

"I don't know where your shoe is, Paris," I said, trying to steer the conversation in another direction.

Her grin only grew as she stood taller and stepped into the bedroom fully, her arms folding over her chest. "Just admit it…"

"Admit what?"

"I did good."

"Good?"

"With Ethan. He's perfect for you, isn't he?"

I couldn't argue. What I didn't want her or anyone knowing, was how quickly I was falling.

The memory of his touch burned me through the night, and I'd found my fingers slipping beneath white sheets to caress my own skin, imagining it was him and he was there with me, touching me again.

"He's lovely," I offered quietly, my body flaming at the memory.

"Oh, boy," Paris whispered. "This is going to be fun."

Reaching behind me, I grabbed a white scatter cushion and launched it at her head, unable to stop my smile from exploding as she laughed and teased me before she ran out of the room.

With a groan, I threw myself back onto my bed, my fingers sliding through my hair and tugging tightly while I stared up at the ceiling, unable to get Ethan goddamn Walker out of my mind. He made me feel like a giddy virgin waiting to be destroyed by the over-experienced lothario. The likes of Matt Cooper and Jack Parker couldn't compete with him, and I'd been all the way with both of them. Even though I thought they'd been satisfying at the time, that one intimate minute with Ethan had proved just how naive of a sex life I'd had.

He was going to wreck me, and I was going to devour every second of the destruction.

Glancing at the clock by my bed, I realised I had three hours to get ready for our date later that night. I had no idea where we were going, only that I wanted to get there quickly. Three hours felt like a lifetime away from him, and I knew just how dangerous that made him in my life.

My phone rang suddenly, the sound of the Foo Fighters *All My Life* making me reach for the phone and smile when I saw who was calling.

"Hey, Lauren." I grinned.

"Hey, doll face. How's it going? Sorry I didn't call you back last night. There's busy, there's hectic, and then there's my life which is, quite frankly, just unfuckinbelievable."

"It's fine. I know your schedule is crazy."

"That's the understatement of the decade." Lauren chuckled. "What's the matter, anyway? What shit do you need my help with?"

God, I loved Lauren. Straight to the point, cutting out the fat, and only speaking the truth in her heart, I'd quickly grown to rely on her more than either one of us realised. After Paris got herself in trouble all those years ago, Lauren had helped me track her down and keep her out of trouble, her sleuth ways proving to be a big helping hand in the destruction of Paris's ex-boyfriend and drug dealer, Jason Dagson.

"What makes you think I need your help?"

"Because you only ever call when you're struggling."

I gasped, sitting upright in bed. "That's not true. I don't. I—"

"Cool it, Iz," she cut me off. "It's a good thing. I like knowing I'm the woman you rely on to drag you out of the shit when you're too far in it."

"Fine. You got me."

"I know I do." She laughed again. "Now give me the lowdown. I live for this shit."

I did as I was told, telling her about what had happened to Ethan's club, wondering if she'd heard anything on the grapevine. She hadn't. The likes of Club Crystal were too small a fry for Lauren to get wind of, but in her usual, dependable manner, she vowed to dig deep and get her team to look into it for me.

"Thank you," I said, feeling somewhat relaxed about it already. "But keep yourself out of trouble, okay? I don't want you getting caught out for me on this."

"I don't get caught, sweetie."

"Of course not." I smirked.

It didn't take her long to end the call. When I threw my

phone on the bed, I stood up and went to my wardrobe, opening it up to have a look inside.

So far, Ethan had seen me in jeans, in sweats, and in my pyjamas. Tonight, I wanted to look special for him. I wanted to look like someone worthy of being on his arm, and I knew myself well enough to know I wasn't the person to bring that out in myself.

Clinging onto the wardrobe door, I closed my eyes and gave in to what I knew I had to do.

"Paris?"

She appeared at my door less than thirty seconds later. "Yeah?"

I turned, looking at her through helpless eyes, not needing to say a word.

"Sure, I'll help you, Izzy." She smiled, her face coming to life with the prospect of using me as a Barbie Doll.

"Thank you," I mouthed.

"We're going to make you so pretty; he won't make it to his car without being able to touch you."

***

I stood in front of my wardrobe mirror and smiled.

Paris hadn't gone overboard.

I was wearing tan platform wedges that made the slender muscles and definition in my bare legs pop, along with a little strappy black broderie summer dress that ended halfway down my thighs. She'd buffed and polished every inch of my skin, finishing off her masterpiece by draping a long silver necklace over my head that fell in between my braless breasts. My hair was down and free, my natural beachy waves falling over my shoulders, and I had my old Levi's denim jacket on, too, to keep me warm. This was Manchester, after all.

It felt like I'd been waiting a lifetime until Ethan rang the bell at Casa, and when he did, my body flushed with heat, and I went to him on jellied legs. With a deep breath for bravery, I opened the door, my smile bursting to life the moment I saw him turn and take me in.

"Hey," I said brightly.

His eyes ran the length of my body. Down my legs and right back up until the hazel burning with intensity met mine. "Jesus."

He stepped up and into my body. His fingers skimmed the flesh of my thigh at the hemline of the dress. He watched me closely as his fingers trailed the line back and forward, then he leaned in to brush his lips against mine in greeting.

"You look stunning."

"You don't look so bad yourself."

"This old thing? Figured I'd make an effort this time."

"I was talking about your face." Reaching up, I pinched his chin between my finger and thumb. "Kinda like it, in case you couldn't tell by this stupid smile I'm wearing."

"You're making it impossible for me, you know."

"To do what?"

"Take things slow." He pushed against my hand, pressing his lips against mine and held them there as he growled the rest quietly. "You're making me want to taste you again, and here you are in a dress."

"*And* heels," I pointed out, raising my brows.

"We should probably leave now." He pulled away, his hands sweeping mine up and giving me a tug. "I have something planned, and we can't be late."

Ethan pulled me from the house and leaned back to shut the front door, brushing his chest against my arm as he did. He led me towards the street, his smile proud when he stopped by a grey car with a small flourish.

"This is Lucy, my Mustang. She's also known as the other

lady in my life," he announced, leaning in to open the door for me. "She's the reason you had McDonald's on our first date."

I blinked up at him. "You *own* a Mustang?"

"Yep."

"Wow."

"She's been my dream car since I was four," he said proudly. "It was the first thing I bought when we started making a profit at the club."

I found myself stepping around Ethan and running a hand over the bonnet with reverence. I moved to the front of the car, taking it all in. "She's the most beautiful thing I've ever seen."

"She used to be."

"Huh?"

"Before you."

I glanced up at him, a smirk playing on my lips as I tried to ignore the heavy thudding of my heart. Keeping my eyes trained on him, I pressed both hands on Lucy.

"Okay now, Lucy, I know he's yours and you had him first. I get it. You probably want to take a sharp right at some point and throw me into the door. If I had to share him, I'd feel that way, too. But you heard him just now, and when he says things like that, it's impossible for me to stay away." I rubbed her carefully, my smile growing as I looked at Ethan. "So instead of being enemies, let's find a way to be best friends, okay? I'll look after you, and I'll let you keep him to yourself... occasionally."

Ethan's smile turned hungry as he watched me. His hands white-knuckled on the frame of the door. "You are a dangerous woman, Izzy Moffit. As much as I would love to acquaint you and Lucy more intimately, we have someplace to be."

"Sorry." I sighed softly, looking down at Lucy before I whispered, "I love you already," and I skipped around the car, not wanting to ruin any plans he may have made.

CHAPTER SEVEN

Ethan

Seeing Izzy at the door in heels and a dress had almost been more than my control was capable of. Then she'd fondled Lucy, and all rationality had gone right out the window. This woman was more dangerous than I'd ever anticipated. She'd cast a spell over me, and I was helpless against her. I also couldn't find it in myself to give a shit.

Putting the car in gear, I pulled away and headed in the direction Adrian had given me. He'd set everything up in his family's hanger as they were all currently in London along with their private jet. He'd even had a catering service arrange the food. He paid his debts tenfold.

I was able to keep my eyes and attention on the road for all of two minutes before it was drawn back to Izzy. She'd shifted in her bucket seat, her skirt riding up those luscious thighs and giving me more of a view. I was trying to remember how to speak when I finally came to a stop at a set of traffic lights.

"Thanks again for your help yesterday," I said. It was that, or *let's scrap the date and screw*.

"You okay?" she asked casually. "You seem kind of… tense."

"Not tense," I corrected. "Just really fucking distracted. By you. In a skirt."

"Should I have worn trousers?"

"You wouldn't have been any less distracting," I said, reaching over to touch her thigh, my hand inching under the hem of the skirt, and squeezing her gently. "If you'd worn trousers, I wouldn't have been able to touch you like this."

Her thighs pressed together, her body shifting lightly. "Do you feel that?"

All I could feel was warm, soft skin and heat, but I played dumb. I glanced over at her in question before I pulled away when the light turned green.

"That spark. Is it just me? Or do you feel it, too?" There was no embarrassment to her voice. Her question was genuine, and she was looking at me with wide eyes and a waiting smile. "Am I crazy?"

"I felt it the moment I kissed you on your doorstep two nights ago."

"Thank God," she sighed happily, her head falling against the headrest.

"Weird, huh?"

"Really weird. I can't say I've ever felt that with anyone before."

"I feel like that shit should probably freak me the fuck out."

"Me, too." She grinned. "You look really, really hot tonight, by the way."

"Thank you." I chuckled. "You look absolutely stunning."
And entirely too fuckable, I thought, heading onto the motorway.

Izzy's thighs moved again, but never once did she try to remove my hand. "Want me to help you drive? I can gear up and down for you. Or you could practice more of that self-control of yours and take your hand back."

I slipped my hand down towards her knees and grinned over at her. "I'm going to get you to our destination safely."

"That would be appreciated." She chuckled to herself, turning forward again. "Want me to talk shit while you focus on the road?"

"Feel free."

"Well, my day has been epically long. I worked, got distracted, deleted everything I wrote, then tried to work again only to get distracted… *again*." When I glanced her way, Izzy was staring out of the windscreen, a small smile tugging at her lips as she ran a hand through her long, wavy blonde hair. "After that, I spoke to a friend, hung out with Paris, and got ready for tonight with you. My favourite colour is mint green, but I hate mossy colour greens or anything that's tinged with shades of brown. Those colours make me feel heavy, and I prefer to feel light. I want to travel more. I haven't done that enough in my life. Sometimes when I'm bored, I practice perfecting my own handwriting. I love the swirl of ink on white paper. I also love nachos as much as I do Corona, and I've yet to find any food that beats them. I haven't had my hair cut in such a long time I'm actually scared to go to the hairdressers now for fear of them judging me about my split ends. I go on rollercoasters even though I secretly hate them. I don't know why I do that, actually." She paused to release a carefree sigh. "I have a million pairs of Converse. Not enough heels—according to Paris. And…" Her smile grew bigger. "I've had more butterflies in my stomach with you in the last three days than I've had with anyone else in the last ten years."

Damn, she had a way of making me pay attention. She was stunning in her bravery. I hadn't ever been fearful of telling someone the truth. If it was hard or unfortunate, I exercised some restraint and delivered it in the best way I could, but the way she just dropped these little facts in my lap was more of a turn-on than I knew what to do with.

She turned to look at me again. "How's that?"

"I can't get enough of you, Izzy."

"Things may change. I'm a lot to handle." Even though that smile stayed on her face, I thought I saw a hint of sadness wash over her. "One day at a time, right?"

I smiled back at her in response.

When I finally turned into the small airport, I slowed as we approached the guard gate at the back that led to the private hangers and handed the guy my license.

"Been expecting you, Mr Walker. It's hanger four."

"Cheers, mate," I said, taking back my license and dropping the car into gear as he lifted the security gate. I chanced a look over at Izzy and grinned. "Curious?"

"More than you know."

"You'll know soon enough," I said, following the signs to the hanger and pulling slowly inside.

The place was empty of anything apart from a surround system set out in a square where I'd been told to park facing the back wall of the hanger. I turned off the engine and glanced over at Izzy again as a few people stepped in and placed small tables and buckets on either side of the car. They backed away, merging into the shadows as the doors closed behind us, casting us into darkness.

"You ready?" I asked, picking up a remote from the table on

my side of the car.

She was scowling as she looked at me, shaking her head and smiling. "I have no idea what is happening right now."

Pointing out of her window with the remote, I smiled gently. "I pay attention, gorgeous. I have the best nachos around, as well as Corona bottles on ice. And this…" I pointed the remote in the general direction I'd been told to, and I hit play.

The opening credits started to roll after the usual production logos flashed brightly. A long piano with the neon word BANDSTAND rolled on the wall being used to project the movie onto, but my eyes were on Izzy.

Her reactions played out in slow motion, her hands falling behind her as she shuffled to the very edge of her seat before she gripped the dashboard and took it all in. The music from *Road House*—one of her favourite movies—filled the hanger, and I glanced down to Izzy's thighs, watching the goosebumps flare to life over her skin.

"Holy shit," she mouthed. She was in a trance, her wide eyes on the screen before she blinked wildly and turned to look at me. "You did this for me?"

"I figured this was a more acceptable date. Not a chicken nugget in sight."

"You did this… for me?" she repeated on a whisper.

"Yeah, Izzy. I did it for you."

"Why?"

I pressed pause on the remote and leaned over the console towards her. I could see her features in the light from the screen and ran my index finger down her jaw slowly. "You really have to ask?"

She shook her head again. "This is crazy." Her smile erupted, a huff of nervous laughter bouncing from her chest. "*You're* crazy."

"I'm crazy about you, Izzy." I bent over the middle console, pressed my lips against hers, and stayed there. "You deserve so much."

It took her a second, but when she accepted it, she reached up to cup my cheeks, and she held my mouth against hers, leading the kiss between us for the very first time with nothing held back. Her tongue slid over mine, the massaging of her lips more than either one of us could handle as she gave herself to me. I let her guide me, following her lead and enjoying every damn second of it until she broke away and held my face in her palms, her eyes searching mine.

"Our first adventure." She smiled, lighting up the whole fucking hanger with it. "Thank you."

I would have done anything to keep that smile on her face. Izzy was a natural beauty, everything about her was attractive to me, but this elated joy was what I wanted to aim towards every day.

"The first of many," I said. "You ready to watch? Or can I kiss you some more?"

"I like you, Ethan, but if you're trying to come between Patrick Swayze and me, we may have a problem here."

CHAPTER EIGHT

Izzy

The two of us laid over the bonnet of his Mustang, hidden under the hanger while Patrick Swayze kicked arse.

This is the kind of thing I write about—dream about, I thought to myself over and over again, unable to tame the crazy smile on my face. The cheek ache had set in as we talked easily. Even when the conversation grew serious, I couldn't make it go away, and I couldn't stop casting glances his way.

Ethan Walker was fucking hot. Insanely hot, actually, and even though I had a feeling he knew he was attractive, he did nothing but make me feel like a queen.

He was all man, with ripples over the muscles of his arms that made me swallow back my desire constantly. His strong jaw and few-day growth made my fingers itch to touch him. But most of all, the thing that got me every time were those hazel eyes of his. The way they stared at me, studying every part of my face with genuine curiosity, and the sparkle he held in them. Sure, he could be a gentleman. He'd proved that enough already. No matter how hard he tried, though, he couldn't completely hide the animal side of him—the one that was dying to switch off the movie and move this into the back seat of his precious Lucy.

He was currently leaning back, his body twisted my way as he rested on one elbow, glancing between the screen and me, while I was sitting upright, eyes now glued to the tragedy happening in front of me.

Wade Garrett was about to meet his maker, and I couldn't hold back the anger that resided inside of me every time I saw this.

"Oh, no. No, no. Not again. She's fine, Dalton. Doc doesn't need saving. Go to Wade, go to Wade."

Ethan rubbed my back slowly. "Tragic, isn't it? No matter how many times you yell at them, they never listen."

"It breaks my heart."

Ethan shuffled closer to me on his side before he balanced his beer against the windshield and linked our fingers together. The music turned dramatic when Swayze took off to get his revenge.

I could feel Ethan staring at me.

I turned to him. "What?" I smiled.

"You've completely pulled my attention away from one of my all-time favourite movies, and you're not even sorry, are you?"

"Should I be?"

Ethan smirked. "No."

"Then stop moaning." I leaned down to place a soft kiss on

his head before I deposited my beer on one of the nearby tables and laid back to be by his side. "I could get through life like this. Being spoiled is more addictive than I ever thought it would be."

Ethan slid his hand over my stomach and gripped my hip with a gentle squeeze. "You should probably get used to it. I'm hoping to spoil you stupid."

"Tell me more."

"I'm not going to tell you, beautiful." He gazed at the screen before looking back at me, rolling so his body was pressed against mine, his lips brushing the lobe of my ear. "Have you ever orgasmed on the bonnet of a car while watching Swayze before?"

I swallowed, feeling a rush of breath leave me.

"Have you, Izzy?" he whispered.

"Never," I breathed.

The hand on my hip traced a slow path down my hip to my thigh, sliding slowly up under the material of the dress. "Do you want to?"

"W-what would Lucy think?"

He fingered the edge of my underwear before slowly moving closer to the inside of my thighs. "I really don't give a shit what she thinks."

A knee raised without my permission, my foot sliding up the bonnet, causing my thigh to nudge him closer. "Okay," was all I could breathe, my eyes unblinking as I stared at him, waiting, wanting.

Gripping the waist of my underwear, he tugged it down over my hip just enough for him to have full access. Taking his time, Ethan ran his index finger over the sensitive flesh, his eyes studying me as he teased in slow strokes. He slipped between my folds with a quiet growl in his throat—his slow movements now circling my clit with the same teasing intensity.

My chest began to bounce, and my lips parted as I closed my eyes and lost myself to his touch.

Ethan applied more pressure with his finger, and his breath moved closer, bathing my cheek, neck, and then ear. He ran his tongue along the edge, and his breath hitched as that single digit between my thighs ventured down through my slick sex.

"You look fucking beautiful like this," he whispered, pushing inside of me in a slow stroking motion, his voice trailing off in a heated growl as the movie played on behind him.

But fuck the movie.

Fuck Swayze.

Fuck everything and everyone who wasn't Ethan.

My eyes flickered open, misty with arousal as electricity shot through me, and I sought him out. I wanted—needed more. I wanted this to last forever.

He held my gaze as he slid that one finger from me, his thumb brushing the sensitive bud of my clit as he did. He paused, his lips curling in a satisfied smile as he studied me. His gaze flickered to my lips only briefly before he moved again, thrusting two fingers back inside of me, his erection pressing against my hip. He applied more pressure with his thumb against my clit, and I felt it *everywhere*.

My eyes closed again, and I imagined him inside me, both of us naked, his touch everywhere, and his mouth in those places, too. I was about to lose my mind. The reality of him was so much more than the fantasies I'd already had.

I was also about to come.

The thrusts were slow to begin with, Ethan stroking inside of me as he retreated, then he pushed deeper, seeking more, groaning as my body tightened around his two fingers. Slow didn't last long, though. He timed his thrusts with my breaths, his own picking up as he rocked his hips against my side, his thumb applying pressure in the same rhythm.

That tight knot of tension in my stomach grew, making my hands fly to twist in my hair as I arched off the bonnet.

"Fuck," I panted. "Don't stop that. Don't…"

Pushing his body closer against mine, he fucked me with his fingers. The pressure of his thumb exchanged for the heel of his hand grinding against my clit as his index and middle finger pressed deeper inside me.

A second later, that knot in my stomach turned to fire, and it spread out, shooting down my legs, and forcing my body to tighten around his fingers as I came, hard.

"Jesus Christ," he growled, his hand slowing, feeling and stroking as my body slowly relaxed. "I could watch you do that all fucking night."

Despite struggling to catch a breath, I let my hands slowly fall to my stomach, and I turned to him, my face completely flushed.

"I could let you," I panted softly.

Ethan moved his hand from between my thighs in a slow drag, his fingers lingering on the intimate parts of my body before sliding them out completely. His body rolled closer, almost covering mine as he stared down at me, all hint of humour now lost to his arousal.

"Be careful what you wish for, Izzy."

I've wished for you my whole life.

He slipped his fingers into his mouth, his eyes still holding mine, watching my reaction as his tongue darted out, then fell over the curve of his bottom lip. I'd barely had time to draw a breath when he was on me, lips covering mine, his tongue pushing into my mouth hungrily.

I reached for him, wrapping my arms around his neck and holding him to me.

"I should behave myself," he growled against my lips.

"You should," I breathed out, not meaning a word of it.

"You think that's possible when I can taste you on my lips?"

"Don't ask me. I'm about three seconds away from asking you to fuck me already."

Ethan's breath hitched at almost the same moment as a heavy door swung shut somewhere in the darkness of the hanger. The growl was more frustration this time as he reached down between us and pulled the skirt of my dress down, covering me up.

"The fucking timing."

"What was that?" I asked, looking around him as my hands dug into his shoulders.

"Probably the people who were hired to set this up checking up on us." He groaned, his hand pressing against his crotch as he shifted. "The movie finished."

I glanced down at his jeans, a small smirk growing before I looked back up at Ethan's face. His misery was clear, and I couldn't help the small huff of laughter that bubbled in my stomach. "At least something got seen through to the end."

A small laugh blew his breath over my cheek. "There I was thinking about putting my head up your dress, and you hit me with that. You're a cruel woman."

"Overthinking leads to disappointment. Next time, just do it." I wrapped my arms back around his neck, pressing my forehead to his. "Although, maybe one day we'll look back on this moment and be glad we got interrupted before we did something we planned on waiting for."

He smiled down at me, kissing the tip of my nose as a young man approached us slowly from the shadows.

"Was there anything more we could get you, Mr Walker?"

Ethan looked down at me with his smile back in place. "You

want more nachos or Corona?"

"I'm good, thank you. Couldn't fit another thing inside me," I answered through a soft smirk that soon turned into a huge grin.

Ethan choked out a laugh, trying his best to keep a straight face as he thanked the guy. The moment the figure blended with the shadows again, he let go, a bellow of laughter falling from him as he dropped his forehead to my shoulder.

"I'm never going to be bored with you around, am I?"

"Not if I can help it."

CHAPTER NINE

Ethan

After one of the best nights of my life, I wanted nothing more than to take up Izzy's invitation to come in for a cup of tea when I dropped her off at home. I was sure she'd meant the request innocently enough, but my driving need to do a million dirty things to her, just to see that exquisite euphoria on her face again, made it a gamble to accept. I wanted to do this relationship thing right for her. The rules she'd set in motion may have been out of the window as a whole, but slow was the one thing I was going to respect. I'd wanted the date to be about her, and leaving it where we had ensured it stayed that way. Even if kissing her goodbye had lasted for an hour.

Izzy Moffit had exceeded every fucking fantasy I'd had about her. All those years thinking about her hadn't done her justice. The more time I spent with her, the more I lusted after her. I just couldn't get enough, and I hadn't masturbated so much in my fucking life. Even as a teenager, I'd had more self-control.

"You are a lost cause, mate," Scott said, pulling my attention away from my phone, where I'd just shot a text to Izzy. It had been less than twenty-four hours since our date, and I'd been dragged to the local pub by Scott and my brother Dean. They hadn't seen much of me since that first date I'd had with Izzy, but it was our pub night, so I was there as requested.

"I ain't even sorry about it."

"Course not."

Dean scoffed at me from the other side of the table. "Din't think I'd see the day ma big bro got pussy-whipped."

"Keep it coming. Just remember I'm going to pay your dumb arse back tenfold when some poor lass is stupid enough to want to spend more than a night in your bed."

"Nevah gunna happen."

I nudged Scott in the ribs. "He might be right. What lass would put up with his shit?"

"He can barely talk English," Scott joined in with a laugh.

My phone pinged, and I looked down at the screen, grinning at Izzy's reply to my simple *hi!* I'd sent.

Izzy: Rich? Is that you?

Scott glanced over my shoulder and guffawed, even as I palmed his face and shoved him away.

"Can't you dickheads find something to amuse yourselves with?"

I typed my response.

Me: I can be anyone you want me to be. Rub me and see what happens.

I hit send and glanced up at the two fools gawking at me, open-mouthed.

"You shagged her yet?" Scott asked. "Only a girl who is a fucking dynamo in bed should have this much power over another human being."

"Why is my sex life such an interest to you two? You've never been this interested before."

"*You've* never been this interested before."

"He's right, E." Dean pointed his bottle at me. "We learned everything we know from you."

"Speak for yourself, dickhead," Scott interjected.

"You know what I mean."

My phone pinged on the table, and the two of them groaned. I gave them both a 'fuck you' glance before grinning down at my phone like a fucking idiot.

Izzy: I've seen what happens when you get rubbed…

My smile grew.

Me: What are you wearing?

Scott glanced over my shoulder and shook his head in defeat. "Deano, you up for a game of pool? We lost this fucker to his phone already."

I barely heard Dean's reply or noticed them getting up from the table as I took a mouthful of beer and waited for Izzy's response. I already had the phone in my hand when the tone for a new message pinged.

Izzy: Wait. Let me send you a picture. Words can't describe how hot I look. You need to see it for yourself.

It took her another minute to follow through with that promise, and it was the longest minute of my life.

Izzy: Photo attached.

I opened the picture and let out an involuntary laugh as I stared at the picture. Her gorgeous long legs were the main focus, and I appreciated the length as much as I always did.

The amusing part was a pair of shorts with penguins in various positions, and slippers that looked like she'd shaved a dog to cover. Only Izzy could get away with an outfit like this and somehow manage to sex the fucking thing up.

Me: You take sexy to a whole new level.

Me: What are your tits doing?

I glanced up only long enough to catch the eye of a waitress and ask for another beer before my phone pinged again.

Izzy: Hold, please.

Izzy: Photo attached.

The second picture came through quickly, showing Izzy laid on her side, her tits nestled together beneath a thin, white vest as she rested her head on a white pillow on her bed. She was makeup-free, her long, wavy blonde hair spread out around her, and the small smile on her lips made her eyes crinkle at the corners.

Izzy: They're just waiting around to be felt up.

Me: Is that an invitation?

I hit send as someone slid a beer onto the table and dropped into the seat opposite mine. I didn't bother glancing up. The only person I had any interest in was on the other end of my phone.

I waited, grabbing at the beer and drinking. We'd opened a tab, so there was no reason for anyone to hang around. When my phone pinged again, I woke the screen up.

Izzy: You're in danger of becoming obsessed. I can feel it.

Me: Too late.

I hit send and glanced up impatiently.

It wasn't Scott, Dean, or even the waitress sitting there, as I'd suspected. Looking at the familiar face there, I was pretty fucking sure I would never have expected Tommy to be sitting with me. My smile faded slowly.

"Well, if it isn't Manchester's finest entrepreneur," Tommy said in that low, rough, immediately threatening voice. He sounded like part of the old school Krays' squad, and his face was marred with scars.

"Tommy. Been a long time," I said, my eyes searching the bar for Scott and Dean, hoping to fuck they stayed away. Although they knew about the darker parts of my past, they didn't know the finer details, or who they involved, exactly. Tommy, my old boss, and drug pusher was dangerous. I'd got away from him once. Very few managed to do so, and that fact wasn't lost on me.

"Hmm." Tommy's eyes narrowed, his smile never leaving his face. "That it has. A long while."

I hated the motherfucker almost as much as I hated Jason Dagson, but I also knew what he was capable of. Seeing him this soon after the club had been tossed told me my suspicions were right on the fucking money. He'd been responsible for everything I'd lost.

"What can I do for you?" I asked calmly, my tone polite.

"What do you think you can do for me, Walker?"

"After over a decade, I can't fathom."

"You could start by at least pretending it's a pleasant surprise to see me." He shuffled in his seat, glancing to the side before focusing on me again. "After all, we spent time together once. You knew things."

"Things that are irrelevant now. As I said, it's been a long fucking time."

It was a gamble talking to him the way I was. He wasn't someone to be messed around, but I'd spent too much of my life avoiding him and the other bastards to even so much as show him that they made me nervous. Once he knew he had you, you were his, and I wasn't ever going to be in his debt again.

Tommy's smirk lifted his cheek, and he studied me for far too long, doing his best to make me uncomfortable with nothing more than a look. I held his gaze until he leaned back and huffed out a humourless laugh, one hand resting on the table while the other fell to his thigh.

"Lots to catch up on." His nostrils flared, and he raised a brow. "How are things?"

"What do you need, Tommy?"

"Found a nice girl? Got any kids?" he asked, ignoring my tone completely. "Found that suburban life yet?"

As if on cue, my phone chimed on the table in front of me. One glance at the screen, I saw a bubble with Izzy's name on it. I couldn't even think about her with Tommy sitting in front of me. It felt like dropping a toothbrush into a toilet. I wasn't going to let her get touched by this if I could help it.

"Mate, I appreciate the small talk, but please get to the point."

His smirk turned into a slow grin. "Mate?"

I raised my brows. What I remembered of Tommy wasn't much considering I'd been high as a fucking kite most of the time, but I did know he liked to bait people. I'd seen him doing it. He would start a conversation, calm as you like, never raising his voice as a way of intimidation, and it worked. Being on the other end of it was fucking disturbing, but I couldn't afford to chase the baited trap he was laying out. I wanted no part of his shit, and I sure as hell didn't want to expose Izzy, and by association, Paris, back to this life. So, I waited him out, saying nothing in response.

"I didn't think so," he eventually said, his voice eerily quiet. His eyes drifted down to my left hand before glancing at my phone, which lit up with another message before he finally focused back on my face. "I was sorry to hear about that girl you used to fuck around with. Thought that, when I saw you, I'd come over and pass on my condolences." He tilted his head to the side and slowly drummed his fingers on the table. "What was her name again?"

"Jessica."

"Right."

I exhaled heavily, my chest expanding and deflating slowly.

"Nasty business we used to be in. A lot of people got hurt because they couldn't quit using."

I felt my jaw tense at his words. "It was a shitshow."

"And then you somehow got out."

"Yeah, I got clean and moved on."

"Good for you." He sniffed up, his eyes penetrating mine. "It's always good to hear that some got… lucky."

I tried my damn best not to react the way I wanted to. "Indeed."

His chest bounced, but no laughter came out. "Noticed there's no ring on your finger. Probably best you keep women away, I guess, after what happened with the other one. Women always did bring you nothing but trouble."

My phone started ringing and vibrating on the surface of the table before his last syllable was free. Tommy's eyes dropped to the screen as his lips curled in that sociopathic smirk of his. Having Izzy this close to this animal made me feel sick. So, I ignored her call.

Tommy chucked his chin and gestured to the phone. "Don't ignore that on my account."

"It can wait."

"I'm not sure *My Blondie* agrees," he said as the call ended, only for it to start up again. Izzy was eating out of the palm of

Tommy's hand, and she didn't even know it.

"You know what it's like. They get a taste of your dick and they just keep wanting more."

"It's not like you to turn away a fuck toy."

"I'm done with that piece of arse."

Even saying it in my head made me feel sick. Tommy thought he had me, and I couldn't let him think he was winning. I also couldn't let him know who *My Blondie* was.

The phone kept ringing, though, which only seemed to amuse him all the more.

"You should tell her then."

"What?" I scowled.

"Tell her." He gestured to the phone. "Tell her you're not interested."

The smirk he was wearing said he'd already won this little fucking battle, and he had. If I didn't pick up and tell her to fuck off, he'd know she could be used against me. If I picked up and told her to fuck off, there was a chance I would lose her, and he would win.

I'd rather suffer that way than let them get hurt. I reached for my phone.

"Walker," I barked down the line, hoping to Christ she'd hear the tone.

"Texas Ranger," she said, mimicking my voice before she laughed softly. The happiness within her flowed down the phone before she let off a dreamy sigh. "Hey, you."

It broke my heart knowing what I had to do.

"What can I do for you, love? I'm in the middle of something."

"Oh," she said quietly. The long pause that followed was filled with Izzy confusion. "Sorry. I, erm…"

I tried not to react. Every knuckle in my hand ached to

make a fist and knock Tommy out. My jaw ticked and twitched as I forced it into some semblance of relaxation, while my chest turned to lava.

"What do you need?" I asked her sharply.

"Need?" she repeated, her voice rising.

"Why did you call?"

"I called... for... you."

Tommy raised a brow at me and tilted his head in waiting—waiting for me to say the words I needed to say that I knew would break Izzy's heart when she'd specifically asked me not to.

"Yeah, no longer interested. Sorry." I swallowed and hung up the phone, too afraid that if I heard her response, I would ignore my better judgment and grovel. I glanced up at Tommy and shrugged. "Where were we?"

His face lit up with amusement, and rough, sadistic laughter made his body rock. "Never gets easier, does it? Being a ladies' man." Leaning forward, he rested his arms on the table again and lowered his voice. "Although, I'd have thought you'd have been well-practised enough not to turn green when you told them to fuck off, Walker."

Tommy's eyes searched mine, so many silent threats and words going unspoken before he tapped his hands on the table, stood up, and tugged on the lapels of his jacket.

"I'll leave you in peace," he said smugly. "A pleasure, as always. Until next time."

The sick son of a bitch didn't wait for my *fuck you* to him before he walked away, slipping into the crowd at the bar. I stayed frozen in my seat, my hand white-knuckled around my phone as I watched the door, waiting for him to head out before I reacted. He'd somehow known Izzy meant something to me, and he was flexing his fucking muscles just to inflict misery into my life.

He had.

I fucking hated myself for what I'd just done.

He left the pub with barely a glance in my direction. I offered a tilt of my chin in the way of farewell before I was on my feet with my jacket and keys in hand. I didn't bother heading back to the pool tables. I caught Scott's eye on the way out, and he nodded, looking only slightly concerned.

I needed to see Izzy and explain. Even if I had to drive to Liverpool and back to make sure I wasn't followed.

CHAPTER TEN

Izzy

"Paris?" I called out as I ran down the stairs, throwing my denim jacket over my shoulders and pulling my hair out of the collar. "Paris?"

"What's up? What's up?" she asked, meeting me at the bottom of the stairs, her dark hair wild as she rubbed a sleepy eye.

"Sorry. Were you sleeping?"

"I may have nodded on the sofa, yeah. Fuck, Iz. You sounded frantic. What the hell?"

I was frantic.

No longer interested. Sorry.

I'd been stupid. Stupid, stupid, stupid to let the walls around my heart fall down after just three wanky dates with Ethan Wanky Walker, but I couldn't tell Paris that. She didn't need the stress, and I didn't want to make her feel like shit for putting him in my path, only for him to do this to me…

The way they all did this to me.

"Sorry," I said, pushing my hair behind my ear while holding my car keys in my hand. "I have to go out, that's all."

"Out where?"

I don't know. Anywhere. "I said I'd go meet Lauren quickly."

"The reporter chick?"

"Yeah. She has a job for me down in London. She wants to talk to me about it tonight."

Paris wasn't stupid, though, and the not-so-subtle glance she gave my outfit said everything she didn't. Apart from my denim jacket, I was wearing grey jogging bottoms, the same white vest I'd texted Ethan in, and my white Converse. As far as business meetings went, I was already tanking it.

"I… she… I'm just meeting her at her rented flat in town. She suggested pizza and wine while we talk business."

Paris smirked and folded her arms across her chest. "Izzy, if you're going to see Ethan, just tell me you're going to see Ethan." She reached out to play-punch me on the arm, but my numb body was too broken to fight it off, and her punch made me rock to the side before I looked up at her, trying my best to school my face.

"Not Ethan," I said quietly.

"Oh shit," she whispered, her own face falling. "What's happened?"

"Nothing."

"Do not lie to me, Izzy Mary Louise Moffit."

"I just…" Blowing out a breath, I pushed my hand through my hair and held it behind my head. "Everything is happening too quickly, and I think I got a little carried away with myself."

"What do you mean?" She scowled. Her protective edge

was already out, ready to flex its claws and slash through any threat.

"He's just not as into me as I thought, and I feel a bit stupid about that."

"What the hell did he do?" Paris stepped forward, a hand resting on my arm. She was the biggest pain in my arse most days, but when it came to it, I loved her like no one else in this world.

"He said he's no longer interested, and then he hung up the phone."

"Ethan said that?" She frowned.

"Yeah."

"You sure *Ethan* said that?"

"He was crystal clear, Goose."

She searched my eyes for another moment before she stomped her foot. "Fuck!" she growled out. "I'll kill him. I'll actually kill him."

"No killing. I'm okay. I just need to get out of here."

"I'll cut his balls off and I will—"

"Paris!"

"... throw them to the rabbit! That's what I'll do."

"Stop it." I slapped her face gently, forcing her to blink and look back at me. "Stop it. I don't want any of that. I'll handle Ethan myself. Whatever's got into him, I'll deal with it. I meant it when I said I was taking charge of this new world we're creating. No more being weak. No more getting others to fight my battles. I'm strong now, and I know when I need to get out of here and go for a drive."

"So, you're not really going to Lauren's place?"

I offered her a sad sigh. "See you in the morning?"

"The *morning?*"

"I'll be safe, I promise."

"Oh, hell no, Mav."

"Paris," I warned. "I'll be fine."

Grabbing my bag off the bottom of the staircase, I offered her as many reassurances as I could before I bounced down the pathway and hopped into my Mini, throwing my bag in the back before I got behind the wheel. Once alone, I didn't feel so brave, but I white-knuckled the steering wheel anyway, giving myself a moment before I turned the key in the ignition and pulled out into the road.

No clue where to go.

No idea what the hell had happened.

Only knowing one thing:

I'd been a goddamn idiot all over again. This one was going to ache like hell to try and recover from.

CHAPTER ELEVEN

Ethan

It took me over an hour to travel the usual ten minutes to Izzy's house. The paranoia that I was being followed insisted that I drive around Manchester a couple of times before creeping down her street to finally talk to her.

I'd thought about calling her, but this was a conversation we needed to have in person. I needed to see her face when I confessed about my fucking past and how it tangled with Jason Dagson, Tommy, and Paris. I needed to lay it all out for her, but when I slowed outside her house, her Mini was gone.

She wasn't home?

Glancing at the clock on my dash, it read after eleven, which wasn't that late, but it seemed unusual from what I knew of Izzy. Paris's bike was in its usual spot, though. If I had to go through her, I would. Izzy was my main priority, and I wasn't afraid to admit I didn't like her being out this late, possibly alone, when Tommy had just threatened me.

I checked the street behind me before I pulled into a free parking spot and turned off the engine. I waited another ten minutes out of paranoia before I climbed out and headed to the door with a nervous ball of tension in my gut. Driving around, I'd convinced myself that if I could just see her, I could fix it. Now, I wasn't so sure.

Sucking in a deep breath, I rang the bell and waited.

I heard the shuffling inside the house long before the door was opened. I heard Paris mumbling on the other side, and I tried to school my face and hide the disappointment as she pulled it open.

She glared at me; her green eyes narrowed with fury before she stepped out and punched my arm with a set mouth and defiant jaw.

"Ow!"

"Not interested. *Sorry,*" she bit out before she tried to slam the door in my face.

I stuck my foot in the jam and slammed my palm against the surface. "I lied, Paris. I *lied.*"

"Yeah, so she said. Lied all the way through. Bye, Ethan. Sorry I made a mistake with you." Paris tried to push against the door, but I was too strong, managing to hold it in place.

"Not being interested is the *only* thing I've lied to her about," I growled, slapping the door with my palm. "Goddammit, Paris, would you just… fucking… *listen*?"

She stopped in her tracks, glaring at me through narrowed eyes. "You have thirty seconds."

"I was in a situation. I was just trying to protect Izzy. I need to talk to her… to explain. Would I be here if I wasn't interested? Have you ever known me to chase *anyone*? Jesus!" I finished on a reluctant sigh, my shoulder coming to rest against the door as my chest tightened again. "Paris, please."

"What kind of game must you have been playing to tell her you weren't interested? I don't get it."

"No games. I wouldn't play those when it came to Izzy." I eased up the pressure on the door as she relented a little. "I promise I will tell her everything, but I need to tell her before I tell you. Where is she? Is she safe?"

Paris's eyes narrowed. "Why wouldn't she be safe?"

"I'm asking you to trust me here. Just… please. Call her; ask her to come home. At least then you'll be here if she wants me gone, right?"

Paris's shoulders softened, and she stepped back into the house, letting go of her fight. "I don't like this, Ethan. You've known her for a matter of days, and she's been upset twice. The stats aren't in your favour, and even though I've always thought you were a good guy—the sole reason I set you up with her—she has to come first. She does come first. You know that, right?"

"Right now, she's fucking everything." I didn't give a fuck how that sounded.

Reaching around into the back pocket of her jeans, Paris pulled out her phone, swiped through it, and lifted it to her ear, never taking her eyes off me.

It seemed to ring forever, the echo of it filtering through the hall as we waited and waited and waited.

"Goose, I'm fine," Izzy's voice said, just as Paris clicked it on speaker, still looking at me.

"Where are you?"

"Driving."

"Where?"

"Places."

"Be specific, Mav."

"Why?"

"I'm just wondering."

"Does drowning in misery count?" She laughed sarcastically. "That's all your getting from me."

I felt like a complete wanker hearing that tone coming from her. I'd made her sound like that. I was starting to think I should have given Paris the money shot at the family jewels for what I'd done. Instead, I rolled my hands, asking her to go on, to try and get an answer or get her back here.

Paris was clearly torn in two between protecting Izzy and helping me. It was obvious to anyone how much I fucking adored Izzy already, and she could see that. She could probably feel it, too.

"Mav, as much as I love your dramatics, for my own sanity, I need to know you're safe."

"Why wouldn't I be safe?" Izzy asked the very same question Paris had asked me only moments earlier.

"Because you were frantic when you left here, and I know what you can be like when your emotions are high."

"My emotions aren't high. They're fucking rock bottom, Goose. I feel like an absolute moron." Izzy groaned, and it sounded like she slapped her hand on the wheel. "I thought he was different. What is it with me? So, he had the most amazing forearms I've ever seen on a living human being. Great. So, his jaw alone made me want to scream out like Sally when she met that idiot Harry. Whatever."

"Erm, Izzy…"

"So, his fingers were pure magic. So, his voice made me break out in goosebumps every time I heard it. That doesn't *mean* anything." Izzy slapped the wheel again. "It doesn't mean anything, right? It's been three days. No four. God. Is that all it's been? Jesus. I really am pathetic.

"Izzy," Paris said, her smirk in place as she stared at me now.

"I hate that he's not what I hoped he would be, Paris. I hate that I got it wrong again."

I probably should have stopped her little rant before it gained traction. It was something I'd grown used to in those four days but hearing her confirm that sense of rightness I'd felt with her made me pause. When I glanced up and saw Paris staring at me expectantly, I stepped forward and nodded.

"Iz, I'm trying to be that man for you. I fucked up, I know I did, but I need you to come back and talk to me so I can explain."

Silence.

That was her only response.

Paris winced, her face scrunched up as she waited. "Mav? You there?"

"I... Why is he there?" Izzy asked her best friend with no emotion in her voice as she spoke. "And why can he hear me?"

I retook control. "I'll explain everything if you come back. I promise. The only lie I have ever told you is that I wasn't interested. Just... talk to me."

That silence grew thick again, the wait torturous, but when she finally spoke, I almost wished she hadn't.

"Not interested. Sorry. Goodbye, Ethan."

The phone went dead.

I stared at the phone in Paris's hand even as the light dimmed and the screen went black. I was so goddamn angry at myself—so angry that I'd played right into Tommy's hands. I pushed my fingers into my hair and stumbled back from the door, feeling the ache in my chest almost immediately.

"Fuck. *Fuck!*" I met Paris's eyes, shaking my head in denial even as a rational response formed on my lips. "I'm sorry, Paris.

I never meant to hurt her."

I didn't wait for a response. I stumbled away from the house and down to Lucy. I slipped behind the wheel and stared blankly at their house as the door closed. I pulled my phone from my pocket and dialled Izzy's number, waiting for her to answer.

She didn't.

Her bubbly voice asked me to leave a message, and I couldn't deny her the request.

"I know I hurt you," I said, starting my car. "I told you I would try not to do that, but I promise you I have an explanation that I am more than willing to give you if you'd just answer your phone or come and see me."

I gave her my address and hung up as I pulled away and headed down the street towards my apartment. Then I called again and again, begging shamelessly, asking for a chance to explain—asking her to come and see me.

When I got home, I locked the door and deadbolt to stop Scott and Dean coming in and forcing me to talk. I texted Izzy instead, the same requests and invitations and apologies filling up space on the screen before I eventually gave up for the night and laid on my bed, staring at the ceiling.

Waiting.

Hoping.

I even prayed a little.

I didn't fall asleep, and it was the only reason I saw the phone light up my room with a message.

I rolled to the side and picked it up off the bedside table, swearing when I dropped it before I could see who it was from. The alarm clock said it was 3:15 a.m. Without looking, I knew.

Izzy: I'm outside.

It was all it needed to say.

I took off downstairs, realising my feet were still bare when

I pushed out of the security door and into the night beyond it. Not that my odd state of undress mattered. The thought was gone the moment I saw her leaned against her Mini, arms and ankles crossed, hair in waves falling around her, those unfathomable blue eyes, which were on me.

She wasn't happy, but she was there, and it was all the hope I needed.

Everything inside me unclenched at the sight of her, and I made my way across the car park.

CHAPTER TWELVE

Izzy

I eyed him all the way, my heart screaming one thing while my head growled another. I hadn't planned on giving in. I'd wanted to stay away, even just for a night, but damn him and the things he'd said on his messages. Damn him for having wormed his way into my heart enough already for me to give a shit.

Damn me for being so weak.

Weak or not, I was going to play at being strong even if it killed me. I'd spent too long being the girl who ran away. Now I was the woman who stood firm, faced her problems, and dealt with the consequences.

No matter what that meant in the end.

I glanced down his defined bare chest, my heart rate picking up as I took in his grey jogging bottoms—ones very similar to the pair I was wearing. Only he made his look *way* more appealing than I could ever hope to pull off. His hair was a mess, sticking out in places, and his wide eyes were locked on mine, unable to look away. He seemed nervous. It wasn't an emotion I thought I'd ever see on him.

I didn't say a word or move an inch when he came to a stop, not two feet away from me.

"Izzy." The longing in the word was laid out as he took me in.

"What?"

"You came."

The lump in my throat rose, forcing me to swallow. "Don't make me regret it."

"Will you come inside?"

"I have something to say first."

He nodded in agreement, his arms still fidgeting at his sides as he studied my face, waiting.

"You can be the most beautiful man in the world. You can take me higher than anyone ever has, and you can offer me the world… but if you switch hot and cold, treat me like dirt, or make me question myself even once, the other stuff means nothing. Those are just moments—words. Actions are what count. Do you understand me?"

"I didn't do any of that to hurt you, and I sure as hell didn't change my mind about how I feel about you." He reached out, his hand finding mine in the crook of my arm. "Just let me explain, and if you don't like what I have to say then I will leave you alone. If that's what you want."

I stared down at his hand on mine for far too long. It didn't make sense to me, the way his touch made me want to throw myself into his arms every single time. It had been a matter of days, and this panic of mine wasn't just about tonight. Deep down, I knew it was about so much more.

Glancing up at him, I searched his eyes, looking for any sign of a man who would hurt me the way Jack had done. All I saw staring back at me was a man who didn't know how to salvage this mess we'd found ourselves in.

"Okay," I said, my voice breaking.

Ethan's fingers tangled with mine before he stepped back, his arm stretching until it gave mine a gentle tug. He tipped his head towards the building behind him. "Come inside."

I followed him, letting him guide me into the building, through a security door, and up some stairs, the two of us moving slowly. Ethan kept glancing back at me, and I looked up at him with wide, expecting eyes each time, hating the tension between us.

He stopped outside a black door on the top floor that had sleek metal numbers attached to it. He pushed it aside, his arm sweeping in an invitation for me to go first. I stepped inside, my movements somewhat cautious, and I heard the door click shut behind me.

"Can I get you a drink? Beer, tea, Johnny Walker?"

This wasn't *just* an apartment. The floor space was bigger than my house would be laid out flat, the living room and kitchen were open-plan, yet so far apart, it felt like they were miles away. The red brick walls made it warmer than it should have been. This was a man's home, but a man with classic taste, and I suddenly felt a little embarrassed about the shitty teenage-type bedroom I'd shown him with pride.

"Iz," he prompted, his tone careful.

"Whiskey. Neat," I said quietly.

"Make yourself at home." He headed towards the kitchen to make our drinks.

I spun around in slow circles, taking in all of it before the back of my knees hit his sofa, and I turned to look down at it.

It was brown, soft leather, and looked like I'd never get off it if I dared to sit down. Glancing over at Ethan, I saw him casting glances my way almost nervously as he poured the drinks. I perched on the arm of his couch, my hands resting on my knees as I waited for him.

I hadn't made my mind up about how long I would be there.

This was the make or break of something that hadn't even begun.

Ethan headed back to me, handing me a glass as he pulled the coffee table closer to where I was sitting, and he perched at the edge of it. He held his glass in both hands, suspended between his legs as he watched me.

"I hate myself for what I did to you tonight, Iz. It was a shitty thing to do, but it was the only way I could protect you." He stopped, taking a mouthful of whiskey and letting it settle before he continued. "I considered that the attack on the club was random for a while, but tonight I realised that my first suspicions had been right."

"How can hurting me save me? Who would ask that of you?"

Ethan drew in a long breath, knocking back the last of the whiskey in one go before he set it on the table behind him and clasped his hands together.

"I think…" He stopped. "Or maybe I know, it was Jason Dagson's right-hand man that destroyed the club. Tommy is a dangerous bastard, and he doesn't like his boss being fucked around." Ethan rubbed at his chest awkwardly.

My spine stiffened the second that name was spoken, the blood rushing from my head, making me pale as I stared at Ethan.

Jason Dagson.

Paris's ex-boyfriend.

The abusive manipulator who ruined her life, and almost took both of ours a few years ago.

Ethan had just brought a ghost into the room with us, and all I could do was stare at him helplessly.

"Why are you saying that name?" I whispered. "Don't say that name. Daggs… he's in prison now. He doesn't exist in the real world."

Ethan met my eyes. "But *Tommy's* not in prison, Izzy, and Tommy does what Daggs tells him to do." Sighing, Ethan reached out and cupped his hands around mine. "They tried to kill me for what stupidly happened between Paris and me all those years ago. I messed with Jason's girl. They wanted me gone. They'd already set a trap for a girl I went to school with, and they sent me along knowing I would get caught up in the crossfire. They wanted us both dead. I lived; Jessica died. They've left me alone since, and I've avoided them for the most part, but I have a feeling I know why Tommy is leaning on me now. I think you do, too."

I couldn't blink—my heart felt like it stopped beating.

This couldn't be happening. This couldn't be the reality of Ethan—that he was tangled up in the history and mess of someone like Daggs. He was too perfect for that. He was the dream. He wasn't like them.

I was scared to death to ask the next question because the instinct in my gut told me I already knew the answer.

"How did Tommy and Daggs try to kill you?"

Ethan looked down at our hands, his cheeks ballooning as he blew out a long breath. "I…"

"Ethan?"

"They poisoned some heroin."

"Heroin," I breathed out, my face falling.

"Yeah." He nodded once, and I saw the shame in that single

movement.

"Drugs?" I whispered.

"It's a long story, and one I will tell you everything about if you want to know. It was a year of my life, and I've been clean for a decade. That single attempt on my life was enough to scare me straight. The point is, they knew Paris worked at my club, and when Tommy showed up at the pub tonight, he was fishing. When you called, all I could think about was him using me to get to you two, and I couldn't let that happen. I panicked. I tried to make him think you were just another girl I was messing around with. Fuck, Iz, it made me sick to do it, but I had to."

The last seven years of my life flashed through my mind, from the point of me finding Paris broken in that old factory, to this moment right here, sitting opposite this man, my hands shaking as I stared at him.

"If this Tommy was fishing, it wasn't for information on Paris. He knows where she lives. He's known for a while, Ethan. They both have. That's why…" I blew out a shaky breath. "That's why I had to threaten Daggs all those years ago to stay away. That's why I handed over evidence to the police that eventually led to him being put behind bars when he fucked up off his own back. If Tommy was asking questions, it was probably because of me."

"You?" His lips parted.

"He'll want revenge for everything I did."

"He's not going to touch you. You know that, right?" Ethan growled. "I won't fucking let that happen."

"I'm not scared," I said quietly. It was only partly a lie. If they wanted to drag me down, I'd at least make them work for it first.

"Izzy," Ethan sighed.

"You're trembling," I said, squeezing his hand in mine

tighter. Dropping my glass down beside me, I wrapped my other hand around his, trying to calm him.

Ethan rested his lips against the back of my hand and shook his head. "I'm not scared; I'm fucking angry. The thought of them coming after you makes me crazy. Whether you want me in your life or not, I won't let those bastards get close to you."

"I know."

I did. I could feel it pouring from him—this need to wrap me up in bubble wrap already. None of it made sense after so little time, but it felt nice. It felt warm and safe, and I was so tired of living life on my own, climbing beneath cold sheets and trying to stay strong for the world. I could be a hell of a lot stronger with someone like him wrapped around me during the fight.

I shuffled closer, my arse perched on the edge of the arm of the sofa. "We're at least safe here in this apartment tonight, though, right?"

"A hundred percent."

"Good." I pulled away from him, stood and shrugged out of my denim jacket to drape it over the sofa. I picked up my glass of whiskey and dropped myself into the corner of his couch, feeling his eyes on me the whole time as I turned to stare out of the huge floor-to-ceiling arched window at the end of the apartment. "Then I'm going to sit here, I'm going to watch the sun come up, I'm going to drink your whiskey, and I'm going to ask you a million questions until you fall asleep."

"Then what?" he whispered.

I turned to look at him, staring into his tired yet welcoming eyes. "Then we'll go from there, okay?"

CHAPTER THIRTEEN

Ethan

I watched Izzy getting comfortable on the supple leather of my sofa, and I tried to calm the rage that coursed through my blood. I had an opportunity to spend time with her, to salvage whatever it was we were building, to beg her forgiveness. Four fucking days and I was hers whether she wanted me or not.

It was crazy considering how far I'd run from commitment my whole life.

Maybe my mum hadn't just been a hopeless romantic.

Standing, I moved to the other end of the sofa and dropped onto it, letting out a small sigh as I sank low. Ignoring the chirp of surprise, I pulled Izzy's feet into my lap and squeezed, feeling better having some contact between us.

"Consider me an open book. Ask your questions."

Izzy took a sip of her drink, watching me over the rim of the glass before she lowered it into her lap.

"No lies?"

"I'll never lie to you."

"What got you clean? How did you do it, because when I dragged Paris through that, it was like walking her through Hell, and I know she couldn't have survived it alone."

"No easing into this." My eyes were on hers. "I actually died twice before they revived me. The bad heroin made it difficult for them. My dad was still my emergency contact at that point. I'd been so fucking lost to the bullshit I hadn't bothered changing it. He put me in rehab. It was a bare room with a plastic bed, and it fucking hurt, but after that, and endless hours of talking about how I felt, I never wanted to go through it again. Once I left, I had Scott and Dean looking after me." I brushed a hand over my hair. "I don't recommend it."

"You don't speak to your father now?"

"No reason to. He's a bastard."

"Something else we have in common." She smiled flatly, tipping her drink to her mouth again.

"You don't get along with your old man, either?"

She rested her head on the sofa, her eyes never leaving mine. "Careful what you ask on this one. There's a simple answer, and then there's an answer you'll hate—one that could make you see me differently."

I breathed in through my nose and held it for a moment. "Nothing will change the way I see you, Izzy."

"Thank you," she mouthed sweetly before dragging in a breath and exhaling her emotions. "Next question: why didn't you get out of town once you were clean? Why did you stick around Manchester? Surely you could have taken your club anywhere in the world."

"Manchester is home. Manchester was where I got a sight of

you occasionally, where my best mate and his family were. It's where Deano, my kid brother, had planted his roots. It was a risk, but I wasn't going to let them chase me out of the only place I'd ever called home."

"Me?" It was the only part of what I'd said that she seemed to pick up on, a hint of a blush tainting the peaks of her cheeks. "You're telling me I was one of the reasons? A girl you got a glimpse of a handful of times?"

"You were my *Great White Buffalo*. A unicorn." I shuffled back into my corner, not feeling even slightly embarrassed by my confession. "That first time I saw you, I knew you were something special."

Her smile broke free, despite her trying to control it. God, I lived for that smile.

"Great White Buffalo?" Her brows rose. "I sure hope that had nothing to do with the size of my arse."

"You've never seen *Hot Tub Time Machine*?" I asked, chuckling.

Izzy just shook her head, waiting for me to go on, her toes curling in my grip as her legs straightened and stretched.

"A woman so perfect you can't quite believe she's real. A once in a lifetime kind of woman. You. *My Great White Buffalo*."

Her cheeks turned from pink to red quickly, and I couldn't help but notice the way her nipples tightened beneath the thin vest she was wearing without a goddamn bra.

"I don't know how to respond when you say things like that."

"You don't have to say or do anything. You asked me to be honest, so that's what I'm doing."

"Maybe you should have got out of Manchester. Met some other unicorns."

I took in every curve and line of her face and smiled. "There's only one unicorn, beautiful."

Izzy released a soft sigh. "Why did you wait? Why not get to me sooner?"

"The man I was back then wouldn't have been any good for you: the drugs, the rehab, the constant working to keep ahead of the cravings. I wouldn't have been the man you deserved. I'm probably still not, but at the risk of freaking you out, I don't think I *could* give you up now."

"Talking like that could get you in trouble."

"I'm already in trouble."

"Me too."

I reached for her and pulled her towards me until she was straddling my thighs. Her hands pressed against mine as she looked down at me. I linked our fingers unapologetically, needing to touch her and think of anything but the position she was in. "Maybe the trouble cancels itself out then, and now we're just in it together."

"I'm still mad at you," she said with no conviction at all.

"You're entitled to be. I was an arsehole."

"Don't do that again."

"The last thing I ever want to do is hurt you."

"You never want to hurt me?"

"Never."

"Funny." She pushed against my hands, her smile growing. "Because I can feel a very painful surprise coming to life behind me."

"That will be a very pleasurable kind of surprise. I can promise you that."

She huffed a laugh that stayed behind her pressed together lips, never looking away from me as she curled her fingers around mine.

"I have no doubt about it. But not tonight."

"No. Not tonight." I paused, glancing down where she was hovering over my thighs. The sight of it made me swallow. "You may need to distract me with more of those questions, though."

Izzy groaned and shifted herself completely. She was soon curled up beside me, one of our hands still a tangle of fingers between us. It was close enough to appease me. A little.

She asked about Dean, Scott, the business, and even Jessica at one point. For hours, I spoke, answering everything she wanted to know about me. In quiet moments I was able to ask her a few things of my own. She was fascinating to talk to and enchanting to listen to. I couldn't keep my eyes away from her mouth when she rambled. Izzy always managed to get a random lip nibble in when she was thinking about what to say next, those crystal blue eyes shining with humour when she told stories about her friends.

The sun had risen when we both fell quiet for more than five minutes, and by that time she was curled up like a kitten against my side, her blonde hair was splashed over my bare chest.

It was in those moments of silence that my mind wandered to the one topic she hadn't hit upon yet. The one influence in my life that still held so much weight for me.

Dropping my chin to my chest, I brushed my lips over the crown of her head, unsure she was still awake. Then again, it was probably the only reason I had the courage to say what I did.

"There's one person you haven't asked me about yet."

"I know," she whispered. "But as someone who doesn't like to speak about her own mum," she tilted her head back and looked into my eyes, "I didn't want to ask you a question that could make you sad again."

I twisted a couple of strands of her hair around my finger. When it came to my mum, I was still a lost little boy who really wasn't sure how to process what had happened. I just knew that I didn't want anything between Izzy and me that would be avoided in the future. It was proving too easy to be an open book around her.

"Mum died in a stupid, senseless accident when I was nineteen." It still hurt to say it out loud, and for the first time, I glanced away from Izzy, unable to be *that* raw and vulnerable. I swallowed twice before I could go on. "She was the one who held the family together. It never gets easier, and I miss her every day, even knowing how much I let her down."

"Hey," Izzy whispered. "You don't have to do this."

I slowly drew my eyes back to her and gave a sad smile. "I don't want there to be anything we can't talk about. This isn't easy for me, but the more you know, I hope the more you'll understand who I am. Everything good about me and in my life comes from Mum. The club… that came because she thought ahead and made sure Dean and I would be all right if the worst happened. I love the place, but there isn't a day goes by that I wouldn't trade it all in to have her back."

"She sounds like an amazing woman."

"She was."

I pulled Izzy closer and breathed deeply. It was easier to speak about Mum than I'd thought it would, or at least, Izzy made it easy for me to talk. Whatever it was, I felt a small weight falling from my chest as we smiled at one another in quiet understanding. "Thank you."

"For what?"

"Listening. Being so damn easy to talk to." I stopped, editing myself for a moment before I went on. "For being here."

"I'm glad I came."

"So am I," I said, the sentiment repeating in my head twice more. I let the two of us lapse into silence for a while, my thoughts a scramble of sound and images. I thought about the letter Mum had given me with the inheritance she'd set up for us. Those words I'd doubted so much when I'd first read them suddenly came into startling clarity. I was stroking Izzy's arm while so lost in thought, and when I eventually climbed out of my own head again, her breathing had changed into that steady rhythm that belonged to sleep.

Izzy's hand rose, resting over my heart, and a soft whimper fell from her lips while she slept. "I like it here," she sighed.

I liked her there too, and with Mum's letter so close to the surface of my mind, I mumbled the one like that had scared me the most when I'd read it. The line that I'd never thought I would fully understand. The line that was suddenly the only thing that made sense to me with this gorgeous woman in my arms.

She'll be kind and loving, offering a safe place for you and your hidden but tender heart.

CHAPTER FOURTEEN

Izzy

I slept like a baby.

There'd been no dreams.

No waking with fear.

No wondering where I was when my eyes eventually flickered open sometime around noon.

I simply laid there against his warm chest, feeling ridiculously safe in a world that was trying to tell me we were anything but that.

Rubbing my cheek against him slowly, I breathed him in, wishing I could stay there in his arms forever. I knew Ethan was awake when he shifted under me, his hand around me, stroking the sliver of skin between my vest and pants that had been exposed in sleep.

"You awake?" he whispered.

"No."

"I like that answer," he groaned, wrapping himself around me.

He smelt amazing, and I found myself closing my eyes as I inhaled more of him, wondering for just a second what it must be like to wake up every morning next to this man and feel his tender touches against my sensitive skin.

"You know what I like more?" I asked sleepily.

I felt the huff of laughter from him rather than heard it. "If I knew that, you wouldn't be such a mystery."

My smile grew against him. "There's nothing mysterious about me. Especially not when I'm given coffee."

"Ah, the magic word."

Ethan shifted, but rather than moving me, he pulled me against his chest and rose from the sofa with me in his arms. He headed to the kitchen, swearing when his feet met the cold hardwood between the two rooms, and then he deposited me on the island counter, the surface of it cool against my arse. He stepped away, but his hands caged me in, landing on either side of my thighs as he grinned at me.

"What kind of coffee do you like?"

It was at this point that I was *very* aware that I hadn't brushed my teeth… or my hair, and there he was, looking as edible and smelling as delicious as ever.

Fucking men!

I leaned back on my arms, attempting to make it look cute as I pulled my shoulders together, created some distance, and whispered, "Surprise me."

Sinking his teeth into the tip of his tongue, Ethan pushed back from the counter and opened one of the many cabinets to begin pulling what he needed from them. He glanced over his shoulder at me as he pulled out a French press.

"I'm trying to impress you again."

I sat taller. "You really don't have to try anymore. You know that, right?"

Abandoning the coffee he'd just dumped into a grinder, he stepped towards me, his hands gripping my knees gently. "As a man, you learn that when you meet a woman out of your league, you must pull out all the stops."

"If you get any closer, you're going to realise that I'm not as out of your league as you think." I raised my brows at him. "You got a bathroom around here I can use? Preferably one with some toothpaste in it?"

"Up the stairs. I have a new toothbrush in the cupboard by the sink. I can use my old one for another week." He winked at me. "And I won't ever subject you to the guest bathroom that Scott and Dean use. I like you far too much for that."

I smiled sweetly as I slid from the island and eyed him until I was on the other side of it. When I looked to the open staircase by the huge floor-to-ceiling window, I found myself pointing at it like an idiot. "Just up those?"

"That's the badger."

"The badger," I mouthed, finding myself adoring him more and more with every passing second.

I walked away, aware of his gaze on me as I began to climb the bare wooden stairs that led up to a glass bannister. I'd been so wrapped up in Ethan—in us—since arriving, I hadn't thought to look around or ask what was up here. I generally thought an apartment was over one floor, but what did I know? Nothing, apparently. The second I hit the top step, I found myself freezing, my hand clutching the bannister as I stared into what was obviously Ethan's open plan bedroom.

A bed I could only presume was super-king-sized sat in the middle of it, the headboard against the wall to my left. The space around it was huge, with very little to clutter it up. My eyes fell on the thick, plush, dark grey carpet my toes were suddenly sinking into, and I found myself wiggling them before I glanced up again and let my mouth hang open. This was like something out of a magazine, and it made my bedroom look like a twelve-year-old girl's. Ethan had decorated it tastefully, with whites, warm greys, and navy blues being used as the colour themes. At the far end, I could see a door that I assumed led to the bathroom he'd sent me to.

Yeah, he'd sent me up here alone, knowing he was going to leave me speechless, hadn't he?

"Ethan?" I called out, not moving.

"Yes, beautiful?" he shouted back from below.

"Can I live here?"

"You may want to test the bed first." He teased. "Have a good bounce on it. It's what I do when no one's here."

He didn't have to tell me twice. I walked quickly, and the second I was close enough, I let my hands sink into the incredibly gorgeous, thick duvet. Pushing down on the bed, I gave it a few bounces before I leaned back and laughed to myself.

"Definitely moving in! Clear out your wardrobe. I'm never leaving this place." I practically ran back to the glass bannister and leaned over it. "In fact, I don't even need clothes. I'll just live here naked. I'll never have to leave. There's nothing out there in the world for me anymore. Only this apartment. Forever."

Ethan gazed up at me from the kitchen, his smile broad. "Deal, but if you walk around naked, I am too. And that means a permanent erection from me." Holding a spoon, he pointed up at me. "You may want to check out the monster wardrobe before you relinquish clothes."

"You're a permanent erection already," I teased.

"Only around you."

I couldn't help it—I found myself bouncing on my toes and squealing like a girl before I ran back across the room to investigate this monster wardrobe. Just as he'd promised, the walk-in-wardrobe just off the mega en-suite bathroom was big enough to hold my clothes, plus the entire contents of H&M and Topshop. It was only a quarter full of Ethan's smarter work clothes, and a few casual pieces on the side. He didn't look like he needed much, which was why I found it a little confusing that this place was so… roomy.

The vision I'd had of Dandy, Lily, and Paris around the tiny table of my old apartment sprung back to mind, as did the reason I moved and bought Casa in the end. In that vision, the ghosts of my youth had warned me that one day I'd need a bigger place. A place where a man who would steal my heart would end up living. A place that could hold his world in mine. A place where we could be happy and in love.

I had to wonder if Ethan had had the same thought too.

Hearing him whistling to himself downstairs snapped me out of my trance, and I did what I'd rushed upstairs to do. I fumbled around his ridiculously clean bathroom, found the new toothbrush, and gave my teeth a clean while I stared back at my own reflection, taking in how I seemed to look so different this morning.

My cheeks were flushed—a permanent state of being in the last week.

But my eyes seemed brighter somehow. My hair was as wavy and manic as ever, but the smile that tried to take over my lips, even as I brushed my teeth, was unmissable.

Finishing up, I rinsed off the toothbrush and left it on the edge of the sink. I stared at that toothbrush for far too long, wondering what it would be like to always have one sitting there—one that was my own, that belonged to no other woman but me—before I eventually shook my head and banished those ridiculous thoughts to make my way downstairs.

Five days, Izzy.
Five fucking days.
Your life was ruined in forty-two last time.
Slow it down.

Those were all the things my head was screaming at me.

My heart? That was singing love songs from the 80s while imagining how good it would feel to finally lose the name Moffit and replace it with Walker.

Fan. Fucking. Tastic.

Ethan was still at the counter, plunging the coffee with slow, practised patience. He cast a quick glance over his shoulder when he was finished.

"I'm going to follow your lead and brush my teeth. Help yourself to coffee, milk is in the fridge, sugar is in the drawer by the fridge." He stepped closer, grinned, then headed upstairs, taking two at a time.

By the time I'd made myself a coffee and settled back at the island, I'd fantasised about what rug I would put over by the fireplace, where my desk could live, and what our children would look like. Ethan had a way of taking me away from reality, even when he talked about everything wrong in our past and current lives. Right now, like this, after sleeping on his chest and still being able to smell him against me, I was in the clouds, living in an alternate universe.

I couldn't find it in me to want to leave.

Ethan beelined for me when he made it back downstairs. Ignoring the coffee, he stepped between my legs, cupped my jaw, and crushed his lips against mine.

When he finally pulled away, I was smiling like a fool as my eyes fluttered open.

"If you'd have done that straight away last night, I'd probably have forgiven you in front of my car."

"Now she tells me," he mumbled, his thumbs trailing over my skin. "If I'd done that by your car. Would you have come in and found the mecca for your Converse in my wardrobe?"

"Stop it," I said weakly, batting his chest. He couldn't possibly know the insane thoughts running through my mind, and no way in hell was I about to tell him.

Five days, Izzy.

I spun away from him and reached for my coffee, bringing it up between us as I eyed him. "Any more surprises around here that I should know about? A pet poodle hiding in the West Wing? A naked butler about to pop out from the cleaning cupboard? Mrs Doubtfire anywhere with a hoover?"

His eyes diverted to the series of doors on the other side of the apartment before he tried to distract me with a smile, and he dropped his hands from my cheeks. "I have a piano." With a wink, he turned around and started making his coffee.

"Jesus," I sighed. "You play?" Of course, he played.

"I did," he replied, reaching for the milk.

"Did?"

He turned slowly, coffee in hand as he leaned back against the counter. "I haven't played since my mum died. I bought the damn thing thinking I could, but sitting down at the keys, I froze. I wasn't that great to begin with."

"Why do you freeze?"

"I used to play to please her. Mum loved watching me, and she would always laugh when I started playing one of her favourites, like Elton John or Cat Stevens. I was high one night, and a piano piece came on. I could have sworn I heard her laugh. After that, I just couldn't do it."

"I understand." I held his gaze. "But you used to play to please her and make her laugh when she was alive. No reason for you to stop trying to please her and make her laugh now, right? She sounds like she was worth it. Even if it does reveal the real reason you freeze up." I pressed my lips together and waited. "If you've got a talent, you should use it. No matter how dusty it appears on the surface."

"Maybe one day."

"One day. That's good enough. It means my dream of recreating that scene from Pretty Woman, where Richard Gere takes Julia Roberts over the piano, may still come true."

"I may have to watch that movie now." He crossed the space between us and slid his mug onto the counter beside me. With his hands palm down either side of me, he leaned in again, his nose now trailing the line of my jaw. "Taking you over a piano will be on my must list." He breathed in and released a stream of air over my neck. "I should warn you that list is growing."

"Am I allowed to know what's on that list?"

Ethan ran his knuckles in a feather touch over the taut skin of my erect nipple, his jaw tipping down so he could watch. "The first is taking you on this counter. Devouring you like the feast you are."

My mouth opened to say something, but nothing came out.

"You want me to keep going?" he asked, the knuckle of his index finger stroking a half-moon around my nipple.

"My head says no, but my nipple says yes."

Dropping his hand, Ethan rested his forehead on my shoulder, breathing heavily. "I'm sorry, Izzy. I'm going to trust your head on this."

"And what if I want to trust yours?" I dropped a hand between us and dragged the side of my palm along the line of his dick.

Ethan growled, pushing himself against my hand.

I closed my eyes and felt him there, imagining how he'd take control and rid that knot that was burning like fire in the very pit of my stomach. I imagined lying back, my legs falling against the island counter, and staring up into his heated eyes. I imagined all the things we'd do together to rid this tension that was building and becoming impossible to ignore.

I wanted it.

I wanted *him* so badly—the lack of sex was driving me insane.

But then I imagined my first time with him in that beautiful bed upstairs. How the two of us would spend the night together, laughing and drinking. How we'd have touched and teased for hours on end before we came back here, turned off all the lights, and let the moon light the way to his bedsheets.

We both wanted it.

Just not like this.

Blinking back into reality, I removed my hand and slid it around the mug again before looking up at him through bright, needy eyes.

"Head over heart, it is."

CHAPTER FIFTEEN

Ethan

The woman kept me on my toes. She drove me crazy in the best kinds of ways, never did what I expected her to, and I couldn't get enough of it. Spending the night with her in a completely platonic way was becoming a habit. She and I had a chemistry that neither one of us could deny, but this insistence on derailing that train was only serving to build that tension between us. I wanted her to the point that I was reverting to a teenage version of myself. This included masturbating in the shower, which was exactly what I did, while she sat downstairs in my living room because if I hadn't, I would have convinced her to come to my bed with me and broken my promise to her.

I peered over the bannister as I dressed, watching Izzy gazing out of the substantial portrait windows at the city beyond. Her hair rested in a shaggy halo around her, and her thumb was being gnawed at the cuticle.

"I can make you something to eat if you're hungry."

She glanced up at me, her smile breaking free. "I'm not hungry. I'm frustrated."

I started down the stairs, never taking my eyes from her. "About?"

"Just… things. You ready to head to mine?"

"Just things?" I smiled, stepping in behind her and pressing a kiss to her temple. "I'm an open book, and you're *things*?"

She tapped my nose. "Isn't it great being in a one way…" Izzy cut herself off. "Never mind. You ready? I should shower too. You're all fresh, and I am the exact opposite."

"Could you finish a sentence first?"

"Any sentence? Okay. I think we should go. That work for you?"

I crossed my arms and smirked.

Stepping closer, she pressed her hands over my arms and rose on one foot, the other kicking out behind her. "*Please,* can we go, Ethan Walker?"

I stole a quick kiss and smiled. "Acceptable, Miss Moffit. After you."

"Can we agree never to use my last name again? I hate it." Izzy wrinkled her nose and began to walk towards the door, grabbing her denim jacket from the back of the sofa as she went.

I grabbed my keys and coat and followed her to the door. My mind took a left turn while I took a right, but I shut that shit down before I freaked us both out.

"Did I hear Paris calling you Maverick?"

"Yeah." She tucked her hair behind her ears while I locked up. "You know, from the film Top Gun? I'm Mav. She's Goose. It's this stupid thing we started when we were ten. It's just never left us. Sometimes I forget her actual name is Paris."

"I call Scott wanker and dickhead more than I use his actual name. In fact, do me a favour. The next time you see him, call him one of those. He's more likely to answer to it."

"I think I can manage that." Izzy held out her hand in an unusually surprising move, and she waited for me to take it with a nervous look in her eye.

I slipped my hand into hers with ease, offering a squeeze in encouragement. It was that fucking natural to do. I'd never been a hand holder, but there I was, grinning like a fucking idiot, and I didn't want to change a thing.

I followed her home at a sensible speed with Lucy growling below me as I watched the woman in the car ahead of me, head-bopping and her beautiful hair flying out the window as she drove with her windows open. It was almost disturbing how much I wanted to know what she was thinking about. It was even more disturbing to imagine her going home and taking the same kind of shower I'd had. Disturbing and distracting. Sticking the radio on didn't help. The Foo Fighters started singing about *Everlong,* and my eyes found hers in the rear-view mirror as she pulled onto her street.

She picked up my hand again when we met outside her house, and I let her take the lead as she led me inside and to her sunny room with a promise to be right back.

I poked around the things she had on display. Pictures of her and Paris as teenagers were everywhere, both of them maturing as they went along. I picked one up of her in the T-shirt I'd first seen her wearing. She was with Paris, but only half in the screen making a funny face. She looked happy. That smile I was starting to crave was firmly in place.

"Oh, no. Which picture are you looking at? Is it the one of me with neon butterfly clips in my hair that Paris made me wear, or is it the one with the disastrously bad blue eyeshadow?"

I glanced up and instantly became thoroughly distracted at the sight of her in a fluffy white towel, her wet hair sticking to her damp shoulders.

Fucking hell, I was hard... again.

I couldn't remember what I was doing because all I could think about was touching her. I turned the frame around and swallowed.

"Ah," Izzy said softly, a smile brightening her face again as she took it in and stepped closer until she was standing behind me. "One of the better ones. The happier ones."

I cleared my throat, and half turned. "This was the top you were wearing the first time I saw you."

"Seriously?"

She smelled amazing.

She looked amazing.

She looked accessible.

Down, Walker.

"Yep, that was the one. You still have it?"

"Rule number one of being a superfan: you never get rid of your apparel." Stepping away from me, she got to her wardrobe and rummaged through it, her back to me as she dug out a T-shirt and started to open it up in her arms. "Okay, so it's a little tighter on me now, but..."

She didn't finish what she was saying before she pushed it over her head and arms and pulled it down over her braless breasts, tugging it down over the towel around her before she shimmied that down to her hips and turned to me.

"Still fits." She beamed, holding her arms out. "Kinda." She cringed.

I stared at her for the longest time. My nineteen-year-old self was suddenly very present. I wanted to fuck her seven ways from Sunday in that top. I always had. That was one of the many

fantasies that she'd starred in over the years. Faced with her—
the reality and the fantasy—I was fucking certain I was about to
explode.

"I…" I had nothing.

Izzy lowered her arms slowly, her fingers finding the edge of
her T-shirt as she glanced down at the giant logo in the centre of
it. "Maybe it *is* too small now. I think it's like a men's small or
something. I dunno."

"You're positively fuckable."

That got her attention. Her head snapped up, and her eyes
bore into mine.

I stepped closer, balling my hands at my sides to stop myself
from reaching for her. "Do you have any idea what you're doing
to me right now?" Reaching out, I picked up one of her hands
and placed it right over my erection with a small smile, my hips
rocking at her touch. "If you want me to be able to function
today, you cannot wear that."

Her face turned beetroot red, but the twinkle in her eye
was the thing that brought the smile back to her lips. "Message
received. Loud and clear," she said quietly, pressing her lips
together to stop herself from laughing. "No Foo Fighters."

"Unless you want to be eaten alive."

"Down, boy."

"You have your hand on my dick, and you want me to calm
down?" I pressed myself against her palm and groaned. "You
may have to give me a minute."

A small chuckle escaped her before she glanced down at
her hand and slowly started to peel it away. "Perhaps now would
be a good time for me to leave you alone while I go and talk to
Paris about everything. You can take all the time you need," she
said suggestively, looking back up at me. "Bathroom is down the
hall, on the left if you need it."

"Second time today. I blame you," I said, releasing her hand and readjusting myself. "You're bad for concentration and good for my libido."

"Second time?"

I smiled at her, raising my eyebrows.

"Jesus," she squeaked. "While I was downstairs waiting for you?"

"TMI?" I stepped closer to her, my fingers trailing her collarbone.

"I wish you'd said. I could have given you a… hand." With a shit-eating grin, she stepped past me, swatting my arse behind her as she began to walk to the door. "Make yourself comfortable. Keep it clean. I'll be right back."

I watched her arse as she strode out in the towel and slapped my hand over my chest as the door closed. The woman had no idea how sexy she was, and it just added to her appeal. Even the image of her hand wrapped around my dick was enough to make me fucking crazy. I doubted I could do that much more without fucking her on the first available surface.

Was this what dating was? Being so distracted by another human being, it was all you could think about? It wasn't even sex. It was her smile—the way she seemed so fucking surprised when I complimented her. Her absolute bafflement at my reaction to her. She was funny, sarcastic, and unapologetically herself. Spending time with her was almost as imperative as breathing, which was why I was going to hate my suggestion when I finally got my mind back on track.

I needed to focus because I needed to keep her safe.

I paced her room to get my control even close to normal, and then I collapsed onto her mattress, staring at her ceiling as I waited. My mind was finally focusing on what I needed to do, who I needed to speak to, when she strolled back in.

"You okay?" she asked with a half-smile. "Don't look at the T-shirt. I'm about to get changed so you don't have to suffer anymore."

I threw my arm over my eyes and released an exaggerated sigh. "I'm perfect, just horny."

"I hear ya." She chuckled to herself. The door shut behind her, and I heard her begin to make her way around the room—a wardrobe door opening here, the gentle huffs and sighs falling from her as she went about getting changed. "Let me change the subject for you—for both of us. I spoke to Paris and told her about Tommy, the incident at the pub, what made you say what you said. Just so you know, she isn't mad at you anymore. Fuck." She hissed. "Just stood on a hairbrush. Keep your arm over your eyes. My towel slipped."

"Izzy." The word fell from me as a growl.

"Oops. Sorry."

"You're not helping me focus here."

"Focus. Right. Let's focus." A drawer opened and closed, Izzy's tiny little breaths falling free as she went about dressing… hopefully! "I've told Goose to be vigilant, but honestly, she doesn't seem that worried. I don't know if she's putting on a brave face, or if she knows something we don't, but she isn't buying into the theory that Tommy seeing you in the pub means we're all about to, well, kick it. Which is good, I guess. It means she's stronger now. It means she's not the girl she was seven years ago."

"That's good. Panic doesn't help any of us." I blinked against my arm. "Can I look now?"

"Wait." Another small grunt fell from her before she exhaled heavily. "Okay. You're good."

I pulled my arm away and grinned at her. She was standing at the end of the bed wearing jeans that looked painted to her curves, and a black jumper that was entirely too big for her. She looked... perfect.

I pushed up to my elbows. "You look beautiful."

"Knock it off." She grinned, tugging down the sleeves on her jumper.

"You're going to have to learn to accept compliments." I met her eyes and smirked. "Even if I do like that shade of red on you."

She crawled on the bed until she was on all fours beside me, her wet hair falling forward as she stopped an inch away from my face. "You love to make me suffer, don't you?"

I cupped her cheek. "Compliments aren't designed to be torture. Just an honest appreciation of what I see, and fuck me, do I appreciate what I see when I look at you."

I leaned forward, my lips brushing hers gently as her blush rose again. She rocked closer to me, seeking more, only to stumble when her phone rang from her back pocket, sending her sprawling over my chest.

CHAPTER SIXTEEN

Izzy

Lauren's tone was manic as she waffled on down the phone, her breaths heavy and sound of her heels clicking against the street almost as loud as her damn voice.

"Lauren," I called out as I reluctantly peeled myself off of Ethan's chest and rested my back against the wall with my legs draped over his.

"... and then this shit lands in my lap, and I've got no one left to turn to."

"Lauren."

"It's like you cannot get the staff these days.

"Lauren."

"Do you hear what I'm saying, Izzy? No one. There's no one I can rely on like I can rely on you."

"Lauren!" I snapped, my eyes shifting to Ethan before I

mouthed a sorry and focused back on the call. "Slow down. I can barely hear what you're saying. Are you okay?"

"No," she practically growled. "I'm surrounded by idiots."

"Talk me through it, Lo."

She did, eventually calming enough to give me the finer details and explain why she was so enraged. One of her copy editors had let her down at the last minute by daring to need an emergency operation to remove her appendix, leaving Lauren in the lurch with no back up to turn to. She had a paper to release and no one to fill a spot. I knew what was coming, and I couldn't deny the twist in my stomach it left me with as I stared at Ethan, who had no clue what the hell was happening.

"You know I wouldn't ask you if I didn't have to, Izzy," Lauren sighed.

"You haven't actually asked me anything yet," I reminded her quietly.

"Are you going to make me say the actual fucking words?"

"Sure am."

"Jesus shitting Christ. Not you as well."

I smiled instantly, unable to help it. "Lauren…"

"After all the favours I've done for you in this lifetime as well. The nerve!"

"Need I remind you that every single time I ask for a favour, *you* are the one to tell *me* to quit beating around the bush and to get to the point?"

"You're such a smart arse."

"So people keep telling me." I grinned at Ethan, who simply stared at me expectantly, his brows raised, making him look totally swoony. Uch. Maybe that knot in my stomach was from looking at him rather than Lauren's call.

"Fine," Lauren sighed, interrupting my dreamy stare. "Izzy, will you please accompany me to London?"

My face fell instantly. "London?" I cried. "What the hell is in London?"

"Didn't I mention that? Well, shit."

"Lauren," I groaned for what felt like the hundredth time.

"It'll be an adventure. All expenses paid by me. It won't cost you a thing. I'll pay you so well, you'll be able to throw twenties on your bed and use them as a duvet. Maybe throw that new fancy man of yours on top of it and make out like—"

"Woah, wait, what? How do you know…?"

Lauren laughed for the first time, her genuine amusement pouring through the speaker. "You know I have eyes everywhere. He's a total fucking hottie. Can't say I blame you for wanting to jump his bones. I wanted to rub his picture against my nipples just to be able to say he'd once gotten me off."

My face fell into the palm of my hand, a thousand butterflies setting themselves free in the pit of my stomach.

"Say you'll help me, Iz," she pleaded.

I peeked up at Ethan through my parted fingers, a heavy sigh falling free as I looked at him. I'd not even known him a full week—not properly—and the thought of not seeing him made me feel a little too uncomfortable.

"When would you need me?" I asked Lauren quietly.

"Tomorrow morning. I'd put you on the five-thirty train."

Closing my eyes, I tried to swallow down the instant no that was desperate to fall from my lips. But this was Lauren, and she'd never asked me for a fucking thing. She'd been there for me when no one else had. She'd gotten me work when I was down and out, had my back from wherever she was in the world, and done me so many favours; I'd lost count of how much I owed her.

"Can I call you back in ten minutes?" I asked her.

"I need to know in five."

"Five," I repeated. "Okay."

I ended the call, dropped the phone in my lap, and looked at Ethan.

"We may have a change of plans."

"Something come up?" he asked, pushing my damp hair out of my eyelashes with his index finger.

"It's my friend, Lauren. I think I told you about her. She's a bit... stuck. Apparently, I'm the only person who can help her at such short notice." I wanted to stop wasting time, throw myself at him, and dull this ache within me when he looked at me the way he was doing then. Such a simple, yet tender gesture set my heart galloping and my knees weak. "She wants me to go to London, and I don't think I can say no."

"Then don't." His finger traced along my hairline. "I'm not going anywhere. I'll be here when you get back."

"I know, but we said we'd stay close after everything. I'd be leaving you, Paris, the house..." and that was the grand sum total of my life. "Shouldn't I be here?"

"Iz, the reality is that you're going to be safer there. Paris can call me if she needs me, or I can send one of the bouncers over to stay with her here while you're gone, and I can look after myself. If you need to go, do it."

"You don't need to do that. She mentioned some guy she's keen on earlier. If I'm not here, she'll probably go stay with him and have a little fun." I wrinkled my nose at Ethan. "You should know my inner control freak is telling me to stick around."

"My inner caveman is telling me to keep you close, but you still have a life to live, and you being safe means that I can sleep knowing you're that far away from Tommy and his goons."

"And how will I sleep knowing you're near him?"

"You can always call me before you go to bed."

I smiled and raised my brows.

"We could have some fun with that." He smirked.

Dropping my phone on the bed, I moved to lean over him, forcing him to rest back on his elbows as I held my weight over his body. "Maybe a little distance will do both of us some good, too. I'm becoming dangerously obsessed with your face." I grinned. "As well as other things."

Ethan's smile widened. "How do you feel about dick pics?"

"I'd prefer a video call to be honest."

"Sold."

"Me, too," I whispered, my eyes dropping to that mouth of his before I pressed a soft kiss against it and let my eyes close.

It was only London.

It wasn't *that* far away.

I could do this. I'd done it for thirty-one years before him. But that was the thing with Ethan goddamn Walker. Once you had one hit, I had a feeling there was no going back.

After just five days, I could finally understand how Chloe felt after losing him.

How they all felt, actually.

***

The journey to London was boring, and I was only twenty minutes in. My laptop held nothing of interest. Neither did my phone. The magazine I picked up looked bland, the words all bleeding into one big blurry mess as I yawned again and tried to shake it off.

Ethan had stuck around for a while after I called Lauren back to tell her I'd help. Having him hanging around my bedroom made me wonder if that was what it had been like for girls growing up who had had normal boyfriends. That giddy feeling I got whenever I glanced his way was something completely new to me. The butterflies I got every time I heard that deep, velvet voice made me wonder how I'd lived without it all my life.

I'd never experienced desire like it.

Matt Cooper had been somebody else's from the start.

Jack Parker hadn't ever really been mine. I was swept up on some wild ride I couldn't get off until it was too late. He took away my loneliness.

He didn't feed me with life the way Ethan had done already. None of them did.

I wanted to sit on the edge of the bed, cross my legs, and just stare at him as he laid there with that soft, contented smirk of his always in place.

He made everything exciting. Even packing to go to London.

Now, here I was, travelling farther away from the one thing that made me happy… and I was sulking. Big time.

My phone rang, displaying Lauren's name.

"Don't worry. I'm on my way," I answered.

"Good morning, sunshine!" she chirped.

"You sound way too happy for…" I pulled the phone away and checked the time before I pushed it back into place, "Five fifty-seven. Christ alive. I've only ever known one five o'clock in my day."

"Welcome to the world of journalism, where the people at the top of their game never sleep."

I groaned again, letting that be my only response.

She went on to tell me about what we'd be doing for the next few days, and I tried to concentrate as much as I could, my thoughts drifting to hazel eyes, a strong jaw, and stubble I wanted to trail my tongue over. My thighs squeezed together every time I pictured him until Lauren said something that really did catch my attention.

"What did you just say?" I asked quietly, my eyes peeling open to glance around at the other few passengers on the train with me.

Lauren sighed and cleared her throat. "We'll talk about it when you get here."

"You said his name, didn't you?"

"Yeah, I did. I told you I'd figure this out for you, Izzy."

Jason Dagson.

She'd been digging and was confident he was still in prison. Only Lauren hadn't stopped there. The words 'chance' and 'interview' followed by 'if you wanted me to' stood out, and I found myself growing cold.

She had created a chance to step inside the prison where Daggs was serving his sentence, and Lauren was asking me if I wanted her to approach him as one of her interviewees.

Don't rattle that cage.

Don't rattle that cage.

Do not rattle that cage.

That was my most prominent thought as I stared out through the window and watched the world sail by in a fast stream of green, brown, and blue.

Say no, Izzy.

Say. No.

CHAPTER SEVENTEEN

Ethan

A bang at my front door disturbed me from a deep sleep. After leaving Izzy's the evening before, we'd spent a couple of hours on the phone before she'd gone to bed for her early train. After a couple of nights of very little sleep, I'd crashed hard, and that was the last thing that I'd remembered.

I rubbed my hands over my hair before dragging them down my face as I chased the last of the sleep away. I rolled from my bed with a growl of warning. If it was my neighbour trying to tell me about the sighting of a strange cat near the building, I was quite possibly going to swing for the fucker.

I grabbed my phone from the bedside table and checked the screen to see if I'd missed a message from Izzy when I saw a cumulation of fifteen missed calls and messages from Dean and Scott, along with a *Good Morning* from my girl. It answered the question of who was at my door. Especially as I'd apparently put the chain on without thinking.

"E!"

"Calm your tits, Scotty," I grumbled, making my way towards the door.

"Where the fuck you been, mate?"

I threw it open, leaving it that way as I headed to the kitchen for some much-needed coffee. "You're gonna have to be more specific."

"You were supposed to meet the insurance assessor this morning."

"Shit!" I'd forgotten about that when I'd switched off my alarm last night.

"You took off from the pub like you had a fire lit under your arse, didn't message either of us, then you went off the fucking grid. Dean and I tried to call you this morning after Sapphire walked the assessor through. We didn't know what to think, you—"

"One question at a time, for fuck's sake." I put the kettle on as I got my thoughts in order, more than aware of Scott leaning against the island, staring daggers into my back.

"Walker?"

"Jenkins."

"Fucking give me something to go on. This is a side of you we ain't seen in a long time."

"What does that mean?"

"You know damn well what it means. We're worried."

I'd learned my lesson a long time ago about lying to Scott. I tended not to go that route these days if I could help it. "Fine. Tommy paid me a visit in the pub."

"What?"

"Tommy. Dagson's right-hand ma—"

"Why was he there?"

"If I had to take a guess, I'd say he was putting out feelers, shaking me down to see what came loose after the hit on the club. He's never been one to shy away from shit. He wants something, but he wasn't eager to get to the point. Izzy called while I was talking to him. As soon as he saw her name on my phone, he took too much of an interest."

"You went after him?"

"What? No." I turned and looked at Scott. "I'm not a complete fucking moron. I went to see Izzy. When Tommy acted interested in who she was, I was a bastard to her on the phone. I acted like she was nothing. I told her I wasn't interested because *he* was watching me."

"You fucking idiot."

"Pretty much." I snorted.

"What happened?"

"We talked it out. She went to London this morning for a job with a bird named Lauren, so I slept in."

"Why did she leave?"

"Work, but I feel better knowing she's away for a little while. Especially if Tommy is sniffing around."

"So, where we going then?"

"*We* ain't going anywhere," I said, easing the plunger into the French press. "I'm going to see what Tommy's up to, and you're going to get the club sorted."

Scott stared at me like I'd grown two extra heads. His lip quirked to the side, waiting for the other shoe to drop. He'd be waiting a long fucking time. Even when I'd been high as a fucking kite, I'd always done my best to keep Scott away from that part of my life. I wasn't going to put a target on his back when I was just being thorough and making sure Tommy was pressing buttons rather than issuing any real threats. The last thing I wanted was to put anyone else in Tommy's path and give him more ammunition. Whatever Tommy was after, I was going to be the one standing in his way. I was already on his radar.

"You can keep looking at me like that but I ain't sucking your dick."

"This isn't a joke, Ethan."

I turned to pour my coffee, not wanting Scott to see what I was really feeling. I could handle threats against the club and me all day long. It was the threat against Izzy that drove me fucking crazy. The thought of the bastard breathing the same air as her made violence surge through me. I wasn't even sure how to process this new emotional attachment to Izzy, and I couldn't put it into words for Scott to understand. How could I when I didn't even understand it myself?

"You don't have to do this alone."

"It's nothing. I'll just be following the twat around, Scott—making sure he's keeping himself to himself."

"Then why do you look so fucking worried about it?"

How did I tell him that, after less than a week, I was scared to fucking death of losing Izzy? That after five days of spending time with her, she'd come to mean more to me that I could ever find the fucking words to explain. How the fuck did I even begin to find a way to describe the way I felt about her?

Izzy Moffit had been a force of nature in my life, and I was okay with that.

"I'm worried that he's going to start taking his frustrations out on the people I care about."

"Then let me help."

"No."

"You're a stubborn twat." Scott sighed.

My phone buzzed on the counter in front of me, and I felt the immediate goofy smile as I saw Izzy's name flash up with a new message.

> ***Izzy: London is bloody big! Who knew?***

> ***Me: You know what they say about the size of a city, right?***

"You have it bad. You should see your face right now," Scott chuffed out with the first sign of humour since he'd walked through the door.

"Jealous?"

"Am I fuck."

"Liar."

My phone buzzed from the counter again, and it instantly had my full attention.

> ***Izzy: If it's big, so are its socks?***

I started laughing, ignoring the smirk on Scott's face.

> ***Me: It's overcompensating for something. Manchester misses you!***

"Don't look at me like that." I dropped the phone to the counter and glanced up at Scott again as I poured my coffee.

"Like what?"

"That *isn't it sweet* look. I know you, fucker."

Scott raised his hands, palms facing me in surrender. "I honestly didn't think Ethan fucking Walker would be the first of us to go down that rocky path of—"

"Shut your face."

I picked up my phone as it buzzed again, and I turned my back to him.

> ***Izzy: You have me grinning in London. I don't know how you do that so effortlessly.***

> ***Izzy: Seriously nearly just got run over by a black cab. Pray for me.***

I groaned to myself. I was trying my best to keep her alive, and she was playing in traffic. I was fighting a losing battle.

Izzy: Stop worrying. I can see your frown from here. I'm fine. Do you honestly think I plan on dying before I've felt you inside me?

Me: GOD. FUCKING. DAMN.

"What?"

"What?" I asked, looking back over my shoulder at Scott.

"You just fucking swore at your phone, mate."

Had I?

Probably.

Jesus.

Me: Come home. I'll bury myself inside you and not resurface for days.

"Probably best you head out. I'm about to call my girl, and your virgin ears can't handle that shit," I told him.

Me: I'm going to call you now, Izzy. Be ready!

Izzy: Can't speak. I'm in the shower getting myself off.

Izzy: Kidding. OMG! I'm so sorry. I'm about to head in a meeting. Raincheck? Will this do?

Izzy: Photo attached.

I opened up the picture to see a fresh-faced Izzy beaming brightly at the camera, her eyes creased at the edges, and her cheeks, as always, flushed. Her hair was blowing behind her as the bright blue sky framed her perfect blonde halo, making her light up even more than usual.

Izzy: I'll call you this afternoon x

She was stunning, as always, but Scott picked up on the disappointment, his chuckle at my frustrated sigh made me ready for solace.

> *Me: Call me when you're alone. I'm greedy, and I want you to myself. Knock them dead, beautiful.*

I dropped my phone again and drained my coffee.

"Can you take care of shit at the club for me or not?" I asked Scott, ignoring his goofy smile.

"Fine. Whatever. Just remember you can call me in. I'm not made of porcelain, dickhead. You don't have to fight this war alone."

***

I'd forgotten how boring it was to sit outside of a club for hours on end. The mind-numbing thump of fuck all happening settled in only two hours after I parked outside of the club that I'd followed one of their dealers to. I'd have thought I was in the wrong place if it hadn't been for two more faces that I recognised scurrying in like sewer rats.

Four hours later, and I was ready to pull my nails off just to keep things interesting.

I hadn't seen Tommy, but I'd seen *his* version of himself—a lad I'd known as Aaron when I'd been mixed up with them all those years ago. Like Tommy, Aaron had been wearing a suit. He looked for all the world like he belonged as a foot soldier for the Krays. They were trying to look like businessmen, but business meetings rarely went down in seedy clubs with half-naked girls being paraded in and out for entertainment. I wasn't sure which was worse. The possibility of Daggs being back out, or Tommy having taken control of his dominion.

I shuffled lower in the seat of the rental car as the door to the club swung open, and a young woman stumbled out of the door. I blinked as she weaved a couple of feet down the street before leaning into the wall for support. It was a look that was still too familiar for comfort, and one that reminded me too closely of the life I'd fallen into for a year. Had that been how I'd looked? That wasted and worn aura that screamed how fucking high I was—how much I depended on that chemical shit to take my next breath. Had this lass tried to convince herself that she could stop anytime she wanted?

It made me sick to think about it.

I contemplated helping her for a full minute before the opportunity passed and the door swung open, a drugged-up lad laughing and tottering after her. I watched in appalled fascination as they kissed and dry fucked against the wall for all the world to see. It triggered a vague memory of a pub, and Scott walking away from me in disappointment. I shut it down before it had a chance to gain steam. There was nothing good in those memories, and nothing would ever come of searching through them. They were better in that box I kept them inside of, so I locked it back up and moved my attention to where the club door was open just enough for someone to look out of. The couple were being watched. I just hoped their fate wouldn't be the same as Jessica's.

Several different versions of this scene happened as the light faded and the night took over, but my patience finally paid off when Tommy left the club with two blondes on his arms. He headed to an expensive-looking Audi parked down the alley.

I waited for him to pull away and get ahead of me before I pulled out and followed him to a house on the other side of Manchester. It wasn't anything special, but I figured it had to be his. An Aaron clone was leaning against the gate. He lifted his chin as Tommy entered, his hands pushed deep into his pockets.

I spoke to Izzy on the phone, sitting there watching the lone light glowing in the upstairs of Tommy's house. After that, I drove home and climbed into bed, calling Izzy again to say goodnight and tell her quietly what I would like to be doing to her.

On the phone, Izzy was as dirty-mouthed and horny as I was, but I had no problem imagining her blush or the sparkle of her eyes as she spoke. I was determined to get her to touch herself while she was gone… just so she would hurry back to me.

For four days, I followed this routine.

I watched Tommy's every move, but the only focus he had was on his business and the endless string of women he took home to fuck. I was bored, and absolutely convinced he'd shown up that night to rub my face in the fact that he'd managed to get through my defences at the club. He'd wanted to remind me that he still held power.

I went to work on the fifth day of Izzy's absence, and I finally fell into a normal routine with a six-pack of Corona and my gaming console that night, waiting for her to call. Now the panic was over, a weight felt like it had been lifted. I wasn't going to be complacent when it came to Tommy, but for now, we had peace. The upside of this little experiment of mine was that if he tried anything, I knew where the fucker laid his head down at night. I finally had a small edge over him, and I wasn't afraid to use it to protect the things that mattered most to me.

CHAPTER EIGHTEEN

Izzy

It was a good job I'd packed enough to stay in London for a month. Five days in and Lauren was showing no signs of allowing my release.

"You're all I've got, Iz."

"I just wish you'd have let me know the score before I got here, that's all," I whined at her during dinner one night in some super fancy restaurant I definitely couldn't afford on my own.

"You'll be reunited with lover boy soon." She smirked at me.

It couldn't have come at a worse time. Being away from him was an itch I couldn't scratch, and that itch wasn't being helped by the constant texts, picture messages, and phone calls. Distance, as it turned out, really did make the heart grow fonder, and I'd been pretty fond of him while laying against his chest.

The two of us checked in morning, noon, and night. I was at

the point of losing myself to this romance bullshit, too, because I'd even ignored texts from Paris twice now, and that hadn't gone unnoticed. She'd text me during two very intense sex-flirt chats with Ethan, and I'd vowed to reply later, only to forget completely.

I loved her. She was my sister from another mister. I missed her, too.

It was just different with Ethan.

I missed what I hadn't actually had, and that was a really weird feeling to carry around with you on the streets of London.

So far, Lauren and I had worked so many hours, I was losing track. It was Ethan's constant messages of reassurance, and him checking on Paris without her knowing, that was allowing me to relax.

He's one of the good ones, my heart kept telling me.

Fuck him already. I don't need to tell you which part of me that was.

Lauren and I finished dinner that night and walked back through the foyer of our fancy hotel.

"Nightcap?" she asked, chucking her head in the direction of the bar.

"I think I'm going to head to bed. I'm knackered, Lo."

"Mmhmm." She smirked.

"What?"

"Knackered, huh?"

"Yeah." I tried to fake a yawn, but it didn't stick, and it ended up looking way too obvious that I was a big, fat faker. "So tired."

"Right."

"Why are you looking at me like that?"

"It's like you don't even know how bad of a liar you are, even though people tell you constantly."

"Oh, fuck off."

"Izzy Moffit never turns down a drink. Especially not when it's on me."

"Fine! I'll have a damn beer if—"

Lauren cut me off, holding her hand in my face. "Save it. Go to your room. Slip under those sheets. Call your new boyfriend and rub those thighs together, girl."

"He's… not my boyfriend…" I said quietly as I pushed her hand to the side and offered her a smile I couldn't deny myself.

"Still. So. Bad. At. Lying."

Raising my middle finger, I held it between us for a few seconds before I turned on the heels of my Converse and made my way upstairs to undress. Lauren may have gotten me in a little pencil skirt and cream shirt type thing, but I was not wearing the fuck-me heels she'd thrown at me for the meetings. She could either take me with my comfy feet, or she could find someone else to bail her out. Thankfully, she hadn't had any choice but to let me wander around her world in my comfy footwear.

I was in my hotel room and out of my clothes in record time, taking only a two-minute shower before I wrapped my hair up into a bun on the top of my head, brushed my teeth, and then made my way to the bed.

It was big.

Everything in London was big.

The thought instantly had me thinking of Ethan, which was fast becoming a common occurrence.

I slipped between the white bedsheets, turned the television on with the remote, and then I picked up my phone, already smiling before I even spoke to him. First, I had someone else to check in on.

Me: You staying out of trouble?

Paris: Define trouble.

Me: Look it up in the dictionary. Your face is next to it.

Paris: I'm giving the phone screen the middle finger.

Me: Stay safe, Goose.

Paris: Always, Mav.

I always felt better once I'd taken care of family first. The next text came with a giddy heart and tingling fingers.

Me: Busy?

Ethan: I am now… My girl's messaging me.

His girl. The smile on my face was ridiculous.

Me: Your girl? I should probably tell the guy in my bed to get out then.

Ethan: I never was the jealous type, but that may change.

Me: You've never been jealous before?

Ethan: Once. I was in the Arndale centre. You were there, and there was a guy…

I had no idea what he was talking about. My memory was about as good as Dory's from Nemo, and that was on my best day.

Me: You're going to have to help me out here.

Me: Also… I really am starting to think you're a real stalker/psycho, you know.

Ethan: I don't think you saw me that time… and I tried to warn you about the stalking thing before. It's too late now.

Me: Am I falling for a serial killer?

My smile lasted approximately five seconds before I realised what I'd said, and I found my thumbs hovering over the screen as I closed my eyes and prayed he didn't read into that. Even if it was true.

Ethan: I'm not that interesting. I just had an uncanny habit of being in the same place as you at random times and making the best of getting some wank bank material. Was that wrong of me?

Me: Terribly wrong.

Me: You need help.

Me: You should have said hello.

I meant that, too. No matter what Ethan said about him not being in the right place mentally back then, there was such a huge part of me that could imagine how the years would have been so different with him around. I didn't believe he'd been this bad guy he made himself out to be. He was just a little lost. I'd been lost, too. Together, we could have been something more... complete.

Me: And you should also have smacked the guy who was apparently making you jealous. Rage helps, so I hear.

Ethan: Baby, if wanking over you is wrong, I've been wrong half my life... and sometimes I wish I would have. If I'd said hello then, I could be in bed next to you now, sliding inside of you instead of touching myself... again.

My thighs slid together at the same time as my grin exploded. He spoke about sex, flirted, and referenced everything he wanted to do to me so casually, his words made my stomach flip every time. The excitement and anticipation were building, and I had no idea how either one of us were going to last when the time came for us to fuck.

> *Me: I wish I was there to help you out. Hand or mouth.*
>
> *Ethan: Fuck, Iz. I wish you knew what you did to me.*
>
> *Me: Ditto.*
>
> *Ethan: Photo Attached*

A part of me knew what it would be before I opened it, but nothing, not even the inkling I'd had, could have prepared me for the sight of Ethan's hand wrapped around his hard dick. My inhale was sharp, and I felt the jolt of electricity hit my nipples while the pit of my stomach burned like fire. My arse cheeks clenched together, and I took a minute to stare at it, wishing he was next to me. Wishing I could reach through the phone and touch it, tease it before I sank down onto it and lost myself to him.

There were no words that could tell him what I thought, so I did the only thing I could do.

I showed him.

> *Me: Photo attached.*
>
> *Ethan: How long do you think it would take me to get to London in Lucy? I want to be between your thighs. I want to taste you before I fuck you. I want to spend the night taking you over and over again until we both fall asleep, then start right up again the moment you open your eyes. You're the most beautiful thing I have ever set eyes on.*

He was trying to kill me. The air left my lungs in one long stream, and I immediately slid down on the bed, the hand between my legs now slipping through my already-wet heat as I read and reread his message over and over again.

I imagined all the things that Ethan would do to me.

All the ways he'd caress me.

The places he'd taste.

The way my heart would pound beneath him.

The way my legs would tremble and my knees would shake as he brought me to the edge over and over again.

I could barely find the strength to reply as I touched myself and fell into the blissful bubble of pornographic images that featured him and only him.

> *Me: I'm going to pretend you're here, touching me, whispering those things in my ear. I want you so badly that everything hurts.*

> *Ethan: I can't promise to be a gentleman when you come home. I want to make that promise to you, for you, but all I can think about is being inside you, and it's making me crazy. I want to watch that gorgeous face as I fuck you slow and hard. I want to hear my name on your lips while you come. Tonight, think about that night when I fucked you with my fingers on Lucy because that's what I'm thinking about…*

I was struggling to breathe as I let my head roll back on the pillow, and I thought about that night. The feel of his fingers inside me. The way his breaths washed over my cheek and my neck. The things he said with that ridiculously sexy voice of his. Most of all, I remembered the pressure of his hard dick pressed against my thigh, and what it would have been like if I'd have rolled onto my side, hitched my skirt up to reveal my naked arse, and let him slip himself inside me.

All my focus went on the spot between my legs as I let the

phone fall to the bed and imagined Ethan's tongue replacing my finger. Ethan's hands holding mine above my head as he fucked me.

Ethan.

Ethan.

Ethan.

The pressure built and built, and I tried to hold onto the amazing climb until I couldn't take it any longer, and my body tightened, the jolt of ecstasy tearing through me as I came hard, and let the orgasm ride through me in perfect waves of pleasure.

By the time I recovered somewhat, I was pushing a hand through the damp edges of my hair, while struggling to regulate my breathing.

I'd never done anything like that with anyone before—not in a way that I'd truly enjoyed to the point of me already trying to figure out if I was still too sensitive or to go again. That's what he did to me. The very memory of his face. The thought of his hands in mine. The thought of his smile when he looked at me like he wanted to eat me alive.

> *Me: You should know that was good. Really good.*
>
> *Ethan: Ditto.*
>
> *Ethan: When are you coming home? I need to see you.*
>
> *Me: Not soon enough. I don't need a job, right? I can live off of you even though we've only known each other for less than two weeks.*
>
> *Me: Rumour has it, it'll be three days.*
>
> *Ethan: Too long. I want to be inside you now!*
>
> *Ethan: Let me call you. I want to hear you come.*

Instead, I called him, enjoying the anticipation I felt from nothing more than hearing his voice—a voice now so familiar and so comforting, I had no idea how I'd survived without it all these years.

"Hey," Ethan said, his voice hoarse and breathing laboured. It gave me a brand-new fantasy to touch myself over, the thought of him lying next to me after sex, speaking to me that way.

"Hey."

"You still naked?"

"As the day I was born. Just a bigger arse and really sensitive nipples now."

"I'm looking at the picture you sent me. It's burned in my mind."

"You won't need a picture soon."

"Can't come soon enough. I'm seriously contemplating getting in the car, just to sit in the corner of the room and watch you fucking yourself."

"If you expect me to do anything for myself when you're in the room, you're crazy," I whispered, pressing my thumb to my bottom lip. "The only things my hands will be touching is you."

"Jesus Christ, I think I'm hard again." There was a rustling. "Hey, yep, there's the man."

I chuckled lightly, my head falling against the pillow as I rolled onto my side and brought my knees up. "Ethan?"

"Yeah, baby?"

"Those things you text me before… will you whisper them to me now?"

"Which part? Driving down there and sliding inside you? Fucking you hard and slow all night? Watching your beautiful face as I make you come over and over again? Eating you alive until you scream my name? Those things? I can do that all night because all of it is true. I want you so fucking badly, it's making me crazy."

I slipped my hand between my thighs again and closed my eyes. "Everything. I want all of it. Everything you have to give."

CHAPTER NINETEEN

Ethan

My new favourite sound in the world was Izzy pleasuring herself. I'd spoken to her for hours, guiding her touches, telling her what I would be doing to her if I were there. My voice became hoarser the harder her breathing became. Guiding my hand along the length of my dick, I let my words fall away and allowed my grunts and groans to tell her exactly what I was doing to myself.

It was the best sex of my life to date, and I'd been hundreds of miles away from her.

When I finally drifted off to sleep, listening to her breathing down the line, I felt like I had the beginning stages of carpal tunnel syndrome.

Three more days away from her was beginning to sound like Hell on Earth. Which was why I was sitting at my desk working on getting the papers back in order. There was a very real possibility I would break my dick if I continued the way I was going at the moment. Insatiable seemed to be my word of the week.

I didn't give a flying fuck. I'd never been so happy in my life. It even made the monotonous office work more interesting as I lost myself in thoughts and mental images of Izzy and exactly what I was planning to do to her when she finally got home.

I was in one of these fantasies when a knock on the doorframe pulled me back into my reality.

"Boss?"

"Yeah?" I asked, still holding a wad of paper in my grip.

"A girl came in looking for a job. She doesn't have an appointment. Sapphire isn't here, and Scott is taking a delivery out back."

"How long's Scott going to be?"

The girl shrugged in surprise. "You don't want to see her?"

Not really. "If I'm the only one, show her in. Does she have a CV?"

"She wants to dance, not do your taxes."

"Send her in. If Sapphire gets back, send her up… or Scott."

"You got it."

I went back to what I was doing with the paperwork and tried to find some semblance of order, sticking them into files, hoping that the accountant wouldn't shoot me if it were all in the wrong place.

"Mr Walker?" The sultry purr of the woman's voice had me glancing up from the paperwork. I waved her in, before looking down at the file I was working on.

"That's me. You here looking for a job?"

I could hear her heels against the thin carpet, and I cringed as she perched her arse on the edge of my desk expectantly. She was one of *those* kinds of interviews—the kind I used to thrive on. The kind I was now feeling disconcertingly uncomfortable with.

"You want to take a seat?" I waved at the chair in front of my desk and glanced up at the dancer again. She was beautiful, with chocolate brown eyes, creamy soft skin, dark curls, and generous tits. She could have walked straight out of a porn magazine. This was the kind of woman who once upon a time I'd happily have asked to shut the door and let her seduce me like this one was trying to do. She had been the fun part of the job, but as she ran her tongue over her bottom lip, all I felt was… uncomfortable.

Was this monogamy?

Was this what it was like to want a woman so badly that nothing else hit the radar?

Or was I broken?

I chose the former. A single idle thought about Izzy told me I wasn't broken.

"I'm comfortable here," she purred again, folding her legs and showing entirely too much of herself.

"That makes one of us." I pointed to the seat again, giving her a look that said enough.

Flustered, she slid from the edge of the desk, almost falling into the seat in front of my desk. Her cheeks pink in embarrassment.

"So, you're looking for a job? You realise that we're closed for a couple of weeks?"

"I… I'd have to give notice at my other job, anyway. I figured it would be a good time to interview."

"Where did you work before?"

"Stripes."

I paused. Stripes was a strip club in Liverpool.

"Hello, beautiful," Scott said from the door, his smile warm.

The dancer beamed.

My part of the job was done.

"Could you give us a minute…?" I paused, waiting for her to fill in the gap of her name.

"Harlie. My real name is Jenny."

"Give us a minute, Jenny."

She smiled again, and I pushed Scott out of the office and into his down the hall. "You're taking the interview."

"Are you telling me that Blondie has you so wrapped around her fingers already, you can't get it up for *Jenny*?"

"I could if I wanted to. I just don't want to."

"Fucking hell. I never thought the mighty eldest Walker would be the first to fall."

I smiled.

I fucking smiled.

No denial.

No embarrassment.

Just a fucking smile.

"I really hope you get a taste of this one day, Scott."

With a slap on his back, I left his office and sent Jenny his way, closing my door behind me so I could get my Izzy fix for the afternoon.

CHAPTER TWENTY

Izzy

I'd lied.

I wasn't returning to Manchester after three days. On the second day after that first intimate call between Ethan and me, I was getting the late train home from Kings Cross, and I had a plan in mind.

Lauren waved me off at nine o'clock that night… after taking me to a very exclusive spa that afternoon to work the knots out of my back, wax every inch of my skin, and smother me in fancy oils and lotions that would have Ethan drooling within seconds of seeing me.

"I like you like this," Lauren had said at the entrance of the station, her finger twisting through a lock of hair before she let it fall free. "Happiness. It's a long-overdue look on you, Izzy Moffit."

I smiled like an idiot, pretty sure the muscles in my cheeks were becoming perkier than the ones in my arse. "See you in a few days?"

"You will." She nodded. "We'll talk about the other stuff then."

She was referring to Daggs—a topic we'd skated around over the last seven days. A friend she knew wanted to go 'Ross Kemp' on the prisons of North England, meaning Lauren had a chance to slide into a seat and ask to interview a few inmates.

"It could be a real chance for me to sit opposite Daggs, look in his eyes, and drop in some sly questions for him to trip himself up on, Izzy," she'd said.

"Yeah. And it could also be a chance for you to get a target on your head. No deal."

Lauren wasn't going to let this go though, and the determined glint in her eye told me so.

After a quick kiss and a promise to chat soon, I boarded the train and stared out of the window. The excitement rose with every mile we passed, and those nervous butterflies began fluttering their pretty little wings again. So much so that I had to press a hand to my stomach to regain control.

Ethan had no idea what was about to happen.

I only hoped I could pull it off.

The journey was torturous, so I shot off a few texts to him, teasing with a promise of tomorrow night instead of today. When I was an hour away from home, I picked up my mobile, hit up Google for the second time that day, and hit call on Club Crystal's number.

"Can I speak to Scott, please?" I asked the woman after she'd answered.

"Who is it?"

"His sister."

"Right." She laughed roughly, before calling out for the man himself.

He came to the phone eventually, but not before taking his time and offering some flirtatious words to the women around him. I barely knew the guy, but I eye-rolled anyway, thinking *typical Scott.* Maybe I was taking all of Ethan's opinions and storing them as my own.

"Hey, sis!" he cried through an obvious cheesy grin. "Twice in one day. I knew you wanted me. Wait, no, you're my sister now. That's weird."

"Shut up, idiot." I laughed. "I'm about an hour away."

There was a pause before Scott hissed through his teeth. "I was hoping to get out of here before then. This place is creepy as fuck without punters in at night."

"Sorry." I cringed. "We set off a little late. If you can't help me now, it's no problem. I can leave it. It was just an idea—"

"Listen, Blondie, I can give E shit all day long, but even I can see how strung up he is. Trust me. You'd be doing me a favour by letting this guy get his end away sooner rather than later."

I buried my forehead in the palm of my hand.

"See you at Piccadilly in an hour?"

"Thanks, Scott. I really do appreciate it."

"I bet you do." The phone clicked off, leaving an echo of his rough laughter in my ear as he went.

Suddenly, I wasn't just excited; I was nervous, too. Everything around me blurred until I couldn't think straight, and the heat in my cheeks throbbed, making the whole carriage feel insanely warm. I shrugged out of my denim jacket and stared down at the incredibly summery, thin, strappy, yellow dress I was wearing.

"You okay?" came a voice from the seats opposite me.

I turned at once, looking up to see a scruffy, yet somewhat

handsome looking man staring back at me. His eyes were piercing blue, and his smirk was cocky as hell, hidden behind a long, straggly, blonde beard. My eyes fell to his long, dark coat, filled with tiny holes, and his hands, which looked dirty and rough.

Everything about him said avoid.

Everything but his eyes.

"Yeah," I croaked, quickly clearing my voice and wafting my hands over my cheeks. "Just… warm."

He huffed and nodded, his smile turning down as he acknowledged that statement. "Sure."

"What does that mean?" I scowled.

"Nothing." He shook his head and raised his brows. "Unless you think it means something."

"Sorry?"

"What for?"

I frowned harder and looked away as I rested back against the seat and tried to ignore the weird tingling down my spine.

Ethan will kill you again if you get murdered by a stranger on the bloody train!

Paris, too.

Don't die three times, Izzy.

"You know," the stranger said through a long sigh, turning on his side and leaning an elbow on the pull-down tray in front of him. "It's been a long time since a girl got flustered over me. Whoever the fella is that's making you go red, he's a lucky guy."

"What… how do you know that?"

"What?"

"That I'm flustered over a guy?"

"Kinda written all over your face. How long have you been a thing? A day? A week? A month?"

"Less than two weeks," I found myself admitting quietly,

not knowing why the hell I was speaking to this guy who looked homeless. My eyes drifted down his body again, and I noticed a small, overused rucksack sitting by his booted feet.

"You're wondering if I'm homeless, aren't you?" he asked outright, forcing me to look back up at his face and see the twisted smirk he was wearing. "Spoiler alert. One hundred percent homeless."

"I didn't say—"

"Your face gives you away more than you realise."

"Apparently so."

I couldn't understand how such a good-looking guy could end up in that world, which was an insane thought—like some kind of misguided, fucked-up view that only ugly people could end up at the bottom of the barrel, scraping by, desperate for a hand up. I imagined him without the facial hair, or the overgrown hair resting over his shoulders. I imagined clean skin, moisturised lips, and hands that had been scrubbed. Beyond what he was, he could have been everything to someone.

"You going to him now? The lucky guy?"

"Yeah," I whispered.

The man nodded and looked to the front of the carriage, watching as the conductor came down the aisle.

"Shit. Time for me to leave," he said, groaning as he reached for his rucksack, grabbed hold of the back of the seat in front of him and hoisted himself up. "If this geezer asks, I had a ticket, okay?" He smirked.

My soft laugh surprised me as I looked up at him. "No problem…" I paused, waiting for a name.

The guy turned his smirk into a bright grin. "Just call me Gnome."

"I'd rather not." I laughed again.

Surprisingly, he laughed too, glancing once at the conductor before he stepped out into the aisle and said one last thing in my direction. "My bet is that he's sitting at home, way more nervous than you. Don't second guess it. Go for it. One life, and all that shit. You should live that shit for you and nobody else."

Then he disappeared, leaving me to stare at the approaching conductor with my mouth hanging open as the train came to a stop at the station before mine, and the doors behind me opened just in time for… Gnome, apparently… to jump off.

"Did that guy have a ticket?" the conductor snapped at me.

"Sure."

He looked at me dubiously before he shook his head and mumbled something to himself, leaving me to wonder what the fuck had just happened as that stranger's words drifted through my mind.

One life.

No shit.

When I got off at Piccadilly, I saw Scott waiting for me like a giddy boyfriend, which only made me roll my eyes even more.

"Knock it off," I said, trying to sound sterner than I felt as I approached him, dragging my suitcase behind me.

Scott whistled, looking me up and down before he took the case from my hand and swapped it for a silver key. "Fucking hell, Blondie, he's gonna jizz in his jeans before you even touch him."

I reached out to slap him, completely mortified that the world and all their dogs seemed to know I was, hopefully, about to get laid.

"Just take me to him, please." I smiled sweetly.

"With pleasure." Scott held his arm out, and I hooked mine through it, feeling bizarrely at ease with this man I barely knew.

***

I sat in the front seat of Scott's car for a second, just looking up at the building Ethan was inside of. Lucy was sitting outside, gleaming in the moonlight. My cheeks flushed again with the memory of the way he'd touched me on the bonnet of that car.

"Nervous?" Scott asked, for once sounding sincere rather than a moron.

I turned to him and shook my head, smiling. "Not even a little bit."

"You should be. He's broken girls in two with that thing before."

"Jesus Christ, Scott," I laughed. "That's my cue to go. Thanks for hooking me up." I waved the silver key at him and opened his door.

"You remember the code for the front door panel?"

"Yeah."

"And you sure you can manage your case on your own up those steps?"

Leaning down, I peered back inside at him. "You know, the caring side of you is much more appealing than the cocky arsehole side. You should show it off more."

"Yeah, yeah, whatever, Blondie."

Before long, Scott was driving away, and I was standing at the front door of Ethan's apartment building, typing in the code to let me inside. When it opened, my skin prickled with goosebumps. I couldn't believe this was happening—that I was being *this* woman—but after the last seven days away from him, needing him more than ever, I also knew it felt right.

I made my way upstairs as carefully as I could.

It was after midnight now. I'd lost track of time. All I knew was that Ethan was meant to be sleeping—his text message had told me so only an hour ago when he said he wanted an early night, so he was rested for my return the next day.

He had no idea.

I slipped the key in the door, careful to make as little noise as I possibly could. The heat and nerves wrapped around me again, making my breathing louder than normal, and I had to will myself to do this and do it well.

Once inside, I shut the door behind me, cringing when the small click sounded like a bomb going off in the silence of Ethan's very own apartment palace. The moonlight shone across the shiny wooden floors, but other than that, the place was in darkness.

He was sleeping.

The grin on my face exploded, and I slipped out of my Converse as carefully as I could—my denim jacket too, leaving my suitcase by the door. Before long, I'd tiptoed to the stairs leading up to his room, and I stared up them with a desperately racing heart pounding hard against my chest.

I made my way upstairs, and when Ethan came into view, it felt like that rapidly beating heart just... stopped.

I stared at Ethan in awe.

His golden skin shone for me under the thin stream of moonlight, and I knew with everything I possessed that this was going to be the most amazing night of my life. I was his now. He was mine.

His head was tilted to one side against the pillow, one arm behind his head while his other rested on his naked abs. Only one leg was tucked under the duvet, while the other hung out, curling around the sheets as he slept peacefully.

He looked so fucking perfect, I almost considered not waking him.

That consideration lasted less than a second.

Standing at the top of his staircase, I hitched up my floaty yellow summer dress, and I slid my underwear down my legs, kicking out of them. For now, the dress was staying on. I wanted him to peel me out of something, but I also wanted him to feel how wet I was for him already.

I wasn't the innocent girl either of us had once known. I'd become unleashed, and that feeling of power surged through me, pushing me forward.

Ethan's soft breaths filled the air, a small sigh of disruption falling from his slightly parted lips as I crawled on top of the bed as carefully as I could before I threw one leg over his torso and hovered over him in a straddle.

He didn't even know the effect he was having on me as I stared down on his peaceful, handsome as hell face. Had I known of it until now?

An emotion rose in my chest, so strong and foreign, I didn't recognise it enough to let it linger, so I swallowed it down and blinked away the blurriness in my eyes as a smile broke free. Leaning over him, I circled my hand around one wrist, slowly doing the same to the one resting on his stomach before I pushed that above his head, too. I lowered my arse down onto his semi-hard dick, wondering if he was dreaming of me—hoping he always did.

Then I leaned forward, my lips brushing over his to rouse him fully. It took him a second, and his lashes fluttered wildly as he tried to get his bearings before his head rolled back, and he opened his eyes to take me in.

"Izzy?" he croaked.

"You're even better than I remembered," I whispered through a satisfied smile.

A smile curled the corner of his lips, growing wildly the more he woke up until it was beaming from him. "This is either a really vivid dream, or I'm the luckiest goddamn man alive, and you're home."

"I'm home."

I was. Right there with him, that's exactly what it felt like. Home.

"I got sick of dreaming. Tired of waiting. I'm ready," I whispered, brushing my lips over his and squeezing his wrists.

I felt him harden beneath me, his chin dipping to his chest as he looked between us. "You need to make an entrance like this more often."

"I wanted to make an impression."

"With that dress on, you're a ray of sunshine." He pushed his wrists against my hands experimentally and grinned. "Now that you've got me where you want me, what are you going to do with me?"

I pushed his wrists back into the pillow, my smile growing wider as I stared down at him, my hair falling forward.

"You're going to stay right there," I told him, not giving him a chance to argue. "And you're going to stay still until I tell you otherwise. Aren't you?" I raised a brow.

His hips rose under me. "Welcome home, baby."

Every time he called me baby, my insides clenched like he had a direct password to my ovaries.

My hands slid down his arms until they found their way to his chest. My teeth clamped down delicately on his bottom lip, and I dragged it out, releasing it only when I had to before I sat upright and took a moment to stare down at him. My hands roamed over the smooth, tanned skin of his chest, tracing the curves of every defined muscle with fascination.

"I don't even have the patience for foreplay. We've been doing that all week. I've never been more turned on that I have been for the last seven days." I dragged a nail over his nipple, my eyes finding his as I let it fall farther south until it stopped at the edge of my yellow dress. My hand slipped under my skirt, and I raised my arse to remove the duvet that separated us. Tossing it to the side, I settled back in place, my nipples painfully tight as I reached between us both and finally curled my fingers around Ethan's thick, hard dick. "I just want you inside me."

My own slow smile made everything tingle, and I watched Ethan's face through my arousal as I moved his cock, taking in the way his eyes widened and his lips parted as he waited for the moment. Then slowly, ever so teasingly, I positioned him right where I wanted him, and I sank down, clenching around him as he filled me.

Ethan's breath left him in a rush, his eyes sliding closed as he pushed his head back against the pillow. Both his hands dropped, pushing under the skirt of my dress, gripping my hips as he raised his own from the bed in pleasure. Holding us together, as though memorising the feeling of it.

His eyes eventually fluttered. The hazel locked into mine as he loosened his grip on my hips, giving control back to me.

Pushing my hands against his chest, I leaned closer, staring into his eyes as I began to move, feeling every inch of him pressing against me, hitting spots I didn't even know existed before him, as I rose and fell with strangled breaths falling from my parted lips. His fingers squeezed my hips, and he had the nerve to turn me on even more by looking at me like I wasn't real—like this moment wasn't happening.

"You feel so good," I groaned just as he pushed into me again, the thrust of his hips getting harder.

He sat up slowly, his hands holding me against him, the new angle pressing him against a sensitive spot inside of me. Releasing one hip, his hand pushed into my hair and fisted the strands tangled around it, his mouth stealing a passionate kiss as our bodies moved in that steady motion together.

"Ethan…"

"Yes, baby?"
"I want you to ruin me."
"I thought you'd never ask."

CHAPTER TWENTY-ONE

Ethan

Ruin me.

The words stoked the fire already in full ignition and set me in motion.

Izzy had officially blown my fucking mind.

I tried to keep my shift in control slow at first, my hand pushing farther up under her dress, needing to see her, wanting to feel her, and trying my best to push the dress up over her head sensually… but my movements sent another rush of tension between our bodies, and Izzy clenched around me, chasing away my last grip on self-control.

I wanted her.

All of her.

Desperation had me peeling the dress from her, my arms banding around her waist as I flipped us in a move that I wasn't really sure how I managed to pull off. I knelt back the moment she was settled and let my eyes trace every line and curve of her beautiful body. She was magnificent. Her blonde hair was fanned out over my bed, her creamy flesh covering every inch of her. The tight, taut skin of her nipples tightening more as my hands finally found her thighs and pushed them farther apart to study her perfect pussy.

Gripping my dick, I leaned in, running the lengths of her wet folds as I hovered over her, my eyes capturing and holding hers. There was a moment between us—the smiles on our faces heated, needful, and wantful—and it was that moment that I chose to slide back into her, my eyes taking in her every reaction.

Izzy gave in to it as she pushed both hands into her hair and dug her nails into her scalp. Her swollen lips parted, and her chest bounced every time she dragged in a breath.

She was perfect, but as much as I wanted to take her all in, I would have to wait for the second round because her clench around me demanded I move. I would have given her the heart from my chest if she'd asked for it. There was no taking my time now, the rock back had her mouth open in a small O, but I glanced down, watching as her body accepted mine again, and the hunger took control.

With a hand on her hip, I took selfishly.

Every push of my body against hers moving her farther up the bed until my hand was on the headboard, sweat beading on our flesh as I took and took and took and took. My mouth covered hers after the first of her cries, swallowing the sound as I ground deep and rocked before retreating.

Izzy's body bowed off the bed, her chest pressing against mine, and the new angle had her breath rushing from her. The hand I'd been gripping on her hip slid between our bodies, the index finger finding her clit and pressing down, circling.

I felt her gasp, and I buried myself inside her deeper and harder than I'd thought was possible. She felt fucking amazing: tight, wet, demanding. Her body worked with mine, hips rising and seeking more as our breaths turned to grunts and every thrust sought more. My sudden need to be under her skin was almost painful.

I tried to slow down and ease her through it, but I was too deep—too lost in this moment with her. I was always an instant gratification arsehole in the past, thinking about how I was feeling, how good I felt. Still, I'd always known Izzy was different. Even now, my body damp with sweat and pushed as deep as I could be inside of her, I couldn't help but watch her. Watch her teeth push into her bottom lip, the tremble of her chin as her breaths stuttered into her lungs, the fair lashes dusting the freckles on her cheeks as she fell into a place deep inside her head.

Two weeks.

Two weeks, and I was so fucking head over heels for this woman, I felt a twinge of fear mix in with the ecstasy coursing through my veins.

"Izzy, look at me, baby," I grunted at her, grinding myself into the cradle of her hips with a groan.

Her eyes were glazed when she did, her hands moving as one gripped my bicep while the other slid over my heart again. She stared at me in a way she never had before, and for a moment, I thought I saw a perfect reflection of what I was feeling looking right back at me.

Was she feeling this too?

The sight of it, that flicker of—shit. I swallowed the word as I growled in pleasure. Every muscle in my body was trembling as I strove to push deeper. To be under her skin and be a part of her. Flicking my thumb over her clit, I felt Izzy buck below me, the sensation of her hips twisting, making that pulsing start in my veins. The echo of my old self demanded I just go, take, but I wanted to see her come. I wanted to see her face when I buried myself inside, so I waited her out. Her blue eyes were heavily lidded but held mine, reading everything I wasn't saying.

Her nails dug into the skin over my heart, and a small smile curled her lips as she lifted her head from the pillow only an inch. "It's okay," she panted, her voice barely a sound. "I feel it. Go with it." Her head fell back, and she lifted her legs higher, wrapping them around my back and squeezing her thighs tighter. "I like it here," she ground out, a seductive moan rumbling in her throat.

I dropped my head, my forehead coming to rest between her breasts. Right over her heart. The part of her I suddenly wanted the most. The strange angle of our bodies set off a chain reaction. I felt Izzy's legs tighten around my waist when I pressed a kiss to the side of her breast, and I glanced up just as her head fell back against the pillows, and she came undone. The tightness of her around me undid me. I felt the tension, the tightening, the ache. My body hammered into hers, thrust deep enough for our bodies to become one. I held her to me, needing that closeness, and then let go, the only thought in my head so loud it deafened me.

I was in love with this woman.

I was in love with Izzy.

Collapsing against her as her legs went limp, I rolled to the side, panting heavily as I tucked her against me. I couldn't breathe. I didn't want to breathe. I didn't want the moment to be over. I wasn't sure I would ever be ready to let her get out of this bed again.

"Damn," I sighed.

I felt her smile against me before she looked up and

unleashed her crystal blue eyes on me. "Surprise," she said through a mischievous grin.

"I can live with surprises like that," I said against her hair, still unable to catch my breath. "I'd say go away more often if you come back that horny, but I'm not sure I can have you gone that long again now."

"The last two weeks have unleashed a side of me even I don't recognise," she panted. "I'm excited to see what the next two bring. And the two after that." She rose on her elbow and brought her lips level with mine. "And the two after that. You see where I'm going with this?"

I smiled up at her, peeling some of her hair from her bare shoulder. "You're mine now. Just accept that, and we're going to be fine. I like to think I'm not stupid enough to let go of something this good." I probably should have been embarrassed by that confession, but I wasn't, not after that self-revelation when I was balls deep inside of her.

Love.

Love.

I was in fucking love with Izzy Moffit.

"We *are* good together, aren't we?" She beamed, her hand finding my stomach and stroking it slowly. "Amazing, actually. Every other couple will compare themselves to us and our awesomeness from this moment on, and if they don't, they should."

"They really should," I mumbled, brushing my lips against her throat. "Every relationship should have a goal." I trailed small kisses down her chest and pressed my lips just above her nipple. "Every woman should be this distracting when they're naked."

Izzy's skin rippled with goosebumps, but that didn't stop her from pressing a finger under my chin and forcing my attention up to her smirking face. "So, we're doing this? No miscommunication here. No second-guessing. No reading between the lines. I've just said the word couple, and you've mentioned relationship. We're together now? You and me. Just us."

I held her gaze, letting her see that every word was an honest one. I pressed my hand between her breasts, my palm over her heart. It hammered wildly, telling me exactly what she was feeling.

"Izzy, I am all in when it comes to you." I smiled, flickered my eyes down to my hand, and back up. "I like it here."

"I like you there, too," she whispered, her smile exploding as she stared down at me, her eyes becoming misty and her cheeks flushing even redder than they already were.

"What are you thinking to make you blush like that?"

"How right it feels."

I couldn't stop touching her. The hand over her heart was being pummelled with the constant slam of her heart, and it just made me want her all over again. Her words slammed right into my own chest and made it impossible to do anything but smile, even as my lips brushed the shell of her ear.

"Ditto," I whispered softly. "You and me against the world."

I pressed against her, slowly easing her back down to the bed. I caged her in with my arms, my hands pushing her hair back from her face in slow strokes.

I pushed up on my forearms, studying her face.

"What are you doing?" she asked me quietly.

"I'm taking note of all my favourite spots on your body. Your freckles captivate me." I kissed the tip of her nose. "I can't help but smile when you curl this cute nose because you're trying to figure shit out." I kissed her lips. "Those are self-explanatory. Want me to go on? I have a lot of favourite spots on you, baby."

She chuckled sweetly. "You surprise me every day, Ethan Walker."

When she looked at me that way, that deep way of seeing past what everyone else saw. When she gave me that smile that said, *yeah, I see you*, it made my chest ache. I'd never let anyone close to me, certainly never *this* close. Part of me actually believed it was because I was holding out for her. I'd have probably waited another three lifetimes. This feeling was more than I knew how to put into words.

"Have you considered that's because you bring out the best in me?"

"*Baby,*" she said, mimicking my voice as she ran a finger down my cheek. "You ain't seen nothing yet."

She slid from under me and rolled from the bed, completely unabashed as she headed to the stairs, her pale flesh bathed in the moonlight. She was fucking stunning. Every curve was like it had been sculpted. Her arse was tight, the muscles in her back elegant, and her legs… I wanted to have them over my shoulders for hours.

"Where are you going?" I asked, my eyes on her arse.

When she reached the bannister, she glanced back over her shoulder. "After sex that good, people usually light up a cigarette. I don't smoke, so I figured I'd grab us both a beer before I find myself jumping your bones again. That okay?"

"Jesus Christ, you really are perfect. Hurry back, I'm not done with you yet."

Izzy bounced down the steps, her laughter trailing behind her. "If you ask nicely, I'll even make you a sandwich." I heard her footsteps hit the wooden floor in the living room.

"About that moving in thing…" I teased.

I rolled onto my back, my hand pressed over my pounding

heart as her laughter rose, and the sound of the fridge opening told me she'd reached the kitchen. I allowed my mind to wander back to her wake-up call, the weight of her hovering over me, her eyes flashing in the darkness, that determined bite of her bottom lip as she reached between us.

Fuck.

I was getting impossibly hard again.

The things this fucking goddess did to me.

Being buried inside of Izzy had been better than anything I could have come up with in my imagination, but I knew there was no way in hell I was even close to being through with her body tonight.

She hadn't screamed my name, yet… and she would. Multiple times.

"Are you on your way back yet?" I shouted, palming my erection.

CHAPTER TWENTY-TWO

Izzy

The sun had risen hours ago, highlighting our damp skin as we lay tangled together, not letting an inch rest between us.

My arse had been in the air.

My legs over his shoulders.

My mouth had been wrapped around his cock.

I'd watched as he'd tasted me, the slow lick of his tongue making me orgasm over and over as I twisted his hair in my fingers and held him like my life depended on it.

I was starting to think it did.

"I want to hear you scream my name."

"I don't scream," I answered confidently.

"You will."

Fuck, he'd been right.

My arse cheeks ached, and my thighs burned. Every inch of

my skin was marked in some way, yet the deep-seated feelings rushed through my blood, making me fall into a blissful bubble of pure and utter contentment every time he slid back inside of me.

Ethan had just taken me for the fourth time, each time getting more attentive and lasting longer. The second his name escaped me, all raspy and shrill, his face lit up in victory, and his eyes darkened as he pounded into me again and again. The muscles in his shoulders, arms, and torso strained beneath his sweaty skin as he began to climax.

He collapsed on top of me, breathless and exhausted all over again, his cheek pressed against my breast, and his body weighing me down.

I could have stayed beneath every inch of him that way for the rest of my life. I no longer needed adventure. I didn't need thrills. I wanted to avoid everything that existed outside of this apartment.

"Mine," I panted through a smile, pushing my fingers through his hair.

Ethan pressed his lips to the side of my breast, his fingers tracing my ribs. "Hmm?"

"I said you're mine. I was having a smug moment... being a little self-indulgent about owning you now."

Lifting his head, Ethan rested his chin on my chest. "You realise that I probably won't ever be willing to let you get out of this bed again?"

"I don't think I *can* get out of this bed again." I chuckled. "I'm broken. I'm pretty sure my legs won't hold me anymore. My skin is red. My lips are swollen. I have cheek ache from smiling too much and don't even get me started on the way it feels between my thighs. I'd say you're stuck with me."

"I could draw you a bath, but that would mean moving."

"Stay where you are."

He lifted his head. "I don't like thinking of you hurting."

"It didn't seem to bother you when you were sinking your teeth into my arse cheeks earlier."

"I can't be held responsible for what I do when you're bewitching me with your magic vagina."

"Magic, huh? I'll take that as a compliment considering your reputation, Mr Walker."

He nudged my thighs with his hips. "This is the only one that counts in my eyes. I can't get e-fucking-nough."

"You're insatiable."

Wherever this chemistry and heat had come from between us, it was dangerous. The way he wormed his desires into my mind to become my desires should have been frightening. The lack of fight I put up when he told me what to do between the bedsheets should have unnerved me, considering how easily I'd fallen before.

All my 'should haves' melted away to become… nothing. The only thing I felt being with him that way was pure happiness.

Trouble wasn't enough now. I was heading towards disaster, and I couldn't have been more excited about it.

***

Paris's squeal had me pulling the phone away from my ear as I sat on the toilet, sneaking a call to her in Ethan's bathroom.

"Shh," I laughed quietly, eyeing the door.

It was sometime later that afternoon, and like a typical giddy woman falling hard, I needed to talk to my girlfriend about everything I was feeling deep inside.

Desire.

Passion.

Lust.

And another L word I was refusing to acknowledge so soon.

"You sound so happy. I can't help it," Paris cried. "Oh, Izzy. This is it, isn't it? This is everything we wanted for you."

"It's early days, Goose. I don't want to get ahead of myself, but—"

"Don't do that! Don't dampen this high you're riding."

"*But,*" I repeated slowly, pushing my thumb against my bottom lip to control the smiles that just wouldn't leave me for a minute. "God, I've never felt anything like this."

"Never?"

"Not once."

"Not even with treehouse boy?"

"Are you kidding? I was teaching him most of the time." The memories of Matt Cooper lasted for a split second before they faded away—the boy I once thought I'd cared for now being replaced with the handsome face of the man downstairs, waiting for me. "Everything with Ethan is so…"

"Mind-blowing?"

"Intense. I feel like he was meant to be. Does that make me sound like an idiot?"

"A dreamy idiot." I heard the grin in her voice. "I've never heard you talk this way, Mav."

"I never thought I would."

"I'm happy for you."

"Thanks, Goose."

"I miss you, too."

"I know. I miss you. I'll be home soon. I just need to… you know…"

"Enjoy Wonder Boy's dick for a while?"

"Something like that." I laughed again, crossing my legs and resting my elbow on my knee. "You keeping that fucking rabbit alive?"

"Yep. The rabbit's still breathing. I'm still breathing. Casa is still standing. It's like," she gasped, "it's like I'm an actual adult, Mav. Who'd have thought it?"

"Not me, that's for sure."

"Arsehole."

"I love ya."

"Love you, too."

"I'd better go. Call me if you need me for anything, okay? Anything at all."

"Yes, Mum."

"Good little peasant child."

After I ended the call with Paris, I shot Lauren a text with nothing more than a winky face to let her know that everything had gone to plan. She sent me a row of kisses back, followed by a second text that read **Fuck, yeah!**

When I tried to stand again, everything ached, and I groaned as I stumbled over to the sink and gripped onto the edge, taking a moment to look at the woman in the mirror staring back at me. I barely recognised her. Wild hair, rosy cheeks, and sparkling eyes made me look like a woman I didn't know—someone who went after what she wanted in life. I grabbed a hold of it with both hands. My skin was marred with Ethan's touches, and I traced a few of them by my shoulders with the tips of my fingers, unable to control the smile that broke free as I did. I pushed down the yellow strap of my sundress, which I'd slipped back on when I'd taken a moment to stand by Ethan's giant window and stare out over Manchester.

I wanted to be naked again for him.

I imagined us together all night. Waking up together. Eating lunch, talking over the kitchen island… maybe even watching a movie curled up in each other's arms.

My eyes rose up to my face, and I stared at myself again,

feeling a small bubble of laughter bouncing in my chest.

"I really, *really* like it here," I whispered.

CHAPTER TWENTY-THREE

Ethan

I'd never spent a weekend with a woman before, but Izzy was proving to be a lot of firsts for me.

We'd spent a couple of hours watching movies and cooking dinner together. Actually, I cooked, and she watched, distracting me while sitting on the counter in one of my old and comfortable oxford shirts that dusted her thighs.

The thought of having that all day every day was appealing, so when I finally had to let her go early on Monday morning, my empty apartment suddenly seemed too empty, and I was eager to get back to work.

I'd fallen in love with her.

Jesus Christ.

Love.

I'd never thought I would see that day.

I never thought those would be words I would let vibrate

around my head and pulse through my veins. Especially not after two fucking weeks.

I was beginning to realise that I didn't have much choice.

My long-fractured heart had run away without me, slowly piecing itself back together, and I was following it blindly, hoping to hell my first love wouldn't be my first heartbreak.

All the thoughts about love inevitably made me think about my mum and the letter she'd written to me. It also made me think about the ring I had sitting boxed up in my mini-safe in the wardrobe.

You need someone who will hold your full attention and challenge you every single day.

I thought about Izzy again, the very woman who had broken down every one of my fucking walls in two weeks. The woman who strolled through my mind when I least expected it and made me think about what I was doing. Izzy had made me feel more than I had any right to feel. She also threw that one question at me in quiet moments when we were just holding hands or being together.

Why didn't you say hello sooner?

I was starting to ask myself the same thing.

I hadn't been ready when I'd seen her at nineteen. Mum had *just* died. The trauma was less than a week old, and I was drowning myself in alcohol to escape. Approaching her very well could have saved me from myself and that bastard of a year that followed, but at nineteen, I had been a dickhead. I hadn't cared about anyone but myself. Rhiannon had been proof of that.

When I thought back to the times I'd bumped into Izzy when I was clean—like the library, the park, the pub, behind the club, and even the shopping centre—I was kicking myself in the arse for not having the balls to approach her because it had been fear then. I hadn't felt good enough, even when I was bedding every bird I came into contact with.

I'd always had my Blondie up on a pedestal, just out of my reach.

All those years I'd wasted.

All that time I could have spent with her was now gone.

I liked to think we'd made up for some of that over the last few days, and damn if it didn't make my dick twitch again when I thought about her. Izzy had been fearless, allowing me indulgences, even when I was too exhausted to do much more than curl up behind her. She'd willingly thrown her leg back over my hip and guided me inside her.

Thinking about those slow hours of long, tender fucking was torture now I was in jeans.

I hadn't been lying when I'd said I was hers, and here was a prime example of that. I was supposed to be focusing on the repairs to the club, and all I could focus on was Izzy Moffit and her magic pussy.

I pulled my phone from my pocket. If we were in a relationship, I didn't have to play those fucked-up dating games anymore.

Me: I miss your sweet, round arse.

I must have had a goofy smile on my face as I stared down at my screen. I found myself doing that a lot, and it hadn't gone unnoticed. For the third time that morning, Scott sauntered past singing The Cure's *Lovesong*.

"Dickhead," I grumbled, not really meaning it. I was in too good of a mood to be bothered by his bullshit.

"Me?" He chuckled. "I ain't the one walking around the place like I just got off a four-day horse ride, *pardner*." Pushing his thumbs through his belt loops, Scott did a bow-legged strut farther away, his legs parted wider than necessary while whistling the *Bonanza* theme tune.

My best mate was a funny fucker.

"Remind me why I call you my friend, arse wipe?"

"Because life would be dull without me," he said, nodding at the phone in my hand. "Tell Blondie hi from me."

I glanced down at my phone and smiled at her name.

"Fuck off, Scott."

"Love you, too, dickhead."

> *Izzy: You took a picture of it, didn't you?*
>
> *Me: I took a picture of everything. You've got the most gorgeous body I have ever seen. Can I see you tonight? Even if it's just you crawling into my bed and letting me fall asleep with my arms around you.*
>
> *Me: You're the best sex and the best night's sleep I ever had.*

I looked up as another ping from the delivery door went off.

"I got it," Scott shouted from the back.

I smiled down at the phone, waiting for her reply, only glancing up when Scott wandered back in.

"What's up?"

"The police finally got some enhanced photos of the arseholes who broke in." He was shuffling through a stack of images. One eyebrow raised. "Every last one of the bastards had their hoods pulled up and bandanas covering their mouths."

He handed me the images after I pushed my phone in my back pocket, and I flipped through them, studying every pair of eyes visible. Not one of them looked familiar, and there were three of the bastards.

"Could be fucking anyone."

"Could be," I said, going through them a second time. "But even if it was Tommy, he could have hired random lads to toss the place. I'm certain he came to the pub that night to gloat. He knew there was nothing pointing in his direction. He knew the police wouldn't run any kind of test on the body fluids just to find out who smashed and grabbed."

"He wanted to rattle your cage."

"Shake me up. Push my buttons. Swing his dick around."

"We should still keep an eye out."

"That's why I've updated the camera system. The fuckers disabled the old one and stole the hard drives, but this one is state of the art and it backs up to offsite storage. They can smash all they like, the files will still be available."

"You're also keeping the old system?"

"Yeah, they don't need to know we upgraded. The cage the hard drive is in should look like we put a bit of effort in at least. I also updated the locks, and you've seen our office doors."

"You honestly think they'll try again?"

"Depends how much I piss them off. Even if it had nothing to do with Tommy, statistics say that places that have been robbed have a higher percentage of being hit again, for no other reason than they have all new shit to steal."

I threw the pictures on the new bar top and looked around my club. With a fresh coat of paint, upgraded upholstery and poles, the place was looking brand new again. We'd gone with a different colour, better materials, and higher quality poles, all thanks to the amazing insurance I paid too much for.

My office had a fancy couch, desk, office chair, paint, and a fresh start. Izzy was the only woman I would ever want to fuck in there now.

"Maybe they did us a favour."

Scott threw a glance my way. "Maybe."

"Either way, it's done now."

Scott moved behind the bar slowly and pulled out two of the new glasses and set them the right way up on the counter. He pulled out a bottle of Johnny Walker.

Fuck.

I knew what was coming next, even as my phone buzzed in my back pocket.

"Bit early for Johnny, ain't it?"

"It's after twelve."

"I don't have to have alcohol to talk about her." Scott looked at me and smirked. "That's what you were gonna ask me, right?"

"How deep in are you? I saw what she was wearing Friday."

I raised my eyebrows.

"How the fuck did you think she got a key to your place, E?"

"Thank you."

Scott's laughter was from his gut. Shaking his head, he studied my face. "That answers that question."

"Great. White. Buffalo."

"*Great white buffalo*," Scott whispered.

"Don't let me fuck it up, mate," I said, pulling my phone from my pocket as it sent a reminder alert.

"Like I've ever been able to stop you."

"Would you stop me now?"

"Why the fuck would I stop anything that put that goofy-as-shit smile on your face?" He chuckled and continued pouring the Johnny Walker. "It's good to see you happy."

I was happy. For the first time in a really long time, I was genuinely happy. I looked down at my phone and read the message on the screen.

> ***Izzy: Keep saying things like that, and I'll end up pregnant.***

My laughter sputtered from me.

"Speak of the foxy devil."

I flipped him off before I responded.

> *Me: Tele-communicative insemination. We could make millions.*

Her response came quickly.

> *Izzy: No amount of money would be worth missing out on the practice now I've found you.*

> *Me: I want to see you… Soon. I'm needy and pathetic, and I blame you entirely.*

> *Izzy: Just checking my diary. Hold, please.*

> *Izzy: According to my very busy schedule, I can fit you in around… now.*

I looked around the club and over at Scott, who was watching me, a smirk of knowing firmly in place. I didn't have to say a word. He just rolled his eyes.

"Go."

"You sure?"

"I got this."

"I'm reconsidering letting you gaze at my arse as I walk away."

"I knew you loved me, tosser."

I glanced down at my phone, texting as I walked to my office to get my things.

> *Me: Pick you up in fifteen?*

> *Izzy: It's a sunny day. I'm working in the garden. We can go out if you want, but I can wear a lot less clothes here.*

> *Ethan: Sold.*

I managed to get in and out of my office without being side-lined by a contractor or employee. I even got out of the back door without the usual offenders tracking me down with their endless need for direction. I breathed out a sigh of relief as I slipped into Lucy and headed out. At least I wasn't the only one in this relationship who was eager. It also didn't hurt that the image of her in bed, naked, was driving me to go a little faster than I normally would have. By the time I pulled up outside of her house, only ten minutes had passed since our last text.

I didn't see Paris's bike parked in its normal place, so I considered just hopping the fence and going around the back to surprise her, only changing my mind when I reviewed the scare we'd both had last week.

I knocked and waited instead.

"Come in!" Izzy called out.

I did as I was told, closing the door behind me and peeking into the front room to see if she was there. The Neanderthal in me hoped she would be on her bed.

"Where are you?"

"In the kitchen. I'm making nachos!"

I huffed out a laugh, and made my way down the hall, rocking to a dead stop when I found her in the kitchen.

She was in the kitchen, all right. All of her was in the kitchen.

Naked.

On glorious display.

I slapped my hand on my chest, unable to form words at the sight in front of me. Izzy had her back to me as she gently swayed her body from side to side, humming a tune to herself as she fastened the lid back on a jar and dropped it on the counter.

Slowly, she glanced over her shoulder and looked right at me while sucking something from her thumb. The second she did, she grinned and raised a brow.

"Hungry?"

There was only one thing I was hungry for, and she was as naked as the day she'd been born. I stalked towards her, pulling my shirt over my head as I did.

"Absolutely starving, baby."

CHAPTER TWENTY-FOUR

Izzy

The week passed by in a blur, filled with all the cliché things the world attached to romance. Endless kissing, handholding, rolling around between the sheets at ridiculous times of the day. We screwed in bed, on the sofa, over the kitchen island, against walls. If there was a surface Ethan could push me against, he found it and used it to the best of his abilities.

Boy, were his abilities good.

In thirty-one years, I'd never experienced sex like it. I couldn't get enough, and lucky for me, neither could he.

Work had always been my focus, and now I was putting it aside at every opportunity. I had so many deadlines coming up, but I couldn't find it in me to care when hazel eyes looked at me the way they were doing at that moment, or when strong hands took my weak body and did what they wanted with it.

It was a beautiful spring evening, and Ethan had finished work early—again—to take me to the movies. I had no idea if he even planned on watching anything we paid for. I could see what was going through his mind as he thought about dark corners and roaming hands. Not that he needed an excuse to let his hands roam.

My arm was hooked through is, and I was pressing into him as we walked through Manchester, surrounded by people.

"What did you say we were watching again?"

"Fast and Furious Six. Fast cars." He winked at me. "And for you, Paul Walker."

"You give me great sex, *and* you give me movie star porn, too? You're the greatest boyfriend *ever*."

"Boyfriend?"

"That okay?"

Ethan stopped, his head swivelling before he dragged me into an alley and pressed me up against the wall there, his smile bright. "I think that's the first time you've called me your boyfriend. I think I like it."

"You think?" I whispered.

"I know." He brushed his lips against mine in a teasing sweep. Not relenting as he pressed his body against mine. "I really fucking like it."

My hips pushed against his. "I'm really fucking glad my *boyfriend* really fucking likes it when I call him my *boyfriend*."

Ethan growled under his breath. "My *girlfriend* is about to get fucking fucked up against a fucking wall if she keeps going." He ran his nose along my jaw, his lips pressing into the sensitive flesh just behind my ear. "What do you say, beautiful? Me. You. A manky wall? If I kiss you right now, I'm not going to be able to help myself." He pressed his erection against me. "Maybe we should just get in Lucy and head somewhere I can make you scream without an audience."

Just as he said it, my head turned to the side to see a group of teenage boys looking our way and laughing, all with their hoods up, while one with a cigarette in his mouth narrowed his eyes and smirked right at me.

"I think if you undress me here, you're going to have to get over your issues about sharing me. We have spectators."

Ethan glanced to the end of the alley, his body easing up from mine as he straightened and confidently turned in their direction. One by one, the lads started walking, shouldering one another and laughing. All except the one with the cigarette.

I didn't like the vibes he was giving.

"Ethan," I said, trying to pull his attention back to me. "We should go." The last thing I wanted was any trouble from a young kid, or for Ethan to have to warn him away. I had a feeling if anyone even looked at me the wrong way, I'd see a side of him I'd yet to imagine could exist. Ethan was warmth and security, passion, and protection—but I didn't have to have seen it already to know he was capable of hurting anyone who got in his way. His body was stronger than strong… his passion even more so.

Ethan looked down at me, the hard edge to his jaw relaxing as he offered me a casual smile. He offered me his arm as the kid finally huffed out a disgusted laugh and followed his friends, leaving the two of us alone.

"You okay?" Ethan asked me gently, his other hand reaching out to slide my dishevelled top back into place.

"Yeah." I nodded, looking up at him. "Are you?"

"All good." He walked us back out to the street and headed towards the cinema. "I can't imagine being that ballsy when I was that age. I was a dickhead with my mates, but I always treated people with respect."

"I agree. You were a total chicken shit. Couldn't even find the courage to walk over and talk to the young girl wearing the T-shirt you liked." I smirked, nudging his shoulder with mine to try and lighten the mood.

"I regret not taking that chance every single time I kiss you. I could have you knocked up for the third time by now."

"Third time?" My eyes popped, and I stared at him as we walked down the street. "You want three kids?"

He shrugged casually. "Not a clue. I'm rounding down. I can't keep my dick to myself where you're concerned. But you're smart, so the odds are that after ten years together, my swimmers would have caught you out at least three times."

The grin on my face was ridiculous.

It wasn't always the profound things he said that had that effect on me. It was the little things he dropped into conversation like this, and the way he laid out his entire thought process without any filtering. It made me feel close to him already.

"Marry me," I teased, leaning into him and gripping his bicep in both my hands.

"What? No getting down on one knee because I'm a lad?"

"If I get done on my knees, I know the only thing coming out of your mouth will involve the words suck and dick."

"That's the double knee, baby. Double knee. One knee is a different experience entirely." He stopped walking and grinned down at me. "But seeing as you have blow-jobs on your mind…"

I laughed with everything I had, dropping my head to his chest for a moment before I looked up at him again and shook my head. "I'll give a hundred blow jobs, but there'll be no one knee from me. Marriage is…" I cut off, swallowing, despite my smile.

Marriage was nothing more than a joke in my eyes—a few

words exchanges and a certificate telling you *congratulations! Everything's gonna fuck itself up right now for the rest of your life.*

Tilting my head to one side, I narrowed my eyes and made that smile of mine bigger. "You did say we were going to see Paul Walker tonight, right?"

"You wanna back that pony up there? Marriage is…?"

"Something we do not need to be discussing after three weeks together." But my responding laugh was off, and when I glanced over Ethan's shoulder, I thought I saw the very demon I was trying to avoid staring back at me.

Floppy black hair.

Hands tucked into jean pockets.

A smirk I hated.

Narrowed eyes and a tilted head.

"Jack," I mouthed, blinking hard and forcing myself to turn away. I backed up from Ethan suddenly, before I opened my eyes again and looked back to where I thought I'd seen Jack Parker.

A man with floppy dark hair turned away, and a woman ran up to his side before hooking an arm through his and laughing much the same way I'd just been laughing with Ethan.

That wasn't Jack.

It couldn't be.

He hated Manchester—hated me.

That was nothing more than…

Than…

"An illusion," I whispered, mouth open and eyes blinking hard.

"Marriage is an illusion?" Ethan asked, glancing back over his shoulder, one eyebrow cocked. "You okay? You've gone crazy pale."

"I…"

"Izzy." Ethan stopped us again, turning so he was standing in front of me. "You look like you've seen a ghost."

He isn't here.

That wasn't him.

He's never coming back. You're free.

I stared into Ethan's concerned eyes. "I think I just did."

Ethan glanced up and over my head, searching the street behind me before dropping his gaze back down to me. "What just happened, baby?"

"I don't know." The panic rose in my chest, but I kept my focus on Ethan, using his face to calm me. "It's been forever. I haven't seen him since. I don't… I can't even remember what he looks like. Not properly. I've changed. He will have too. We were talking, and then I thought I…"

"Who?"

"Jack," I whispered.

"I don't know who that is."

Taking a deep breath, I held his gaze, knowing I couldn't keep the truth in.

"He's the guy I married, Ethan."

CHAPTER TWENTY-FIVE

Ethan

The look on Izzy's face, the drip white pallor, wild eyes, and thin white line of her mouth all told me that even a chance sighting of a man that looked like her ex was not a good thing. I'd known she'd been married. She'd told me as much when we'd had the exchange in the library. She'd said it had been a bad deal, but the trauma that rolled from her was shocking.

It was shocking enough to make me want to resort to violence with whatever the fuck had put that look of horror there.

"Okay, baby," I said gently. "Let's get off the street."

Glancing around us, I steered her towards a little coffee shop across the road. I ordered us both coffee and slid hers in front of her, along with several packs of sugar.

"You all right?" I asked carefully.

She nodded once. "Yeah."

"You told me you were married, but you didn't say it was this bad. What the fuck did he do?"

Izzy dragged her cup closer, wrapping both hands around it before she looked up at me. "I don't want to tell you all this because I don't want you to see me the way I saw myself back then."

"You remember what I told you about my past? People change. I see who you are now. I just need to know what the fuck made you look like that out there."

"I feel nothing for him. I need you to know that. The pain he caused me isn't because he walked out on me less than a day after we said our vows. The pain is there because I'm mad…" She paused, shaking her head. "I'm furious at what I allowed him to push me into when I knew—I *knew* with all of my heart that he wasn't who I wanted. I was just… lonely."

"He was a manipulator?"

"Massively." She laughed, no humour in it at all. "He said he saw me on the plane we were both on when we flew out to Cyprus, and he knew there and then that he wanted to *know my story*." Izzy rolled her eyes. "What he meant was that he was alone, he saw I was alone, and he also saw that I was weak. He thought he could have a little fun—see how far he could push me and what I'd do for him. I was pathetic." Her voice dropped off on the last word, and her jaw tightened as she swallowed. "I knew him for forty-two days, and even when I knew he was going to walk away, do you know what I did?"

"Whatever the answer to that is, it doesn't fucking matter, Iz. Not to me."

"It does matter, Ethan. It really fucking matters," she hissed quietly, her fire shining through. "When a man you barely know looks at you like you're worthless, and you beg him to stay just so you don't end up bitter and lonely, that matters. When you let someone in that way and allow them to push you over without putting up a fight. That matters. When you tell a man you love him because that's what he wants to hear, and he doesn't bother to say it back to you. That matters. I won't ever be that woman again. She's too much like my mother, and I have already lived through that life once. I am not going there again. Not ever."

"None of that is on you, baby. You're not that woman anymore, and no man will ever have that power over you again, not even me. I can see that fire in your eyes. I've felt your fight. You're beautiful, sexy, and sinfully tempting, but none of those things would mean anything if they didn't have your strength, incredible sense of humour, intelligence, and stubbornness behind them. You're sarcastic, witty, and hard-headed when you want to be. You're also loyal, full of heart, and fucking passionate." I bent over our hands and pressed my lips to her knuckles. "Please… just trust me to see you for who you really are."

Izzy stared at me for the longest time.

The way she always did.

Then she took a deep breath, sank back in her chair, and told me everything.

She told me how the bastard had manipulated her—how he hounded her relentlessly to go the extra step. How she knew it wasn't right but was so lonely, she couldn't deny that she'd become a slave to his rotten attention. She lost herself to the dark memories she'd tried so hard to lock away in a secluded corner of her mind. Her eyes welled with tears, but Izzy wouldn't let a single one drop. Not for him. Not for the woman she hated back then, either.

When she told me about the morning he coerced her into telling him she loved him, only for him to then walk away without returning that affection, a part of me wanted to storm out of that fucking coffee shop. I want to track down Jack Parker and show him how my fist was capable of manipulating his face.

But she was more important.

She told me of the way he left her only twelve hours after their marriage, using her love for Paris as a reason—like she had to choose.

The weak fucking prick.

When she'd finished, her shoulders relaxed, and Izzy looked up at me, waiting and expectant. I knew what she was expecting, too, but if she thought I was going to run or see her differently, she had me all wrong.

"So, there you have it," she said quietly, barely blinking as she watched me.

I studied her right back.

"It wasn't your fault, Izzy. Not one bit of it."

"I can admit to my mistakes.

"Being lonely enough to give someone what they want doesn't make you the bad guy. It does make him worse than dirt. You were in a vulnerable spot, sure. You opened your heart to try and heal it, and that motherfucker took advantage of you. Fuck Jack Parker for what he did, but you're mine now, and I'm yours. You got me?"

"How does a man as thoughtful as you have such a fucked-up reputation? All I see is a miracle."

I gave her a subdued smile. Picking her hands up from around her cup, I kissed her warm palms and held them safely in mine. "I've done some shitty things in my life, Iz, but for you, I want to be a better man. A man who deserves you."

"I'm sorry he ruined our night, even if it was just a memory. I want that to be the last time."

"It's not going to make me think less of you."

She leaned over the table, turning her hands in mine. "I've never wanted you to take me to bed more than I do right now," she said quietly, that naughtiness that I liked to think was reserved for me shining through her innocent blue eyes. "You turn tragedies into fantasies whenever I'm with you."

"Then let's rent a movie, get some takeaway, and get naked."

"Sold… to the man with the eyes I can't say no to."

***

The old adage that time flies when you're having fun finally meant something to me. Time with Izzy was more than fun. It was consuming and immersive. There wasn't a second that went by when I wondered what was going on outside our little bubble. I was new to the whole relationship thing, and Izzy was now the longest one I'd ever had.

I had no idea what I was doing, and this was never more evident than when Sapphire pulled me aside one evening and asked what I had planned for our month anniversary. That's when I realised that I knew absolutely fucking nothing. My question of whether or not that was an actual thing was met by several glares from dancers strolling past us. I deduced my answer from that.

Month anniversaries were a thing.

Right.

Now I knew this, I had to take the initiative and plan something to celebrate.

There was a place just outside of Manchester that I'd adopted as my own years ago. A spot I thought Izzy might appreciate as much as I did, so I put together a picnic—with the help of Scott's mum—and grabbed a couple of blankets and camping lanterns before I picked Izzy up.

It was almost dark by the time we got to my spot

overlooking Manchester. The lights were slowly beginning to flicker on all over the city as the sun set, but we were far enough out that the first of the stars had started to show through. I watched Izzy as she took in the city laid out before us, the wind blowing her hair and dress around her. She was more beautiful than ever. I couldn't take my eyes off her.

"What do you think?" I asked, handing her a Corona.

She turned to look at me, tearing her eyes away from the view before her smile broke free slowly. "I like it here."

"Me, too," I said, leaning in to kiss her temple as I held out a small box for her. "Happy anniversary, baby."

I was no good at any of this romance stuff. So, I'd gone with my gut and bought her a dainty necklace. It was a small hourglass that had suspended crystals inside of it. I felt ridiculously nervous as I waited for her to take it.

"What's this?" She turned the box over in her hands, looking down at it.

"An anniversary present."

"Wow." Her eyes widened. "Never had one of these before." Her small laugh seemed like it was for herself rather than me before she opened the box, and she traced the necklace with her index finger. "It's beautiful," she whispered.

"It's the first time I've ever given one," I admitted. "I was informed it was customary, but I had no idea what to get you. Now I feel awkward as fuck." I pushed her hair over her shoulder as I watched her.

"From where I'm sitting, you're winning at life." Her grin could have lit up the night sky when she traced her finger over it again. "Do you want to tell me why the hourglass?"

"I wasted so much time, so it's to remind you that I'm not planning on wasting another second I have with you. Cheesy, right?"

"Cheesy, beautiful... words I'll never forget." She pressed her lips to mine—a soft kiss filled with gratitude—and when she pulled back, she held the box up between us. "Want to help me put it on?"

I pulled the necklace from the box carefully, and eased it around her neck, waiting for her to sweep her hair aside so I could clasp it into place. I let it fall against her pale skin, and I pressed my lips against where it landed, breathing her in.

She rubbed it between her thumb and finger, her eyes trained on me. "Am I making you fall in love with me, Ethan Walker?"

I had no idea if she was being serious or not.

She had no fucking idea how in love I was with her. There was no falling where Izzy was concerned. I'd crashed into love with her, and I wasn't willing to look back now.

"You make it so easy."

Her face fell for just a second as she searched my eyes. Was she looking for a lie? She wouldn't find it. But Izzy, I was learning, was the master of hiding her emotions when she felt she needed to.

I ran my fingers along the curve of her bottom lip. "Now for the cherry on top."

"Yeah?"

"I brought nachos."

CHAPTER TWENTY-SIX

Izzy

We spent the night under the stars.

Lucy held our arses in the palm of her hands, and Ethan and I looked out over Manchester like it wasn't the same place we'd both grown up in—instead like Hollywood; a place filled with hills I'd never noticed, lights I didn't recognise, and views I'd never seen before.

When I'd joked with Ethan about him falling for me, I thought I'd seen a flash of something in his silent response. Maybe that was the hope in me willing it to be the same emotions I was feeling for him.

Or maybe it was real.

He showed me things that felt like love.

He gave me things that represented that, too.

He made me feel loved—more loved than I'd ever felt in

my life without having to break my bones for it… literally. Love with Ethan didn't feel cruel, vindictive, or borrowed. Love with Ethan was light, yet suffocating, too. It was easy but heavy—like the comfiest duvet I'd ever laid under.

He'd chosen to celebrate one month together. One. Month. He'd bought me a gift I already treasured and couldn't stop touching. A month with Ethan Walker made me excited for a year, ten, a hundred, and if the laws of life would allow it… a billion.

I couldn't imagine ever getting bored of him.

Because he turns my tragedies into fantasies.

Since the words had slipped from me without thoughts, the truth of them had hit me like an arrow to the heart. Was it possible that we were fated? That life had made me wait for…

This.

Here.

Now.

Climbing back into Lucy, I couldn't control my smile. Behind the wheel, Ethan looked completely fucking fuckable. The forearm porn was out, leaving no sleeve for his heart to rest on. No. For tonight, that was in the palm of my hand, and I wanted to hold it tight, squeeze it with reassurance, and never let go.

As he put the car in reverse, he glanced in the rear-view mirror, and I took the opportunity to rest a hand on his solid thigh, letting it slide between his legs as I studied him.

"I need you to know something."

Ethan glanced down at my hand, smiled, then glanced back at me expectantly. "What's that, beautiful?"

"I've had the best month of my life."

He gave me a sly smile in return and echoed my earlier words back at me. "Ditto."

That was all I needed, and as he pulled out onto the road, I let myself sink into the leather seat beneath me, part high on Corona, part high on life. A life I couldn't ever have imagined. A Wonderland, at last.

Ethan kept glancing between me and the road until we hit the first blind bend only for him to slam the brakes on, causing us both to jolt forward in our seats. A black pimped-up car I didn't recognise was on the wrong side of the road until it swerved and forced Ethan to stop abruptly. The car flying past us suddenly beeped its horn in a quick succession that sounded like a taunt.

"You got your seatbelt on?" he asked, turning in his seat to glance out the back.

I tugged on it in response, not understanding the look in his eyes. "Yeah. I'm fine." I scowled lightly. "No thanks to that idiot."

Reaching over, Ethan grabbed the lap strap and pulled, tightening the seat belt over me before sliding Lucy into gear and pulling away with a jolt of speed.

"I'm not convinced it was some random idiot," he said in response to my glance his way.

"What does that mean?"

"Nothing," he whispered dismissively, checking all his mirrors as lights flared from behind us.

I glanced over my shoulder, my curiosity spiking before I looked back at him and saw the worry etched on every one of his features.

"Ethan?"

"It's fine, Iz."

"Bullshit."

Ethan glanced at me, his foot pressing down on the accelerator, making the engine growl. "I'm probably being paranoid, that's all."

My body pressed against the seat, and my hand clutched the edge of it. I could sense what Ethan wasn't saying. I could feel it, too.

"You think it's them? You think someone just tried to run us off the road on purpose?"

"I don't know what to think other than it would have to be a fucking idiot to be on the wrong side of a road on a hairpin turn, and then for them to turn around and chase us down. If it's not them, it's kids playing stupid games."

I spun again in my seat, glancing out the rear window, but Lucy wasn't made for people to be observant. She was fancy, and all I could see behind us now was a pair of headlights getting closer. "They followed us."

"Let's not jump to conclusions yet. I'm going to get us back into town, and we can lose them there. Then I can drop you off and circle back; see if I can figure out who they are." He hit the accelerator again, Lucy's tyres squealing as he took a corner too quickly.

"You want to leave me? No! What? No."

"I don't *want* to leave you," Ethan growled, shifting and checking his mirrors. "The last fucking thing I want to do is leave you, but you'll be safer than in the car with me where they could hurt you."

"Wrong answer. Try again."

"You think for a second I'm going to risk you?"

"Do you think for one second that I'm going to risk *you?*" I glared at his profile, fingers twisting into the leather seat. "Try. Again."

Ethan swerved around a branch in the road, the back end of the car fishtailing for a moment before he corrected and straightened out. The car behind us swerved and swayed, too, sending light bouncing through the car.

"Izzy, please. I need to know you're safe. I can *focus* if you're safe."

"And what do you think I'm going to do if you drop me off at home? Huh? Focus? No. You don't get to do that if I don't." I glanced back again, noticing the car getting closer. "Where you go, I go."

"Do you have any fucking idea what they'll do if they realise the woman that I'm in love with is in the car with me?" He took another curve too fast—his palm slamming on the steering wheel as he straightened out and glanced behind him.

"I don't care as long as we're—"

I stopped... my words now drowned out by his.

The woman I'm in love with.

"What did you just say?" I asked, too quietly as my voice got stuck in my throat.

"I..." Ethan cut himself off, the growl of the engine dying away as he eased off the accelerator. He glanced in the mirror again, then studied the road ahead of him.

"Tell me."

"I said I'm in love with you." He let his eyes flash to me briefly, his foot pressing down and making the engine scream in protest, an odd joyful and knowing smile painting his lips. "I love you."

I stared at him.

Hard.

Words I'd longed to hear falling from a dream's lips.

Ethan turned the wheel, his eyes on the task, and that confident smile never fading until I had nothing left to do but speak.

"You... love *me*?"

"Fuck, yes, I do!"

"Now?" I cried, eyes popping, just as he took a hard left. "You're telling me this now?"

"I—" He still had the smile on his face as he shook his head. "I wanted to say it a dozen times already. I planned on saying it after a romantic night…" He slowed at a junction and ran the light when it was empty. "When I was looking you in the eyes, holding you, just before we drifted off to sleep. I wanted that perfect moment for us, but it came out now. I mean it, and I won't take it back. I'm sorry it wasn't perfect, baby, but, yeah, all right? I love you."

I didn't need perfect. I needed real, and he was the realest, truest man I'd ever laid eyes on. All I could do was stare at him before I swallowed hard, glanced behind me to see lights fading away, and then looked back at Ethan.

He loved me. This incredible man who was too good to be true loved me.

No tricks. No games. No lies.

Only love.

I love you, too.

But I couldn't say it. Not like this. I needed to be near him. To touch him. To look in his eyes and make sure he could see what I felt deep inside.

"Ethan *goddamn* Walker, I need you to find a way to lose these guys quickly and stop this car," I croaked, emotion taking over as my skin burst to life, rippling with goosebumps. "Or I'm about to take this seat belt off while you're still driving, throw myself in front of you, and risk my life for three words I need to hear again."

The muscles in Ethan's forearms tensed briefly as he gripped the steering wheel and glanced behind him again. We were closer to town now, and he knew where he was. Taking half a dozen consecutive turns, he slipped Lucy down a back street and parallel parked, so we were hidden between two skips. His eyes locked on the mirrors for a moment before his attention moved to me, a bigger smile lighting up his face.

"You were saying?"

I unfastened my seatbelt and watched as he slid his seat back before I practically threw myself at him, straddling his waist and staring down on his disgustingly handsome face. My hair fell between us, and I grabbed his cheeks.

"Say it again."

"I. Love. You." He enunciated every word for me.

"One more time." I grinned.

"I love you, Izzy." He chuckled, his hands warm on my back. "I love you."

Something like gratitude exploded in my chest.

He meant it, and the realisation that this is how love was meant to feel made my insides clench, and my heart pound against my chest.

"I love you, too," I told him, dropping my forehead to his and pushing myself closer to him. "It's insane, and it scares me, and I'm nervous, and I'm terrified, and I love you."

Ethan trailed his hands up my spine and twisted my hair back, his hazel eyes locked on mine. "You're the only woman I've ever said that to, Izzy."

"You're the only person I've ever said it to and meant it." I sighed with nothing but happiness. "Loving you feels like the most natural thing in the world when everything else has always felt like a fight."

"Jesus, I'm kicking my own ass for waiting so long."

"It doesn't matter. None of it matters. All that does matter is that you're here, saying these things... while parked between two... skips. After being chased to our almost deaths." I arched a brow. "Nothing says I love you quite like being surrounded by

Manchester Skip Hire slogans."

He loved me.

"If it weren't for the smell, I'd be buried so deep inside of you right now you'd never forget the feel of me."

"Take me home?"

"I thought you'd never ask."

CHAPTER TWENTY-SEVEN

Ethan

"It's a fucking zoo out there," Scott said, kicking my office door closed behind him as he waved a bottle of bourbon at me. It wasn't my usual poison, but it had been a present from Sapphire for the grand reopening.

I was sitting at my desk, my lips curled into a smile I hadn't been able to rid myself of since Izzy had said she loved me. I hadn't meant to say those three words to her in reaction to being chased down by a random car that probably belonged to one of Tommy's goons. I wasn't sure when I'd planned on saying it because I'd been afraid it would scare her. But hearing those words back was a better fucking high than most of the drugs I'd tried.

My Blondie *loved me*.

I found my smile growing.

I was finally alive.

Happy.

Happier than I could remember ever feeling before, and it was all because of the remarkable woman I'd lusted after since I was nineteen years old now being in love with me.

"You're starting to look creepy with that perma-smile painted on your ugly mug," Scott drawled, waving the bottle at me.

"What, you don't like seeing me happy?" I slapped my laptop shut. I'd been trying to search for the car that had followed us. I only had a partial registration, so it was proving difficult. They'd taken all the branding off the car, but I'd narrowed it down to an Audi or BMW.

"Mate, you know me better than that. I just like giving you a hard time."

"What's new there?"

Scott shrugged; his smirk bright. I was pretty sure there was something going on in his life, too, but I also knew that he would only tell me when he was damn good and ready. Asking him would only escalate the sarcasm or force him to shut down on me, and I was in too good of a mood to push my normal sardonic responses to get a rise out of him.

"You realise that you're going to have to put in an appearance downstairs sooner or later?" Scott asked, wandering to the other side of the office and grabbing two heavy tumbler glasses from the drink tray there. "You can't be up here having phone sex with your girl all night. The dancers want to see you. The bored housewives want to admire you. The punters want to celebrate with us."

"I was just finishing some admin shit."

Scott slid the glasses on the gleaming polished surface of my new desk and filled them both with the bourbon. He grabbed his own glass before falling back into the new leather chair and swirling the amber liquid in the glass.

"Then let's have a quick personal toast. To the rebirth of Club Crystal," he said, holding up his glass.

I raised mine, mimicking the flick of it against his before taking a long pull and savouring the burn. The bourbon was the expensive shit, meaning it was far smoother than most.

"Wait, wait, not finished yet." Scott leaned forward and topped up my glass when I knocked back the last of it.

"My apologies. Please continue."

Scott raised his glass again, his smile full of sarcasm now. "To love."

I smiled and drank, watching the smug grin on his lips fade into genuine surprise. Scott had been taking the piss, pressing my buttons, and he had probably expected me to jump into defensive mode and deny, deny, deny.

It's what I would have done before.

Love had been one of those words I'd scoffed at.

Fuck that attitude now, though.

I wasn't stupid enough to pull that shit and deny how I felt about Izzy again. I'd learned my lesson the hard way.

"Wait. You're in love with her?"

"Mate." I laughed and took a drink, my smile popping right back into place when I swallowed. "I think I always have been."

"Is that why you shagged every bird in Manchester *but* her for the last decade?"

I thought about that, surprising him again by finally eliciting a laugh when I flipped him my middle finger.

"Jesus Christ. You're pussy whipped *and* disgustingly in love. Where the fuck is my Ethan Walker?"

"Your Ethan Walker?" I huffed. "When have I ever been yours, big boy?"

"You know what I mean. You've been smiling like a dickhead for days now."

"Get used to it." I pointed to my smile. "This is here to stay."

"Fuck me, you don't do anything by halves, do you?"

"What's the point? I love her, I like spending time with her, and I adore waking up to her. What would denying that do? Other than serve to insult her... again."

"You almost make love sound appealing."

I threw a pen across the desk at him simply because he'd made love sound more like he was saying dogshit. He shifted, and the leather creaked under his weight.

"So, you've thought about the fact that this could be the last woman you fuck in your life?"

I knocked back the last of my bourbon, trying my best to hide my smirk behind the rim of the glass. If the question was designed to scare me, it wasn't working. I'd had a lot of sex in my life, some of which I wasn't proud of. The thought of being with Izzy every night for the rest of my life, however, was appealing. I didn't think I could ever really explain how amazing sex with Izzy was *every fucking time* without getting into explicit detail, and the thought of Scott having those images in his head ensured that wasn't ever going to fucking happen.

"I'm happy for you, E, really," he finally said, the humour fading a little as it was replaced with a warmth I rarely saw from the dickhead.

"I'll drink to that."

Scott raised his glass and polished off his bourbon before pouring himself another. He offered me the bottle, but I declined. I was hoping that Izzy would be at my place waiting when I got there, but if she wasn't, I wanted to drive over to her house and crawl into bed beside her.

I was *that* guy.

"I know that look," Scott grumbled, gripping the neck of the bottle and rising to his feet. "You gotta make an appearance before you slip out the back and disappear for the night. Let's go, lover boy."

"I'm just—"

"Thinking about the holy grail between your girlfriend's legs, yeah, I got it."

I rose from my desk, resigned to the fact that my solitude for the evening was now officially over.

The club was in full swing by the time we made it downstairs. The dark room had thin lines of colour painting the walls from the laser lights Scott had insisted on. The subdued lighting over the booths and poles had been added in after the renovation. They now highlighted those beneath them tastefully. We also had a new sound system that made the floor under us rumble with the bass of one of my favourite tracks.

The moment we stepped out of the back area and into the club, the lad we'd hired as DJ announced us like we were fucking royalty. Appreciative chortles and raising of glasses in cheers came over us in waves, and smiling faces greeted us both, offering to buy us drinks as the beat resumed. Most eyes eventually roamed back to the girls working the poles.

I slipped in behind the sanctuary of the bar with the staff, while Scott mingled out on the floor, raising the bottle to me in a toast. I needed to put a barrier between myself and some of the more enthusiastic women who were willing to shower me with the attention I'd have lapped up not so long ago. I smiled in welcome and thanks, flirted mildly with them, but made damn sure I never gave anyone the wrong impression as I helped to serve drinks. With it being the grand reopening night, we had offered a decent discount on cocktails, which always brought in a rowdy, thirsty crowd.

It also brought in unfamiliar faces.

"Hey, boss."

I leaned into Stacey, one of my bar girls, so I could hear her better as I uncapped two bottles.

"Don't look now, but there's a guy totally checking you out."

I served the drinks and took the money, dropping the change into the jar Sapphire had insisted on when the customer waved the change away. I headed back to Stacey, grinning. I was free to flirt with her as much as I wanted. She liked women as much as I did.

"Can you blame him?" I teased, slinging an arm over her shoulders and using the opportunity to see who she was looking at. "You've seen me, right?"

Stacey chuckled and mumbled something about modesty as I scanned the bodies pressed together.

The guy wasn't difficult to find. He was leaning casually against one of the booths, his arms crossed tightly over his chest as he glared at me with unrestrained hatred. He wasn't checking me out in the way Stacey had implied. This felt more like he was sizing me up, wondering how he would fare in a fight. I'd seen that look a hundred times in my life, across every boxing and bare-knuckle ring I'd been inside of. Why would this stranger be staring at me this way?

As much as I hated to admit it, I'd probably fucked his girl at some point.

I'd always tried to avoid taken women over the years—there were plenty of single women around without dipping into that pool—but at the end of the day, I could only take their word for it, which meant that shit sometimes happened.

I almost felt bad about it. Now that I had Izzy in my life,

thinking about another man touching her drove me fucking crazy and laser stares like this suddenly made much more sense. I watched him cautiously as the guy shifted, pushing his dark hair back from his face, but he made no move to approach me. Not even when I made it evident that I'd seen him, and I lifted my chin in greeting.

"He looks pissed," Stacey chuckled playfully. I dropped my arm from her and stepped away to serve another customer.

She wasn't wrong.

If looks could kill, I'd have been chopped liver.

I didn't want to start anything tonight if I could help it. I went back to working the bar, smiling, flirting, and chatting with people as the rush thinned out and a steady stream trickled through. Some of the regulars had made their way in now we were open again, and they had insisted I'd take shots with them. I'd given them tequila but shot water for myself, a small part of me on high alert as we began nearing capacity. I didn't think we'd been so busy since we'd opened.

I checked my phone when I could, grinning at the texts Izzy had sent, and shooting off replies and photos of me with my back to the crowd so she could see how fucking crazy the place was. Sharing these little things with Izzy had given them more significance. Every little victory had become larger because I had someone to share it with. This was another one of those anomalies that I'd heard about but never believed.

I enjoyed seeing the club like this. The dancers were happy, the people watching them were having a good time, and the alcohol was flowing. This was the kind of thing I'd envisioned when we'd first opened. What I'd been building up to all these years.

It was gone 1:00 a.m. when I decided I'd had enough for the night. Scott was comfortably in a booth surrounded by women,

Sapphire had several men transfixed with her pole acrobatics, and the DJ had found his happy place. I wouldn't be missed by anyone but Stacey, who was practically shoving me out of the door anyway. I scanned the floor on my way to the office and found the same guy staring at me from the spot he'd been in earlier. He barely blinked at the half-naked beauty on the pole, four feet in front of him—not even when she shook her arse at him, which was suspicious.

I didn't want to start any shit. Not when I was this close to getting out for the night. But there was a nagging in the back of my mind. A warning that had me changing directions and heading right towards him.

He held his ground, but by the time I made it through the crowd to the other side of the dance floor, he was almost out of the front doors. He stopped in a circle of light by the pay booth and looked back at the club, eventually finding me in the spot he'd just vacated, then he smirked and pushed his way outside.

I didn't like it. Not one little bit.

CHAPTER TWENTY-EIGHT

Izzy

"You can stop that any time you like, you know."

I turned to Paris as the two of us walked down the street on an unusually glorious day in May. "Huh?"

She eyed me over the top of her fake Ray-Bans. "Haven't you noticed how much I'm wearing these sunglasses lately?"

"Not particularly."

"Well, I have, and it isn't because we're having good weather."

"No?"

She looked forward again and pushed her glasses back into place. "I have to wear these every day now. Your smile is blinding."

That only made my smile bigger. "Do you want me to say

sorry?"

"Would you mean it?"

"Nope." I laughed.

Her smirk rose, and she wrapped an arm around my shoulder. "Then don't bother. Just remember who your chief bridesmaid is going to be when you walk down the aisle and become Mrs Izzy Walker."

I shrugged her away, trying not to let the thoughts of marriage ruin yet another day. It killed me during moments like this that I hadn't shared the truth with Paris about my brief time with Jack, but she'd had her own ghosts to deal with, and mine just didn't ever seem relevant.

Funny how ghosts have a habit of tracking you down when you're at your happiest.

"There will be no talk of marriage. That's your dream, not mine," I teased, nudging her shoulder before the two of us parted to avoid a lamppost.

"Oh. That's right. You're the girl who dreams of peace. I forgot."

"I may have adapted that dream a little now."

"Please tell me it involves bondage."

"You have no idea." I smirked, the visions of Ethan's naked body beneath mine as I rode him taking over. That feeling of having him filling and teasing me, his eyes locked on mine the whole time, and that look he would give me whenever we made love.

Fucking love.

God, I adored it.

The ecstasy of life with him in it made me want to stick out my arms, tilt my head to the sky, and spin around endlessly.

"You're doing it again," Paris interrupted my reverie. "Your smile is going to stop traffic, Izzy."

I came to a stop in front of her, palming my cheeks. "I can't help it. It's like someone has stuck a bloody coat hanger in my mouth, and my cheeks can't fall down."

Paris plucked at a strand of hair that had fallen free from its ponytail before she glanced down at my light blue, flowery summer dress. "You've even gone all girly on me. I've never seen you in so many dresses as I have done since Ethan came along."

"He makes me feel sexy. I've never wanted to look this way before."

"You know he'd want to bone you if you were wearing a bin bag, though, don't you?"

"Oh, I know." I smirked.

Paris laughed, hooked her arm through mine, and started to guide the two of us closer to town. "You sent him nudes yet?"

"Yep."

"Has he sent you them?"

"Yep."

"So, Ethan Walker's cock is on your phone right now?"

"With my mouth wrapped right around it in one photo, too."

"*Damn,* Moffy Moo. You're a naughty girl now. You'll be exchanging your I Love Yous next."

"Been there, done that, got the T-shirt."

"What?" She stopped us in our tracks, her face falling genuinely for the first time. What I saw staring back at me wasn't surprise or happiness. It was hurt. It made me panic for just a split second until I realised why she would feel that way.

"It only happened the other night, Paris. You've been out a lot. I've been busy too. I didn't not tell you for a reason. I just wanted you to see my face when I said it."

Paris peeled her glasses away, and she stood tall in front of me, those beautiful green eyes of hers searching every inch of my blues.

"Sorry," I eventually said.

"Don't be sorry. Just promise me something. Promise me we'll always be best friends."

I frowned hard. "You think I'm so shallow as to forget you exist now since I have a pretty guy to look at?"

"That's not what I meant."

"Then what *did* you mean?"

"That I want us to keep telling each other everything."

I wanted to lie to her then. To tell her that there wasn't a single thing in the world she didn't know about me, because lying to her would make her happy, and all I'd ever wanted to do was make Paris Hemsworth happy. But lying would mean that I was breaking a promise before I'd even made it, and this new life I was creating meant so much to me, I wanted it to be as authentic as possible—needed it to be for it the happiness to be real.

"I can't stand here and say that I'll never keep anything from you ever again. You shouldn't do the same for me. Sometimes we get caught up in life. All I can do is promise to always try my best to be the friend you need me to be. You'll always be the girl I want to share my life with."

"Damn you and your words, Mav."

I grinned brighter, flashing my pearly teeth in response.

"And damn you for making love look so good."

"It's my new favourite shade of me." I fluttered my eyelashes and puckered up.

"I think it's my favourite shade of you, too."

***

Ethan was working again that night. After the club had reopened, he'd received some great exposure in the press who'd taken pity on him and Scott, and the fact they'd been attacked that way. They were getting busier with each night that passed, and even though Ethan assured me it would settle down, I was happy for him.

Since the incident with the car chase that had led to our declarations of love, nothing much had happened, but I still couldn't seem to shake off one small issue.

Lauren: If you want me to go inside and get close to the enemy, I'll need to know soon, my little beauty queen. I appreciate the big, throbbing cock that's taking up your vagina at the moment, but time's ticking...

Me: It is big…

Lauren: And you're smug.

Me: I totally am. ;)

Me: Re: the inside job. I don't know, Lauren. It seems like it could be dangerous.

Lauren: You know I live for this shit. Don't sweat it. Let me know by tonight, either way. I'm happy to give it a hard pass if you truly think that's the best thing to do.

Me: Appreciate you.

Lauren: Just not as much as the big, throbbing cock.

Me: **no comment**

I sat at my desk, staring out of my bedroom window. I didn't want to rattle any cages that held sleeping lions, and even though we'd had a couple of scares here and there, would this help? Would being so close to Daggs benefit any of us, or would it serve no purpose apart from having Ethan kill me when he found out what I'd done?

Ethan.

I picked up my phone to scroll through a few pictures I'd taken of us both. Hazel eyes and a face I'd come to rely on stared back at me. The huge smile on his face made my heart skip a beat. The two of us had tried to take a selfie, only he'd whispered something utterly rude in my ear a second before he hit the button. I'd erupted into a fit of laughter, my eyes scrunched tight—my face all cheekbones and teeth while he looked as smug and handsome as always.

I already knew I'd do anything for that man.

Anything.

If all my nightmares had led to this dream, I'd endure every one of them a thousand times over if he was there waiting for me at the very end.

Me: I love you.

Ethan: I love you. You thinking about me?

Me: Always. I can't concentrate on work, and I have a deadline to hit. All I can think about is when we'll next be naked together.

Ethan: Now good for you?

Ethan: Was that too eager?

I laughed to myself, knowing all too well how he wasn't joking. We were a matter of weeks into this thing that was uniquely us, and I'd seen on more than one occasion how he was willing to throw his business to anyone who could catch the keys so he could escape and be with me.

Me: I really wouldn't get any work done if you were here. And YOU have a business to run. Do I really need to be the sensible one in this thing? I was hoping I could just turn up with boobs for you to play with, and let you do the rest.

Ethan: I think we're fucked. But I don't mind going down if it's with your boobs in my hands. Seems like a good trade-off. Now, go work so I can come and fuck you later… Please x

Me: **types faster than the wind**

Me: See you soon x

This was more than a honeymoon period, that much was obvious. I felt it deep down inside, in places I never knew love could exist. Trying to imagine how that could multiply in a month, a year, two years blew my mind.

I'd do anything to protect it now.

Dropping my phone on the desk, I put my fingers to the keys and typed a single sentence before I found myself picking it back up again.

Me: Set it up.

Lauren: Consider it done.

Like I said.

I'd do anything.

Whoever was trying to ruin this…

They wouldn't stay hidden for long.

CHAPTER TWENTY-NINE

Ethan

I had my hood up as I drove Dean's old banger through the car park of Tommy's club. Row by row, I scanned the cars there looking for the one that had followed us. It had become a small obsession of mine. With Izzy on deadline, in and out of meetings and needing to focus, I needed a project. Work was running more smoothly than it ever had before, and I wasn't required, which left me feeling like a spare part, so I found something to do.

Protecting Izzy from these arseholes seemed as good a plan as any.

I had yet to find the black car at Tommy's, and this had been my third trip this week. Dean didn't seem to give a shit that I was using his project car, so I didn't feel guilty about asking. It blended in with the rest of the cars hanging around the car park by the club, where Lucy would have stood out

I parked up at the far end under a large tree that made me seem less conspicuous, and I watched the foot traffic in and out of the building, as well as watching for the car to roll through. They didn't give a shit who they got high in these places. Kids far below the legal age to drink would stumble out looking completely fucked, eyes as big as saucers, while jittery hands groped whatever was next to them.

As long as Tommy and his suppliers had their money, their culpability ended at the point of sale.

I'd only been there for a couple of hours when a young couple stumbled out in the early evening. They'd barely made it down the narrow alley between the club and the building next door when the girl was on her knees in front of the lad she was with. I looked away. That old familiar shame crawled up the back of my neck and gave me odd flashes of those moments I'd had when I'd been high. Those memories had always scared me so much in the years after rehab that I'd go and get tested just to make sure the last all-clear hadn't been a fluke. Every year since my drug days, I'd made a point to do it, and every time they came back clean. I was one of the lucky ones. I'd always had condoms on me, and I'd always used them except with Izzy. She and I seemed to agree that skin to skin was the only way—thank you birth control.

This was the third night I'd seen a couple in some form of copulation since I'd started driving out here. It was uncomfortably commonplace, but tonight was the first time I'd seen them disturbed. A group of four lads passed them on the street and stopped to watch—all of them laughing and pushing at each other, even as the girl pulled away, wiped her mouth with the back of her hand, and grinned up at them. Three of them left in a hail of pushes and laughter, but one stayed behind, allowing the swaying girl to approach him.

The scene triggered a more recent memory. One of Izzy and me the night she told me about Jack Parker. I sat up, narrowing my eyes as I tried to focus on the kid's face and the smirk he was wearing. Was it the same kid? If it was, had he been following us, or was it a coincidence?

I let my attention flicker to the others as they headed inside the club, and I glanced back to where the girl was flirting with the ringleader. I was poised, ready to approach him when he finally peeled the girl off and walked away laughing. Seeing his face, he clearly wasn't the kid we'd seen that night, but the familiarity was enough to make me believe he could be a part of the network Tommy had. He would see the opportunity in having these cocky teens working the streets for him. If he wanted to keep his image clean, he had hundreds of these little bastards looking for a quick pay out.

I needed to get the fuck out of there.

Hanging around for several nights in a row was making me feel itchy and dirty. I hadn't spoken to Izzy all day because she'd said she was in a meeting, so I picked up the phone, making her my drug of choice.

Ethan: How busy are you?

I dropped the phone back into the seat and headed to Dad's garage, where I could trade this rust bucket out for Lucy and then head elsewhere. I'd hoped to head to Izzy's, but she still hadn't replied by the time I got into Lucy. I was torn on whether to go to work or go home, so sitting in front of my Dad's garage, I tried Izzy again.

Ethan: Baby? You still in your meeting?

I drove around the city and past the club to make sure the black car wasn't there, hoping to kill some time so I would get a response from my girl, but there was nothing.

It had been at least an hour since I'd sent the first message, and this kind of radio silence wasn't usual—not even when she had meetings. It was more out of concern that I finally pulled over and stared at my phone. Izzy and I always replied, and even if we couldn't, we tended to let the other know that. I'd have the 'mouth-zipped' emoji enough from her now to actually enjoy it.

Unnerved, I dialled her number and waited for her to answer.

She didn't.

There was a part of me that was beginning to panic, and I was scowling at my phone where her picture appeared on the screen telling me she was calling.

"Hey, baby, I was starting to worry."

"Hey," she said through a tired sigh, not sounding like Izzy. "Sorry. I just had some work I needed to… finish up."

"You sound weary. Everything okay?"

"Yeah," but she went too high-pitched for it to come off as genuine. "Bad day in the office, that's all. You okay?"

Paris had always told me that her best friend was an awful liar, and I was beginning to see that for myself. She'd had a bad day, but she was making an effort not to tell me why. Bad idea or not, I started driving towards her house.

"Want to talk about it?"

"Erm." I heard some noise in the background. Maybe her jumping off her bed. Some papers being moved around. "Not really," she eventually groaned and blew out a breath. "Is the club busy?"

"I've left for the day."

I heard a small bang, followed by her cursing under her breath, as though she'd knocked or walked into something. "That's good," she croaked. "You heading back to the apartment? Getting some R&R in?"

"Actually… I'm a couple of streets away from you."

"Oh." She cleared her throat quickly. "You're coming here then?"

"That okay?"

"Sure."

I turned onto her street and headed to the usual spot I parked in. There was something wrong. I could hear it in the tone of her voice, the quiver in her breaths, and my girl was never as much of a klutz as she was when she was nervous. I had no fucking idea what had happened to make her freak out like this, but I didn't like it, and I liked it less that she was trying to hide it from me.

"Will you come and let me in?"

"I'll be right down."

Izzy ended the call, the usual enthusiasm I was getting used to not there tonight. It took her longer than necessary to make her way downstairs, but when the door flew open, and I took her in—standing there in those duck pyjama bottoms and a white baggy T-shirt—I looked up to notice her face was pale and her eyes dark… even if she was smiling at me.

"Hey," she said softly.

She looked like she'd seen a ghost.

I reached out for her. My body stepping into hers as my hands cradled her jaw, angling her face to mine. Her skin was almost cool to the touch. I searched her eyes, the blue lacking that usual sparkle that belonged only to her.

"What the fuck happened?" I held back the *who do I have to kill?* that screamed from the back of my mind.

She blinked up at me. "What do you mean?"

"Baby, you're drip white. You look…" I didn't want to say bad because she never looked bad, so I searched for something more fitting and less insulting. "You look sick."

Her smile grew slowly. "Just so you know, arriving on your woman's doorstep and telling her she looks sick isn't always the best way to get some action." She wrapped her hands around my wrists and slowly stepped back. "I'm just feeling a little bit rundown at the moment, that's all. You know how it goes. Deadlines, work, and stuff. I'll be fine tomorrow."

"I'm not here to get some action. I'm here because I'm worried. You look like you've seen a ghost."

Izzy opened her mouth to speak before she closed it again and studied me for a moment. Same action. Different girl tonight.

She swallowed carefully and let go of my wrists. "Do you trust me?"

"You know I do."

"Then grab a beer from the fridge before you follow me upstairs. You're going to need it."

Izzy slipped away without further explanation, making her way up the stairs and leaving me to stare after her. I headed to the kitchen once she was out of sight, and I grabbed two beers from the fridge before I followed her up, taking two at a time. I slipped into her room and nudged the door closed behind me with my foot. I watched her staring out of her window with her thumb cuticle between her teeth.

"You realise you're freaking me the fuck out, don't you?"

Accepting the beer I held out for her, she dropped it onto the desk in front of her and smirked without humour. "Don't worry. I'm not pregnant or anything."

It hadn't even crossed my mind, but I found myself blinking at her as that image stamped itself on my retinas.

Jesus Christ.

She turned to look out of her bedroom window before she finally reached over and yanked her curtains closed. She spun around and perched her arse on the edge of the desk, gripping it with white-knuckle force with both hands.

"Not that I'm trying to scare you even more… but you might want to sit down for this."

"Iz, spit it out already."

Her head snapped up to me, no light in her eyes. "I did something today. Something I know you're going to hate, but an opportunity presented itself, and I knew that if I told you what I had in mind, you'd shut the idea down before you even had a chance to hear me out. Before I say anything, let me make two things clear: I did what I had to do, and I don't have any regrets." Her eyes searched mine before she took a breath.

"Izzy…"

"Lauren, my editor friend, had a chance to work with a friend of hers on some research to go inside some of Britain's most dangerous prisons. She asked me if I wanted to work with her on it."

"Visiting prisons?"

"Visiting prison*ers*," she corrected.

I gripped the bottle in my hand harder, making the long-healed joints ache. "What aren't you saying?"

"When your club got hit the other week, I phoned Lauren and asked her to look into it. She knows people everywhere. I wanted her to find out if there'd been any rumblings from anyone as to who might have come after you. After we spoke, she contacted me again and asked what was going on. I mentioned to her, after the way she'd helped me with Paris, that we suspected old enemies were circling." Izzy gulped again, her knees rocking from side to side as she studied me. "So… Lauren suggested using this research she needed to do for her friend as a way to get in front of one particular enemy, face-to-face. One in prison. One who had all the answers." She paused. "Daggs."

I stared at her, my mouth open and heart pounding like a fucking steam engine in my chest. My head turned into chaos as the thoughts and possibilities pounded against my skull with relentless knife points.

"Ethan, I—"

"Tell me you're fucking kidding," I choked out as my hand trembled around the glass that suddenly felt too fragile. "Tell me you weren't in the same fucking room as that animal. *Tell me* that you didn't just put your fucking self in his goddamn path and paint a fucking target on your back."

"Technically, I was in the room next to him," she said quietly. "He didn't see me. He couldn't—"

"*Fuck*, Izzy!" I snapped.

She flinched, but remained unmoving as she stared at me with nothing but conviction for what she'd done—the danger she'd put herself in.

"You think that makes a fucking difference? You were in the same fucking building as him, while someone you can be *associated with* is interviewing him, asking him questions that will lead right back to the two of us. What the *fuck* were you thinking?"

"If you'd let me tell you—"

"I don't know if I want to hear it!"

"Look, Lauren got a friend of hers to interview Daggs. We had a plan before we went in. She even gave us different names and ID before we walked through the doors. The guards there were pretty accommodating to protecting our privacy while inside. I… I know how it sounds, really, I do, but this wouldn't happen again. We'd never get this chance to figure out if he gives a shit about us or not." Izzy stood, pushing herself up but keeping her distance from me, her skin growing paler. "Ethan, please, just…"

My ass hit the bed before I was aware that I'd made the decision to sit, my face dropping to my free hand as I fought to find somewhere beyond the blind fucking fear that was rising like bile. All I could see before me was the past, and it made my stomach turn violently.

"Do you have any idea what happens when you underestimate these guys? I do. I've seen it, Iz. I barely fucking survived it... but hell, you and Lauren have it all under control. What could possibly go fucking wrong?"

"Don't do that."

I pushed to my feet and stepped towards her.

"Do you have any fucking idea what it does to me when I think about you in danger?"

She took a step back, her face hardening. "And what? Because I'm the female here, I have to wait to be rescued? I have to sit by and let you patrol the streets every night, coming back to lay in bed with me while you stare at the ceiling, your brain practically ticking with ways you can stop all this? I told you. I told you when this all began that if you're in this thing with me, you're going to have to be prepared for me loving you the way you love me. If, in your eyes, that makes me reckless, then hell, I guess *me and Lauren having it all figured out* is what you're going to have to deal with. Because I'm not going to stop, Ethan. You don't get to tell me how I love you. Not now, not tomorrow, not in a decade."

She was panting, staring at me as her chest bounced.

"Fuck," I whispered to myself.

She'd known. Somehow, she'd known that I drove out there every night obsessing about the fucking car, driver, Tommy, and that I was hunting. I should have known she'd figured it out. I was as guilty of underestimating her as she was of underestimating Daggs.

"You're not doing this alone. Get that in your head before the next words fall out of your mouth." She sighed.

"I'm not trying to treat you like a damsel. I'm not trying to be a hero, either. The only thing I want is for us to have a shot at a normal life together—one where we're not looking over our shoulders every fucking second. You saw what Daggs did to Paris. I saw what he and Tommy did to Jessica. I can't lose you like that, so forgive me if the thought of you being that close to someone that I fucking hate absolutely terrifies me."

"I want that normal life, too," she said, her shoulders softening as she stared up at me. "But I need you to understand that I'm not out there trying to get myself killed. I'm trying to let us live. I wouldn't do something stupid with someone like him. I'm not that much of an idiot, Ethan."

"You know what scares me the most? I would burn it all down for you. The whole fucking world."

"Yeah, well, right back at you. I'd do the same for you."

"I'm slowly beginning to realise that." I raised a hand to cup her cheek. "We're tinder and flame, baby. Maybe I should feel sorry for them."

"You should." Her lips twitched for the first time. "I'm a hard arse."

I pressed my forehead to hers. "Have I told you how much I fucking love you?"

"Not recently. You have told me what an idiot you think I've been, though."

"Tell me everything that happened."

"Everything?"

"*Every*thing."

CHAPTER THIRTY

Izzy

I could see him.

He wasn't more than ten feet away, and even though I knew he couldn't see me in return, that cold shiver of dread crawled down my spine as I stood there behind the one-way glass and took him in.

Jason Dagson.

I'd never been this close before.

His skin was worn, hard leather on a round head. The arrogance oozed from him like slime, his smirk never fading as he took in Hugo Ferrera—an associate Lauren had drafted in to keep us both out of the way.

A list of questions had been prepared, and Hugo was already halfway through them, while the rest of us beyond the glass studied Jason Dagson like a lab rat.

"He doesn't look real," *Lauren whispered.*

I was too busy chewing my thumbnail down to the cuticle to respond. He wasn't ever who I'd imagined Paris lusting after, never mind falling in love with. All he offered her was an optical illusion that looked like love from a certain angle. Usually the one on the opposite side of his favourite fist.

"Mr Dagson," Hugo said for the tenth time. "Part of the research we're doing is looking into the insights of criminals' motives."

"That's why you people push paper, and we push… people," Daggs said slowly, his voice rough like rocks dragged against porcelain. One ankle rested on his opposing thigh, and his hand tugged at that ankle as he rocked back and forth, the movement so subtle, you became obsessed with watching how he managed to make something so irritating look like a threat. "You look into the whys and hows too much. You think criminals need a motive?" He shook his head. "Most of the time we do it because we can."

"For fun?"

"Fun." Daggs huffed in response, his eyes drifting to the window we were hiding behind before he smirked and looked back at Hugo. "Yeah. Fun."

"So, you don't believe people can be conditioned to be this way? Childhood traumas? Poverty? Addiction? Their DNA demands the thrill of it all?"

"If you're asking me if I believe some people are fucked in the head, I do. Most of the people I trusted turned out to be just that."

"Care to expand?"

"Can you guarantee this will be put out there?"

"If you want it to be."

Daggs' smirk grew slowly, the dark, evil twinkle in his eyes making my skin crawl.

"You can write my enemies' names on every billboard you can find if it makes you happy. Anything that lets them know I'm coming."

I stopped breathing, the gulp of air I tried to take getting lodged in my throat.

Was he talking about me? About us?

That man sitting there referenced his revenge so casually that it made my forehead prickle with beads of sweat.

"Izzy."

He was coming for me.

"Izzy."

For Ethan.

"Izzy!"

For Paris!

I sucked in sharply when Lauren gripped my arm tight, and my eyes burned when I blinked because I'd been staring at Daggs for too long, hoping a single look could make him drop dead in front of me. I wanted that. I wanted him to die right there, today, so I could bear witness to it and never have to whisper his name as long as I existed.

"Did you hear what he just said?" Lauren whispered, leaning in.

Scrunching my eyes tight, I shook my head and stared back at her. It was only then that I realised she was smiling while I must have looked ready to keel over right in front of her. "What?"

"He gave a name. Listen." *She gestured back to the interview taking place beyond the screen, and I found myself taking a final step closer, even as Daggs' voice echoed all around the room we were standing in.*

"So, this Tommy," Hugo started. "He's the one who betrayed you?"

Daggs nodded slowly, the cocky smirk falling from his face as he tensed his jaw and narrowed his eyes.

That was the face of the man who'd tried to kill Ethan. The man who'd beaten Paris and had her run off the road, almost killing her, too. He'd hurt those I loved, and all I could think about was storming through into the next room and tearing his throat out with my bare hands. Until he uncurled his legs, rested his handcuffed hands on top of the table, and leaned closer to Hugo.

"Maybe you were right. Maybe I was right, too," Daggs drawled out. "Everyone in this prison has done something they thought was fun, only to land themselves behind these bars, bound by cuffs, and limited to so much shitty daylight, we might as well grab a noose and cut ourselves loose to end it. But you want to know the one motive we all have in common?" He paused, lowering his chin. "Revenge."

Hugo physically paled before him, Daggs' presence so terrifying, even my hands were trembling from a distance.

"Some of us will die in prison, and that will be everything we want and more because we're willing to hurt those who hurt us if we ever get out. My former brother..." He ground his teeth together, flaring his nostrils. "He betrayed me in the worst way. More than anyone else ever has. Being double-crossed and clueless has been bad for my reputation, Mr Ferrera, and I don't like any fucker messing with my reputation. You want a good article for your research?" He smirked again. "Quote this: I'm one of those bad guys who's willing to do whatever it takes to get out of here, shoot my enemy in the balls before I slam that gun up through his skull, and then I'll take a piss on his dead body right before I enjoy the finest smoke of my motherfucking life. And you can send that quote to Tommy, with love... Jason Dagson."

"Right." Hugo gulped not so discreetly.

Daggs' smile drew up on one side. "Is it now time for us to discuss whether or not I ever plan on finding God?"

I sat opposite Ethan on my bed—legs crossed as I finished my story and waited for him to stop staring at me like I had three heads.

"Tommy betrayed Daggs?" he finally said. "How? Did he say what that betrayal was?"

"He didn't exactly give bullet points, but he said enough when Hugo pressed him a few questions later. Something about a setup, and Tommy planning on getting Daggs put inside. He just kept going on and on about revenge, Ethan. It was twisted. He wasn't shy about it, either. Lauren said they'll never let him out if he talks like that in there, which would suit us just fine, I know, but…" I picked at the bottom of my pyjama bottoms, staring up at him and offering a shrug of my shoulder. "What if we've had it all wrong so far? What if it's *Tommy* who is coming after us of his own accord. Not Daggs. He never once mentioned Paris or anything to do with her."

"It's not completely out of the realm of possibilities." Ethan looked down at my hands. "Tommy's building himself an army of his own. I wasn't sure at first, but you remember those lads that stared us down?"

I frowned. "The perverted kids watching us in the alley?"

"He's got dozens of them in and out of his club on a daily basis. I'm pretty sure they're dealing for him, but I think they're probably his eyes and ears, too. Tommy was always smart and level-headed. He had that scary as fuck calm to him, while Daggs lost his mind and skull fucked you. If Tommy knows Daggs has figured out he's double-crossed him, he's going to cover his back and his assets."

"So, this could be something and nothing. We could just be a part of his games, but we're not the big target here. If Tommy is trying to build himself some kind of defensive empire, maybe he attacked your club so you'd *think* it was Daggs, and that would put another target on his back rather than Tommy's?" I twisted the material around my finger, my brain running at a hundred miles an hour suddenly. "We could be just… unfinished business he wanted to fuck around with."

"Shaking shit up and seeing what comes loose. Maybe he thought Daggs was reaching out to former associates? Maybe Tommy thinks you're the key to keeping Daggs inside. You're one of the few to pull it off and make the charges stick."

The thought made my stomach twist into a tight knot. I didn't want to be the key to any of this. I wanted to pack a bag, book a flight, jump on the next plane and get out of here. I wanted to stay in my bubble with Ethan—too loved up to see the rest of the murky world outside of the walls we lived in.

"Or maybe," I whispered, "the two of us have spent so many fucking years being paranoid and looking over our shoulders, we're trying to make this about us because we're not used to feeling happy. We're waiting for someone to burst the bubble for us."

Ethan brushed my hair back from my face. "Maybe."

"We could always book that flight I mentioned."

"Where would we go?"

I let myself drift into the daydream, a wistful sigh falling free as I looked up to the ceiling. "Somewhere hot, where I'd be in a bikini, and you'd be tanned and oiled up all day long. Warm beaches. Cool seas. Lots of sex. Zero reality." I looked back down and smiled at him. "Or we could stay and fight because we both know neither one of us knows how to run away from those, apparently."

"If we stay and fight, we do it together."

"I can throw a surprisingly good right hook, I'll have you know."

"One day, I'll tell you about my fighting days, but I can show you sometime?"

"My ridiculously handsome boyfriend, who is full of charm, sweet words, huge, warm hands, and gives me sex so good I can barely walk straight… was also a *fighter?*"

"I was. I won a ten-grand tournament with a dislocated shoulder. I'm badass, baby."

A shiver of appreciation ran over me. "And here I was thinking you couldn't get any more perfect."

CHAPTER THIRTY-ONE

Ethan

Trying to protect Izzy by being overbearing clearly wasn't an option.

My woman was a fighter. She met threats head-on and didn't look back to think it through until after the fact. She'd made it more than clear that I could get on board and deal or take the next train out. I actually found her assertiveness sexy as fuck, and equally terrifying, so I'd offered to teach her how to protect herself.

I would have loved to have taken her to Albert's Gym and introduced her to the old man, but with Tommy suddenly showing interest in the place, it just wasn't feasible. Instead, I took her to the place that still held my secret stash of cash from those fights so many years ago.

The guy behind the desk didn't so much as blink as we came in. I was offered the usual chin lift of greeting, and Izzy was welcomed with a wink before he went back to what he was doing. The gym was tucked into the back of an industrial estate, and it didn't advertise, so it wasn't as though we had many people to contend with. We ended up being the only ones in the small ring in the backroom, which left me able to lock the door behind us.

"Nothing fancy, but it'll get the job done," I said, releasing her hand and dropping my bag. Izzy looked as sexy as fuck in her old, torn Rocky shirt that hung loosely over her running gear as she gazed around the place with curiosity.

Grabbing what I needed from my bag, I slipped into the ring and held the ropes apart for her. She was so agile; she was up and through them with little effort and immediately started to bounce on her toes. Training her wasn't going to be easy when all I could think about was wrapping her up in those ropes and fucking her or eating her alive.

Either option seemed feasible at this point.

"Where do you want me?" she asked innocently.

"That's a loaded question."

"Only to a pervert."

"Guilty as charged, baby." I smirked, swooping down to pick up the boxing pads I'd brought with me. "You wanna show me what you've got?"

She shrugged, looking unfazed. "I can try. I've never done this like you have, but…"

Slipping my hands into the pads, I took a stance, holding them up for her to focus on.

Her face changed as she stared at the pads, took a fitting stance of her own, and threw a right, left, right at me before she paused, looked up, and quirked a brow. "Like that?"

Holy shit. Could my woman get any hotter?

"Beautiful." I cleared my throat and at least tried to remain focused. "Now put all of your weight behind it like you mean it. You're not going to hurt me." I slapped the pads together. "That's what these are for."

She smirked, but more to herself, as though she'd just shared a private little joke with no one else. "Right." She nodded, moving quickly to repeat the move twice over, throwing six consecutive punches at me before she bounced back and brought her eyes up to mine. "Like *that*?"

Fuck if I wasn't hard.

I should have known she'd have that kind of power. Her lithe body was my favourite thing to study, and her muscles and strength were hidden away under that smooth skin.

"Beautiful." I tapped her left shoulder, widened my stance, and nodded. "Raise the elbow on this arm and follow through. You've got power behind your punches already, but this will give you more. Hit me with your fist, follow through with your elbow. We're fighting dirty."

She did exactly as I told her to, her concentration clear every time I gave her a move and told her to strike. Even on the odd occasion where she stumbled, she would straighten up, set her mouth into a thin line, and go again. Beads of sweat began to collect around her hairline, making stray strands of hair stick to her skin, and she would blow them away at the end of every move before she looked up at me for approval.

She was a fast learner and definitely wasn't afraid to apply herself.

Every move I gave her was made with precision and clarity, and she switched them up on me when I least expected it, impressing me even more. She had the basic knowledge and mechanics. We found ourselves working harder with every combo and correction.

"Now you need to defend. Focus on the attack but be aware

of the returns. Come at me with the last combo you did but pay attention to my legs and body. In a drag-out fight, there are no rules. You have to be prepared for anything."

"No rules," she panted, planting her hands on her hips. "So, it's all about the element of surprise?"

I raised the pads to cover my face, watching every twitch of her muscles. "Yes."

"Got it." Izzy took her stance again, eyeing me and waiting for the right time to strike. When she thought I least expected it, she ducked, leaned forward, reached out, and tickled my balls in surprise before jumping back with a beaming grin on her face. "Like *that?*"

"Well, fuck, Izzy…" I didn't finish the sentence. I growled and pounced, my hands shaking off the pads as I pulled her close and pushed us against the ropes. We stared at each other, both of us out of breath. "I might get upset about you doing that to someone else, but you have the concept down."

"You can't get upset if it saves my life."

"This is true," I said, angling her back to the ropes and gripping her wrists gently. "It's definitely a distraction." Spreading her arms along the ring, I twisted the second level of ropes with the first and carefully locked her arms at her sides. "Just like I'm distracting you."

I stepped back and looked down on her with a heated smile. A bead of sweat trickled between her breasts as she heaved in air. Her arms pushed out on either side of her now tied and tangled in the ropes.

"I'm not distracted. This is all part of my plan. I've actually got you where I want you." She grinned adoringly.

"*I'm* very distracted. You're damn sexy when you're sweaty and kicking arse." I smirked and stepped closer to her, my fingers slipping under the Rocky shirt and sliding along the hem of her leggings. "I have fingers and a tongue that are just itching to explore you, I thought you should know."

Izzy's smile was mischievous. "Fair warning: I'm in defensive mode, so if you go down, be prepared to go *down*. Know what I'm saying?"

Pressing my hand against her damp, sweaty stomach, I slid my hand between it and the material, pressing my mouth against her ear as I slipped my palm to her mound. "Dying with my tongue on your clit doesn't sound so bad to me."

Her hips pushed away from the ropes, her chest expanding. "A true attacker wouldn't care whether they died or not. Surely they just want to get the job done?"

My middle finger eased between her slick folds and circled her clit, too lightly to do anything but stir her arousal, while I licked the small expanse of sensitive skin behind her ear. "I'm feeling reckless."

"You're feeling horny," she corrected in a whisper.

"I always feel horny when I see you work up a sweat, but this…" I pulled my head back and glanced at her arms tangled in the ropes. "This is a fantasy." I thrust my finger deep inside her with the last word, my mouth dropping to her neck and pressing my lips there on her sharp inhale. I fucking lived for that sound these days.

Her head rolled away, exposing more of her neck, and Izzy closed her eyes as she ground herself down on my hand. "I'm about to lose this round," she rasped.

"You can bet your arse on that, baby." I pressed another finger inside of her, my other hand working the material down over her hips as I teased her and pumped in slow, dramatic strokes.

Izzy let herself sink against the ropes, giving herself to me, and to this fantasy. "Fuck, I love the way you touch me."

I was so hard, it was uncomfortable. The things this woman did to me made me fucking crazy, to the point I wanted to lose myself in her for days and never resurface. I sank to my knees before her, moving slowly and dragging her leggings down with me, removing them and her trainers swiftly. I watched my fingers as they thrust inside her pussy, and I groaned when her body tightened and gripped them inside her.

I took my time leaning into her. My eyes rising to her as I blew a stream of cold air along the heated folds my fingers were sinking between. The bastard in me wanted to hear her plead for more. The desperate boyfriend in me wanted to devour her whole. The horny fucker in me wanted to take my time and ease every moan and groan from her beautiful mouth.

Izzy's chin dropped to her chest—her lips parted as she panted for breath and stared at me with heated eyes. Her thighs tensed before a small smirk tugged at her open mouth.

I watched her face as I slowly pulled my fingers from inside her. With my hands gripping her thighs, I placed one and then the other over my shoulders until she was all I could see. Pushing my face to her, I ran my tongue between her folds and flicked at her clitoris, pushing closer and closer until I was close enough to roll my tongue over her, sucking and nipping intermittently with my teeth. I used the roll of her hips to my advantage, the taste of her filling my mouth and leaving me hungry for more.

Every sound spurred me forward. I worked my mouth against her, feeling the tense of her thighs as she grew closer to that edge I was beginning to become so familiar with. I read every move and every sound until my tongue slipped inside her, and she came undone around me. I watched with pleasure as her toned arms tugged against the ropes, and her perfect body arched around me. Breathless moans of pleasure fell around us both as I slowed my desperate moves and took in her exhausted state.

I wasn't finished. Nowhere near it. I barely gave her a chance to catch her breath before I rose to my feet and gripped her arse in my hands. With her legs still half over my shoulders, I thrust into her, the spring of the ropes sending her rocking back against me. I was so deep inside of her that our bodies ground together, and her fading orgasm gripped my dick as I angled deeper and rocked inside of her.

I watched Izzy watching our bodies' connection. I took in every flutter of her eyelashes and twitch of her mouth as I retreated and paused. She was already panting from the first orgasm, and even under the Rocky shirt and a sports bra, I could see her chest trembling as she waited for me to move again.

I loved her like this. I loved *us* this way.

I waited for another breath.

Then another.

I waited for her eyes to meet mine, filled with that demanding impatience I craved. Then I thrust into her again, my smug face alight with passion for this incredible woman who was capable of fulfilling fantasies no one else ever could.

We stayed locked onto one another as I used the tension of the ropes and sank deep inside of her. Over and over again, our bodies met and ground between us. The two of us groaned wildly, drowning in pleasure as my impatience and need grew. My grip moved to her hips and tightened, my thrusts turning into pounds as the sight of her teeth sinking into her bottom lip made my balls tense. I was worried I was bruising her for a second before her body jerked, and her chest arched.

She mouthed something as her head fell back between her shoulders, and her pussy gripped me, not wanting to let go. It was all it took for me to follow. The sight of her, the sound, the feel all came together and mingled with that impossible love I felt. It sent me over the edge to join her, one deep thrust connecting our bodies as my arms trembled, my head and heart screaming out emotions I'd never had before when I came inside her.

The moment the last of my energy escaped me, my body leaned against hers in exhaustion, and I sank to my knees, Izzy's body following me down even with her arms still caught in the ropes.

I moved us so she was sitting over my thighs, the two of us breathless, her arms up high, and her eyes aimed low on me.

She was everything.

My head fell against her chest as my breaths sawed in and out. The fabric under my cheek was damp from sweat, and I couldn't get enough of it—of her. Reaching out, I flicked the ropes and unlocked her arms from their prison before guiding us both to the mat, grunting as she sprawled flat over my chest.

I was never going to get bored of fucking this woman, and when she wriggled sleepily above me, I started to get hard again. My breath huffed from me in a laugh as I reached up to brush loose strands of her hair back from her face, and I took in her sleepy blue gaze.

"You ready for round two?"

"Jesus," she gasped.

CHAPTER THIRTY-TWO

Izzy

The mornings spent in the gym soon became my favourite—usually because the two of us would end up a sweaty mess, kissing against walls, his warm hands roaming over my tight skin any chance he could get. He made me feel like a deity, and it was benefitting every part of my life.

Including my writing.

Ethan was my muse, my reason for waking up with a smile on my face, and the drive I needed to push forward. I'd caught up on my deadlines in between working out, screwing my hot boyfriend, and seeing the world in a brand-new light. We had worries, but none of them could dim the shine on this little thing called love that was uniquely ours.

It was another Friday night, and the two of us had decided that a night out in Manchester was what we needed—to be among other people, surrounded by life, and to let the music take over our souls. We were becoming so engrossed with one another, leaving whatever room we locked ourselves up in was now considered hard work. He was my oxygen, and I was his every cure. It was dangerous, losing yourself to someone like that so easily, and I'd never been so excited to drown in danger before.

His hand rested on the top of my arse as we walked to the door of a bar Ethan had suggested, and my heart skipped a beat when he squeezed it before he let his palm drift to the small of my back, and he guided me inside.

The first song I heard was Robert Palmer's *Addicted to Love*. I turned to look at Ethan with a bright smile shining from behind my ruby red lips.

"I know that smile," he said, grinning back at me.

"You have no idea what's going on in my mind," I teased, grabbing his hand.

"Maybe you should whisper it into my ear." He headed to the bar and flagged down the girl serving drinks behind it.

Grabbing his shoulder, I rose on tiptoes and whispered to him, "I was just wondering if this was a building we could spend time in and make it out without fucking each other."

"Doubtful."

I laughed and fell back down, turning to the bar to look around as I tucked some hair behind my ear, which had come loose from my high ponytail. "I don't know. I think we have a shot in this place. It's busy enough for us to people watch. There's music to distract us. The DJ isn't too hard on the eye, either. I can always let my eyes drift his way if you're proving too much for my ovaries again."

"Yet, you're still the biggest distraction in here. That means I'm going to be thinking about fucking you the whole time we're here."

"Remind me why we came out again?"

"I think they call it socialising." Ethan winked as two beers were placed in front of him.

I plucked one from the bar and wrinkled my nose. "Sounds awful."

We made our way to a high-rise booth at the side of the bar with just enough privacy for us to talk, but enough going on around us for me to do some of that people watching I'd joked about. I used to do it when I was alone, in the days when Paris had disappeared, Jack had left me, and all I had for company was myself. Looking back on those days now felt like a lifetime ago. Maybe even two.

I'd transformed into someone I barely recognised.

This was happiness.

I slid into my leather booth while Ethan slid into his, and I tugged down on my way-too-short leather skirt and readjusted my shoulders in my T-shirt.

"Is this a favourite place of yours?" I asked, just as the music shifted to a Guns N' Roses track that the majority of the bar recognised, their enthusiasm showing as they began to dance and sing along in their little groups dotted around the space. "I had you down as more of a strip club kinda guy."

"It's a pole dancing club," he said with an amused quirk of his lips. "And this place used to be one of my haunts." He pointed to a table of men at the back who were slowly getting drunk. "I used to go to school with those arseholes. The guy with the piercings had a Halloween party every year. He stopped having them after the *incident*."

"The what?"

"Did you ever see that movie with Cameron Diaz and Selma Blair? The one where Selma Blair gets a dick stuck down her throat?"

"I am *so* worried about what you're about to say next."

"Mr Pierced over there was getting head from a lass, and they had the unfortunate mishap of re-enacting that scene. Everyone at the party paraded through there offering hints and tips. Someone even suggested singing like in the movie. As you can imagine, a bunch of drunk arseholes killing themselves laughing and singing *Champagne Supernova*... he decided the tradition should end there."

I stared at him, blinking, my lips parted.

"It's how we all learned he had a Prince Albert." He made a motion with his hands and started to laugh. "He avoids most of us like the plague now."

I turned back to look at the guy before I faced Ethan again and leaned forward. "Dude, where the fuck did you go to school?"

"About two streets down. We called it Hell."

"Sounds hella funny compared to where I went. Our school was hella boring compared to the prince back there."

"Ah, the stories I could tell. Remind me to tell you about the time my younger brother was caught with a girl by the long jump pit. Then you can give him a hard time when you meet him."

"Do you want me to?" I asked without thought. "Meet him, I mean?"

"Of course, I do," Ethan said, leaning to rest his hand over mine. "Just don't judge me by that twat. That's all I ask."

"Trust me. I don't judge *anyone* by their families. The thought of someone doing the same to me is one of the things that terrifies me the most." I said it light-heartedly, but the memory of my family tugged at the old scar they'd left, reminding me that I was sadly alone apart from Paris when it came to loved ones. "I'm sure your brother is great. Just like you." I smiled.

"He's a dickhead, but I love him." He paused. "I hate the look that you get when you think about your family."

"What look?"

"Sad. Disappointed. Full of loneliness." Reaching out, he brushed his thumb down my cheek.

Full of loneliness.

Those words described my childhood. The disappointment and physical pain, I could deal with. The loneliness had been what had left me cold my whole life, too scared to get close to anyone beside Paris and the man sitting opposite me.

I looked down at my drink. "Yep. That about describes it."

"Will you tell me. One day? When you're ready?"

I glanced up again. "It isn't about whether I'm ready or not, Ethan. I know the story. I know the beginning, the middle, and the end. I know every step of it, chapter by chapter. It's about when *you're* ready to hear it… because it isn't pretty."

Ethan studied my face. "You know, I keep thinking I can't love you more than I do at any given moment, and then you say something like that, and I just fall deeper." His palm rested against my jaw. "I want to know everything about you. The good and the bad."

"Then ask me," I said quietly. "Ask me anything you want, but don't say I didn't warn you when it makes your chest burn and your fists shake."

"Not here," he said quietly. "Maybe we can open a bottle of scotch at my place one night. We can talk, get shitfaced drunk, and then fuck all night until the bad shit goes away."

"Have I told you today how much I love you?"

"You love me?" He grinned goofily.

"Little bit."

"Ditto."

Just like that, he took the moment and flipped it back around, leaving the two of us with smiles on our faces and a promising night ahead. Where once the mere mention of my parents would have left a dark cloud over my head for days, now it was merely a blip—an overcast few seconds on an otherwise glorious day. Maybe I was healing? Maybe pretending the two of them didn't exist was finally weakening the memory of them both?

Or maybe, quite probably, it was nothing but the Ethan Walker effect.

We spent the next couple of hours barely moving, except to go to the bar. We laughed, talked about Paris, Scott, and Dean—who I was officially desperate to meet after Ethan regaled me with story after story of his brother, who apparently couldn't speak a single word of English properly without some ridiculous Mancunian crossbreed accent attached to it.

I was tipsy, Ethan was hot, and I felt like the luckiest girl alive to have his adoration in the middle of a crowded bar. The music changed to become a little more up-tempo, and the lights had dimmed as the night wore on, throwing shades of green, blue, and neon pink across our faces.

"I feel like I'm having to shout to hear you now," I called over the table to him, the warm fuzz of alcohol refusing to let the smile fall from my face.

"We could call it a night? Go home and get naked."

"Is that all you think about? Getting me naked?"

"About eighty percent of my thoughts."

"And the other twenty percent?"

"What we'll do while we're naked."

I smirked, tilted my head and gestured to the exit. "Let's get out of here."

"Let me head to the toilet first," Ethan said, hopping up and pressing a kiss to my lips.

He disappeared, and I took a moment to look around the people gathered close by. As much as I loved the hustle and bustle of city life at times, when it got this crowded, I always felt the need to retreat. To find a quiet spot to admire the things I loved, and to let my thoughts make sense again.

I let my mind drift, imagining the night of laughter and passion ahead of me, and my cheeks ached as I sat there smiling to myself like an idiot. Until someone pulled me from my daydream.

"Excuse me," came a feminine voice.

I looked up to see a woman who I'd guess was in her early forties, smiling at me. Her red hair was scraped back into a harsh tail, and her eyes slanted upwards at the edges because of it. She reeked of posh perfume, and her makeup was a palette of mismatched colours.

"Hi."

The woman pointed at Ethan's empty seat. "Are you guys leaving?"

I glanced in the direction of the toilets before looking back at her. "Erm. Sure. My... boyfriend has just..." I pointed to the loos.

"Mind if we take your seats before someone else snatches them?"

My brows rose. "I... yeah. Of course." I couldn't blame the woman for trying her luck. The place was packed, and the seats were limited, but I couldn't help feeling like I was being shoved from them by the way she looked at me like *no* wasn't even an option for me.

Sliding off and hopping down, I waved a hand at the booth. "Be my guest."

"Thank you." Her smile was kinda sleazy, and she glanced

over her shoulder before she crooked a finger and signalled for someone to join her. A bald guy with an intimidating face drew closer, his shoulders back, and his chest pushed out as he fastened the single button in the middle of his jacket. He approached like he was royalty, and the woman fussed about in front of him, pushing our empty glasses to the side on the table before she slid into her place.

I couldn't stop staring at the bald guy.

He looked like he could crush a child's skull in the palm of his hand, and that wasn't necessarily to do with his size. It was more the way he carried himself.

When he was standing next to me, I smiled brightly and then pressed my lips together, waiting for him to say thank you.

He didn't.

With nothing more than a tip of his head in the direction of the woman behind me, he slid into his seat, unfastened the jacket he'd only just fastened, and he rested his arms on the table to lean in closer to her.

I looked away, mouthing the word 'rude' under my breath as I hitched my bag on my shoulder and turned back to wait for Ethan. I found him quicker than I expected, but he'd frozen in place just outside the toilets, and his eyes were wide, his skin pale as he looked at me like he'd just seen a ghost.

CHAPTER THIRTY-THREE

Ethan

I couldn't fucking breathe.

Tommy Lloyd was sitting in my empty seat.

He was sitting in my seat, and he was less than three feet away from Izzy, who was watching me with curiosity like I was doing something fucking interesting. I wasn't. I was frozen in fear. Tommy could grab Izzy in less than a heartbeat, and it made me sick to think about.

I took a moment before I tried to relax the tension that flowed through me. I didn't want to freak Izzy out, and I sure as hell didn't want Tommy to see how freaked out I was. I headed forward, dodging bodies that stood between Izzy and me, and I tried not to look at the bastard sitting behind her. I rocked up and grabbed her hand with a smile, and then I led her away calmly without glancing up. Tommy was an intimidating cunt, but I was more worried about the goading look I'd be sure to see. When it came to Izzy, I was protective, more than I had been of anyone in my life. I wasn't sure I could control myself if he said or did something that so much as insinuated a threat.

I felt her resistance as Izzy glanced back over her shoulder, pulling her body weight away from mine. Without a clue who she was looking at, she offered a weak smile in the direction of Tommy and the woman he was with.

"Uh, bye," she said, with a feeble wave of her free hand.

I glanced back, keeping us moving. Tommy's gaze swung towards us, and my insides froze, right up until he turned back to the woman he was with like he'd never seen us before in his life. I let out a long breath and held open the door for Izzy, looking over at the table one more time to see nothing but a conversation between a couple like any other.

Jesus.

I followed Izzy out and pulled her to me, a quiet huff of relief falling free as I studied her expression.

"So, I'm guessing you've never met Tommy before?"

Her frown was immediate. "Why are you talking about Tommy? I thought we were going home to get naked and have fun."

I dropped my forehead to hers. "That *was* Tommy, Izzy." I gestured to the pub with a tip of my head.

"Who?"

"The guy who took my seat."

"The bald guy?"

I stared at her, my brows rising as I waited for the penny to drop.

"Oh my God." She spun her head in the direction of the door.

Jesus, I loved this woman. It was moments like this when that innocence of hers shone through. It made me wish this hadn't been an issue.

I stepped back and tugged on her hand. "Let's get the fuck out of here."

Izzy planted her feet firmly, her frown growing deeper again as her eyes drifted between the door and me. "Wait a minute. The rude fuck? The guy with no manners? *That's* Tommy?"

"His lack of manners is probably the more pleasant part of his personality."

"But… isn't he meant to hate us? Isn't he meant to be coming after us? Because that man in there barely even blinked at me, Ethan."

I started us walking again. "I don't know why he blanked us, but I'm hoping that it stays that way. One less fucking problem to deal with, right?"

Her legs quickened to keep up with me, her hand squeezing mine. "I've never seen you look like that before." Izzy's eyes darted up to mine. "You were scared, weren't you?"

"He was too close to you," I said as I hailed a taxi.

"Stop walking." Izzy tugged on my hand, digging her heels in. "Look at me."

I did as she asked, every part of me feeling jittery as I checked every dark alley and shop door along the street. I only met her eyes when I was sure there wasn't something I was missing.

"Stop it," she ordered quietly.

"What?"

She stepped closer. "I'm tougher than I look. When I need to be, I'm tougher than even I understand. I need you to know that. I love the way you love me. I love the way you want to keep me from harm, but I'll always be okay. Trust me on that. I've been fighting since I was a child."

I had no idea how to explain what was going through my

head without sounding like an arsehole. I trusted that she was more than capable of looking after herself. She'd gone after Daggs and nailed his arse to the wall when every other person had folded under his intimidation.

I pressed her palm to my chest, just over my thundering heart, and I held it there. "Do you feel that? You feel how hard it's pounding? My need to keep you safe is purely selfish right now. I know you can look after yourself. I've never doubted that, but I hate you being this close to the bastard. I hate not knowing if he has his little minions watching us. At the risk of freaking you out, I can't lose you, Izzy. You're the most important thing in my world."

"You're not going to lose me. I'm not going to lose you. Nobody is taking us away from each other."

I sighed heavily in response.

"Okay?"

"Can we maybe go home and get naked now? I need to be inside you."

Her lips twitched at the same time as her eyes misted over. "Whatever makes you feel better. Whatever you need."

"How do you feel about Barbados?"

"Is this a swanky new sex position I haven't heard of? I never know with you."

My laugh came as a snort. "No. I meant the country. Us on a beach away from this madness sounds like a fucking great idea. Scott wouldn't mind looking after the club, you could write, I'll get us the best internet package they have. You, me, surf, sand, and lots of sex. What do you say?"

"As in reality, not fantasy?"

"I'm serious."

"I can't think of anything I'd love more."

***

I left Izzy sleeping in the next morning. After staying up until the early hours of the morning trying to perfect our version of tantric sex, she needed the sleep. Seeing her sprawled out on my bed was possibly the sexiest thing I'd seen in my life. I hated the mornings I woke up alone. Even as rare as they were these days, I lived to open my eyes and see that mass of blonde spread over the dark grey of my sheets.

I was on my third cup of coffee, looking at some of the hotels and beach houses in Barbados, Jamaica, and several other islands in the Caribbean, searching for the perfect place for us to escape to for a couple of weeks. I'd been serious the night before, it may not happen as soon as I wanted it to, but we would go, and we would come back the same pasty white colour because unless we were fucking on the beach, we wouldn't be in the sun much.

I'd found a small beach hut that would serve what we would need, and I was leaning in to get a closer look when the door crashed against the chain I'd set.

"Who is it?" I called out quietly, snapping the laptop shut.

"E, for fuck's sake, open up."

Dean.

Shit.

I glanced upstairs and hopped up from the sofa, shutting the door and unchaining it. I stepped aside before Dean could come in.

"Izzy's asleep. Keep your fucking voice down, don't be a jackass, and for fuck's sake, speak English."

He waltzed in, swaggering around like usual, his cocky grin in place as he gave me the eye. "Got your end away, lad?"

"That isn't English, dickhead. Do you want coffee?"

Dean straightened up and pretended to nudge an imaginary tie around his neck, his lips pursed. "One would excuse one for not bin' proper." He laughed and nudged me on the shoulder with his fist. "Fuck, yeah. Am gasping for a brew."

I headed towards the kitchen and started on a fresh pot, gazing over my shoulder when Dean staggered back to try and get a look up at my bedroom.

"Why you out at this time of the day on a Saturday? Aren't you normally in bed until the afternoon?" I asked him.

Dean rose on his toes as if that was going to get him a closer look. His neck was strained when he spoke again. "'Ad a mate who needed his motor fixin' up. Decided I needed to see our E and grab a free brekkie." He pointed up at the glass balcony. "Blondie butt naked up there?"

I picked up a coaster and lobbed it at his head. "Don't be a dickhead. I know it's hard, but I have faith in you, little brother. I'd hate to have to lock you in a room. She actually wants to meet you. Let's not make her regret that decision."

"Want me to go up 'n' show her how nice I am?" He grinned at me like a little bastard.

"I don't want to scare her." I stepped towards him and ruffled his hair. "You're an ugly cunt, mate."

He batted me away. "Fuck off 'n' get ma brew ready, dick. I need to take a piss."

"Bacon butty any good for you?"

"If ya weren't taken now, I'd fuck ya myself." Dean disappeared down the hall with a laugh trailing behind him.

"That's incest, sicko." I headed to the fridge to grab the bacon.

I didn't normally have much in. I'd been something of a workaholic before I'd had my date with Izzy. These last few weeks, though, I'd spent more time in my place than ever. I wasn't even sure I knew if my high-tech oven had a grill to cook the bacon until I opened it and found what I needed.

The place was beginning to smell like bacon within seconds, and I was looking for the ventilation fan switch when I heard stirrings from upstairs. I poured three coffees, fixing Dean's with the indecent amount of sugar and milk that he used, and then I set up Izzy's.

I heard her steps on the stairs, and I glanced up only when she was tiptoeing behind me in the kitchen. I looked at her messy blonde hair, sleepy blue eyes, and a T-shirt with the words *Top Gun* printed over her tits… but barely covering her underwear. Her arse cheeks were on full display.

"Oh, shit, baby… you look good. But, uh—"

Izzy blinked at me, barely awake, but Dean's voice cut through both our thoughts.

"*Woah,* that's what I'm talkin' 'bout, sweetcheeks!" he cried as he came back into the kitchen area. "Nice to meet ya, indeed." He laughed.

Izzy's head rolled his way, her eyes widening, and her face falling.

"For fuck's sake, Dean." I shook my head, turning Izzy around and guiding her upstairs. "Watch the bacon, dickhead."

I managed to set her on the bed with a grin.

"I think you made a lasting impression on my baby brother."

She looked utterly mortified, but the pink was returning to her cheeks as she pressed her palms to them. "*That* was Dean? Dean, your brother? Dean, who has just seen my bare arse before I've even said hello?"

I chuckled, brushing her sleep mussed hair back from her face. "Don't worry, you'll be able to get him back eventually. He's a terrible drunk who does anything you ask him to."

She opened her mouth to say something, only for the two of us having our attention pulled towards the staircase as Dean sang *Danger Zone* from the bottom step.

"I can take him in a fight, just say the word," I said, unable to do anything but smile. I hated seeing her so mortified, but Dean could make any situation light. He never took life too seriously. Still, he didn't sing in tune either. "Dean! Bacon!"

His laughter trailed away, and Izzy turned back to me.

She let her hands fall into her lap. "I guess there's no point hiding my arse up here when he's already seen it."

Pressing my lips to her forehead, I headed into the bathroom and grabbed a pair of sweatpants from my wardrobe. Heading back into the bedroom, I offered them to her.

"For my sanity. And for the record, if you took him on, he might actually enjoy it." I winked at her. "Let me go and save the bacon. I have coffee down there for you when you're ready."

She took the pants from me and smiled. "I'll be down in a second."

"Love you," I said, stepping back and heading to the stairs where I could see Dean in the kitchen, still humming.

CHAPTER THIRTY-FOUR

Izzy

Despite Dean insisting on calling me sweetcheeks every time he spoke, I was quickly allowed to put the unfortunate introduction to the back of my mind. It turned out Dean was, in fact, hilarious. A younger version of Ethan, he had his brother's eyes and charming personality, but that was where the similarities ended. Where Ethan was smooth, Dean was as much of a doofus as I was. He laughed at his own jokes. He was secure in everything he did and whatever came out of his mouth. Down to the fact he was happy to sit in front of me, scratching his balls, talking about some girl who'd caught his eye.

Even though Ethan gave him a hard time, it was clear to see that he was also insanely protective of his younger brother. He loved him.

He was protective of everyone he loved. Including me.

Their bond was a beautiful thing to watch. I had to wonder what it would have been like to grow up with a sibling to share your parental burdens with.

The three of us had been sitting in Ethan's apartment, talking for over an hour when Dean got a text on his phone that had him groaning.

"Fuckin' 'ell."

"Everything okay?" I asked, tucking my feet under my bum on the sofa while Ethan shifted his hand farther up my thigh and gave it a squeeze. He'd barely let me go since we returned downstairs. Not that I was complaining.

"Another mate a mine, wantin' sommat for nowt."

I tried to decipher what he'd actually said, a small laugh falling from me as I glanced at Ethan and saw him rolling his eyes. The way Dean spoke was beyond weird, and I made a mental note to ask Ethan what that was all about once we were alone. They'd grown up together, that much I knew. So how they could carry and present themselves so differently was fascinating to me.

"Do you enjoy what you do, Dean?" I found myself asking when I turned back to him.

"Fixin' up motors? Sure as shit do, sweetcheeks."

"Ugh, that name's not going away anytime soon, is it?" I groaned, letting my head slump down to rest on Ethan's shoulder.

"You'll forever be my lil sweetcheeks now." Dean laughed, jumped to his feet, and shoved his phone into the back pocket of his jeans. "Catch ya later, E?"

Lifting his chin, Ethan smiled at his younger brother. "Later."

"See ya, sweetcheeks." Dean winked and made his way out

of the apartment, leaving Ethan and me to watch him go.

When the door slammed shut behind him, I angled my head up to Ethan. "Think he liked me?"

"Definitely. He made an effort to speak human."

"*That* was him speaking human?"

"You should hear him when he's excited about something. All his words melt into one long one, and it's indecipherable."

"Why does he speak the way he does? He sounds like a mash-up of *Snatch* and *Cool Runnings*. It's so confusing."

Ethan studied my face for a moment, his smiling dialling down just enough for me to notice. "Mum was a teacher. I think he just liked winding her up, but then he didn't stop, and when she died, it stayed for good. You get used to it, and you can always hear his dumb arse in a crowded room."

I could have apologised for making him think about his mum, and I could have asked him if he was okay, but as someone who had loved and lost, I knew how much I hated that. I didn't want people to be sorry. I wanted people to feel comfortable enough around me to allow me to talk about the ones I missed without having to go grey in the face.

"What did she teach?" I asked, leaning back to look at him fully, lifting a hand to the back of his neck so I could trail a finger over his skin. "English?"

Ethan chuckled. "How did you guess? You can see why Deano took so much pleasure in fucking with her. Still, it was always their thing, and I think he secretly enjoyed the time she spent trying to break him of bad habits. He had English for that. I had music."

"That's right. My little piano playing hottie." I pushed my fingers up the back of his hair and down again. "Your mum was responsible for that?"

"I remember some things clearer than others when it comes

to Mum, but I must have been about eight when I came home from school to find her playing classical music. She only ever did that alone. The piece she was listening to was Moonlight Sonata, and I can still see the look on her face. So, I wanted to make her that happy. I asked for lessons. I don't think we could really afford it looking back, but she made it happen, and the first time I played one of her favourite songs for her on the piano, I saw happy tears."

"You're the kind of guy who will learn something just to make someone else happy. That makes you pretty special."

He moved us, so we were lounged on the sofa, his legs framing my body. "I think my old man would disagree with you."

"Your old man is an arsehole. Let him come at me."

"He wouldn't stand a chance against you, baby."

"He clearly doesn't know you like your mum did. I'd fight him just for disrespecting that." I glanced at him, letting my smile fade. "You shouldn't give a shit what someone like him thinks. If I ever have kids, I'd want them to be just like you… in every way."

Tightening his arms around me, Ethan finally released a chuckle. "I think I would prefer our kids to be like you. Gorgeous, thoughtful, loyal, loving, and kind."

"Oh no," I laughed, trying to ignore the way my tummy flipped at him mentioning *our* kids. The thought of a future like that with this man made me feel like I was soaring through the skies on wings that wouldn't ever fail me. "We're not putting my family's DNA on any kids. I got lucky. Believe me." I sighed, the smile still on my face as I looked back up at the ceiling. "We don't need any of that."

"I have all the time in the world and a fantastic bottle of Johnny Walker if you feel up to it."

"What's it like?" I asked quietly.

"What's what like?"

"Having nice memories of a parent. Having a sibling—someone to share things with."

Ethan relaxed under me. "Memories of Mum, I wouldn't trade for the world. She loved Dad, and she knew who he was, so she loved Dean and me enough for ten of him. Having Dean, especially after she died, made days bearable. I can't put into words what it was like, Iz. I also can't imagine the Hell you must have walked through. You don't have to say a word for me to see that."

I let my head roll his way, and I searched every inch of his perfect face.

That trust was building, forming something impenetrable, and before I could stop myself from speaking, words seemed to fall freely.

"I don't want to make you feel guilty for the good times you had as a child. I'm just intrigued. Like Paris with her dad… I used to watch them together and think, *what must it be like for a father to use his hands to hug his daughter rather than strike her?* A part of me grew up thinking that violence, blood, anger, and abuse was the norm. So, when I ask these questions, I'm not trying to compare. I promise. I'm trying to understand. I'm trying to imagine what it must feel like to look at a parent and not feel such… hate."

He searched my eyes, a slight twitch of his jaw catching my attention. "Tell me everything."

"I don't want to hurt you."

"I can't change the past, but I can promise to have your back in the future. I want to know all of you. Every freckle, every hair on your head, and every detail that made you this fucking perfect creature I can't seem to get enough of."

My eyes filled with tears, contradicted by the warm smile that tugged at my mouth.

I loved him.

So hard, it hurt some days.

He deserved to know all of me, the way he'd let me see all of him.

After taking a deep breath, I began the story of my childhood. The nightmare of a youth filled with learning how to fix a broken mother. How she'd climb into my bed on a night, cold and clammy, with blood dripping from her head, arms, and chest, and how my father would then chastise me the next day for staining the sheets with her blood. I watched Ethan's jaw tighten, and his muscles tense every time I mentioned how Terry Moffit—the man classed as a father according to my stupid birth certificate—would teach me to fight one moment with a look of pride on his face, only to then put me to the test the very next.

The memories of those nights I'd tried to forget attacked me, but I remained calm. I didn't cry. The tears simply lingered there as I spoke, unleashing a lifetime of shit that I'd tried to bury for far too long. With every word I spoke, I felt lighter, even if I did detest knowing that I was passing the pain on to Ethan.

He, as patiently as ever, listened without judgement, his fingers stroking my hair, my shoulder, my arm... anything he could touch to soothe me as I went through the timeline of my shitty upbringing. There were no memories of the happier times my mum had once promised me existed—the toddler years before I could really answer Terry back, where he would look at me like he loved me rather than something he hated. But I told Ethan about those apparent times, anyway. I guess I wanted to imagine they really had been real.

The teen years were the hardest to cover, and when it came to me recalling the morning after I'd left Matt Cooper's house, only to go home and get dragged across the threshold on my knees like a stray dog, I struggled to get the words out of my throat.

Not because of fear. That emotion was anger. And maybe a tinge of sadness.

I blinked hard, letting the first tear fall before I looked up into Ethan's eyes again, using him as the anchor that could and would ground me.

"As soon as I could escape, I did. I ran to Paris's house more fucked up than ever before. It wasn't really fair of me, but I did it anyway. One look at me, and she and her dad let me stay with them. I think they'd been waiting for me to quit life with Mum and Dad for a while. Daniel—my Dandy," I said through a sad smile, my cheeks flooding with warmth at the memory of his face. "He treated me like another daughter. I don't know what he did to Dad, but neither him nor Mum came looking for me once I'd told them not to. I think that was Daniel. I think he made sure they stayed away. Truth is, I don't think he could bear to see me bust up like that anymore. None of them could. Not even me."

Ethan stared into my eyes; his expression completely blank.

"That's it." I shrugged weakly.

"You know the only thing I think about right now is how fucking extraordinary you are."

"Yeah?"

"Jesus, Iz, you literally grew up in the middle of Hell—a hell no kid should ever have to endure, and you came out the other side one of the strongest people I've ever fucking met."

I swept that stray tear away on my face, a humourless laugh falling free. "I always promised myself that I'd grow up to be better than them—that I'd be different. I can't change what they did to me. I can't undo the damage. I know I've been single and alone for so long because of my fear of twisted love. I haven't been strong. I learned how to avoid having to fight… for the most part. Loneliness was easier."

"I wish you could see what I see when I look at you. What I saw in you for all those years that you had no idea I was even looking. When I say you're extraordinary, I fucking mean it. You're too compassionate to be your father, and you're too strong to be your mother."

"I'll take that."

"I mean it, baby. You're your own woman, and you make your own goddamn rules."

"I didn't realise until now how much I did need to get this off my chest. Telling someone else about it… it reminds me it was real, and it's okay that it was. It's been and gone now, and I'm me because of it. I'm ready to live for the future."

"I want to be your future."

"You already are."

With that, Ethan kissed me, and I was lighter than I'd been in years.

CHAPTER THIRTY-FIVE

Ethan

I wanted to murder something.

It didn't matter what it was. I just needed to beat at it until it and my fists were swollen enough to satisfy my thirst for blood. It's why I'd chosen to bury myself inside of my girl. My choices had been to make love to her until we both came enough to exhaust us… or slip out and hunt down the motherfucker who had called himself her father.

Staying with her had been the right choice.

The scent of her filling my senses had a way of calming me that not many things were capable of. I didn't lose my temper often, and very few things really got under my skin enough to light that kind of fire in me, but this did.

Knowing I couldn't change it.

Knowing there was nothing I could do to erase that pain.

Knowing that cocksucker was still dragging in breaths.

It all made me crazy. Even after almost eight hours of sex.

I think Izzy had popped home just for time to sleep, while I was stuck in my head, kicking my arse for being such a pussy about my dad. I couldn't understand what would be in a man's head to treat his woman and child that way. When I thought about a future with Izzy, I saw love and laughter twisted together. Happiness, and the occasional knock-down, drag-out argument that would lead to hours of make-up sex. Izzy had as much fire in her as I did, but that was always words, never violence, and never anything neither of us would be able to take back.

I'd meant what I'd said to her before I'd lost my mind and explored every inch of her damp skin. I thought she was extraordinary. Not just because she survived her parents and the death of the one man she'd seen as her true father, but also because when she'd allowed herself to trust enough to marry a man she barely knew, she was brutally burned, yet, still managed to move on, save her best friend, buy a house, work her ass off, and then let me into her life.

Why couldn't she see what I saw so clearly?

I was going to be the last person she'd have to let in her life that way. I already knew that I would marry her beautiful arse one day in the future. I had no fucking doubts when it came to this woman. I just needed a distraction now. Preferably before I did an Internet search for the address of Terry Moffit.

The gym seemed like a good choice considering how much energy I had left to burn even after the exhaustion I felt had settled into my bones. I was too thirsty for a fight.

I changed quickly, grabbing my bag before I headed out. I was already outside Albert's when I realised my mistake, but I couldn't stop myself from going inside. Donna had been married for three years now, and Albert had been ancient when he'd recruited me a decade ago, but he still seemed as immortal as ever when he crossed his arms and grinned at me across the room.

"Long time, no see, Walker. You spoiling for a fight?"

After dropping my bag, I leaned in to give him a one-armed hug. "Just need to get rid of some frustrations, and I missed your scintillating conversation."

"You say the nicest things, you little bastard." He slapped my back in his usual way, genuinely happy to see me before he shoved me away with a feigned irritated growl. "The backroom is clear if you don't want to mingle."

"Cheers, old man."

"Less of the old."

I raised both my hands in surrender. "I forget you vampires don't count in regular years."

I heard Donna's cackle, and I grinned at her as she stuck her head out from the office, her youngest propped on her hip. "Don't let him fool you, E. He's missed your cheek."

Spreading my arms out, I smiled at her. "I live to please."

Donna narrowed her eyes in my direction, her usual attempt to get a read on me finally paying off as a flash of enlightenment lit her features, and a wide smile blossomed. "So, that's what that looks like on you."

"Huh?" I scowled.

"You're in love." She beamed.

"Is that what that smell is?" Albert asked, shoving me again with a huff of laughter.

"I'm happy for you, E." Donna bounced her son on her hip, his fair curls bouncing with every sway of her hips. "'Bout bloody time, too."

"Yeah, yeah." I grinned. "She was worth the wait."

"It's a good look on you."

I gave her my usual cocky smirk. "You always said that about my smile."

"Case in point." She waved her free hand at me, her attention moving back to the office where her eyes rolled. "I'll catch you later, E."

I offered her a wave before heading to the back with Albert tailing me as I wrapped my fists and started my usual warmups. He sat on the edge of the ring and watched me, offering little tips where I was failing.

"So, what's got you so worked up you have to try and gut my bags?" He said it casually, but he was offering an ear like he always did.

"Shit that I have…" I gave the bag another combination, sending sweat trailing between my shoulder blades, "no control over."

"You craving?"

"No," I huffed out a quiet laugh. I hadn't thought about getting high in weeks, that nagging now only pertained to my newest addiction, and I'd just had eight hours in my own personal Heaven. "Just fighting ghosts and memories, old man."

"Seems like a pointless endeavour."

"It's better than the alternative," I said, stopping and resting my fists against the bag.

"Not completely a ghost, then?"

"Not fully, but this has helped."

"Now who lives to serve?" He winked, his hoarse laugh forcing a smile from me. He opened his mouth to speak again when a ringing came from the direction of my bag.

"Bleeding hell, Walker, what have I told you about those electronic leashes in my gym?"

"A distraction."

He waved a hand at me with a growl as I crossed the room

and picked up my phone anyway. The club emblem splashed across the screen.

"Walker."

"Hey, boss," Sapphire sang in her twangy accent. "We need you for a crisis. One of the girls came in a little worse for wear."

"How bad?"

"I think it's best you decide that for yourself."

It was bad then.

"Heading that way now. Just set her up in the staff lounge and stay with her. I'll be there as soon as I can."

"You got it."

I disconnected, throwing an apologetic look at Albert as I dialled another number. He threw up his hands in protest, but I just shrugged in response as I waited for an answer.

***

Worse for wear had been an understatement.

Sophia was a twenty-year-old dancer who had just discovered she was almost three months pregnant and was choosing to deal with the news by drowning herself in cheap tequila. The litre bottle she was gripping in her hands was nearly half gone, and not one of us had been able to persuade her to stop fucking drinking from it.

"How about… you grab her, and I grab the bottle?" Scott offered unhelpfully, sounding as desperate as I felt.

"Because that won't traumatise the fuck out of the girl?"

"Does anyone know who the father is?"

I cringed as Sophia tipped the bottle and took another drink from it. The word 'father' seemed to be one of those trigger words for her. Even from where we were huddled by the door whispering.

"Clearly a sore spot, dickhead," I muttered, pulling my vibrating phone from my pocket and answering without looking at the screen. "Walker."

"Uh oh. You're using your boss voice, while I'm over here still floating in my post-orgasmic state. Who's upset you?"

I slid from the room, my voice softening at the sound of hers. "Crisis at work, babe. We have a dilemma."

"What the hell has Scott done now? Or who has he done?"

I choked out a laugh. "Don't let him hear you say that. He may have a coronary. It's actually one of the dancers. She's in a bad spot, and we can't seem to help. Sending her home isn't really an option,"

"Oh no," Izzy's voice softened. "What happened? Does she need a lift home? I was just driving out for a milkshake. Maybe I can help."

"You think you could?"

"I can try for nothing.

"We need all the help she can get. I hate to ask, but… we're out of options."

"You didn't ask. I offered. I'll see you in ten. I apologise in advance for the state of me."

She didn't give me a chance to reply before she ended the call, and true to her word, within ten minutes, Izzy was pushing her way through the club. She was wearing the same baggy grey jogging bottoms she'd worn the night she forgave me for the incident with Tommy, along with the same white vest, her trusty denim jacket thrown over her shoulders. Her hair was wild, her eyes seeking me out as she stumbled in and tried to find me.

I glared at a couple of the customers who'd spotted her and were checking out her arse. Sweeping her into a hug, I lead her to the changing rooms. Sophia was pushed into a corner of the sofa. Her arms around her legs, the bottle clutched in one hand as she stared around her like a caged animal.

I kept us both out of earshot but stayed close enough that

Izzy could see what was going on. "She's just discovered that she's pregnant and we can't seem to un-weld that bottle from her hands. We've tried everything, short of pinning her down, and that seems like it would be too excessive. Any ideas?"

"How old is she?" Izzy asked, pressing her hand filled with her car keys to her chest. "She looks so young."

"She's twenty. She turned twenty last week, actually. We had a party." I gave her a look that expressed how much I was regretting that particular decision now.

"Twenty," Izzy mouthed, her sad eyes widening for just a moment before she let out a sigh and dropped her keys inside her jacket pocket. She took a moment to study Sophia, the way she did so often with me when she was trying to put her thoughts in order. Was that a part of her that had come from her childhood— the need to process things in front of her before she spoke? I had no idea, but when she turned to touch my arm, Izzy shook her head. "I have no idea what I'm doing, just so you know. The only thing I know is that, if that were me, I wouldn't want a damn thing fixing. I'd want someone to let me cry."

"Cry?" I scowled lightly, not understanding.

"Trust me. It's a girl thing. Mind if I go to her?"

I swept my arm towards the couch, resisting the urge to kiss her before she went. "Be my guest."

Izzy moved across the room slowly, coming to a stop in front of Sophia before she crouched down in front of her. She kept her distance just enough to entice some curiosity from my employee. Sophia looked up through devastatingly sad eyes, a small scowl creasing her forehead as she stared at Izzy.

"Hey," Izzy whispered.

Sophia didn't respond with words, but her eyes were scanning the face of the incredibly attractive woman in front of her like she couldn't believe she was real. I knew that feeling all too well.

"I hear there's a party going on over here," Izzy said quietly. "Mind if I join you?"

Sophia blinked, a set of fresh tears falling down her cheeks, but other than that, she remained silent.

"Izzy," Izzy said, pushing her hair back from her face and offering Sophia a smile. "Hi. I should probably have started with that, right?"

"What do you want?" Sophia asked quietly.

"Nothing." Izzy shook her head carefully. "Nothing at all. Well, apart from maybe some of that tequila, if you feel up to sharing."

Sophia glanced past Izzy to me. A look of confusion was etched on her face before she looked down at the bottle of tequila in her grip.

"Or you can keep it for yourself," Izzy offered in a warm voice. "That's okay, too."

"I shouldn't be drinking this," Sophia sniffed.

"It's fine. You're going to be fine."

"But, I'm—"

Reaching out, Izzy placed a gentle touch on her arm. "Overwhelmed. Scared. Too young for this shit. I know."

Sophia blinked up at her. "Do you know?"

"I'm just here to share your tequila…"

"Sophia," she finished for her. "My name's Sophia."

Izzy's smile came alive, her eyes twinkling. "That's a pretty gorgeous name for a gorgeous girl."

"Really?"

"I'm good at many things, but not at lying. Just ask Ethan."

For the first time since I'd arrived at the club, a sad smile tugged at the corners of Sophia's mouth, and she swallowed as she stared at Izzy. "Well… thanks." She shuffled her feet closer to her, freeing up more space on the couch—a silent invitation for Izzy to take a seat. She wasted no time in doing so, keeping close enough to Sophia without crowding her personal space.

"You know, I've only ever turned to tequila twice in my life," Izzy began. "Once was a celebration. Once was quite the opposite."

"I hate the stuff."

"Me, too. That must mean this isn't a celebration or a party we're having over here."

"Erm…" Sophia croaked. "No."

"Wanna talk about it?"

I stared, open-mouthed, at the two of them, even as Scott and Sapphire stepped in to join me. In three minutes, Izzy had managed to do what none of us had. She'd relaxed Sophia enough to open up, and she knew nothing about the girl. I shouldn't have been surprised, but I was, as well as incredibly proud and in awe of the woman I loved.

Sophia glanced down at the bottle in her hand again. "If I talk about it, it'll make it real."

"Is it real?"

"Yeah."

"Then, staying silent won't help you, Sophia. It'll only choke you from the inside out," Izzy told her, her voice patient and understanding. "I know that more than anyone."

"I don't want it inside me."

"Don't want what inside you?"

Her eyes shot up, red and tired. "A baby."

Izzy didn't react. Her face didn't falter. That soft, sympathetic smile she had in place stayed where it was. "I don't think I'd have wanted that at your age, either. Or maybe I would have, and what would have really scared me was doing it alone."

Sophia swallowed hard, not responding, her fingers

loosening on the neck of the bottle.

"But do you know what I've learned in life?" Izzy reached out, keeping eye contact with the young girl as she carefully peeled the bottle from Sophia's hands, and then brought it to rest below her own lips. "Sometimes, when you feel at your loneliest, you're about to meet a bunch of people who will become your family. Sometimes, feeling like you've got no one actually leads to you getting everything you ever wanted." Izzy eyed Sophia as she tipped the tequila back and took a shot of it, her wince hard as she brought the bottle down and began to cough and laugh at the same time. "Jesus, this stuff is fucking awful."

Sophia's teary eyes creased at the corners, and she, too, laughed at Izzy as she shuddered and cringed.

Izzy held the bottle back out to her. "You want it back? I clearly can't handle it."

Sophia stared at it, her smile fading before she eventually shook her head and rested her hands on her stomach. "You can keep it."

"Are you trying to kill me here?"

"No," Sophia laughed softly.

Izzy carefully dropped the bottle to the floor, and she rested a hand on Sophia's knee as though she'd known her all of her life. "You want a coffee instead?"

"I'm… I'm not meant to have that, either."

"No coffee?" Izzy's eyes popped. "Shit, no wonder you're upset."

Sophia laughed again, a small hiccup bubbling up her throat.

"How about water then? Lots of water."

"Okay." Sophia smiled with nothing but emptiness.

Izzy squeezed her knee and leaned in, lowering her voice. "Hey. It's going to be okay. You know that, right? You're going to be fine. You don't have to be alone."

I felt Scott leave quietly, but Sapphire leaned in as she turned to do the same, her hand on my arm as she whispered to me, "Wow. You've got a keeper there, boss."

I nodded in agreement and felt the squeeze of her hand on my arm as she stepped away. My eyes met Izzy's across the room, and I nodded, heading out to get several bottles of water. Needing one to douse the fire in my own heart, too.

CHAPTER THIRTY-SIX

Izzy

I sat with Sophia for over an hour, reassuring her that she didn't have to be scared. Even though I was terrified for her. My life had been a mess at twenty. The thought of bringing a child into that mess would have made me reach for more than a bottle of tequila. My life had been a mess at thirty, and I still wasn't ready. She had my full sympathies, and now I'd become invested, I promised to check up on her often. If she needed someone to go to the midwife with, I told her I'd be there. If she chose to go down a route that some may judge her for, I told her I'd be there for that, too.

People made mistakes when they were scared.

The bottle of tequila had been her mistake. I could only hope she woke up with a clearer head the next morning.

After calling her a cab, and four of us seeing her off safely,

I leaned back against the wall of Ethan's office and pushed my hair back with a sigh.

"I'm emotionally spent."

"You were phenomenal."

"I'm so worried about her. She's young, beautiful, vulnerable…"

"And calm, thanks to you." Ethan ran a hand from the top of my head down to my jaw. "I should have called you first."

"Hopefully, your girls won't make a habit of that, so you won't need me again."

Ethan dropped into his desk chair and tugged at my hand, inviting me to fall into his lap. "*I* will always need you. The girls, maybe not so much."

I fell into him, curling myself up in his lap. "I know you look after these girls, and you and Scott don't let them work under anything but the best conditions, but I can't help but wonder how a twenty-year-old ends up thinking this is what's best for her. The money I get. The thrill of it all… I get that, too. But where the fuck are her mum and dad, Ethan? Why can't people who have kids just do the thing they're meant to do and protect them?"

"Sophia was brought in by one of the other girls. She left home the moment she was seventeen and never looked back. I think they were super strict with her, to the point she rebelled just because she needed to breathe. This isn't the first time we've had to talk her down, but this was beyond any of us. I think she'd been talking to Sapphire about going to Vegas when she had enough money. She had a dream to be a showgirl."

"Great. This is the girl's dream, and here I am pitying it." I lifted my head and looked up at him. "I should go home. Get some sleep. Let you get back to work."

"I wasn't working. I was at the gym when they called me in.

I could come with you. I promise to let you rest."

I rolled my eyes, smiling. "Because letting me sleep is your speciality."

"The way I'm feeling, tonight may be your lucky night."

I slid a hand between my parted legs, letting it roam over his dick. "Did I break you?"

Ethan's eyes blinked closed. "Jesus."

"Didn't think so." I extracted my hand slowly, pressing it to his chest and kissing his lips. "You plus me equals sex. Every time. Probably until I start developing varicose veins and chin hair. Only then will you give me a night off."

"I can't help it. I love the way you love me."

My heart started to beat faster. "Ditto."

Ethan nuzzled into the back of my neck, a long sigh flowing from him. "Fine. I'll go have a wank while thinking about you. You can sleep, but if you're feeling like giving me one of those *good* mornings of yours, I will not be upset."

"You'll have to leave your door unlocked. I had to give my key back to Scott." I closed my eyes as he kissed my neck.

"You want a key? You can have a key. I have a spare right here in my desk for emergencies."

I froze, my eyes pinging open as I peeled myself away and turned to look down on him. "Did you just offer me a key to your apartment?"

He smiled. "I think that's exactly what I just did."

"But…" I blinked at him. "You were joking, yeah? Like… funny, ha ha, here, Izzy, borrow this key. That's what you meant."

Ethan shook his head. "I want you to have a key to my place. I want it to be another safe place for you—another home. I want you to come over whenever the fuck you want to, whether I'm there or not. I want to go to bed, never knowing whether or not you're going to be there. I love you, Izzy. I can't get enough of you. It's that fucking simple."

He looked like he meant every word as he stared up at me, while I sat there, winded by his love, too tied up in knots to say the things I really wanted to say.

"What are you doing to me?" I asked, a little too high pitched.

"I'm loving you."

"Goddammit," I groaned, dropping my forehead to his.

"What?"

"I just love you so much—it makes me ache inside."

"Then take the key," he whispered, his lips brushing mine.

"Like I can say no to you."

"That's my girl."

He reached around me and opened a small drawer at the top of his desk. He pulled a single key from inside and held it between us, his eyes alight with pleasure. "Yours."

I took it from him, pinching it between my thumb and finger, my eyes locked on him beyond it. "You sure?" I raised a brow.

"Absolutely certain."

I squealed like I'd never done before—a full girly shrill of excitement that had me shaking my head from side to side, my blonde hair going wild before I launched my arms around him, sending the chair flying backwards and forcing a grunt of laughter from Ethan.

Pulling back, I held my hair away from my face and stared down into his eyes. "If you did this just to get laid, well played. There's no way I can go home now. Meet you at your place in half an hour? I'll let myself in before you get there."

He brushed some hair over my shoulder. "Thirty minutes. Be very naked."

"You're about to get the best blow job of your life."

Ethan looked down between our bodies. "You hear that, big man. Blondie's going to give you some love." He glanced back up at me. "What the hell are you waiting for, woman? Get the hell out of here."

With an excited wiggle of my key, I jumped off him and made my way to his office door, not taking my eyes from his. "Don't be long."

"I may just sit in the car park and wait for you to unlock the door. Fuck responsibilities. I want that beautiful mouth of yours wrapped around me." He pointed to the door. "Now, go."

I left him with a bright smile before I slipped out of his door and bounced down the steps as though I'd just won the lottery. I guess I had, only this was the lottery of Izzy Moffit's troubled life, which was finally turning into everything she could ever have dreamed of and more. The key in my hand was as precious as a bunch of expensive diamonds, and everyone I passed in the busy club looked at me with a confused smirk on their faces.

There I was in my scruffy clothes, wearing no makeup, my hair unbrushed, yet I somehow felt like the most beautiful woman in the room.

Because of him.

I waved to Scott and spun around before I skipped to the door. A couple of the girls said goodbye to me, too, and I ignored the lingering looks of a couple of weird-looking men around a table by the door. When I passed a security guy who was standing inside the club, I gave him a pat on the shoulder and told him to have an amazing night. He looked at me like he thought I'd just got laid.

This was better.

Ethan Walker, Manchester's most eligible bachelor, had chosen *me* to give a key to.

This wasn't casual dating now. This was *more*.

It was pitch black when I skipped out of the front doors of the club, my hair swinging wildly behind me, and my smile making my cheeks ache. With a quick glance around to make sure nobody was watching, I did a little dance on the spot and squealed again to myself before I closed my eyes and spun around with my arms out wide.

The future felt so damn good, the feeling of it squeezing my chest tight as if to say *you endured all you did to get to this. Enjoy every second of it.*

When I finally opened my eyes and made my way around the corner to where my Mini was parked, I was on another planet, dreaming of slipping between grey sheets and strong legs. I didn't exist in the here and now anymore, only there, and that was the worst place I could have been.

Maybe if I'd have been in the here and now, I'd have heard footsteps approaching me before the arm lashed out to curl around my throat, cutting off my breath and pulling my back against a hard chest. Maybe I'd have been better prepared to stop my attack.

My hands flew up to try and pull the arm away, but the hold it had on me was an iron grip I couldn't shift, and as my attacker began to heave and grunt in my ear, dragging me farther back into the darkness, I felt the air in my lungs begin to thin.

No.

No.

This wasn't happening.

Digging my nails into the arm, I tried to free myself again when a hiss of pain fell against my ear. I dug them in harder, twisting at the hair and skin I could feel in my grip, and I tried to yank him away as my vision started to blur, only for the arm to tighten around me even more.

"Bitch," they spat in my ear.

And it was with that word that I felt my blood chill, and my spine stiffen.

I knew that voice.

"No!" I cried out, using every last breath I had within me to gather enough strength within my muscles and tear myself free. I yanked on his arm three times, but he was too strong, and I was losing the fight. Within a second, my neck was in the crease of the man's elbow, and his grip had tightened.

My eyes rolled in the back of my head, and I felt myself begin to count down in my mind.

Three…

Two…

Darkness.

CHAPTER THIRTY-SEVEN

Ethan

I was fucking floating when I headed towards the doors. Even doorman Stan was grinning at me as I edged past with a slap on his shoulder. Nothing fucking mattered outside of getting home, but I was planning on popping into the supermarket to pick up some flowers for my girl. I also wanted to see if I could find the same toothbrush and toothpaste I'd seen in her bathroom. There were so many little things I wanted to do. Things that would make her squeal in happiness like she just had when I'd not even planned it.

Love was something I had denied myself, but I sure was making up for lost time.

I was spinning my keys around my finger when I heard the scream. Just one word: *No!* But I knew who it belonged to, and then I was running. I slid around the corner to see a big motherfucker with his arm around Izzy's neck, his bicep tightening as her body fell limp.

The fucker didn't hear me coming. I was on him before he could look in my direction.

The moment I pushed him, he stumbled, releasing his grip and sending Izzy tumbling to the ground. I barely caught her, but I stopped her head from cracking on the path before I laid her down carefully, while still being aware of the arsehole getting back to his feet.

He'd fucked up.

He'd beyond fucked up because I lost all conscious thought and saw red, my body tensing as I clenched my keys in my hand and swung at him. The first hit was met with a satisfying crunch, and I followed it with another, and another, giving his face the same fucking treatment I'd given the bag earlier in the gym. Every grunt, every split of flesh and rush of blood against my fists was followed by a thirst for more until I felt arms around me, pulling and tugging me away.

"Boss. Stop! You're gonna fucking kill him."

Two of my bouncers tried again to pull me back, and I kicked out at the fucker slumped on the ground, my foot connecting with his jaw. I didn't know who he was, but he got every ounce of my fury.

"Your missus is waking up. Calm the fuck down," Stan hissed in my ear.

It was like he knew it would be the only thing to get through—the only thing to push back that fire that demanded more blood and flesh as penance. I shrugged Stan off and turned, finding Izzy on her back, her hands on her throat, and her eyes blinking open.

"Baby?" I dropped to my knees beside her.

She opened her mouth, stretching it out as her eyes rolled. Her jaw clicked, and she blinked three times before she coughed and rolled onto her side. "Jesus... Christ..." she croaked.

"Iz—"

"I'm... fine."

If I believed that for a second, I still wouldn't be okay. It was taking every ounce of my control not to grab her and just hold her. It was only my fear of hurting her more that stopped me.

"Can you sit up?"

She nodded weakly, her body fragile, but that quiet determination shining from her red eyes. "Give... minute..." she said, her words fractured as she went on all fours, her arms shaking as they held her weight. "Ethan," she rasped, sucking in a breath that sounded painful. "Where... where is he?"

"Not as dead as he should be."

"Where?" she repeated.

"He's not a problem right now," I muttered, glancing over my shoulder to where the bastard laid, half-conscious and blinking as the doormen did the usual first aid bullshit they'd been trained to do. "I'm more worried about you," I said, turning back to her.

"Him," she wheezed, not making any sense.

Slipping my hand under her hair to cradle the nape of her neck, I angled her head and studied her pupils, looking for some sign of concussion. "You want to try that again for me, baby?"

Her eyes cleared, and she fell back, resting her arse on the heels of her feet as she reached out to grab my arm. "It's... him."

"Who?" I asked, feeding off her panic.

"My dad."

"What?" I gasped, staring into her eyes.

She didn't have to say a word in response for me to see it was the truth.

"Son-of-a..." I started to rise to my feet. My finger gave her one last gentle sweep along her jaw before I snapped, turned, and charged towards the fucker.

The doormen weren't quick enough to stop me this time. My hands planted against the brick wall, giving me stability, and I started playing football with the abusing bastard's head. It wasn't satisfying enough. I started in with my fists again, barely able to hear the voices over the rushing blood that clouded everything around me.

I wanted to kill him.

I wanted to break him open the way he'd broken my girl.

"For fuck's sake, Stan, grab him before he does real damage." Scott's voice penetrated the wall of sound as three sets of hands tugged and pulled at me, eventually tearing me loose and pushing me roughly against the wall beside the crumpled body.

It wasn't enough.

It would never be enough.

"Get off me," I ground out, pushing each and every one of them away. My nostrils flared, and my jaw was tense as I looked at them like I hated them. The only one I hated was the piece of shit at my feet.

"Boss…" Stan started.

"He's okay," Scott said with a gentle huff of sound. He'd taken my place by Izzy and forced her to look away from the fucking mess I'd made of her father… though she looked to be fighting Scott a little.

I pushed off from the wall and glanced down at Terry Moffit with disgust before finding myself being shepherded away by two of the security people who'd joined the fray. My only regret in this current state was that Izzy had seen me that way. Feral. So out of control and angry.

It was a rare thing for me these days.

Even with that regret, I made my way back to her, my trembling hand landing on her thigh as I sank to my knees. Patiently, I then waited for the fallout.

Izzy's gaze fell to my hand, and she picked it up with both hands, bringing it closer to her face. "You're bleeding," she said quietly.

"I don't care," I panted.

"I do."

I closed my eyes and took her from Scott, my arms folded around her, my legs stretching to her sides as I parked my arse on the ground. "I'm not hurt, babe."

"Did you kill him?"

"Sadly not."

"Shame."

I groaned, letting her go long enough to cup her face and gently lift her head to study her neck in the dim light. "Are you hurt?"

"No," she lied.

Dropping my forehead to hers, I felt emotion wash over me, my voice thick as I whispered the next words to her.

"I'm so sorry."

"What for?"

"I fucking promised you this wouldn't happen."

"Don't do that," she whispered. Her hands came up to my shoulders, and Izzy steadied herself, trying to be strong for me. "Please," she begged. "Don't do that."

Still cradling her face, I kissed the freckles under her eyes and pulled her against me. Breathing as deeply as I could through that residual anger at the man slumped less than ten feet from us. I didn't want her this close to him again. Seeing her body go limp like that... I had to close my eyes and hold her closer to me. I was so lost to the fear of almost losing her that I was hardly aware of Scott slapping my shoulder gently to signal him leaving us alone.

"I'm sorry you had to see that," I said into her hair, glancing over to see Scott toeing the tooth on the ground next to Terry.

She pulled back slowly. "I'm not." Her face was serious—no doubt in her eyes. "I've waited thirty-one years to see that."

I huffed out a cloud of air as I stared at her, a small smile of disbelief forming. She was unbelievable.

"But... I need to go to him."

That smile didn't last long, but as I took her in, I knew that was a battle I wasn't going to win.

I also didn't want to deny her a thing right now. This was Izzy. I would have given her the world, even if I had to die in the process.

"You sure?" was all I asked, trying to keep it as calm as I possibly could.

"Yeah." She nodded once.

"Okay, baby."

"Stay close?"

"Always."

She dropped a kiss to my forehead and slowly began to peel herself away from me. Her limbs were still unsteady, so I helped her stand, and I watched as Izzy's face changed from the soft, loving woman I adored, to a young girl who now had to fight again.

She approached slowly, and I stayed at her back, her hand in mine. I wasn't willing to let her go, not ever after this, but especially not tonight. Not with this absolute cunt of a man blinking up at her. I could see the damage I'd done, and I swallowed my satisfaction at the hard knots already forming on his jaw and one of his eyes. His lip was split in three places, and I was pretty sure I saw another tooth hanging loose behind the bottom one. It didn't look good, but it was less than he deserved.

Terry's attention was focused on me, a look of fear flashing over the one eye I could see clearer than the other, but when Izzy drew closer, he turned his gaze to her, and his face fell instantly.

He was looking at her like it was the first time he'd ever seen her.

Terry blinked wildly, his chest freezing on a sharp inhale as he stared unashamedly.

"Dad," Izzy said quietly, a single three-letter word broken into a thousand pieces.

Terry searched her face, taking her in as though he was trying to recognise her.

His own fucking daughter.

"Isabella?" he finally wheezed through swollen lips. "Is that... you?"

Izzy's jaw set tight as she towered above him, an audible swallow from her filling the night air around us. "It's Izzy," she said firmly.

"Lord, Jesus," Terry mouthed, his face paling as he stared up at her.

I stared down at the man, disgusted. Had he attacked her knowing it was her? He actually seemed surprised to see her. Maybe I'd hit him harder than I fucking thought I had.

Izzy took one of those moments of hers to study him. She glanced back at me only once, as if to check I was still close by before she took another step towards Terry and dropped into a crouch in front of him.

"You're..." Terry began.

"Still breathing," she finished for him. "No thanks to you."

Terry glanced up at me, seeing nothing but hatred staring back at him, before he looked back at his daughter—the little girl he'd treated like a football for years, using her as a sick game to throw around whenever he deemed fit.

"I didn't know," he said roughly, a cough making his body shake and a trail of blood fall from his lips.

"You didn't know what?"

"It was… you."

I crouched beside Izzy, satisfied when he cringed slightly. "What the fuck are you talking about, old man?"

Terry's face scrunched tightly as he tried to push his slouching body farther up the wall, the pain in his features nothing but satisfying to see. When he gave up, realising his body was too weak, he slumped down again and shook his head against the brick wall. All of his fight gone when he opened his eyes and stared at Izzy again.

"It's been so long," he said to her, resigned to his fate on the ground. "You've changed so much. I didn't… I didn't recognise you."

"Good." Izzy's nostrils flared, the heat rising to her once-pale cheeks.

"I didn't know it was you."

"So, this is what you've become?" She snarled. Her lips curled in disgust, her eyes narrowing on him. "No longer happy with beating your wife and daughter, you take to the streets and attack innocent women now?"

Terry Moffit closed his eyes. "No—"

"You get your kicks out of bringing women to their knees, is that it?" Izzy cut him off, her hand rising to the red mark around her neck as she stared at her father. "You could have killed me."

Terry shook his head, blinking one eye open again. "I don't kill anyone."

"That makes it okay then," I muttered dryly. "Why did you attack her?"

"I get told who to hit up, okay?" Terry ground out, the eyes of someone who was once probably strong and powerful, now looking tired, aged, and weak. "I get told who to grab, and I fucking grab them." He looked back at Izzy.

"You're... a hitman?" She scowled. "Is that even a thing?"

Terry had the nerve to smirk, despite his bust-up lips. "Still so naive."

I punched him. I heard someone huff from above me but ignored them as I glared at the motherfucker, scrambling to rub his jaw.

"Be very fucking careful what you say to her, arsehole."

Izzy reached out, placing a hand on my arm, her sad eyes holding mine. "I'm okay," she assured me quietly.

"I have no doubt. That was for me."

A shy smirk tugged at her lips before she turned back to her so-called father. "Your words don't hurt me anymore, Terry. To be honest, they never really did. You can't feel the cuts from blunt blades, and I never loved you enough to let your sharp tongue make me bleed. It's why you always had to use your fists, isn't it?"

Terry's face changed, and I saw a flicker of the man Izzy had to grow up with. His jaw set hard, and his nostrils flared.

It only made Izzy's eyes sparkle and her smile break free. "You're nothing. Nothing more than a waste of space, slumped against a wall, too old to fight, too weak to win."

Terry's body flinched only a fraction, his need to defend his old self and hurt her taking over before he stopped and glared at me through angry eyes.

"Careful. You give me a short fucking fuse," I warned him. "And I'm only just getting warmed up."

Terry stared at me enough to let me know exactly what he thought of that before his body betrayed him, and he swallowed the fear loudly and turned back to Izzy. "Got yourself a little hero, I see."

"Izzy doesn't need saving. She's done that for herself."

Her soft smile in these dark circumstances was typical of her, but she stayed on track, focused on her sorry excuse for a father. "Who put you up to this?"

"Dunno."

"Terry."

"I don't know."

"Unless you want me to set the guy next to me on you again so he can destroy your other eye, I'd start opening up a little. You may be my father, but I have no problem letting karma do her thing."

Terry snarled, opening his mouth to say something before he glanced my way and thought better of it again.

Fucking coward.

Men who beat women always were.

Izzy pulled her mobile phone out of the inside pocket of her denim jacket. "And, of course, there's the police. I bet they'd be super happy to put someone like you away. Especially when your daughter confirms everything you've been up to for the last thirty-one years." She tilted her head to one side and waited him out.

I couldn't be prouder of her. Watching how easily she faced down this man and so much of her past with barely a blink made my chest swell with love. I had a feeling she may pay for it later emotionally, but I hoped this gave her some clarity—some closure on how fucking cowardly and weak Terry Moffit was

"Tick Tock, Terry. Your girl works fast."

Terry spat some blood to the side, never taking his eyes off of Izzy as he did.

"I got a call," he began, his voice rough with pain. "Very few words were exchanged. A guy needed a girl taking care of—

scaring a little. No name. Just a description. Your description. Long blonde hair. About your height. He even described what you'd be wearing tonight."

Izzy's face fell, all her confidence draining to bleed out at her feet.

"Said he'd pay me two grand," Terry added.

"Name," I demanded, my voice coming out as a growl.

"Jay," he said flatly. "Said he'd transfer half the money before, the rest when it was done."

"How would he know it was done?" Izzy asked, her voice quiet.

"He said he'd be watching."

CHAPTER THIRTY-EIGHT

Izzy

My head spun behind me to glance around the car park.

I was going to be sick.

Someone had put a hit out on me, and Ethan and I were sitting here, waiting for them to strike.

"We need to get the fuck out of here," Ethan muttered quietly.

"No," I snapped, turning back to Ethan. "No." I stared into his eyes. I wasn't going anywhere. If someone wanted to hurt me, they could find the balls to do it themselves. If they had to draft in someone like Terry Moffit, they were no threat to me.

Turning back to the thing that was my father, I leaned in closer, the anger rising in my chest.

"You're sick," I hissed. "You need help. You make my skin crawl. You're lower than scum. I don't know how you sleep at night."

Terry stared at me, the two of us glaring at one another with tight jaws and anger in our eyes.

"You're going to tell me who Jay is, and you're going to tell me now, or so help me."

"I don't fucking know," he snapped back.

"Then you're no use to me."

Terry frowned. "What the fuck does that mean?"

I didn't have to look at Ethan before I tossed my phone in his direction, never taking my eyes from my father as I did. "Call the police, E. Tell them we have security footage of my *dad* trying to kill me. Because if this idiot here thinks I'm going to let him walk away and hurt some other poor girl for the sake of two grand, he really has no business sitting in front of me and calling *me* naive."

With a smug, flat grin in place, Ethan started dialling but glanced at me before he hit send. "We could always make sure he was in a wheelchair for the rest of his life."

I tilted my head to the side and stared at Terry. "Then he'd never hurt anyone ever again. Sounds appealing."

"You two think you're fucking Bonnie and Clyde—"

He didn't get to finish.

Only that time, it wasn't Ethan who struck Terry. It was me. The left-handed backhand I'd dreamed of striking across his face for years landed with a brutal sting that sent his already bust-up face flying to the left.

"Bitch!" he hissed, and I quickly struck again with my right.

"Thanks, Dad."

"I warned you about name-calling," Ethan warned, shaking his head. "You're really starting to piss me off. Either give us a name, or things are about to get nasty."

"Jay." Terry rubbed his face, his lips slack as he stared at me like he had no idea who I was. He didn't. Not anymore. "Jay P. That's all I know."

"Jay P," I repeated, immediately sensing a shiver of dread crawling up my spine. "When you say Jay, do you mean the name, or…"

"The fucking initials, Isabella. J. P. Jesus Christ."

I fell back on my arse with a thud, staring at him with wide eyes.

There was only one JP I knew.

Only one I'd ever come across.

But surely… no. It couldn't be him.

"JP," I whispered to myself before I glanced over my shoulder as if I'd find him standing right there, staring down on me with that arrogant smirk on his face. But there was nothing but dark skies and muted streetlights around.

Ethan studied my face before glancing over his shoulder and waving over one of the doormen from the club. "Call this bastard a cab and save the footage from the cameras. Drop that shit in my safe before you leave." The guy nodded and rushed away, but Ethan stood, grabbed my hand, and pulled me to my feet. "You mind staying at mine for a while?"

I held onto his biceps, not really hearing what he was saying as I scanned the darkness in front of me.

He was watching.

All of a sudden, I could feel it.

"No," I said in a breath because I had no intention of leaving Ethan for a long time. Not now I knew who was messing with us.

"Izzy?" he whispered, asking so many questions with my name alone.

I looked back up into his eyes, and I took a deep breath. "It isn't Daggs who's after us, Ethan. It isn't Tommy, either. JP.

There's only one person it could be."

"Who?"

"Jack Parker."

Sliding his hands along my jaw, Ethan angled my face, his hazel eyes locking on mine. "I will kill him before I let him touch you."

"Take me home."

"Give me your keys. I'll have Scott drive your car to the apartment."

I did, digging around in my pockets and pulling out my usual bunch before I scanned the ground. "Shit. Your key. I must have dropped it."

He looked around us, scanning the ground and catching the eyes of the guys helping Terry up. "Anyone seen a key?"

Most of his security staff shook their heads, but it was Scott who dangled a single key with a smirk. "Seriously. Ten seconds has to be a new record."

"Not the time, mate," Ethan said kindly, taking the key from his hand.

I plucked it from his fingers and worried it between my own. Terry was being hoisted up to his feet, and I gave him one last glance before I forced my eyes away and back to Ethan. What was weirder than feeling nothing was knowing that it should have felt weird to feel nothing, but it didn't. I despised the man I saw flickers of myself in when I looked at his face.

He'd once been a handsome man, able to manipulate everyone around him with his fists or his fear. Now he looked weak, old, and pathetic. There was no love in my heart for him, only pity. There was no warmth in the memories, only ice-cold nostalgia. Hate was too strong of an emotion to describe what I felt.

Emptiness.

That's all there was.

Nothing.

Holding the key up to Ethan, I focused on it, twirling it around in my fingers. "You think this is a bad omen?"

"No, just shitty timing."

"Let's go home." I glanced around, searching the shadows. "There's someone I have to call."

***

Ethan didn't stop touching me as he drove the two of us home in Lucy.

The shock of everything was beginning to settle in, as were the nasty red marks and fresh bruises around my neck. My throat was sore, and my voice was already beginning to turn raspy.

When we made it back to Ethan's apartment, he guided me upstairs, and I had the phone pressed to my ear when the two of us stepped inside. Ethan turned on the lights and tossed his car keys on the kitchen island, immediately going to the fridge to grab two cold beers while I waited for Lauren to answer.

"Come on, Lo," I whispered, dropping my phone to the island and putting it on speaker.

"Fuck!" she answered in a flurry. "Sorry, Iz. I couldn't get to my phone. You don't give up, do you?"

"Sorry, Lauren," I countered with an apology.

"Oh, shit. You sound dreadful. What happened?"

"How long have you got?"

"For you, I'll make time."

I looked up at Ethan as I spoke. "I need your help again, Lauren."

"Did that bastard figure out it was us interviewing him? Has he come after you? I swear to—"

"Lauren," I cut her off, trying to raise my voice, but it was breaking whenever I tried to go high, and I immediately had to clear my throat to try and speak again. "It isn't Daggs."

"Who is it, then?"

With another resigned look in Ethan's direction, I began to tell Lauren everything that had happened that night with my so-called father, and the clues he'd given us about who it could be that was messing with our lives… which meant I had to tell Lauren everything about Jack Parker, too. Everything. Including the fact that I'd once walked down the aisle with him.

I had to look away from Ethan when I spoke about that— like my past was betraying him somehow. I couldn't imagine how I would have felt knowing he'd once wanted to marry someone who wasn't me, so I decided to focus on the phone, hating having to even speak my ex's name, never mind discuss everything that had happened.

When I'd finished, Lauren was silent, her usual snark nowhere to be heard.

"Lauren?" I asked quietly.

"Jesus, Izzy," she whispered.

"I know." It was all I could think to say because she was right. *Jesus.* What the hell had I been thinking? Who the hell had I gotten involved with?

"You don't make life easy for yourself, do you?"

"I'm trying to change that now." I caught Ethan's eye from the other side of the island, my face filled with hope, despite the sadness that lingered in my eyes. "Will you help us?"

"You want me to track this Jack Wankhole down? See if he's in your neck of the woods?"

"Anything you can find out would be more help than you realise."

Lauren blew a breath out. "Lady, you know I'll do anything for you. You're my weak spot. The friend I can't say no to. The friend whose happiness somehow means more than my own. If

I can find something out that helps, I'll do it. I want you and Mr Big Throbbing Swoony Cock to live the happiest life together."

Ethan's sputtered laughter came loud in the otherwise quiet apartment. "Mr what was that?"

I was grinning like an idiot, trying to control my own laughter when Lauren took a moment to herself.

"Holy shit," she eventually whispered. "Is that the man himself?"

"Mr Big Swoony Cock, at your service," Ethan offered, winking at me.

"You're on speaker, Lauren," I chuckled, smiling back at him.

"Well, thanks for the fucking head's up." Her voice was filled with amusement. "And don't sell yourself short, Ethan. I actually called you Mr Big *Throbbing* Swoony Cock. I've heard a lot about you. The pleasure is all mine. About that service you offer…"

Ethan leaned his forearms on the counter and glanced up to meet my eyes. "Only fully available to one beautiful lady, I'm afraid."

"Oh, come on. Don't be like that. Hasn't Izzy told you about my magical vagina yet?"

Ethan was chuckling when he responded. "More to the point, has she told *you* about hers? Pure fucking gold."

I was laughing quietly at the both of them. Unable to look away from the light that was returning to Ethan's eyes after he'd been so angry.

"I can see I'm going to have to raise my efforts here," Lauren sighed playfully. "You sound like you're whipped and ready to sacrifice it all for her already. Don't worry. I won't give in. I'm tenacious. Ask Izzy."

Shaking his head, Ethan reached out for my hand, gladly

taking my fingers when I slipped them into his. "I admire your tenacity. If I didn't like you, I'd hook you up with my brother Dean. I think he'd like that mouth of yours."

"Sounds interesting. Send me his number. I'll try him out and leave a review."

"All right, you two," I interjected with a chuckle, squeezing Ethan's hand. "I'm not a jealous girl, but don't test me."

"It's all one fucking way, Iz. Don't worry. You can kick my arse next time you see me."

"I love you too much for that, Lauren."

Ethan bent his head to kiss my hand before he spoke again. "Do you need anything from us? To get the ball rolling, I mean?"

"Just for you to stay out of trouble, which apparently isn't as easy as it should be for the two of you. You know, for a set of newly loved up lovebirds, you sure are finding trouble on every street corner. Can't you stay indoors and screw for a while... just to stay safe?"

"That was my plan for the next ten hours, Lauren."

"Girth *and* stamina. Where can I order one of you from?"

"I'm a limited edition."

"I think I'm in love."

"Aaaand... end scene," I said dramatically, full of humour. "That's enough from you, Lady Horndog. Call me in the morning? Or whenever you get news?"

"Tinkertush, at your service, princess."

We ended the call with smiles on our faces, and I looked up at Ethan when I pushed the phone away and leaned over the island. "And that is what I call The Lauren Effect."

"Tinkertush and sweetcheeks. You could be a crime-fighting team."

"I think my crime-fighting needs some work based on tonight's performance."

"I think maybe I should have walked you to your car after distracting you with my sexual prowess."

I smiled a distracted smile, and I looked down at the bust-up knuckles of Ethan's hand. The blood had dried already, but his hands were swollen, thanks to his efforts on my father's face.

"I can't live my life with you walking me to my car, me looking over my shoulder, and you worrying every time I'm not with you. You can't live that way, either. Whoever it is that's got their sights set on us," I looked up through hooded eyes, "I can't let them win. You know that, right? That's not who I am."

"We're not going to be looking over our shoulders forever." Ethan shook his head. "But while there's a threat out there, I'm always going to worry. All part of this love shit, right? The fear of losing that one thing you suddenly can't breathe without."

I ran my thumbs and fingers over the uncut parts of his hand. "I don't know how I ever breathed without you."

"Ditto."

CHAPTER THIRTY-NINE

Ethan

I'd lied to Lauren about what we'd be doing for the next ten hours. As much as sex sounded like an amazing plan, we'd both been exhausted and emotionally spent. I ran us both a bath and sank into the heat of the water while Izzy gently cleaned the blood from my knuckles, her lips brushing over every one reverently before she dipped them under the hot water to soak them for me. I knew why she had done it. I knew because I did the same with her, my soapy hands running over her flesh to make sure she was real—to make sure she wasn't more broken than she was letting on, and to feel the proof of life under my palms.

Losing her terrified me.

Seeing her hurt made me so crazy inside, I couldn't settle.

Neither could she.

Even as we lay awake in my bed, huddled together, our

limbs twisted, we spoke in whispers, discussing what had to happen next. Even though we both hated the thought of it, we knew we had to finally explain what the fuck was going on to the people it would affect the most.

Paris and Scott.

I considered talking to Dean, but his life had been untouched by the whole thing so far, and I wanted to keep it that way. He also had a way of complicating uncomplicated situations, and this was far from uncomplicated. This was a nest of knots in a tumble drier. The more he kept his distance, the better.

We'd sent texts to Paris and Scott in the early hours of the morning before we both settled down to finally try and sleep. It didn't take Izzy long at all once we fell into our usual comfortable silence. Her deep and even breaths washed over me, calming part of my chaotic thoughts.

I just couldn't shut the rest of my mind off enough to let myself fall with her.

Every blink had the sight of Terry fucking Moffit choking Izzy painted on the back of my lids. Every breath had that fire in my chest kindling with fury. Knowing he was out there and still breathing was making me fucking crazy. I'd sent his arse home in a cab. I'd sent him home to a wife he'd probably taken his frustrations out on while he stewed over his daughter's cheek at refusing to be his victim anymore.

The thoughts piled up in my head.

Would that man's anger drive him to try again?

Would I let him?

Glancing down at Izzy, I shuffled my body out from under hers. Then I slipped from the side of the bed. I watched her for a while, driven for that same need for proof of her life, making me watch every breath she took and released. Even knowing I was being neurotic didn't deter me. It was only after ten minutes that

I was certain enough to slip into the bathroom and dress before I padded downstairs and palmed my keys from the island.

All it took was a blink to get me to my car, and ten more seconds to have Terry Moffit's address and Izzy's childhood house of horrors on the screen of my phone. Before I could stop myself, I was driving through the almost deserted streets of Manchester in the grey light of the impending morning.

I parked outside of the house and got out, leaning against my car with my arms folded over my chest as I studied the tiny house that sat before me. I saw every one of Izzy's stories play out in my mind. I felt the barely-scabbed flesh on my knuckles stretch as my fist tightened over and over, and I forced myself to breathe through it and allow my cooler head to prevail before I pushed from the car and headed to the house where I knocked quietly.

Izzy's mum answered.

She was a tiny, fragile-looking woman, with the same blonde hair and quirk to her lips that Izzy had. It was there that resemblance ended. She was empty where Izzy was full of life, hollow where Izzy brimmed with laughter and energy, cold where Izzy loved so openly with those she allowed close enough. Her magnificence lay only in the girl she'd given life to, yet wouldn't allow herself to love enough to save.

"Terry in?"

The little woman gripped the neck of her robe and pulled the two sides together like *I* was the threat.

"I, uh…"

"I'm Izzy's boyfriend."

"You should probably go."

"Terry?" I called out, respectfully disagreeing with his old lady.

"Look, I don't care who you think you are—"

"I already told you, love. I'm Izzy's boyfriend."

I could hear the creak on the stairs behind her, and I knew Terry was standing just out of sight. The fucking coward that he was didn't want to face me. Again.

"And we don't want anything to do with her standing on our doorstep," Izzy's mum said weakly. The hitch in her voice betrayed her as she looked down at the ground.

"Then maybe your husband shouldn't have tried to kill her last night." I leaned into the door and raised my voice. "Isn't that right, Terry?"

Mrs Moffit's head shot up to study me before she glanced over her shoulder to where Terry was presumably waiting. I saw the uncertainty on Izzy's mum's face. I saw the slight doubt, followed by the accusation she was throwing her husband's way. When she turned back to me, she attempted to shut the door.

"We don't need those lies, either."

I pushed my foot in the jam. "That's okay. He only has to listen to what I have to say. I don't need a two-way conversation because this isn't up for discussion. So, Terry… let me make this clear. If I see you anywhere near Izzy again, I *will* fucking kill you. There'll be no one there to stop me next time. I'll make damn sure of it. You so much as glance Izzy's way, think about her in passing, or allow her to slip into a dream, and I will hunt your arse down and break every fucking bone in your body before I slit your cowardly throat. You can tell your employer the same fucking thing. And you should also know this: I've never made an empty threat in my life. Test me. Let me show you how that ends."

The woman in front of me cowered. Her eyes were wide as she stared up at me as if waiting for a strike to hit her. It was probably the very thing Terry did to her daily. She opened her mouth to say something, but before she could, a shadow appeared behind her, seeming somewhat smaller than he had the night before. His body was limp, and he hugged one side of his ribs when he came into view, a broken, bloody, swollen mess of a man who somehow managed to still set his jaw as though he had a chance.

He glanced at his wife like she was dirt on his shoe, and she stared right back, swallowing only lightly before she dipped her head and stepped back for Terry to take her place.

"You need to leave, boy," he said quietly.

"You're not in a position to tell me what to do, old man."

Terry stared at me through the one eye he could see out of, trying to either intimidate or size me up. "What you gonna do? Go for round two? That make you feel like you didn't fail her in the first place?"

I rubbed my jaw, cocking my head as I forced my lips into a smirk. I had failed her, but I wasn't giving him the satisfaction of seeing he'd hit his mark.

"This coming from the man who failed her for seventeen years? The man who beats his wife still? Jesus, you don't know when to fucking give up, do you? You brought a knife to a gunfight, Terry. I ain't got shit to prove to you, and neither does your daughter. She couldn't care less what you bastards think about her."

Terry blinked slowly, his face blank and expressionless. "I don't have a daughter."

"She doesn't even want you."

"Then we're all happy."

"Keep it that way."

"Understood."

"I'm glad I made myself fucking clear." I motioned to leave. "Good luck with her, though."

I froze and turned back to him. "I don't need luck. You have no idea what the fuck you've missed out on, and you never will. You lost out on the most incredible woman to exist the day you drove her away."

"You don't know anything. You don't know what a whore—"

"Be *very* fucking careful with the next words that come out of your mouth," I warned him, feeling the veins popping in my neck as I stepped closer.

Terry sucked in a big breath, slowly releasing it as he stared up at me. "Consider me told." He smirked.

The smirk crossed a line I'd been toeing since I got there. I reached out and grabbed the scruffy neck of his T-shirt, dragging him out of the door. I threw him to the ground even as his wife squeaked behind me. It was almost insulting considering the horror stories I'd heard about her past.

The old man grunted the moment he hit the ground.

"Here's my problem. I'm beginning to feel you're not taking me seriously, Terry. There's only a limited number of things in my life I really give a shit about, and you're fucking with the top of my priority list. My number one. My girl. And it's really starting to piss me off. I like to think of myself as being rational, but you're like a fly buzzing around my head. You have a choice here. You fly the fuck away, or you force me to take action." I paused as I caught Mrs Moffit moving in my peripheral. "If you're calling the police, you should probably know you're putting him away for a long time, love. I have video of his attack and attempted kidnapping last night. We've got shit on your old man you can't even imagine exists."

"Don't," Terry croaked, holding his hand up to his wife and shaking his head. She immediately shrunk back into the doorway.

"Stay away from Izzy," I growled one last time. "Or I

promise you, I *will* kill you."

Terry looked up into my eyes. "Understood."

I straightened and glanced back at his wife before I dug into my pocket for my keys then stepped over the bastard. I started towards the street and my car, pausing at the end of their path when Terry called out to me.

"One last thing," he said, his voice strained as he struggled to sit up and clutch his ribs.

"What?"

"You might want to knock on a few other people's doors. If you think this thing starts and ends with me, you're wrong." Terry coughed roughly, clutching at his ribs. "Whatever she's done, they're going for her. Last night was only the start. It's why I was sent to fuck your club up, too."

I turned. "You *what*?"

"Figured if you weren't about to call the pigs on me for what happened last night, I might as well throw in what me and a few lads did to your business." He looked at me, deadpan. "Gotta go where the money is."

"Maybe one day I'll test the loyalty of those lads and see what it will cost for them to turn on you." My keys were close to piercing holes in my palm as I clenched my hand around them, the pain of it centring me. "You come near us again, and you'll regret it. That goes for my club, too. If someone so much as tags the walls, I'm coming for you."

"Sorry about your carpets," he muttered, fighting back his satisfied, smug smile. As though those fucking carpets were worth more than his daughter's life.

"Terry," his wife squeaked, stepping forward with her fingers pressed to her mouth as she eyed me with caution.

"You should listen to your wife, Terry."

I walked away, unwilling to let him push my buttons

anymore. If I stayed, I would have to dig him a grave.

I headed back to the apartment, stopping at McDonald's to pick up coffee and breakfast, gutted that they refused to sell me some nuggets so early in the morning. I half expected Izzy to be awake, but I found her sprawled out over the bed on her stomach, the imprint of the sheets embedded in her skin where she'd slept heavily.

I dropped the coffee and food on my bedside table, kicked off my shoes, and I covered her body with mine. My lips pressed light kisses over her cheeks, and I felt my heartbeat begin to calm just from being close to her.

"Baby?" I whispered after a minute or two. I was desperate to hear her voice and see her eyes. "Are you sleeping?"

"Yes," she rasped, her voice weak and broken.

"But I brought you McDonald's… and lots of sex."

Her lips quirked. "I'm too broken for sex, but the McDonald's…" Izzy peeked one eye open, "has my attention."

I wriggled my hips so she could feel me nestled between her arse cheeks. "I think you got that backwards."

"You're insatiable."

I rolled from her back, pulling her with me, so I ended up curled around her on our sides. "Only with you. I got you coffee and a McMuffin. I may have eaten your hash brown."

She gasped and spun around to face me, her eyes sleepy yet wide. "Are you kidding me? That's the best bit!" Izzy glanced down at my clothes. "So, you steal my hash brown, and you dare to wear clothes in bed with me? Who even are you?"

I huffed out a breath. "Fine, you can have my hash brown. The clothes were for your protection. If I stripped, you'd not be able to help yourself, and I have feelings. I'm not just a penis."

Izzy smirked, her fingers finding the top button of my shirt as she looked up at me. "Maybe I can't help myself whether you're in or out of clothes, little penis."

I grabbed her tight, my hand slipping between her thighs and hoisting one over my hip. "Less of the little, you'll hurt his feelings."

Izzy laughed roughly, and it sounded painful, causing her to stop short as she took her hand away from me and pressed it to her neck. "Shit, I sound awful."

"They say a dick in the throat is a healing balm."

"Can't a girl get a morning off after she was attacked?"

"I love you." I chuckled, dipping my head to look at the bruises on her neck. I hated seeing them there as I ran a finger over one, watching her flinch. I knew I couldn't hide my trip this morning from her. As much as I wanted to protect Izzy from so much as hearing her father's name again, I needed her to have all of the facts. Especially before Scott and Paris showed up.

"So, I… I need to tell you something."

"Was I snoring?"

"Yes, but it's not that."

"What have you done?" She raised a brow. "You have guilt written all over your face."

"Don't be mad."

"Oh, hell."

"I couldn't sleep. Every time I closed my eyes, all I saw was that moment when I turned that corner and saw you going limp. It made me fucking crazy. I needed to know he wouldn't try that shit again. So, I drove over there." I said the last part in a rush, watching her eyes as the words sank in.

"Drove where?" she asked quietly, her smile fading.

"Your parents' house."

Izzy just stared at me, waiting.

"I told Terry to stay away from you. Pretty much threatened to kill him if he tried to see you again. He finally saw things my way, but not before he warned us that the person who hired him was motivated. He also admitted he was part of the squad who trashed the club. After that confession, I left before I really did kill him."

It took her a moment to let everything sink in, her eyes searching mine for something... I didn't know what. Until she spoke again.

"Did you see... her?"

"Your mum?"

Izzy nodded once. It was barely a movement.

"Yeah, I did."

With an exhale, Izzy pushed herself up to sitting, turning away from me and looking at the bedside table. "Did you say we had muffins and coffee?" She tried to clear her throat, making sure I couldn't see. "I'm so hungry."

I pushed up behind her, my arms circling her body and holding her tightly, my chin on her shoulder. "It's okay to ask questions."

"Did you get me a sausage or bacon McMuffin? Which one is mine?"

"You can have whichever one you want," I said, pressing my lips to her shoulder.

"Sausage," she said weakly.

"Will you talk to me?" I hated feeling the strange hollowness rolling from her. It reminded me too much of the empty shell that had been standing at that front door. That wasn't my Izzy any longer, that was her mother. She could be whoever she needed to be, but I wanted to be able to help—to be someone Izzy trusted enough to say what she felt because she knew there was no judgment there.

"About what? Terry? Nothing to say. I don't blame you for going there if you think that's what you needed to do."

"And what about your mum." I turned her body and tried to catch her eyes again. She looked up at me, tears she clearly hated welling there.

"She's still there. Good for her. Nothing else to say. She made her choice, Ethan. I wasn't it. I'd rather forget them both and focus on those who did choose me."

"It's their loss," I said, giving her a pointed look.

"I know."

I kept my face serious and leaned in, my lips close to hers. "Remember this: you're always going to be my first choice. No matter what."

CHAPTER FORTY

Izzy

We decided to talk to Paris and Scott at Casa instead. It seemed like I'd hardly spent any time there lately, and since Scott was already vaguely aware of something going on, it made sense for us to make sure Paris was in the comfort of her own home when we told her my father had attacked me.

After spending the day at Ethan's, with his open-plan home and huge bedroom, it felt odd to be back in my tiny double bedroom.

"Do you think she's going to be mad?" I asked Ethan as I tugged on the sleeves of my fluffy hoodie. "About me never telling her I was married? The whole Jack thing?"

"If she is, she'll get over it. It's not like you told everyone but her," he offered gently. "Some things we just don't talk about."

"I told you before I knew who you were."

"You thought you'd never see me again. It's easier to talk to strangers than the people you love."

"When did you get so smart?"

"I've always been smart, babe, I just let my dick do the thinking ninety-eight percent of the time."

I rolled my eyes and made my way to the bedroom door, glancing back at him and holding out my hand. "You and your dick."

He shot me a sexy smirk and rolled from the bed. "Haven't heard you complaining yet."

When he reached me, I entwined my fingers with his and began to lead him downstairs, where Paris was waiting in the kitchen, dancing along to her dad's favourite on the radio, Luther Vandross.

"Wish me luck," I whispered to Ethan, looking back at him.

"You got this, baby." He tapped my ass.

The knock at the door came at just the right time, and Ethan gestured to it, knowing it was Scott. I let him go to answer while I stepped into the kitchen and watched my best friend dance around.

She was lost to the music her father loved, and I hated disturbing her when she was rolling around in happy memories, which wasn't as often as either of us would have liked. As if sensing me there, she spun around with a smile on her face. Her hair was tied back, and she was makeup-free for once. No thick mascara. No bright red lipstick. No heels. Just the Paris I knew and loved—the one I'd grown up with.

"About time you two came up for air." She smirked.

I folded my arms across my chest. "I'll have you know we were talking."

"Is that what the kids call it these days?"

I laughed and shook my head while she grabbed two bowls of nachos and gestured to the beers on the side. "Grab yourself one. There are loads more in the fridge. These are already chilled."

"Is that a fucking rabbit?" Scott's voice drifted from the hall. There was a small commotion before he stepped in, holding the rabbit against his chest with Ethan chuckling behind him.

"Paris, you remember this dickhead, right?" Ethan asked, physically moving Scott out of his way.

"How can anyone forget? Hey, Scott. Feel free to deposit the rabbit by the patio doors in the living room." She grinned at him.

"Killjoy." He grinned back and headed into the living room, leaving Ethan shaking his head.

"That's what happens when you deny your kid a puppy," Ethan said.

"I heard that, you twat."

I found myself laughing as I looked between all three of them. Paris soon followed Scott, and Ethan and I trailed behind. Once the four of us had settled on our chosen sofas and chairs, we made small talk. It was nice for me, and I was probably the quietest I'd been around Ethan in a long time. It wasn't because I was sad or worried. More that I couldn't stop looking at the three people in front of me and smiling as they bantered back and forth.

Scott told Paris she looked good—better than when he'd last seen her. Paris told Scott he didn't stand a chance, and then the banter between Ethan and Scott started up.

They were the male version of Paris and me, filling their chatter with insults to cover up the fact that, actually, they adored one another. It was only when Scott shoved a nacho in his mouth and pointed at my neck, asking me how it was, that the mood turned serious, and Paris's attention turned to me and me alone.

"What's wrong with your neck?" she asked, trying to look at it beyond the fluffy hoodie that came up to my chin.

I tugged on a toggle around my neck and glanced at Ethan for reassurance. He gave it in a single look, which made me turn back to Paris.

"Well, it's kind of the reason we organised this little gathering tonight," I started.

Paris looked between Ethan and me. "What's going on?"

"We have some things to tell you guys."

"What kind of things?"

"Do you remember the other week when I fucked up with Izzy because Tommy was asking questions, and I wanted to throw him off?" Ethan started, his eyes flickering to Scott and back.

Paris pursed her lips and gave Ethan a pointed look. "I do."

"So do I," Scott grumbled under his breath. Ethan shot him another look.

"Neither of us were really sure what the hell we had that he'd suddenly want. The only logical answer was that Daggs had sent him, but even that didn't really add up. A couple of weeks ago, I took Izzy out, and we were followed by a car. It got pretty intense. The faster I went, the harder it came after us. We couldn't shake the damn thing until we were back in the city. It made this one…" he tipped his head in my direction, "worried and curious. So, in typical Izzy fashion, without me knowing, she went ahead and asked a friend for a favour."

I glanced at Paris. "Ethan didn't know, but I called Lauren."

Her face dropped. "You only ever call her when you're in trouble."

"That's not technically true—"

"Izzy."

"Fine. Lauren offered me an opportunity." I took a deep

breath. "A chance to go inside a prison and get near—"

"Please don't tell me what I think you're going to tell me right now," Paris interrupted, her eyes wide before she looked up at Ethan and waited.

"Well," I drew out.

"Izzy." Paris blinked. "Ethan?" She looked at him sharply.

Ethan threw up his hands. "I had no idea, I assure you. This was strictly a go ahead and explain everything after the fact for her. Believe me, I was as pissed as you. I can't stop Iz from doing anything she wants to. You know I would have tried to convince her otherwise if I'd have known."

"You went caveman on her." Scott snorted.

"It was fucking Daggs."

"I am here, you know," I said, a little temper tainting the edges of my already sore throat. I glanced between each of them. "And, yeah. I get it. You think I was stupid, but I got the answers we needed. With Lauren's help, I learned that we're not even on Daggs' radar." I shifted my focus to Paris to see her reaction to that. She gave nothing away as she looked at me blankly. "He's got bigger fish to fry. I really don't think he's coming after us any time soon. The threat from him, for now, is on the back burner."

"You idiot," Paris whispered, shaking her head.

"I'll take it."

Between the two of us, Ethan and I went on to tell Scott and Paris everything that had happened since. How we'd seen Tommy in town, and how he'd barely blinked at us. What had happened the night we thought we'd been followed. Everything we'd tried to hide from those we loved. Until it came to the night before with my father. Paris's face was set to stone as she listened, no sarcastic comments falling from her lips, and no rolling of her eyes as she called me dramatic and told me to get a grip.

She looked worried until she heard the one thing that made her blink and look up at Ethan.

"You gave her a key to your apartment?"

Ethan sighed, unable to stop his smile breaking free. "It seemed like the natural thing to do. The woman gives amazing morning head."

"Jesus Christ," I whispered, letting my head fall into the palm of my hand while Scott barked out laughing, and Paris groaned in protest.

"You're sickeningly in love, aren't you?" Paris asked us both.

"Unfortunately, yeah." I chuckled, peeking up and shaking my head at Ethan.

He grinned smugly. "Unapologetically."

"Fuck me," Scott huffed. "You told her?"

"I didn't tell you?"

"You told me you loved her. You didn't tell me you'd told her you loved her."

"I told her I love her. I tell her every day. Every night. And all the in-betweens." Ethan smirked.

"Are you moving out?" Paris asked suddenly, and when I turned to her, she looked genuinely worried. I hadn't even thought about how it would sound—Ethan giving me a key—or how it would make her feel.

"What? No." I shook my head, gripping hold of Ethan's hand as I did. "Not even close, Paris. It's just a key. Casa is my home, but the apartment is… I don't know how to describe it. Every day there feels like a holiday with him, and I'm enjoying it. We're both enjoying it."

Ethan squeezed my fingers. "The key ended up being a distraction she could have done without. She was on her way out of the club to use it for the first time when she was… attacked."

"Attacked?" Paris almost choked, leaning forward in her seat and looking between the three of us.

I pulled down the edge of my hoodie, revealing the red marks and blooming bruises to her.

The fear rose on her face slowly as her eyes took everything in.

"Who did that to you?" She growled.

I blinked once. "My father," I whispered.

Paris's nostrils flared, and her jaw set tight, her eyes rising to Ethan for clarification.

"I wasn't that far behind her. The moment I heard her cries, I jumped in and stopped him…" Ethan held up his hands, displaying his knuckles, which were red and swollen. "And I made sure to pay a visit to his home, too, to make sure the message was received loud and clear."

"Why would Terry do that to you now? What am I missing?" Paris asked, her angry, somewhat restrained features focusing back on me. "What aren't you telling me?"

"He said he didn't know it was me he was trying to scare. He'd been paid to attack me, Goose. Paid. And the scum took it for two grand. He gave me a name after Ethan had to use his powers of persuasion on him. He said it was someone who went by J."

"Jason," she whispered.

"No." I shook my head, pulling in a breath and releasing it on a sigh. "JP."

"Who the hell is that?"

With one look at Ethan for encouragement, I closed my eyes and turned back to my friend, feeling my heart sink into my stomach when I opened them again. "Jack Parker, and I guess now is a good time to tell you about that time I got married without anyone knowing."

***

She took it worse than I thought she would, probably because her annoyance wasn't aimed at just me and the secrets I'd kept, but at the mention of Terry Moffit again—a man she loathed possibly more than I did. Paris had requested some time alone to process everything I'd told her, including my short-lived marriage with Jack Parker. She'd risen from her seat, frustrated and full of disbelief that I could keep something like that from her, before she'd taken herself upstairs, asking not to be followed.

I felt like shit, and while Ethan and Scott tried to reassure me that she'd get over it in time, I couldn't leave her.

I lasted thirty minutes before I dragged myself upstairs, and I plonked myself down on the edge of her bed, watching as she picked at a piece of thread on her oxford pillowcase, which was pressed in between her crossed legs on top of the duvet.

"It's okay to be mad at me," I told her. "It's been years, and I'm still mad at me too."

"You should have told me."

"You're right. I should. But you came back from Daggs, and you were more important than some idiot I'd only known for just over a month. After time passed, it just never seemed right to bring Jack up."

She glanced up at me. "You were *married,* Mav."

"No." I shook my head. "I signed a piece of paper that lasted a few hours. I was never married."

"I should have been there."

I smiled sadly at her, realising for the first time what this was really about. "You have regrets. I have them, too. I'd really like for us to stop being mad at each other for the mistakes we made along the way."

"It's not just that," she said quietly, looking down at her pillow again. "I feel like…" Paris stopped herself and let her shoulders drop. "I feel like I'm losing you a little bit."

"Losing me?"

She glanced up at me. "I hardly see you anymore. You have all these secrets that Ethan knows before I do. I just…"

I shuffled closer on the bed, pressing my hand on her leg and leaning in. "Paris, listen to me."

She searched my eyes.

"There's only one best friend in my life. No one will ever replace you. No one."

"Promise?"

"On my life."

She rubbed her lips together and held my gaze before a small smile made her lips twitch. "I do like seeing you like this, though."

"Like what?" I scowled, my own smile rising at the sight of hers.

"Utterly fucked up in love." She grinned.

I picked up a scatter cushion from her bed and threw it at her head, laughing when she giggled and threw it straight back.

"Moffy Moo is totally dick-whipped."

"You'll get there, kid," I assured her, picking the cushion up again and holding it above her in warning. "Until then, stop sulking like a baby and get your arse downstairs. Our family is growing… just like we always wanted it to."

CHAPTER FORTY-ONE

Ethan

I was proud of Izzy. Telling Paris about Jack Parker was one of those things she'd never truly wanted to do because she hadn't wanted to hurt Paris. The two of them had a connection closer than most sisters, and the thought of having hidden such a secret from her friend wasn't something Izzy cherished. Worse, Paris took it hard, but they talked it out and still managed to come back downstairs smiling.

I'd been given the third degree by Scott while they'd been up there. He figured something was going down, and he figured I had it sorted. He was more amused that I'd chosen to hide just how, in his words, *dumb-fuck stupid in love* I was.

I wasn't hiding shit.

I *was* dumb-fuck stupid in love.

Deep in it.

If it wasn't for all the shit we had following us around at the moment, I would have already booked those tickets to the Caribbean, and we'd be on a beach together. Sun, sea, and sex. We would be living the dream. Izzy was one of the only women I had ever met that I wanted to lock myself away with and never fucking surface.

We stayed at Casa until Scott made his excuses and left. The lack of sleep was beginning to catch up with me, and I think I fell asleep on Izzy's legs listening to her and Paris talking at one point.

If Paris hadn't been expecting company of her own, we'd probably have ended up in Izzy's bed, but I felt safer back the apartment where we were behind security doors and cameras. Once there, we crashed out together, exhaustion getting the better of us both.

I was first awake again the next morning, and with Izzy's quiet snore-cups still firmly in place, I slid from under her and wandered the apartment, checking the car park and surrounding buildings as I drank my coffee. I felt paranoid as fuck—neurotic, even. I didn't know who I was looking for, had no idea what the douche bag looked like, but my eyes scanned anyway, looking for anything out of place as I sipped my coffee and allowed my mind to wander.

When I felt Izzy's warm body press against my back, my smile was immediate.

"I have bad news," I sighed dramatically, patting her hands as she planted them against my stomach.

"You do?" she mumbled sleepily.

"You actually *do* snore."

"I bite, too," she said before she sank her teeth into my shoulder.

I twisted, one hand holding the coffee cup out as her

teeth grazed flesh, my laughter breaking the quiet peace of the apartment. "Jesus. Vampirism would have been good to know about before I fell in love with you, beautiful."

She looked up at me with bright blue eyes. "I only bite when you talk shit. I don't want your blood, only your truths."

I swooped in, giving her a peck on the lips before dancing out of reach again. "Truth. You snore. Lightly. Femininely. Elegantly. But you *do* fucking snore."

Izzy's mouth fell open, and she stared at me, unblinking. "I do not."

"I'll record you. It's sexy as hell." I slid my mug onto the side table and reached for her.

She hopped back, her brow raised. "Yeah, well, you… I dunno." She flew her hands in the air and slapped them back on her thighs. "You drool. A lot. And you take up too much space in bed."

"I'm also a duvet hog. You still love me, anyway."

"Which could change quickly if you insist on telling me I snore."

I placed a hand on my chest. "Please, tell me how I can make it up to you."

She eyed me for a while, the blush rising to her cheeks. "I need coffee."

"Fresh pot, just made." I winked. "Grab yourself a cup. I'll be right back."

"Where do you think you're going? Coffee was just the start. I have other demands." She kept her eyes on mine as she made her way to the coffee pot. "You don't get off that easily."

I smiled at her, my eyes dropping to her arse cheeks peeking out of the bottom of the T-shirt she was wearing. "Not trying to shirk my debts, baby. I just think I'm ready to share something with you."

"It better not be any more of my bad habits," she mumbled to herself, reaching for a cup. "Or more cartoon drawings of what you want to do to me against that window."

I'd already started walking to the back of the apartment when her words stopped me. "Wait. We can do this later. Let's have sex against the window."

"As you were, Ethan," she called out to me. "As you were."

"Dammit." I took in her smooth, toned thighs, and I shook my head. I needed to think with my dick more. Sex against the window sounded like a beautiful idea, and one I should have considered long before now. Her arse cheeks imprinted against the glass, handprints showing over her shoulder imprints… it would be modern art.

I headed into the back hall where the spare rooms were, and I went to the one door no one ever opened. Outside it, I took a deep breath. I hadn't been inside there since I'd moved in. I'd bought the piano, set it all up, and then couldn't bring myself to sit at it. Mum's pictures were dotted around the room, as well as her record player and records Dean had saved when Dad tried to move them to the attic. Dean had known they'd mean something to me.

I pushed the door open and forced myself to drag in a breath, waiting for the familiar memories and pain to hit me in the gut. I was surprised when it didn't. The memories were there. The pain of her death still lingered in my chest, but my mind was suddenly eager to make new memories, share happier thoughts, and cling to the good shit rather than focus on her absence.

Izzy was still making her coffee when I glanced back at her with an appreciative smile. I couldn't remember the last time I'd thought about Mum without that twinge of sadness. I was grateful to Izzy for allowing me to see life in a new light. I'd clung to that misery for so long, I'd forgotten how Mum's love had felt.

Stepping inside, I approached the baby grand, eased the fallboard back from where it sat protectively over the keys and stared at the ebony and ivory below. Every lesson I'd ever had, every song I'd ever played came flooding back as my fingers hovered over them.

"Izzy? Can you come in here?"

"Where are you—?" she asked, coming to a stop outside the open door.

I held my hand out to her. Not entirely sure of what to say now I was in here.

"Your piano," Izzy said, her eyes wide as she looked up to me. "Are you okay?"

I smiled brightly, beckoning her in with a wiggle of my fingers. "Never been better."

Izzy took my hand, letting me guide her inside before she glanced at the piano. "It's gorgeous."

"I bought it when I bought this place. I moved it in here and couldn't bring myself to play it." I sat on the bench, tugging her down next to me and started to play a classical piece lightly. "I was standing at the window waiting for you to wake up. I was looking for a stranger. I realised in the past two days, you've had to face most of the ghosts from your past. None of them good." I continued to play, my eyes moving to meet hers, my fingers miraculously remembering the path. "I've never faced my mum's death. It got too hard, so I stopped trying. Today was the first time I opened this door and remembered what it was like to be loved by her without it being tainted by her death, the hate of my father, or the rapid decline of my sanity when I discovered that I could lose all of those feelings in drugs."

She reached up to caress my bicep. "Her love for you will always be separate to any bad thing that happens, Ethan. She'd be so proud of you, even when you thought she'd have been ashamed. She'd have been proud because you never stopped fighting."

I missed several notes but bridged it over with a dance of my fingers before I moved into the haunting melody of Moonlight Sonata. "I honestly think I was afraid of the void that was there after she died. She loved so fiercely. So protectively. So unconditionally. Then it was gone. Filling the void with numbness and random sexual encounters was the only way I was able to cope. One day, I got a call from a lawyer. After seeing one of her students going through hell after losing a parent, Mum hated the thought of us having to go through the same. She'd set up a life insurance policy and wrote us each a letter for us to open on our twenty-first birthdays. I've never read Dean's. He's never read mine, but…" I pulled my hands from the keys, the last of the notes hanging in the air. "She saw you coming."

"Me?"

"You. It's always been you."

Her hands fell to my waist, a smile rising. "Tell me more."

I reached out for the frame sitting on the top of the piano. It was a picture of Mum and me. I was only about seven in the picture. I was sitting on the piano bench of an upright, hands on the keys, and she was leaning on the top, her chin in her hand, eyes closed, and her smile bright. I turned the frame in my hand and slid the holders aside before pulling off the back and revealing the letter that I'd hidden there. The ring was sitting in my safe. But the imprint was still on the envelope where I'd kept them together for a while. I pulled it free and held it out for Izzy.

"Tell me that's not you that she's talking about."

"You want *me* to read this?" she asked in disbelief, reaching out for it. "Are you sure? It's so personal."

I swallowed my inclination to make a quip about her seeing

me naked. The moment wasn't right. Instead, I brushed my knuckles over the bruises on her neck and smiled sadly. "You're the only person I will ever allow to read it, and only because I *want* you to. That's all I'm going to say right now. I have a feeling it would freak you the fuck out if I said everything I was feeling. Just… read."

She did, dropping her head to become absorbed in my mum's last words to me.

Izzy took her time, and I watched as her eyes slid from left to right and back again, and the tender way she rested her free hand on her chest when those words became heavy. Her eyes filled with tears, one dropping down into her lap, which she tried to brush away too late before she eventually looked up to me with a sad smile on her face.

"She knew what you needed, even then. She knew who you were from the start."

"And I still doubted her," I mused with a chuckle. "I didn't think you existed."

Glancing back down at the letter, Izzy's eyes roamed over the words again. "Did you keep her ring?"

"It's in my safe."

"Do you… think you'd want to use it one day?"

"One day," I said, biting my lip to hide my smile as I dropped my hands to the keys and started playing Cat Steven's *Wild World*.

I saw the way Izzy's face dropped.

"You okay?" I asked her.

"I… yeah." She cleared her throat and looked up at me with a soft smile. "I love this song."

Considering all the shit going down with Jack, I wasn't going to bring up anything to do with marriage. I knew that's why she'd faltered, and I wanted this to be a happy memory.

"This was Mum's favourite."

"What was her name?" Izzy asked, picking up the picture of her and turning it over in her hand. "She's stunning."

"Julia. You have to talk to Scott's mum if you want the good stories."

"Julia. Hi, Julia," she said to the picture, her smile genuine. "I hope I'm what you had in mind."

"I think you're more perfect than even she envisioned."

She turned to me. "And I think you're trying to get sex against the window." She paused, looking down at the picture again. "Sorry, Julia."

"I'm always going for sex." I didn't look down at the picture. My eyes were on Izzy as her lashes flickered. "Sorry, Mum."

"Play some more for me. See what happens."

CHAPTER FORTY-TWO

Izzy

Ethan's mum's words were repeating over and over in my brain.

She'd left him an engagement ring. A ring to propose to a girl one day.

Would that girl be me?

Would I have to turn to him and remind him what a disastrous take I had on marriage?

We'd been together for a countable number of weeks. Okay, so those weeks had been the best of my entire life, but I couldn't think about putting a curse on us. A life without Ethan now suddenly seemed like a life not worth living, and nobody knew what marriage did to a couple more than I did.

I chose, instead, to focus on the things she said that he saw in me.

The safety net. The kindness. The heart he wanted to show

his weak side to.

The fact he thought I was all those things had my heart pounding wildly in my chest every time I thought about them. I'd never placed value on who I was as a person, not until he'd come along. I suddenly felt like a queen.

With my key to his apartment in my grip, I watched as Ethan left for work the very next day, leaving me in the confines of his home. Once he'd gone, I wandered around it like I was seeing it for the very first time. How many women would have died to be here? How many women had seen Ethan in the past and wished to be the very woman I was lucky enough to be in the here and now?

I thought of Chloe. Of his friend, Jessica, too. I thought of the women in the club and of Sophia, who was young, scared, and naive, about to face a trial even I wasn't ready for.

For everything bad that had ever happened, there was this. This moment of happiness, where nothing was even really happening, except my appreciation for the life I was living coming to the surface. And this life I had with him, despite the hiccups and wreckage along the way, was pretty great.

My only exception.

I opened the door to Ethan's piano room and stood there, not entering, just admiring. Julia's pictures were dotted around, and I suddenly hated the way she was locked away, hidden in a room. Her smile was too bright, as was her love for Ethan and Dean, so I did the unthinkable. I crossed the line and stepped inside, reaching for the first picture I could find of the three of them before I closed the door and walked back to the living room to place that picture on top of the fireplace.

If Ethan shouted at me, I'd take it.

If he thought I'd gone too far, I'd agree.

If he wanted to put it back in that room, I'd let him.

But if he looked at it with a smile and let himself love her like she was still here—still living and breathing, it would be worth the risk.

Sinking back into the sofa, I stared up at the picture and at Julia, who was beaming brightly at the camera.

"So, I know we don't know each other," I said quietly, kicking my feet up to rest on the expensive coffee table in front of me, "but I thought you should know that even when I mess up, I'm one of the good ones. If I ever hurt him, I won't have done it with intention. Your boy has quickly become everything I didn't know I needed. Please, help me keep him safe. Help me protect this thing we've got together. I don't know what I'd do if anything ever happened to him now."

The two of us stared into each other's eyes for a while, until the phone lying beside me on the sofa buzzed to life, with Lauren's name lighting up the screen.

"Hey," I answered, not looking away from the picture.

"I was hoping McDreamy would answer."

"I'm fine, thanks, Lauren. How are you?"

"Disappointed now."

I laughed lightly, rolling my eyes, even though she couldn't see it. "I take it my boyfriend has an admirer."

"What is with that voice of his? Jesus, Iz. It sounds like melted sex. How do you get anything done with him around?"

"I... well, I don't."

"I guess that explains the missed deadlines."

"Hey!" I cried, amused. "I've hit every deadline you've set so far."

"Apart from the one that benefits you. Where is this novel you keep promising me? It's been years now of you saying *one day*. One day needs to be today, Izzy Moffit."

"Don't you start." I rubbed my bare thigh with my free

hand, thinking about the stories I'd always wanted to put out there, before I allowed myself to look back up at Julia's picture again. "But for your information, I'm feeling very inspired at the moment, so who knows?"

"Glad to hear it. Now... I have news."

"About Jack?"

Lauren made a wincing noise down the receiver. "Kinda. But, I don't think I've got the answers you're looking for." She paused. "He took a while to track down, Izzy, but... Jack Parker is apparently hiking around Italy. His social media is locked up, but we managed to crack into it, and he's not here. He last checked in in Sentiero Degli Dei, on the Amalfi Coast."

"When?" I asked, sitting forward, my face falling.

"Yesterday."

"Yesterday?"

"It looks legit, too. His account was set to private, and he has about two hundred followers on Instagram, each one congratulating him on his travels."

"That can't be right, Lauren. Who else could it be? Dad said the guy was known as JP. If it's not Jack Parker, then—"

"Think about it, Iz," she cut in. "He's been gone for, what, seven years now? He's never contacted you. What reason would *he* have to come back and do all this to you?"

I swallowed hard, knowing she was right. The evidence apparently spoke for itself, too. "I know," I eventually said.

"You don't sound happy to know it isn't him."

"At least with him, I knew what and who we were dealing with. I knew we could beat him. Whoever it is now is just a blind face and two initials, and that scares the hell out of me, Lauren. It scares the hell out of me because I cannot lose Ethan, and I can't protect him if I don't know who I'm protecting him from."

***

"Hey, Stan," I said, walking into the club.

"Hello, Miss Izzy. How you doing?" His eyes fell to my neck.

"Better than ever," I lied, smiling through it. "Is Ethan around?"

"You two can't keep away from each other, huh?"

"Something like that." I chuckled. "If he's busy, it's fine. I can always come back later. I just…"

"Please," Stan sighed, shaking his head and reaching inside his blazer pocket for his radio. "Every time he's here without you, he's a pain in everyone's arse. You'd be doing us a favour. When you show up, we're in with a chance of a Christmas bonus." He winked, pressing the button on the radio and bringing it to his mouth. "Ethan?"

Ethan's voice was an amused grumble. "What you got for me, Stan?"

"Trouble. About five-six. Little smirk. Twinkle in the eyes… blonde."

"Sounds familiar," Ethan said, "Is it that Britney Spears bird again? I told her I had a girlfriend!"

I curled my nose up at Stan, and he simply smiled smugly back at me.

"Not sure who Britney is, boss, but this one's called Dave, apparently."

"Dave… Dave…? Oh, Izzy? Yeah, that sounds nothing like Dave, mate." Ethan's muffled laughter followed. "Would you send my gorgeous better half up, please, Stan?"

"Good effort, Stan." I patted his shoulder when he shrugged in resignation.

"Can't get anything past him." Stan gestured to the cameras.

I glanced up at the nearest one, smiling brightly and blowing it a kiss before I made my way to Ethan's office, knocking quietly and peering around the door.

"Hey. It's Dave."

"You're less hairy than I expected," he said, leaning back in his chair and spinning to look at me.

"I have a very demanding boyfriend who likes me to be smooth." I stepped into the room and shut the door behind me. "Hi. Nice to meet you."

"Hi." Ethan grinned back at me and held out a hand and wiggled his fingers.

I went to him, pushing myself between his legs and propping my arse and hands on the edge of his desk, so I was looking down on him. "I have news."

"The tickets to the Bahamas have been delivered, and you're packed and ready to go?"

"I *wish*." I playfully tapped his leg with my foot. "I have news from Lauren… about Jack."

The smile faded from Ethan's face, the edge of playfulness dying with Jack's name. "You spoke to Lauren?"

"She phoned me while I was at your place. She says all this going on can't be because of Jack. He's in Italy, on some hiking trip. She thinks it must be someone else."

"Is she sure?"

"Hundred percent."

"I'm not doubting her or her ability to look for this guy, but how can she be that confident?"

"Something to do with his Instagram. Her team hacked into it, saw where he last posted from. I trust her. Lauren never gets it wrong."

"Do you know what his Instagram name is?"

I arched a brow. "Should I? Come on. I've erased that man from my mind as much as I possibly can. The last thing I ever want to do is track him down."

"Can't say I blame you for that." He paused. "You think it would be hard to fake it? Ping it from an IP address or some shit?"

"It's not him, Ethan," I said quietly. "Lauren said he had a whole bunch of followers congratulating him on his journey. Real people who know where he is. Maybe we're fucking this up. Maybe we're letting paranoia confuse us. It could be random. Maybe it's time to go to the police. Tell them what Terry said."

"Terry's a bag of dicks, but I don't think he was lying about being paid to grab you. I can't even begin to think of another JP, let alone a JP I've pissed off. Can you? When I went around to your parents' place, Terry took the time to warn me that his employer had been motivated."

"Why would he do that? To scare you. That's what he does. It's what he's always done when he's losing. He replaces his opponent's victory with fear."

Ethan's hands dropped to my hips. "I just need to be sure."

"What more can we do?"

"Where did you say Jack was?" Ethan asked, sitting up. "I have a wine distributor with a vineyard in Italy. We could—" Ethan's radio crackled on the desk, distracting his train of thought. "Give me a minute. Yeah, Stan?"

"Fights brewing on the main floor. You want me to eject?"

"Hang on, let me check it out."

Ethan knocked the mouse, sending the screens to life. He pressed a button and scrolled through several images before he sat back and groaned

I left him to it, and I stared at the wall behind him, wishing the start of our relationship didn't have this weird, unidentifiable dark cloud over it.

"This guy. *Again?*" Ethan huffed, rocking back in his seat.

I glanced his way lazily. "Huh?"

Gesturing to the screen, Ethan shook his head. "This dickhead keeps popping up in here. He's an instigator. It's the third time in so many weeks that he just stands off to the side and waits for two arseholes to get pissy before he starts pressing fucking buttons."

"Who is he?" I asked, leaning farther in to try and get a good look at the somewhat grainy image in front of me.

Pressing a couple of buttons, Ethan centralised the screen and began to zoom in on a guy with dark hair. "No idea. He's got a creepy vibe to him, though."

The guy had his back to the camera as he watched on, leaving only his long, wavy hair visible.

I was about to open my mouth and suggest Ethan ban him.

I was going to offer a solution.

I was going to say something… anything…

Until the guy on the screen turned and lifted his eyes directly to the very camera we were looking at, and tipped his beer to his mouth smugly, as if he knew we were watching.

My heart fell into the pit of my stomach, and I hitched in a sharp breath, feeling my blood run cold at the very sight of him.

"Ethan…"

Ethan's eyes flickered off the screen to me, his eyes growing worried. "What? What just happened?"

I stared into the eyes of the man on the screen. "It's him," I said quietly. "It's… Jack."

CHAPTER FORTY-THREE

Ethan

That name.

That fucking name.

Jack.

The moment *his* name fell from her lips, I was on my feet. Rage like lava surged through my veins. My hands were trembling as I tried to keep them gentle with Izzy. The desire to knock the fucker into next week was almost undeniable. He had not only been tipping her life upside down for the past God knew how long, but he'd been stirring up shit in my club as often as he could, too. I needed to take it out on his pretty-boy face—make him bleed. It was only because Izzy was standing in front of me that I had any vestige of sanity left.

"Are you sure?" I asked, voice hoarse.

"It's him," she whispered, barely making a sound as she stared at the screen. "I'd never forget that face."

I gave her a sweeping kiss. "Stay here."

"What?" She snapped out of her daze, turning to look at me. "What are you doing? Where are you going?"

I needed desperately to follow my instincts, to head the fuck down there and confront the little dick, but Izzy's face held me locked in place.

"I'm going to talk to him." The way I said it sounded more like *kill* him. Something I was pretty sure she heard, too.

She gave the screen one last glance, taking in Jack's smug, delighted face, before she pushed herself off the desk and came closer to me, resting her hand on my arm as she looked up into my eyes. "He's not worth you getting angry over. Don't do anything stupid. Please. I can't lose you now."

Jesus, I loved her.

Running my hand along the line of her jaw, I kept my touch gentle as I angled her face up to mine and searched those crystal blue eyes. "I'm going to do my best not to do anything stupid. He's a button pusher, which means I can't promise anything, but he's not going to keep doing this to you, or us. That look on your face right now is the last time he's going to put that there." I kissed her again, my lips lingering. "I love you."

She closed her eyes, looking pained. "Ditto."

"I'll be back as soon as I can."

I kissed the tip of her nose and stepped around her, unable to look back as the anger rushed forward. I barely made it to the door without sprinting, and the moment I was out of her sight, I was propelling myself down the stairs three at a time and coasting past a few of the girls gathering to watch the impending storm of the drunks Jack had stirred up.

I searched the room the moment I was inside it, the coloured lights running over faces and writhing bodies of dancers. The doormen had already injected themselves into the potential shitstorm, derailing the mass fight before it gained traction. Jack was now nowhere in sight.

It was only when I caught Stan's eyes that he guided me in the right direction. Jack was on his way to the door, slapping a girl's arse with a smug smile over his shoulder at me, and then he was gone. Out of the door. I knew my opportunity to "talk" to him was dwindling.

The chicken shit was running.

I started after him, moving as fast as I could without knocking anyone off their feet, avoiding squealing women who were drunk enough to think I was a plaything. Wandering hands made it impossible to get anywhere without leaving half my trousers behind.

When I finally got to the door, I was sprinting. My breaths came heavily as the cool evening air burned its way into my lungs. There was no one outside.

No retreating figure.

No smug bastard.

Not a fucking soul.

A black car suddenly drifted around the corner and hammered its way down the street, fishtailing.

"Pussy!" I shouted, flipping it off and feeling fucking powerless about it.

I watched the polished black car until it drifted around the corner and out of sight, leaving me with rage in my gut and nowhere to aim it.

"Fuck, fuck, *fuck*!" I shouted, dragging the last one out as my hands pushed into my hair. "Jesus fucking *Christ*!"

"Boss?" Stan asked from behind me. One of the lads who'd started to fight was already swaying drunkenly away from the doors.

"We got a fucking problem. Gather the guys up. I need you

to keep an eye out for someone."

CHAPTER FORTY-FOUR

Izzy

I watched as Ethan chased after Jack's retreating figure, and I saw the raw anger on my man's face as he pushed past bodies and tried to grab hold of my ex—the one I couldn't believe was here. He was meant to be in Italy. Lauren told me so. She never gets it wrong.

The cameras gave me no new angles of Ethan when he disappeared from the one I was looking at, and I had no idea how to work his system, so I did the only thing I could do: I went after him.

I was jogging out of the office a second later, the door slamming shut behind me as I bounded down the stairs, my hair falling in front of me, and my denim jacket suddenly feeling too heavy and in the way. The main room to the club was only around the corner, and as I hit my stride down the narrow corridor, a figure up ahead caught my attention.

It stood at the very end, a dark shadow in the diluted light of the space in front of me, and even though I hadn't seen Jack Parker for more years than I could count, a sense of dread spread down my spine.

The way the figure moved, and the long hair it pushed away from its face had me coming to a slow stop, my lips parting as I stared ahead, not really knowing what I was looking at.

The silhouette moved to the fire exit door at the very end of the corridor, and when it pushed it open, a flash of light broadcast a glimmer of the owner's face.

Jack was right there. He was ahead of me.

I glanced to the left, trying to find someone—anyone—mainly Ethan, but the club was busy, and the only one anywhere near was a young dancer with pink hair I didn't know the name of.

The door up ahead slammed shut, Jack's figure now gone, and I quickly reached out to the dancer, grabbing her arm.

She looked down at it before glancing up at me with a confused expression on her face.

"Hey," I said in a rush, trying not to sound as panicked as I felt. "Get Ethan for me, okay?"

"You all right?" she asked, glancing behind me.

"No. Tell Ethan I need him now. Out in the back car park. Be quick. Please."

Her face fell, and whether she truly knew the seriousness of it or not, she gave a gentle nod, and I released her, rushing past to make my way to the fire exit.

My hand was shaking when I pushed on the silver bar, and I took a breath, not knowing who or what was waiting on the other side.

When I stepped out into the dark night, my eyes adjusting to the lack of light, I swallowed down the fear that burst to life in my stomach.

I soon found the face of the man I'd been dreading seeing again. Even in my nightmares.

Jack was perched on the bonnet of Ethan's precious Lucy, his arms crossed, and his hair much longer than I remembered it. It made him look sinister—darker. Creepy.

The second he saw me, Jack's slow creeping smile sprung into place, and all the memories of us together came flooding back. None of them nice, each one nothing more than a reminder of the idiot I'd been and how easily I'd allowed him to ruin me.

I took three steps closer until there were only six feet between us.

Jack tilted his head to one side and flashed his teeth. "Hey, wifey. Long time no see."

CHAPTER FORTY-FIVE

Ethan

"What do you want us to do?" Andy asked, leaning against the wall with his thick arms folded over his chest. "Hold this idiot or kick him out?"

"Hold him. I want a fucking word with him," I said calmly. "I thought he was just some tosser stirring shit up, but this is fucking personal. I need a word with everyone involved back there, you get me?"

"By word, do you mean kick his arse to next week?" Stan asked with concern. "You've already done that once this week, champ."

"Listen—"

"Mr Walker?" a timid voice said behind me. I spun and looked down at Fern, one of our newer dancers who seemed timid until she had that pole in her grasp.

"Can Sapphire deal with—"

"Erm. No. A lady came down from your office just now. A real pretty blonde. She looked freaked out and asked me to get you."

Izzy.

"Freaked out, how?" Stan asked, but I was already moving, pushing away from the admission booth towards the back and my office. I burst through the doors and was halfway up the stairs when I saw the control panel on the alarm system flashing that the back doors had been opened. I hopped over the bannister and headed to the back, pushing out into the dark night.

Izzy wasn't far from the doors, frozen in place, while perched on the bonnet of Lucy was Jack Parker himself.

The smug bastard had the air of privilege hanging around him like a badge of honour. It was obvious he wanted me to react to his presence, and he wanted me to blow my top at having him violate my car.

Any other time, any other place, I would have nailed him to the wall and peeled his skin from his body. But this confrontation was going down in front of Izzy. I wasn't going to let her see that side of me again.

Right now, Izzy was my priority, and she was as stiff as a corpse as she stood in front of me.

I approached her slowly, my arm circling her waist in support as I raised an eyebrow at Jack.

"Not as much of a chicken shit as I thought, Parker. I thought you'd made a run for it in your little unmarked black monstrosity."

Jack's eyes fell to my point of contact with Izzy, and his smile never faded as he stared at it a moment before he looked back up at me. "Ethan, right? Infamous *underground* fighter," he said, his tone mocking me.

"Infamous?" I scoffed in the same shitty tone he'd used. "I wouldn't go that far, but you've done your homework. Congratulations."

I was barely keeping my shit together. I could feel the anger making my every limb shake. Izzy was the only reason rationality was lingering at the moment. I thought I'd wanted to kill Terry, but it held nothing to the desire I felt to end this motherfucker's life.

Jack smirked. "Thank you." He bounced his eyebrows, looked at my hold on her once more, and he turned his attention to Izzy. "He seems nice."

"What do you want, Jack?" she croaked, not sounding like my girl. "Why are you here?"

"I need a reason?"

"Yeah. You need a fucking reason."

"Maybe I just..." he shrugged, "missed you."

"You don't get to miss me."

"Don't I?"

Izzy's nostrils flared. "You can't miss what you never had, Jack."

His smile grew bigger. "You can miss what you never had even more than you can miss the stuff you devoured. Although, I guess I did a bit of that with you, too, didn't I? *So* many times."

That was a line I wasn't going to have him cross. He may have been Izzy's past. He may have been lucky enough to fucking marry her, but there was no way on this earth he was going to talk to her like that while I was around.

"Watch your fucking mouth."

"Oh, he barks." Jack laughed.

"I don't give a fuck who you think you are. Around here, you're nothing. Nobody."

Izzy raised her hand to my arm, squeezing it tight as she looked up at me and shook her head. "Don't," she whispered. "That's what he wants." When she turned back to Jack, Izzy pulled my hand into hers and took a step closer to him. "I'm going to ask you one more time, Jack. What do you want?"

Jack's smile had dropped, and his eyes narrowed in on the way we were holding hands. He remained silent, and Izzy looked back up at me. It was with one look that I knew I wasn't going to like whatever she said next.

"Stay here?"

My hand tightened around hers reflexively. I wasn't actually sure I was physically capable of giving her what she was asking me for this time. It went against every instinct I had, even when I knew she could look after herself for the five seconds it would take me to reach her.

I also didn't know how to say no to this woman.

Planting my feet, I let our hands slip to just fingers before finally letting her go.

Izzy went to him, and she folded her arms over her chest.

"Jack?"

He looked up at her, his jaw ticking, a maniacal look washing over his face before he blinked himself out of whatever thoughts he'd been having.

"What. Do. You want?" she asked calmly.

Jack narrowed his eyes and released a heavy breath. "I was curious."

"About?"

"You."

"Why?" she asked sharply, no patience in her voice.

"Time has made you even more beautiful. Do you know that?"

I was going to fucking kill him.

"Why, Jack?" Izzy pressed, ignoring his compliment completely.

"It's taken me seven years to try and understand you, Izzy, and I'm still no better off now than I was the day I walked out on you."

"And you did." She tilted her head to one side. "Walk out on me. Which I am *eternally* grateful for, by the way. I really wish you'd have stayed away, though. These games you're playing." She glanced back at me briefly before turning to Jack again. "The lives you're messing with... hiring people to hurt me? My own father," she said quietly, shaking her head. "You're sicker than I remembered."

"Sick?"

"Sick, Jack. This isn't normal. This isn't right."

"You don't want normal, Izzy. You want special."

"Whatever fantasy or memory you've got of me in your head, I can assure you, I'm not that girl. I'm not who I was back then, and I sure as hell aren't going to be whoever you need me to be right now."

Jack took her in—his eyes widening as his smile lifted one side of his mouth. "If you'd have been this feisty back then, we could have made it."

"Thank God I wasn't."

Jack pushed himself off the bonnet of Lucy, stepping closer to Izzy.

I moved, too, unable to let him get much closer without reacting. I knew men like Jack Parker. I knew what that possessive move of mine would give him, but if it meant being close enough to stop him from grabbing Izzy, then I would accept that mocking glare of his all fucking night.

He smirked right at her. "I watched you leave, you know. I watched you crying as you left that hotel room. I watched you go home. I saw the sadness—the way your heart was ripped from your chest by my absence. I saw it all, Izzy. I saw you broken."

"You need help."

"You were broken because you loved me."

She shook her head. "I never loved you. I loved company. I loved not being lonely. But you? You could have been *any*one. The only man I've ever really loved is standing behind me. He's kind. Gentle. Protective. Genuine. Real. He loves hard, and guess what? He fucks me harder. And the only thing he does harder than both those things is fight for me, and for us, so I'd be really careful what direction you take this conversation in, Jack. I'd hate to see you end up like my father."

I felt my lips curl into a smile despite our situation. I loved that she understood me well enough to see the lengths I would go to in order to protect her. She wasn't wrong. I would kill for her in a heartbeat and never regret a second of it if it meant knowing she would be safe.

This dickhead, standing before us and pressing as many buttons as he could manage in a desperate attempt to get a rise from us, was less than a man. He was less than a threat.

Izzy loved me, which meant I'd already won.

Stepping up and closing the distance so I was standing beside her, I sized Jack Parker up with clearer eyes. Jealousy and infatuation poured from him.

He wanted her back.

The fucker actually wanted her back.

He thought he could have her, too.

He wanted her to want him in return.

"How often have you checked in on her over the years, Parker? Once a year? Twice?" I asked sharply.

"Enough to know you were stalking her arse just as much as I was, pretty boy." His eyes snapped up to mine. "Don't you play innocent. You've been on my radar a while. Now you've somehow got her to think she's in love with you. I would say bravo, but we both know it doesn't take a lot to get Izzy to fall. Just one or two well-placed promises of love and she's on her back before you can—"

Izzy's hand struck Jack's cheek with an almighty crack that promised as much pain as a punch. It sent his face flying to the right, and when he slowly lifted his head back up, that cheek was red raw.

"Just so you know, Ethan can fight... but I don't need him to. I'll kick your arse on my own if I have to. Not the same woman you left, Jack. Remember that."

I couldn't have been prouder of her, but the look in Jack's eyes when he stared up at her made my blood run cold. I definitely knew his type. He was just like Daggs. He was fine with Izzy being out there while she was alone, but her interest in someone else irked him. Her loving me was making him lose his mind. If he couldn't have her, he didn't want anyone else to. That made him dangerous in a different way.

In a real way.

"Izzy, baby," I said softly. "He's not worth it. Let's go back inside. Now we know who's behind all this shit, I know exactly how to take care of him."

Jack turned to face me slowly. "Take *care* of me?" He smirked. "You have no idea who you're dealing with. Neither of you do." For a man smaller than me, I was surprised to see him take a step closer. "I've been hanging around you and her in some form for years. You've never had a clue about any of it. I've watched you so much that I know you better than you know your damn self. You walk around here with your chin raised, cocksure, wearing your shitty suits, taking another girl home every other night. You screw anything with a pulse—some of them fucking disgusting, even by your standards. I've watched your abysmal attempts at pretending to be decent. I've seen who you really are. I've watched you pine over Izzy while fucking the worst kind of women, you pathetic fucking fool. You think seven or eight weeks with Iz makes you a changed man? Is that what you really think… *Walker*? Because it doesn't. It just means you've gone and got yourself a stage five clinger, and I promise you, she'll wear you down in no time. And when she does, I'll be watching with a smile on my face."

I rubbed my palm over my jaw and laughed sarcastically. "Is that supposed to anger me? Hurt my feelings? Rattle my cage? Or maybe…" I gestured to Izzy. "Rattle my girl's? I know men like you. I know the bullshit you pull over and over again just to get your own way. So, you did your homework about me. Have you ever considered that I've already told her everything about my past? Or are you so emotionally stunted you can't fathom being that open and honest with another person? I don't give a flying fuck *who* you are, Parker. You could be the Queen's cousin twice removed, and I would still pity you. You're a miserable little cunt who can only con women into loving him." I stepped forward, my voice calm as I looked down on him, my eyes filled with hatred. "While I'm genuinely in love with a woman who seems to want to put up with my shit. A woman I would die to protect. A woman I won't let *anyone* hurt again."

I could see how much my words got to him. This close, his eyes hardened, the chill of it polar as he huffed out a breath. I could press buttons, too. I'd taken a lot of shit over the years. I'd taken it from a lot of people, and I was more than adept at letting my cooler side prevail.

Not Jack Parker.

My words hit a place inside that motherfucker that lit a spark.

He rocked back on his left leg before he took a swing at me, and I stayed where I was, smile in place even as my head snapped back, and fire lit my jaw.

I knew where every fucking camera was back here. I had three now, thanks to him hiring Terry Moffit.

It was all I needed to be able to retaliate, and I did. My right hand drew his attention before I landed a fist in the middle of his ribs with my left and heard a satisfying grunt of pain as he doubled over. I went in for another, and another, surprised when he was able to get another swing or two of his own in along the way. The pain spread like balm, surging through me like fire until the need to feel his flesh fold under my fists pushed me into a rhythm.

"Motherfucker," Jack hissed, struggling to hide his pain as he looked up at me through hooded eyes and with gritted teeth. "I'll kill you," he whispered.

Running my forearm under my nose, I rolled into a shrug. "Want me to tie a hand behind my back?"

"There are other ways for me to kill you."

"I wish you the best of luck."

Jack swung quickly, throwing a badly timed right that only sent him stumbling and falling to his knees in front of me. He may have been good at manipulating women, but there was a reason he'd had to hire someone to do his dirty work for him. The man couldn't fight for shit.

"Ethan," Izzy called, stepping closer. When I looked up, her eyes were sad, and she held out her hand. "Stop."

"What?"

"He's not worth any of it."

"But—"

"None of them are," she said quietly. "No more fighting ghosts. They're already dead."

That's all it took from her.

I straightened and backed away with slow steps, barely breathing heavily. The guy was fucking pathetic. If my girl wanted to let him walk away rather than crawl, I would give her that. She wanted closure, and she'd get that in any way she needed it.

She was also right. Jack Parker wasn't worth any of this.

Izzy took my hand and squeezed it tight, a little smile I didn't expect appearing on her face when she looked up at me. "Thank you."

"For you, anything."

"I know."

"I love you," I mouthed silently.

"Dit—"

"It'll always come back to me, you know," Jack groaned, cutting Izzy off and forcing the two of us to turn to look at him as he knelt there on the ground, wiping his mouth with the back of his hand. "That's what it'll come back to every time. Me, Izzy. The first guy you ever let in. When you wonder why he's taken so long to get home from work, you'll think of me. When you lay together on a beach, half-naked and tempted, you'll think of me… of us. I'll never leave you." Jack growled, lifting a foot forward as he pushed himself up to standing, clinging his ribs as he did. When he straightened his shoulders back, he raised his chin. "And every single time you think about marriage, you'll remember me, and you'll run scared, just like the first time."

Izzy sighed heavily. This time she didn't even look at me when she broke free and walked closer to him.

"Maybe you're right, Jack," she said smoothly, her voice no longer shaking. "There'll be times when Ethan walks out of the door and I'll allow a slither of doubt to creep in. There'll be times when I lay next to him and wonder if he's going to leave. There'll be times when he asks me to tell him I love him, and he won't say it back, and I'll have a split second of panic. There'll be so many times you enter my mind over the years." Izzy stopped in front of him, her body relaxed, while Jack's eyes heated, and his grin grew fucking bigger. "You'll be a memory on occasion." Izzy leaned in, dropping her voice. "Like a nightmare I can't quite shake. A distant, blurry memory. A flash of regret. Something that reminds me to stay on my toes and look after myself a lot more than I ever used to. Your face will come up, and it will make me sick. Those moments when I'm with Ethan and I find myself thinking of you will be fleeting, because it's impossible to be with a man like him and have *any* doubts about who I'd rather be with. You were a lesson. He's my forever. And the next time you threaten to kill him, be ready for me to say the same to you."

Before Jack could blink, Izzy had grabbed his shoulders, raised her knee, and planted it right in the middle of his balls.

I cringed in reaction to the pain I knew would follow. Every guy knew what that felt like, and every guy automatically cringed. Even when the bastard who had his balls lodged in his throat deserved it. No one deserved it more than Jack fucking Parker.

It was also hot as fuck to have your woman defend you.

"Baby," I called to her.

She spun around to face me, her eyes wide and waiting. She'd never looked more beautiful.

"Fuck this arsehole." I held out my hand.

She was back next to me in no time, while Jack rolled around on the ground trying to find his balls.

Izzy slipped her hand into mine and sighed. "What is it with us and shitty exes?"

I could tell she felt good about what she'd just done—how

she'd probably been dreaming of that moment since the day Jack had walked out on her.

"They just want what they can't have." I pulled the door to the club open and glanced back at the dick rolling around in agony. "They want what we have."

CHAPTER FORTY-SIX

Izzy

We had the security tapes in our possession, along with a lot of personal evidence to go to the police with. If I had to hand Terry Moffit over to make sure Jack got what he deserved, I would.

I didn't owe either of them anything, and I was done trying to protect anyone who'd ever hurt me.

The only thing I wanted to do now was protect those who loved me. Especially Ethan.

"Shall I follow you to the station in my car?" I asked him as we made our way back downstairs in the club. Ethan had made sure to watch Jack scurry away from the club when we'd been back in front of the cameras, and we'd seen him drive off, the headlights of his car disappearing down the road.

"I'd prefer that we take the same car, at least until they have his stupid arse in custody. I'm not taking any chances with you."

"Mind if we get Stan or someone to move my car around the back? I don't want it out here all night."

"We'll give him the keys on the way out. If Scott's around, we may be able to convince him to take it to my place."

"This is stupid," I sighed. "I feel like everyone in this place is going to get sick of me. They've had to run errands and pick up after me for weeks."

Ethan stopped at the bottom of the stairs and turned to face me. "If they're picking up after anyone, it's me. I'm the nervous wreck here. You're taking it all in your stride."

"I am?"

"Yes." He brushed my hair back over my ear. "If you could hear the noise in my head when I think of this arsehole getting close to you, I think you'd see what I mean. Put your hand on my heart and feel how nuts it's going."

I did as he asked, the heavy beat pounding away against my palm.

"Do you know how hot it is when you get protective over me?" I asked him quietly. "How it makes me feel to know I'm loved like this? By you."

"I have a good idea." He grinned. "Let's go and get this taken care of. Then we can crawl into bed together and pretend the rest of the world doesn't exist for a while."

It sounded like the most beautiful plan. I couldn't wait to start this new life with him—one without a threat, now we knew who had been responsible for everything.

We left my keys with Stan and made our way to Lucy. The two of us were glancing over our shoulders as we went, and even after we'd slipped into our seats and fastened our seatbelts in place, I could feel the tension rolling off us.

"Maybe we should have pinned him down until the police

arrived here. He could be anywhere by now."

"I considered it," Ethan said casually. "I just wasn't going to let him think he'd freaked us out that much. It would only give him more power. Turning our backs on him is a big fuck you to a manipulative shit like that. He thrives on fear."

Ethan started the car and began to pull us out onto the road, leaving me to glance out of the passenger window and curl my arms around myself. I didn't know if the adrenaline was beginning to wear off or if the reality of the situation was beginning to kick in, but I was starting to feel cold.

Jack Parker had been responsible for *everything*. The last person on earth I would have expected it to be. Who else out there could have a vendetta against me?

Ethan headed towards town. I could see his eyes flickering to me and back to the road several times in his reflection before he finally spoke.

"After meeting him, I need you to know that what happened between you and him had nothing to do with you. You know that, don't you?"

I turned to give him my full attention. "Yeah," I said quietly. "I do. I was still an idiot, though."

Ethan lifted a hand, the pad of this thumb brushing over my chin. "Guys like that can make it feel like the earth is moving for you. You have to forgive yourself for the mistakes you made, babe. He could pull this shit with anyone just so he could torture them with it after the fact."

"I guess I just feel so different from the girl I was then. I can't imagine ever having thought he could mean anything to me. When I looked at him tonight, he made my skin crawl. He made my insides shrivel. He made me feel sick." I turned back to the road ahead. "But back then, I didn't have any idea what love was. I thought, as long as he wasn't hitting me like Dad hit

Mum, then maybe that was love. The first guy I ever slept with used me, and I let him. Scrap that. I encouraged him… for years. It was easier to have sex behind closed doors and not have the responsibility of love following it. Jack came along when I was tired, and he made me think that love, perhaps, could be him." My head rolled to Ethan again. "Now I know what it really is, I feel so stupid for thinking it should be anything less than what I have so easily with you."

"I get it. I didn't know what love was until you," Ethan admitted easily. "Being in your life feels as natural as breathing. As powerful and intoxicating as jumping out of a plane. If that makes sense."

I smiled lazily. "Perfect sense."

Ethan navigated the roads, holding my hand where he could until he had to change gears. He didn't keep away from me for long. Whatever Hell I'd walked through, whatever fires I'd endured, knowing he was there waiting to hold me this way at the end of it all made it worth it.

Jack Parker was worth this.

Those snakes I kissed just happened to be a little more poisonous than most.

I blew out a breath, about to ask Ethan if he wanted to stop for takeout, when a pair of lights behind us turned on their full beam, coming impossibly close and making Ethan sit up straighter as he looked in the rear-view mirror. I glanced over my shoulder, but the full-beam was blinding, making it feel like we were staring at the sun.

"Holy…"

"Shit," Ethan growled, finishing for me.

I threw my hands up over my eyes to fight off the bright beam.

"You got your seatbelt on?" Ethan asked sharply. He was

squinting when I looked at him. His jaw tight and his body ready for another fight

I tugged on my belt. "Yeah. What's going on?"

"I don't know for sure."

"Do you think it's him?"

"Considering most of the shit he's responsible for… it has to be."

"Fuck, Ethan." I'd barely got the words out of my mouth when the car behind us drove too close, the front end of it tapping the bumper on Lucy before backing off and flashing their lights.

"Jesus Christ." Ethan's head snapped to look out of both his side windows. The car behind was gaining speed again, closing in on Lucy's bumper.

"Sorry, baby." He dropped his foot hard on the accelerator, running through the gears until Lucy's big American engine growled to life and shot us forward.

He made a last-minute left turn, leaving the car behind to overshoot and smoke to stream from the tyres as he stomped on the brakes and turned. He was farther behind us now, but we were on a straight shot heading out of town.

I gripped the seat, swallowing down the ball of fear that had risen in my throat.

"We've underestimated him," I said without thought.

Ethan rechecked his side mirrors before glancing over at me. "He's never going to win, babe. He may be rich, have connections, and a fast as fuck trash car, but we have him over a barrel. He continues this shit, and he's only making it worse for himself. He also can't outrun Lucy. Dean made sure of that."

"Do whatever you have to do."

"Do you trust me?"

"I trust you."

Ethan nodded, one hand on the wheel, the other on the gears as he took off, the car speeding farther and farther ahead of the lights.

At least for a while.

We were leaving the city behind, the roads getting narrower and darker, hedges rising on either side of us as we shot through them like a marble from a pinball machine. Ethan didn't take his eyes off the road, not even to look out the back.

"He still back there?" Ethan asked tightly.

I glanced back, seeing the lights coming back at us from a distance. "Yeah." I slumped back in the seat, digging my fingers in again. "We need to lose him. He's not going to stop until he's killed us."

"I'm doing my best. I just need to find a turn off that doesn't lead to a fucking farm."

"A farm is better than us being wrapped around a lamppost," I said, a little impatiently. "At least there, we could get out, get help, and hurt him."

"You don't trust my driving?"

"I never said that."

"I know what I'm doing, Iz."

His arms tightened as he navigated another turn, and I reached up for the oh-shit handle above me, feeling my body tense. "Right. Do this a lot, do you? Run from crazy exes. Or shouldn't I ask?"

"That's not what I meant." He slowed and darted around a hard left, a few branches knocking against the glass.

"Oh my God," I winced.

"I've never been chased in my life, but I used to live to drive fast, and out here was the perfect place to do it. It's just… been a while."

"I'm sorry." I scrunched my eyes tight. "I didn't mean that.

It's just... fuck! Why can't we *lose* him?"

"You remember that Fast and Furious movie I wanted to take you to see?" Ethan asked, the car swerving around something in the road. We were going so fast it made everything inside rock from side to side with a slam.

My eyes flew open. "Are you seriously talking about... shit... Paul Walker?"

"More the cars," he said, not taking his eyes from the road ahead. "Dickhead behind us has one of those highly modified motors." He paused as he concentrated on some fiddly turns on the road ahead. "Lucy is fucking fast, but she's probably matched well with his car. That means we have to outdrive him."

"I don't know what that means. I just want to go home."

"Fuck, me, too. Just..." he slammed on his brakes and made a hard right turn down a tunnel of trees. "Motherfucker can drive, too."

"I don't want to hear that. Tell me he's shit. Tell me we're going to be fine. Tell me... anything!" I said, a little too high pitched, losing the grip on my sanity as fear took over.

"Don't worry. I'm better."

"That's right, you are!" I cried, glancing behind me, still gripping the handle above. "You're better. We're better."

"I'm going to get us out of this, baby."

"You'd better, okay?" I croaked, my voice breaking as I fell back into my seat. "Because I'm not done with you yet. I want to do things with you. Grow old, have babies, travel the world, fucking all of it. I'll even marry you as long as it means living. So, you get us home, Ethan Walker, and you do it quickly because I am losing it over here, and there's not a thing I can do to stop it."

"God *damn* that sounds good," he said, his voice almost drowned out by the engine. "I just want to... oh, *fuck!*"

The lights grew brighter behind us—too close. Ethan kept his eyes on the road in front, his hand gripping the wheel so tightly, while his other hand made a bar across my stomach. He swerved violently, barely missing the sheep standing in the middle of the road, and he overcorrected on the other side, making the back end swing out. The headlights behind us went crazy as Ethan navigated to a stop. It was like something right out of a nineties rave before the scream of metal drowned out everything, and the world seemed to play out in slow motion. The car behind us rolled over and over again until it disappeared over a hedge, and silence took over everything.

The ringing in my ears was violent, as was the pounding in my heart as Ethan grabbed my hand.

I didn't dare ask the next question, but I found myself doing so anyway.

"What just happened?"

"Sheep. In the road. I… stay here."

Ethan unbuckled himself and hopped from the car, sprinting to the twisted dent in the hedge highlighted in red from Lucy's taillights.

Spinning around in my seat, I found myself searching for him, my mouth open as I waited for something… anything that would tell me we were safe.

It took a while before Ethan came back, his red silhouette moving slowly. He had a hand over his mouth as he approached and eventually slipped into the car. The moment the interior light lit up his features, I could see how white he was, the stubble making even more of a contrast as he stared out at the road ahead of us.

"I…"

"Ethan?"

"There's… a cliff."

"A cliff?" I whispered, my stomach twisting up in knots.

Ethan stared out ahead of us, his hands rising to cover the bottom half of his face as he blinked slowly. He drew in a breath, his hands moving away and then back to his face as though he was trying to find the words to say.

"He's got to be… dead."

I stared at him, unblinking, my body running cold as my blood turned to ice. Ethan wasn't lying. I could see the disbelief on his face, and in the colour of his grey skin.

"Jack's dead," I said quietly, neither a question nor a statement of mourning. More a whisper of confirmation. Something I already knew by the way my skin prickled and a wave of misplaced guilt rolled over me. "He's dead."

"He must have hit the sheep, lost control, and his car rolled right off the edge. There's no way… I couldn't get down there, but there's no way he could have survived that. The car is on fire. What the fuck do we do?"

My hand found its way to my mouth as I tried to let my thoughts catch up with me, but when they came, they came at once, and I blinked back into the reality of what was happening. I twisted and turned, looking for a phone, my hands trembling, and nausea rising in my throat.

"T-the police. We… we need the police. An ambulance. The fire pe-people. The men. The ones who put out the fires." I scrunched my eyes closed, quickly opening them again. "I need a phone. You… me… one of us should… he's…"

Ethan lifted his ass from the seat and pulled his phone from his back pocket before falling into place and slapping his hand against the hazards. He began dialling the emergency number. I knew the moment they answered, Ethan's face went blank, and his voice steadied enough to bite out the words.

"There's been an accident."

CHAPTER FORTY-SEVEN

Ethan

Jack Parker's death, from early accounts, was deemed just that. An accident.

The police had lots of investigations to carry out, and Izzy and I would, undoubtedly, have to repeat our story a half dozen more times before the week was out. But none of this was our fault.

I hadn't put that animal in the road.

I hadn't been on his ass. He'd been on ours.

As the security footage had shown, he had attacked first and was chasing us for another confrontation.

All of these facts had been repeated over and over to us. Izzy and I had repeated the story so much, we could say it front and backwards. We'd been sitting in Lucy for hours upon hours as the sun rose around the flashing lights of the emergency services. Listening to how dead Jack Parker was from every passing conversation we overheard.

Yet, we were not culpable.

We were not responsible.

We stumbled back into the apartment around ten in the morning, both of us cold, exhausted, and worn out. I hadn't been thinking about sex. Who would when you'd just seen someone fall from a cliff to their untimely demise? But when I'd dragged Izzy upstairs and turned on the shower, our eyes met over the bed.

She looked exhausted. Her blonde hair was a nest of tangles where she'd run her hand through it over and over during interviews and interrogations. Her lips were swollen from her biting them over and over again. Lost in her own mind about the life set alight at the bottom of a cliff. Even her sleep-hooded eyes were enticing.

"Iz?" I said gently.

"I need you."

"Thank God," I muttered, crawling over the top of the bed to get to her.

My lips were on hers before I'd dropped down on the other side, my hands sliding over her morning chilled flesh as I pushed my hands under her shirt and denim jacket. I was driven by want, by need, by the unavoidable and overwhelming craving to feel her alive and against me.

I could have killed her.

I could have killed us both.

"I need to be inside you," I growled, pushing her top up and over her head. "I need to feel you around me."

Izzy's eyes filled with tears, and she wrapped her arms around me, pressing her lips to mine with urgency. Our teeth clashed, and she sucked in breaths through the corners of her mouth, her chest bouncing. "Hold me, Ethan. Cover me in you."

I didn't take my time stripping us down. Clothes were shed and scattered around us. I laid her in the centre of the bed, hovering over her, my body nestled between her smooth thighs. My erection pressed against her welcoming body, as I met those sky-blue eyes below me. I'd loved her before tonight. I'd loved her in every way there was to love a woman, but this moment...

This night.

Looking down on her, I realised she was the reason I was even here.

"I love you, Izzy," I whispered, my body twitching in need.

"I love you more." Her fingers dug into my back carefully—her need as great as mine.

It was all the invitation I needed. With a gentle rock of my hips, I entered her, sinking deep into her heat as the muscles in my arms trembled. I didn't want to rush. I wanted to take my time and make love to her. I retreated slowly before sinking into her again in the same slow movement.

She gazed up at me, her back arching and eyes glowing with something I'd never seen in her before. She was raw, asking me to heal her, begging me to make things right. She was vulnerable, handing herself over with all the trust she possessed... the love, too. It poured out of her without a single word passing those pink lips. I was her everything, and the woman beneath me could let me know that with nothing more than a look. The intensity in her eyes made this feel like more when I'd thought more was impossible.

Every slow, precious slide of my body into hers was a promise to her. A promise to love her, to keep her safe, to never put her in danger ever again. With each promise came desperation and need—a hunger that would only be sated after a lifetime with this woman. Hitching her leg over my hip, I angled myself deeper, taking and giving more as our breaths sawed between us, and our moans of pleasure were swallowed by the other.

She never once looked away. She never once broke contact. Izzy was as all in as I was. I could feel it.

"One day," I whispered as I ground myself deeper inside of her. "I'm going to ask you to marry me, Izzy." I paused, my heart hammering in my chest with all the love I felt for her. "I really hope you say yes."

A tear fell down her cheek as she lifted her palm to cup mine. "One day," she whispered, "I'll say yes."

Yes.

It was all I heard.

My lips crashed against hers. My body beginning a slow pound into hers as I claimed and gave her every part of me that I had left to offer. I didn't care if it was tomorrow or a year or ten down the road... I was going to make this woman my wife.

Her hands found the back of my hair, and she held me closer to her, even when the kiss ended. We made love with our foreheads pressed together, our eyes locked, and my name falling from Izzy's lips like a prayer, over and over again.

CHAPTER FORTY-EIGHT

Izzy

It took a while for me to process what had happened the night of Jack's death. Everything was so clear, yet so blurred at the same time. What felt like a bad dream turned out to, in fact, be our reality, and each morning for two weeks after, I woke up in a cold sweat, panicked, and struggling for breath. Ethan stayed beside me, never letting me sleep alone after it had happened. Not even on the nights where he had to work until the early hours of the morning.

Just like he'd given me a key to his apartment, he had a key to Casa now, and that made both Paris and me feel safer. We were independent women, sure, but there was nothing wrong with admitting to feeling safer with a man like Ethan around.

When he'd climb into bed behind me, I'd smile every time despite the nightmares or bad thoughts, and I'd push back into him because I couldn't get close enough. Not now. Not ever.

Each passing day only seemed to make this love of ours grow.

After a month of dealing with the aftermath, the police called Ethan to let him know that we were officially in the clear. The relief we felt poured out of us in a wild night of pizza, movies, and of course, sex at Ethan's apartment.

It had been the craziest three months of my life.

The best, too.

"Doesn't it scare you anymore?" Paris asked as she sat cross-legged on top of my bed one afternoon. I was writing on my laptop at my desk, trying to beat the sunset so I could go and see Ethan, who was due to finish work early that night.

"What?" I asked her a little absently.

"The whole eternity, together forever, will he hurt me, will we survive, thing?"

My fingers stopped moving across the keys, and I looked out of the window in front of me. "No," I answered honestly. "He'd never hurt me. It's not who he is."

"You're different now."

Spinning in my chair, I rested my arms over the back of it and propped my chin on my hands as I looked at her. She was different, too. We all were. Time could either drag on forever with nothing changing, or everything you thought you once knew could be tipped on its head in a single day.

"I know." I smiled.

Her own face lit up, and she looked at me like a proud big sister, even though I was four months older than her young arse.

"I like it, Izzy."

"Me, too. You look pretty today," I told her, and it wasn't a lie. Her hair was poker straight, like smooth silk, and she'd put on her makeup, making it unusually light instead of smoky around the eyes. She wore a long, black, flowing summer dress, and was currently stroking that damn rabbit on top of my bed.

"Going anywhere nice?"

"Oh, you know." She shrugged, her hands gliding over the rabbit's fur, and her eyes cast down. "Just… out."

"With anyone handsome?"

Her eyes shot up to mine. "No," she lied with a smile.

"He's a bad boy, then? Real hard arse?"

"What makes you think I'm going out with a guy?"

"Because you've got that daydream look about you. The one you wore when we told each other what we wanted from life all those years ago. The one you wore the day we decided to create our very own Wonderland."

"The one you wear with Ethan every day?"

"The very one." I beamed.

"Well," she said, shuffling to the end of the bed and hoisting her rabbit under her arm like an accessory. My eyes drifted up to her, but I kept my chin propped on my hands as I followed her gaze. "If I end up even a tenth as happy as you guys, that'll be me reaching my new dream."

"I wish you and your guy luck."

Walking past me, she dropped her hand to my shoulder and trailed it down my arm. "Love seeing you like this."

"Love you in general."

"Love you, too."

She disappeared out the door, leaving it open just a smidge. "Don't put out in the first hour!" I called out. "I know you're thirsty as hell for sex, but let him buy you a margarita before you flash your fadge."

"Fuck you, Mav," she called back, leaving me to laugh as I stared at the pictures dotted around my room now.

The smile didn't fade as I took each one in. The old ones of Paris and me. The new of Ethan and me that I couldn't have dreamed about all those years before. His handsome face was everywhere, and just looking at all the different versions of his smile had me spinning around in my seat to grab my phone.

Me: How long is it now?

Ethan: Four weeks, two hours, and forty-two minutes. Not that I'm counting.

Our excitement for the holiday he'd promised me was escalating with every passing day. I waited two minutes before responding.

Me: How long is it now?

Ethan: Four weeks, two hours, and forty minutes.

Me: It's taking forever.

Ethan: I know a good way to kill some time.

Me: Sex against the apartment window really speed things up, does it?

Ethan: I can make you come for three hours straight, that's three less hours you're waiting, and three hours I'm not thinking about fucking you because I AM fucking you.

He wasn't lying, either. Ethan could take me up into the clouds and hold me there for an impossibly long time. When we fucked, we did it for hours sometimes, and I swear, in the last three months of us being together, I'd toned up more than ever before. Who needed to go running when I could lay on a bed and orgasm for hours on end instead?

Me: You make my body tingle with a simple text. I like that about you.

Ethan: I live to serve.

Me: It's why I adore you.

Ethan: You still gonna say yes one day?

My grin exploded, and I read his words twenty times with red cheeks and a pounding heart before I found the strength to reply.

Me: One day.

Any day, actually.

But he didn't need to know that.

Ethan: Photo attached

A picture of his strong hand over his heart stared back at me, and it immediately made me copy his pose and take a picture of the very same thing.

Me: Photo attached.

Me: I love you.

Ethan: More, babe. Always more.

"Not even possible," I whispered to him.

CHAPTER FORTY-NINE

Ethan

I stared at the ring that was sitting on the tip of my pinkie finger. It sparkled in the dull light of my walk-in wardrobe as I crouched in front of my open safe. I'd had it cleaned, the diamond sparkling in its setting as though daring me not to put it back in the little leather box I stored it in.

I didn't want to put it back.

All I'd thought about for the past two months was the night Jack had died, and the words Izzy said to me.

I thought about how goddamn close I'd come to asking her to marry me there and then.

The only thing that had stopped me had been not wanting the date of *his* death to be the day I'd asked her to become my forever with any kind of authority and permanence. So, I'd been looking at the damn ring every day since, trying my best to figure out when would be the best moment, when I could ask and not freak her the fuck out as our relationship hadn't even hit the six-month mark yet.

"Ethan?" Scott called out from downstairs, the slam of the door punctuating his arrival.

I set the ring back into the nest of leather and pushed it hesitantly into the safe, where it was now sitting on top of my passport, ready for our holiday next week. I locked it away, rearranging the clothes in front of it, so it was out of sight before I headed to my bedroom.

I peered over the railing at my best friend as he raided my fridge and downed a beer in between sniffing take out boxes.

"You ever eat at home?" I asked, leaning my forearms on the railing.

"Why would I? Your girl practically lives here now, so you always have leftovers, and it's always the good shit."

"You say that like I never buy you the good shit without her. You're not just my whore, Jenkins. I value you."

"Fuck off, dickhead."

"I live here, remember?" I chuckled and headed downstairs, grabbing a beer of my own before joining Scott on the sofa and grabbing a piece of pizza from the box he'd found. "To what do I owe the pleasure of your company? It's been a while."

"Only because you're a love-drunk fool."

"Yet, I still managed to be at the club most nights…"

Scott didn't respond, choosing instead to stuff another bite of pizza into his mouth and wash it down with beer. He polished off that slice completely before he fell back into the sofa and tapped the neck of his bottle in an impatient beat.

"You want to tell me what's going on?" I finally asked. "You've got a girl, right? I know you do because you got that look in your eyes that says you're in deeper than you want to admit, but you've not said a fucking word about her." I tipped the neck of my bottle in his direction. "And that's just fucking weird."

Scott rubbed his jaw and leaned forward for another slice of pizza.

"Scott."

"Just… give me a minute," he grumbled before taking a bite.

I waited for a bite, then two, and a third after that before I lost my patience.

"For fuck's sake, mate. Just fucking say it already."

"It's… I'm in love with Amelia."

Not what I was expecting to hear. Not even fucking close.

"Amelia?"

"I know."

"As in, Amelia, Amelia."

"Yep."

"Your brother Liam's Amelia?"

"E."

I raised the palm of my free hand to let him know there was no judgment from me. I hadn't spoken to her all that much over the years. After she'd married Liam, it had been at the Jenkins' family functions, and that was it.

"How has it happened?"

"It started as just sex, mate…"

"Jesus."

"Now, I love her."

Scott explained everything from how the affair began, to how they got to where they'd ended up—in love. It was a fucking mess, and Liam wasn't a forgiving guy generally, so I couldn't see that ending well. However, it only took a minute of Scott talking for me to know he was as in love with Amelia as I was with Izzy, and I knew there was no fighting that. All I could do was listen and be a friend. We drank more, slowly got drunk, and he eventually passed out.

I hated it for him.

Trying to hide my relationship with Izzy would be a fucking nightmare. Not touching her when I needed to, talking to her when the desire arose… not fucking her against my living room windows when she teased the fuck out of me…

> *Ethan: Four days, fourteen hours, and twenty-three minutes.*

Her response came quickly.

> *Izzy: I can't stop smiling.*

> *Izzy: Make it come sooner?*

My smile was immediate. Just seeing her name on the screen was a bright spot on my day.

> *Ethan: I can make you come sooner. Wanna come over?*

> *Izzy: Come over what? You?*

> *Ethan: I love it when you talk dirty… Come whisper that shit in my ear while I'm in you.*

> *Izzy: You have company, and I hate being quiet when you're fucking me like you do.*

> *Ethan: We can make a game of it. You can try to be quiet, and I can try and make you scream louder. He's drunk and passed out. He won't know a thing! I want YOU!*

> *Izzy: As long as you're comfortable with every second thought being about Scott, wondering if he can hear me, while you're inside me… I mean… okay. As long*

> *as you don't mind.*
>
> *Ethan: Now, I'm fucking hard and jealous… Wanna fuck in Lucy in our favourite spot?*
>
> *Izzy: I get jealous when we're screwing in Lucy. I know you think of her, too.*

I started to laugh out loud, making Scott grunt from the floor where his face was crushed against the rug.

> *Ethan: I can't wait to have you all to myself on a beach in the middle of the Caribbean.*
>
> *Izzy: Photo attached.*

A picture of my girl popped up on screen, her smiling face lighting every one of her features as her lips pressed against a picture of us together. I loved seeing her like this—happy, relaxed, and utterly uninhibited when it came to us. I lived for these little shots almost as much as I lived for those naughty photos she sent at 2:00 a.m. of her hand between her legs as she told me she was thinking of me. We didn't spend many nights apart, but when we did, it was almost as hot as being buried inside her body.

> *Ethan: You are beautiful.*

Those three words rolled around in my head again as I stared at her image, waiting for her response. I almost wished I'd booked the holiday sooner and for much, much longer. I wanted her to myself. I wanted to wake up to her every morning after falling asleep with her in my arms. I wanted to hear her laughter from another room, or the huff of sound she made when she was writing, and her words were being a pain in the arse. I wanted to glance over, knowing she would be there just so I could feel that smile forming on my lips when I saw her face.

> *Izzy: It's because of you. You look good on me.*

> *Everything is because of you.*
>
> *Ethan: You're just a fucking goddess. See you tomorrow?*
>
> *Izzy: I can't wait. ILY.*
>
> *Ethan: ILYM.*

I did love her more—more than I ever could have imagined I was capable of. Throwing a blanket over Scott's sleeping form, I headed to bed, my mind on nothing but my girl and this incredible future I was so desperate to create for us both.

CHAPTER FIFTY

Izzy

Ethan had planned everything, leaving me with very little knowledge of what we were doing or where, exactly, we were heading.

The Bahamas, baby.

That's all he kept saying, and I trusted him enough to let him have his fun. He loved taking care of me, wrapping me up in cotton wool sometimes, and then surprising me with gifts and gestures so thoughtful, he made my soul ache. That ache was out of a disgusting amount of happiness.

After being waved off by Paris, Scott, and the damn rabbit, we'd been chauffeured to Manchester airport, and we drank champagne in the back of the car he'd hired.

I meant it when I told Ethan I'd never had anything like this to look forward to before.

My life had been fairly non-existent. I'd lived through music lyrics and tales of fantasy, where people loved hard and drowned in their affection for their soul mate. I thought I'd lived because I'd lived through others. Now, I was living for me, and that made me feel alive for the very first time.

All because of him.

I couldn't stop smiling, even throughout check-in and airport security. Ethan, however, looked somewhat restless. He took the whole organising thing seriously, and I knew he only wanted everything to be perfect. I just didn't want him to obsess over it so much that he ended up hating the journey.

"Hey," I said once Ethan had recovered his bag from the airport security staff, giving them the side-eye all the while, like they'd tried to steal something from him. "Relax," I whispered, hooking my arm through his. "This is your holiday, too. You could be taking me to a caravan in Inverness, and I wouldn't care."

"I'm just anxious to get there."

"You? Anxious?" I smirked. "Right. This *is* a first, Mr I Can Take on The World."

"I'm getting you all to myself for fourteen days. I want to be there already."

I moved in front of him, tugging on his hands and walking backwards—a move previously dangerous for a klutz like me. He gave me so much confidence, I was certain I no longer walked on this earth; I glided.

"I'm going to be naked for ninety-eight percent of those fourteen days and nights, too. Naked, covered in oil, sand, sea, and…"

"Sweat and me are the end of that sentence."

"Dammit. I was hoping for nachos."

"I'll have to feed you in between fucking."

A visible shiver of excitement ran through me, and that

deep, throbbing ache came to life in the very pit of my stomach.

"I'll take it."

It seemed to lighten him a little, but Ethan only really relaxed fully when we were on the plane. For the first time in my life, I turned left on the plane and was guided towards two very comfortable-looking leather chairs that had enough space to lie back in, with TV screens at the side.

"First class?" I asked stupidly, eyeing him as he pushed his bag into the holder above our heads, and began patting the pockets of his jeans.

"I'm not saying it's gonna be this first class every time we go on holiday, but this is the first for us. I wanted to make it memorable."

"Being with you is enough," I assured him, sinking into my seat with a megawatt grin on my face. I would bring up contributing some money towards this later. Now was not the time to have that particular argument. For all he loved me, when Ethan wanted to dig his heels in, there was no man more stubborn than he.

He bent at the waist, blocking the small aisle behind him as he kissed me. "Just think of it as purely selfish. This way, you can sleep on the flight."

"Always thinking about sex."

"That's what you thought that was?" He smirked, sliding into his seat and picking up my hand to kiss my palm. "I was just thinking of exploring."

"Exploring my body against some freshly cleaned windows, no doubt."

"I love how well you know me."

The flight was an experience in itself. Everything was free, which meant after four hours, I was tipsier than I should have been, and my mouth became dirty, making promises of epic plane sex to Ethan if he could get me to the toilets without being noticed. It killed him to deny me, but first class wasn't exactly private, and the air hostesses were already giving me the knowing eye when I couldn't keep my hands off of him. Those bitches wanted him for themselves. I could tell.

The alcohol made me possessive, too, apparently.

Four hours in, and I decided to slow it down a little. I took a nap, watched a movie, and only sipped on more champagne when Ethan looked at me with a loving smile on his face.

We eventually landed in Miami, then had to take another short plane ride to our final destination in The Bahamas.

It was there, with the aqua ocean surrounding me, and the ten-minute boat ride to our private island, that I lost all sense of speech.

Ethan had rented us a private villa with a personal chef, concierge, and housemaids who would call in only when we needed them. Birdcage Villa at Fowl Cay wasn't real. It couldn't be. This was like something out of a movie. Something out of a millionaire's magazine. Something that didn't belong in my world.

When we stepped onto the jetty, and up into the villa, my heart pounded in my chest so hard, I was convinced it was finally going to break. Every surprise I'd faced in my life, I'd conquered. I wasn't sure I could handle this, though.

I wasn't sure I deserved this kind of luxury.

I wasn't even allowed to carry my handbag inside. The strain of lifting apparently too much for a guest residing in this Caribbean lifestyle.

We had everything to ourselves. A pool, a villa, the ocean surrounding us on three sides, and our own private driveway down to a little beach. I hadn't spoken a word. My eyes were too busy taking it all in until Ethan reached for me inside the living area of the villa and pulled my attention back to him.

"You did all this for me?"

"When are you going to realise that when I say I would move the Earth for you, I actually mean it?"

"I believe you." I smiled, looking at him and only him now. I searched my favourite hazel eyes, wondering if you could ever love someone too much because if you could, I was sure that was the case with him. "Thank you."

He kissed me, long, slow, and heated, before backing away again somewhat reluctantly. He led me towards the back of the house and into the master bedroom with a huge king bed and patio doors that opened to a covered deck and the turquoise water beyond it.

"As much as I would like to unmake this very made-up bed, I was thinking we could swim first. Get nice and wet."

"You have no idea how much I love the sound of that."

CHAPTER FIFTY-ONE

Ethan

I'd watched her face as we'd pulled up at the villa, taking in every one of her surprised blinks of disbelief and the curve of her lips when she discovered something else. It had been worth every penny I'd spent on this trip just for that look alone, but this was going to be a trip we remembered for the rest of our lives.

For me, it was a one-off, so I'd dipped into some of my savings and spared no expense.

The best part of being out here without a gaggle of tourists was watching Izzy explore when she thought no one was watching. I spent hours sitting in a lounger that first day watching her crawl over rocks and venture into the water, her joy lighting up her face like a kid at Christmas. When she would raise her head and seek me out, all I could do was smile in return, feeling happier and more content than I ever had in my life.

I was also nervous as shit.

We'd only been here for two days. As promised, we'd spent time in the ocean, we'd fucked until we'd passed out on a lounger on the porch, then woken up and made love under the stars—the sound of the waves drowning out the natural rhythm of our bodies coming together over and over again.

We were in our own personal Heaven, and I wasn't sure I would ever be ready to leave here when the time came. Here, I knew Izzy was safe. I saw that she was happy, and I adored the fact that all it would take would be one kiss, and we'd find ourselves half-naked and fucking like we had no self-control.

We didn't.

Not out here.

I woke up every morning to her mouth on mine before she rolled me on my back and sank down, her back arching as she rode me, and her cries of pleasure unrestrained.

We didn't spend much time apart, but she was always on the go, exploring, swimming, snorkelling, and walking down the beach, whether I was with her or not. I let her get on with it, and when I felt that twitching energy begin to rise inside me, I jogged out and caught her mid hop from one rock to the other before I swung her up in my arms, laughing at her squeal of surprise.

I could watch her for the rest of my life.

"You want a beer?" I asked, carrying her towards the house where someone had set lunch up for us on the small boat dock. The person I'd organised and booked with had said they were discreet here, but it was like being alone, only with fairies who cleaned and cooked.

"What a ridiculous question."

I dropped her on her feet just inside the door, and I nodded to the deck out back as the breeze swept through. "You head out. I'll grab the beers. Looks like the fairies got your note."

"I *love it* here," she cried, bouncing on her toes before she ran back out to the deck, wearing nothing more than a little white string bikini.

I watched her go, my eyes focused on her sublime arse as she bounced down the steps to the deck and circled the basket and blanket before dropping down and folding her legs under herself.

I was hard again.

It seemed to happen a lot when she was darting around practically naked.

Shaking my head, I headed to the fridge and saw a bottle of champagne in the door of it as I grabbed two coronas. She wasn't the only one the fairies had listened to. I'd asked for the champagne and a few other things, and I would have bet my life that if I went into the bedroom, I would find more of the things I'd asked for hidden in the spots I'd asked them to be hidden in.

Not that it mattered.

I'd changed my mind again.

Like I had every hour or so since we'd arrived.

I probably would in another hour, too.

I was following my gut, meaning I scrapped any plan I had, hoping that the perfect moment would present itself as it had so many times in the past month.

I headed to the deck, shaking the beers and folding myself down opposite her. My smile met hers as I handed her one of the beers, and I chuckled at the not so subtle hijacking of her nachos.

"They any good?"

Her eyes were closed as she swallowed down and sucked on her thumb. "So good," she moaned, dropping her head and opening her eyes again. "So good, I have a plan. Wanna hear it?"

I took a mouthful of beer and swallowed. "Hit me."

She picked her nachos apart, focused when it came to her favourite food. "I say we never leave here." Popping a small nacho in her mouth, she chewed it with a smirk in place, only talking again once she'd demolished it. "I say we fashion some kind of barrier around our villa—because that's what it is. It's ours now. We can make sharp swords with sticks like they do in those films to spear fish. We could use them to survive, and we could use them to warn off any intruders. I'd stay here and write, churn out a book about you. You'd become *the* most loved book boyfriend of all time, earning me millions. Once we have the cash from your charm and obvious good looks to buy this place, we take down the barriers, apologise for the inconvenience, and we buy the villa for twice its value. Happy buyers. Happy sellers." She beamed. "We never have to leave. I can walk around half-naked all day, while you pretend not to be hard on every second breath. It really is a win-win situation."

I eased back onto my elbows and kicked out my legs. "I'm going to be a kept man? I'll start hunting up some sticks as soon as you've fucked me senseless."

Izzy's cheeks blushed beneath her tanned skin, and she swallowed down more food, never taking her eyes off me when she took a sip of her beer, too. "A kept man. I like the sound of that, me keeping you all to myself." She dropped her bottle down next to her, dusted off her hands, and crawled over to me. Staying on all fours above me as she lowered her face to mine. "And I must really love you to choose fucking you over eating my precious nachos and jalapenos. You know that, right?"

"Yep, and I plan on using it to my advantage as much as humanly possible."

I kissed her, slowly and almost lazily at first, resting back on my elbows as she straddled my hips and dictated the speed and intensity from above. Neither of us seemed to care about the world around us until there was a beep from a boat horn, making us both jump.

I'd only just untied her bikini bottoms, so it was probably for the best.

It didn't mean I was going to stop, just move location, so I scooped her up into my arms and rushed to the villa, her laughter trailing behind us as we went.

***

The sun was low on the horizon when I woke up later that afternoon. The rays were falling over our tangled legs, our naked bodies entwined together. Izzy's breaths washed over my chest in her deep sleeping state, and with a turn of my head, I watched her.

I just fucking *watched* her.

I took in those freckles that I loved so much, those fair eyelashes that were longer than they had any right to be, and the subtle upturn of her lips as she smiled in her sleep. Trailing my finger over her shoulder made her mumble my name quietly before she flung herself back from me. Sweat had almost welded us together. She barely seemed to notice that, or the strands of her hair that covered her cheeks.

Love overwhelmed me in that moment.

Everything I felt for Izzy Moffit suddenly welled up and spilled from my heart until I was drowning in it.

This woman—this incredible, extraordinarily beautiful, kind, and loving woman—loved me almost as much as I loved her. After a decade of my life lusting after her, I suddenly had the honour of being hers, and I wasn't willing to waste another second of that time simply being her boyfriend.

Slipping from the bed, I moved slowly and quietly to my bag and dug out the small box. I pulled out my mum's ring before stuffing the box back into the bag and tiptoeing back to Izzy, where I gently picked up her left hand and slid the ring onto her finger with a satisfying burn hitting the centre of my chest at seeing it there.

It felt more than right.

The dying light of the day caught the diamond and sent a small prism of light over Izzy's face, and I knew it was the right day—the perfect moment for this.

I was always meant to be hers, and she was always meant to be mine.

Even when she'd been in and out of my life for years. I'd never seen her coming, but I saw her now. She was all I could see.

Today, tomorrow and every day beyond that.

Smiling with overwhelming happiness, I headed to the open patio doors and watched the gorgeous hues of the sunset alone, knowing Izzy would join me when she was damn good and ready.

It didn't take long for her arms to slide around my waist and her cheek to rest against my back as she mumbled sleepily, "Did I miss anything?"

I smiled at the sky and subtly gazed down at her hands around my waist. She had no fucking idea.

"You're just in time."

Her palms slid over my stomach carefully, and Izzy rose on her toes to rest her chin on my shoulder. Her mouth close to my ear. "I found a flaw in that plan of mine I told you about earlier."

"What's that, baby?"

"I don't want the world to know about you. I'd rather keep you to myself."

"I'm all yours," I whispered, leaning my head against hers.

She pressed a kiss to my shoulder, letting it linger, and I felt every ounce of love I had for her pouring back out to me.

"I love ya," she said through a lazy smile.

"I fucking love you, too," I whispered.

With a sigh of contentment, Izzy slipped out from behind me and came to stand in front of me. Curling her arms around my waist again, she looked up at me. "You okay?"

I grinned down at her. "I'm in paradise with my girl. I couldn't be better if I wanted to be." I studied her blue eyes—saw the slight sparkle in them that had been there since we'd arrived. "What about you? Happy?"

"This much happiness should be illegal." She brought her hands up to the tops of my arms, but her eyes were lost in mine. Her smile bright and carefree. "I'll never forget this feeling right here."

My heart was pounding in my chest. A nervous joy slowly pushed through my veins, and happiness settled around me as I watched her face, waiting for any sign of recognition. "I'll do my best to make sure you never forget it."

"I know you will." She smiled, her hands roaming up to my neck until the tips of her fingers brushed my jaw, and there they continued to climb higher. "But I don't think anything, not one single thing could make this right here with you any more perfect than—"

Her words stopped short, and her eyes fell to the left hand she was now cupping my cheek with, the diamond sparkling brighter than the dying sun behind us, twinkling against her cheek.

If I had any doubt about the way I'd gone about this, it was gone the moment I saw her face.

We weren't a conventional couple.

We never had been.

I'd fallen in love with her from afar long before I fell in love with her in person. She'd always held my heart in her hands, and I trusted her with it.

As Izzy stared at the ring, every ounce of fear and anxiety I'd ever had disappeared.

I knew what her answer would be.

CHAPTER FIFTY-TWO

Izzy

The diamond on my finger sparkled brightly.

I was frozen in place—my mind not working, my heart working too hard, and every word I'd ever learnt to speak suddenly failing me as I forgot to do anything but… look at it.

Too afraid to move quickly or blink in case it disappeared, I simply wiggled the tips of my fingers against Ethan's cheek to check that it was really there.

It twinkled on cue, lighting up my world.

Emotion welled in my eyes, rising up my throat and forcing me to hitch in a breath, my focus sliding to Ethan as I stared at him, mute.

Ethan shifted slowly, his eyes never leaving mine as he lowered himself to one knee and kept my hand pressed to his cheek. He stared up at me, every ounce of love he felt on display when he smiled shyly.

"I've thought of a hundred different ways on how to ask you to be my wife—to tell you I want to spend the rest of this life and any other I may have with you. I've overthought how I could give you that ring in some grand gesture. In the end, this was the only way that made sense to me. Izzy, you're the only woman I have ever loved. I think I loved you the very first time I saw you. Watching you sleep after making love to you all day, I realised I didn't want to waste another second of our lives together. I told you that, one day, I would ask you to be my wife." He pulled in a breath and blinked up at me. "I'm asking you today. Marry me, Iz. Be the only piece of the puzzle that ever fits right, and I will spend the rest of my life making you ridiculously happy."

Tears trickled down my cheeks as I looked at him, the answer rising in my chest without a single doubt behind it.

"Yes," I whispered.

"Yes?" He smiled.

"You and me. Forever. Yes."

Ethan paused, almost breathlessly. A single tear broke free just a second before he rose to his feet, his arms catching me around the waist and spinning me at once. I threw myself around him, closing my eyes and burying my face next to his as more tears fell, and a bubble of laughter escaped.

This was our one day.

The day I never thought I'd want, but now felt privileged to be in the middle of.

His warm body pressed against mine, and my tears mixed with my joy made the strangest, purest laugh fall from me without thought or care. The only thing that mattered was us, right here, in this very moment. A moment we'd never forget so long as we lived.

My god, were we going to live.

"You realise you just made me the happiest guy a-fucking-live, right?" Ethan asked. I could feel his heart pounding against me.

I pulled back to look down at him properly. His eyes were glazed, while mine were puffy and stinging from the overwhelming love I felt. I wanted to look at the ring again, to take it in, hold it up high, and say something profound that would stay with him forever.

But I wanted to look at him more.

"Promise me this isn't a dream."

"This isn't a dream, baby. This is very real. You just said you'll marry me. You're going to be my *wife.*"

I brushed my hands over his hair, somehow ignoring the twinkling diamond sitting on my finger, never to be removed. "I'm going to make you the happiest husband in the world," I whispered.

Ethan carried me inside the room, his smile so big his dimple was beginning to get deeper. "You already have, Mrs Walker."

"I like the sound of that."

"Fuck, so do I." He lowered me to the bed and hovered over me, his arms caging me beneath him.

I looked up into his eyes, loving him more than I ever thought I could. "How long until we seal the deal?"

"I would marry your arse today if I could, but Paris would cut my nuts off and feed them to the damn rabbit."

I laughed freely, running my right hand through his hair while bringing my left hand up between us. The vintage diamond ring was beyond beautiful, filled with history and stories I wanted to discover while living a fairy tale of my own. Spinning my hand around, I pressed it to my chest, holding Ethan's gaze.

"Does it suit me?"

"More than I can even begin to explain," he said, glancing down.

"I guess I was wrong. There was something you could do to make this moment more perfect. I'm so happy I could burst."

"I love you." He bent and pressed his lips against the ring on my finger. He glanced up at me with a small, suggestive smile. "Want to celebrate?"

"I really, really do."

CHAPTER FIFTY-THREE

Ethan

We celebrated all night, starting with dinner and champagne, followed by hours of making love in bed, our sweaty bodies fused until the first inkling of light signified a new day. It was at that point that we decided to give our bodies a rest and take a swim in the perfect turquoise waters.

Not that we did much swimming.

We just clung to one another, the smell of the ocean surrounding us as pinks, purples, and oranges splashed the sky above. I'd proposed at sunset, and we were bringing in the new day together as an engaged couple. It seemed like it was always meant to be that way. Then again, I would have argued that we were always meant to be, too.

Brushing the damp tendrils of Izzy's hair back from her shoulder, I pressed a kiss to her warm, salty skin and left my lips there, my tired body lazily bouncing against hers. I couldn't help the smile when Izzy's eyes darted to her hand again. Whether checking to see if it was still real or admiring the ring, I never really knew at any given time, I just enjoyed seeing the resulting smile.

"I still don't understand how Mum saw you coming," I said against her shoulder, my teeth grazing her flesh.

"I always thought I had a big forehead as a child. Maybe she saw me from a distance."

I dropped a hand under the water and grabbed a handful of her arse.

She pulled back, her smile bright as she looked down on me. "Okay, maybe it was my arse she saw." Izzy laughed softly and curled her arms tighter around my shoulders. "You still believe she was talking about me?"

Reaching up, I ran a finger over her engagement ring, my smile smug. "I didn't have this sized, Iz. I haven't done anything but get it cleaned, and you read the letter. You don't think that was you?"

Izzy's smile faded, and she looked at the ring again, studying it a moment. "Now you've just told me that, maybe I do." Izzy's eyes drifted to mine. "I know how much this ring means to you. I promise I'll always treasure it as something so much more than an engagement ring. For you, and for her."

I bounced us in the water for a moment, not really sure what to say to that. I'd said I love you so much over the past twelve hours, I was pretty sure it was going to become the only three words in my vocabulary if I wasn't careful.

"I know you will," I finally said, tipping her back so her hair became slick again. She was one of the most thoughtful people I knew, but that ring had always belonged to her. Whether she believed it or not.

Izzy clung to me, her hair floating in the water, her eyes closed, and her smile growing again.

"Are you ready?" she asked me.

"Ready for what?" I brushed my lips over her throat.

"For spending forever as my only exception."

"More than ready."

She sighed, full of contentment. "Me, too."

"I already told you, you're mine for this life and any that follows it. Now I've got you, I ain't letting your arse go."

With a splash, Izzy brought herself back up. Her thighs squeezed tightly around my waist, and she pressed herself as close to me as she could get, towering above me with an amazing smile on her face. Her fingers found the back of my neck, and she pressed her tits closer to my mouth, taking one of those moments of hers to savour me again.

"Just checking," she whispered.

I pressed my cheek against her chest and listened to her heart as the sun peeked over the horizon. Neither of us said anything more. We didn't need to. We'd said everything this moment had needed.

For us, our story was just beginning, and we had the rest of our lives together to figure it all out.

It was the two of us against the world now.

I wasn't alone anymore, and neither was she.

Together, we'd take on anything thrown our way.

- THE ONLY EXCEPTION -

SUGGESTED PLAYLIST

The Only Exception by Paramore
Fooled Around and Fell in Love by Elvin Bishop
Lose You to Love Me by Selena Gomez
With You by Jacob Lee
Every Moment by Jazz Morley
You Are The Reason by Calum Scott
Falling Like The Stars by James Arthur
In Case I Don't Feel by Kevin Garrett
Up by James Morrison (Feat. Jessie J)
Oh My Goodness by Olly Murs
Hold You In My Arms by Ray LaMontagne
Move Together by James Bay
Edge of Desire by John Mayer
Beyond by Leon Bridges
Everlong by Foo Fighters
Crack the Shutters by Snow Patrol
You Are The Best Thing by Ray LaMontagne
Start of Something Good by Daughtry
Better Man by James Morrison
Bloodstream by Stateless
NFWMB by Hozier
Intoxicated by The Cab
You and Me by Lifehouse
Rivers by Passenger, Lior
Fire in the Water by Feist
Secrets by One Republic
Kiss Me by Ed Sheeran

ABOUT L.J. STOCK

L.J. Stock has always lived in a world of her own, continuously lost in her imagination. Whether in the forests that backed up to her home in Aberdeen when she was only six years old. The unique landscape of Singapore she discovered at eight, or the rolling woodlands that rolled up to Dartmoor during her teen years, there have always been new worlds to explore.

Now an adult living in Houston, Texas, there's more concrete in the jungle surrounding her, but that doesn't mean there aren't stories to tell. She now has too many. When she's not writing, Louise can be found hanging out with her family. Playing with her crazy pup, or sitting at the computer lost in the creativity of her successful graphic design business, L.J. Designs.

www.ljstockbooks.com // www.ljdesignsia.com
Join my reader group Saintly Sinners Readers Group on Facebook

ABOUT VICTORIA L. JAMES

Victoria L. James is a teenage girl stuck inside a thirty-something-year-old's body. A Corona and nacho appreciator with a ridiculous obsession for all things Rocky Balboa, she currently lives in Yorkshire, England, with her husband and two baby boys. Having had a strong passion for words and stories going as far back as she can remember, she credits her love of literature to her Grandma Bess who taught her that you don't need a lot of money to travel to different worlds, experience new places, and live a thousand lives.

www.victorialjames.com
Join my reader group The J Team on facebook

L.J. STOCK BOOKS

Babylon MC Series
A collaboration with Victoria L. James
Without Consequence: Book 1
Without Mercy: Book 2
Without Truth: Book 3
Without Shame: Book 4
Without Forever: Book 5

The Mortisalian Saga
Parallel: Book 1
From The Shadows: Book 2
Dishonored: Book 3

Standalone:
A Shot in the Dark
A Fight For Ethan
The Only Exception

L.J. Stock Writing as Elle Luckett
The Gilded Knot Series
Reckless Abandon

Club Stigmata Books
The Favor
You, Me, and The Memories
You, Me, and the Crazy Ex
You, Me, and The Stalker

VICTORIA L. JAMES BOOKS

Standalones
A Girl Like Lilac
The Trouble With Izzy
The Only Exception

Natexus Series
Natexus
All The Way
Marcus
Night and Day

Babylon MC Series
Without Consequence
Without Mercy
Without Truth
Without Shame
Without Forever

Victoria L. James writing as Vicki James

Cherry Beats: A Rock Star Romance
Dirty Rock: A Rock Star Romance (Spring 2020)

418 - THE ONLY EXCEPTION -

OTHER WONDERLAND BOOKS

THE TROUBLE WITH IZZY

A THRILL FOR PARIS

A FIGHT FOR ETHAN

THE SECRETS OF SCOTT

THE ONLY EXCEPTION

- THE ONLY EXCEPTION -